"I have what yo... ...ur-gent. His broad-sho... ...iew as his hand slid to h... ...have what I need."

"Yes."

The word had barely passed her lips when, with one quick glance over his shoulder, he pushed her behind the huge screen.

His voice came low and quiet. "If you want to say no, say it now." He shook his head. "Not two minutes from now, not five minutes from now." With one hand, he slowly pulled free the ribbons of her bonnet. "Now, or not at all."

Passion stared up at him. Her breathing came fast, yet she was powerless to slow it. The noisy chatter of voices floated over the top of the screen. This was the fork in the road—her last chance to retreat. This man, this day, these circumstances would never happen again. He was a once-in-a-lifetime opportunity. Could she walk away? Everything she was made of—blood, bone, heart, and soul—begged her to stay. She could do nothing else.

"You have what I need," Passion breathed. She lifted her other hand to her bonnet and, pushing it back, let it fall to the floor. "No reproaches. No regrets." She pulled off her gloves and dropped them. "No repentance."

Passion

Lisa Valdez

BERKLEY SENSATION, NEW YORK

THE BERKLEY PUBLISHING GROUP
Published by the Penguin Group
Penguin Group (USA) Inc.
375 Hudson Street, New York, New York 10014, USA
Penguin Group (Canada), 90 Eglinton Avenue East, Suite 700, Toronto, Ontario M4P 2Y3, Canada
(a division of Pearson Penguin Canada Inc.)
Penguin Books Ltd., 80 Strand, London WC2R 0RL, England
Penguin Ireland, 25 St. Stephen's Green, Dublin 2, Ireland (a division of Penguin Books Ltd.)
Penguin Group (Australia), 250 Camberwell Road, Camberwell, Victoria 3124, Australia
(a division of Pearson Australia Group Pty. Ltd.)
Penguin Books India Pvt. Ltd., 11 Community Centre, Panchsheel Park, New Delhi—110 017, India
Penguin Group (NZ), cnr Airborne and Rosedale Roads, Albany, Auckland 1310, New Zealand
(a division of Pearson New Zealand Ltd.)
Penguin Books (South Africa) (Pty.) Ltd., 24 Sturdee Avenue, Rosebank, Johannesburg 2196,
South Africa

Penguin Books Ltd., Registered Offices: 80 Strand, London WC2R 0RL, England

This is a work of fiction. Names, characters, places, and incidents either are the product of the author's imagination or are used fictitiously, and any resemblance to actual persons, living or dead, business establishments, events, or locales is entirely coincidental.

PASSION

A Berkley Sensation Book / published by arrangement with the author

PRINTING HISTORY
Berkley Sensation edition / July 2005

Copyright © 2005 by Lisa Valdez.
Excerpt from *Patience* copyright © 2005 by Lisa Valdez.
Cover art by Gregg Gulbronson.
Interior text design by Stacy Irwin.

ISBN: 0-425-20397-2

BERKLEY® SENSATION
Berkley Sensation Books are published by The Berkley Publishing Group,
a division of Penguin Group (USA) Inc.,
375 Hudson Street, New York, New York 10014.
BERKLEY SENSATION and the "B" design are trademarks belonging to Penguin Group (USA) Inc.

PRINTED IN THE UNITED STATES OF AMERICA

10 9 8 7 6 5 4 3

A Letter of Some Consequence

July 12, 1824

My Dearest Abigail,

What news I have! I hardly know how to tell you—you, my dearest and most trusted confidante, my girlhood friend and sister of my heart—you, who did warn me so directly and honestly what might happen were I to let my heart rule my head. And how correct you were. For here I am, facing the folly of my feverish desires. Have you guessed my situation? I would not doubt it. But I shall tell you immediately, as I am positive that your eyes are leaping down the page to discover my secret.

I, Lucinda Margarita Hawkmore, am with child! A fact, I know, that in and of itself is not entirely remarkable. But wait, my dearest, for here comes the revelation that will lift your brows ceiling-ward. Do you remember the ravishingly handsome young gardener who I employed to repair my languishing roses? The one with the naughty brown eyes and delightfully thick appendage? Well, it seems that though he was unable to make my roses grow, he was very adept at planting seeds of a different sort, the fruit of which shall spring from my womb, in all glory, some seven months hence.

Now, my dearest, you mustn't chastise me. As you know, I am completely devoted to my new lover, Lord Fentworth. And because I have already born a Hawkmore heir, George, in his usual compliant, husbandly fashion, shall accept this child as his. So there is no harm done. Though George did request that I take measures against his having to play father to any more children not of his making.

I told him I would do my best. And in truth, I have no desire to bear the loathsome burden of more children. As you are aware, I can barely stand the first one. Yet I know nothing of such matters, my dearest Abby, so you will have to educate me. Though, I suppose I am safe for the next several months, which is fortunate, as I cannot bear to be out of my darling Fentworth's arms.

So there it is, my dearest. You and George are the only ones to ever know. You must write to me immediately so that I may know what you think of my little situation. I can almost hear your gentle recriminations now. But as always, I know you shall forgive me.

With all my love,

Your Lucinda

Post Script: I know I can rely upon you to burn this letter.

Chapter One

PASSION

May 4, 1851
London, The Crystal Palace

His hand held her breast.

Passion Elizabeth Dare looked down at the large, gray-gloved hand cupped over the lavender silk of her bodice. It rose and fell with her rapid breath. A black-clad arm curved around her waist, holding her tightly—so tightly she felt the firm press of a body against her back.

Did no one see?

No, the spectators and exhibitors were too busy trying to round up the three scamps who had toppled the tall potted palm, too busy fanning the elderly matron who had fainted when it crashed in front of her, too busy insuring that none of the fine porcelains in the exhibit had been disturbed. Too busy to notice her, who had been swept out of harm's way even before she herself had seen the peril of the falling palm.

His body shielded her from most of the crowd. His hands didn't move and, though the brim of her bonnet hid her view of him, she felt his head tip forward. Was he looking at his hands upon her?

Passion blinked slowly. She felt she was in a dream. A stranger held her with unabashed intimacy in a public place. He smelled of lemon verbena. Why did she feel so safe?

As she turned to face him, her gaze followed the path of her savior's gray-gloved fingers. They smoothed around her waist and across her breast, lifting her nipple to a hard peak. Passion closed her eyes with a gasp. Then, as his hands moved up her arms in a long, unrelenting caress, an infinitesimal spark flared between his glove and her sleeve. The hot tingle penetrated her skin and ignited her nerves. Shivering down her spine, it flooded her womb then shimmied down her legs.

Passion bit back a moan. His fingers gripped her shoulders. Her breasts ached, and she felt moisture on her thighs. How long had it been since she had felt desire?

The low but constant hum of voices surrounded her. She was in the Crystal Palace, Prince Albert's wondrous endeavor to exhibit the world's advancements in manufacturing, textiles, and art. She had come to meet her cousin, Charlotte, in the china, not to be fondled by a stranger! Passion's eyes flew open.

Blue. The eyes she stared into were vividly blue. Blue as the wings of a butterfly she had once seen fluttering by her window. She drew a deep breath. Could she paint eyes that color? Could she capture their intense gaze? Could she draw the particular slant of the dark brows that frowned at her from beneath the brim of his top hat? And what of his wide, sensually curved mouth? By God, but he was beautiful.

His nostrils flared before his hands slid slowly down her arms to her wrists. Passion felt his fingers pressing firmly against her racing pulse. She couldn't move. She couldn't speak. She just stood, trembling, while his hot blue gaze moved over her features.

People shifted past them, around them. Behind, someone laughed loudly, startling her. He cast a quick, almost angry glance toward the source of the boisterous laughter before releasing her wrists. For a long moment, his eyes bored into hers. She stared back, frozen. Finally, he lifted his hand to the brim of his hat. With a nod, he turned and walked away.

Passion's breath rushed out all at once. He was tall, and she followed his broad-shouldered back with her eyes as he moved easily through the crowd. Just as she thought he would disappear entirely into the throng, he paused. She tensed. Her eyes widened as he turned slowly and looked directly at her across the broad expanse of the exhibit room. She couldn't read his expression. What was he thinking?

Her heart leapt beneath her breast as he started purposefully back toward her. She took two shaky steps backward, then turned and hurried into the adjacent exhibit. When she glanced over her shoulder, he was still there, closing the distance between them with a determined, predatory intensity in his eyes.

Passion pressed forward, passing from one exhibit to the next without thought to where she was. Finally, she stopped beside a small crowd that stood listening to a man with a heavy German accent. Clocks. He was talking about Swiss clocks. Passion glanced behind her. A dull thump of disappointment drummed once in her stomach. He wasn't there. She scanned the crowd before turning back to stare at a large grandfather clock with a looming white face.

Disappointment? The big hand clicked forward. Relief, surely. She sighed. Why lie to herself? She had wanted him to follow. Had wanted him to touch her. Just one more time.

The little Swiss man droned on. The big hand clicked forward again, and the heavy pendulum swung—back and forth, back and forth. She stared at it until it blurred. Yes, just one more time. She closed her eyes and conjured

piercing blue eyes and large, gray-gloved hands. Hands
that made her want . . .

A touch! Passion's eyes flew open. Although the brim
of her bonnet acted as a blinder, she could smell him. Bare
fingers pressed on the small expanse of skin between her
glove and the sleeve of her gown. He had found her.

The pads of his fingers moved slowly over the thin skin
of her inner wrist. She bit her lip as he slid one finger inside her glove, pressing it into her bare palm as his other
fingers wrapped around her wrist. Surely he could feel her
blood pounding through her veins.

The Swiss man was still talking. The big clock was still
ticking. No one was watching. Haltingly, Passion turned
her head to look at him. He stood close beside her, staring
at the clockmaker as though he were listening to every
heavily accented word. Yet hidden by the folds of her
skirt, his finger moved slowly and sensually over the
curves and lines of her palm. She closed her hand around
his finger and watched a muscle clench in his jaw.

Polite applause punctuated the end of the clockmaker's
speech. But Passion continued to stare. Her words came
before she thought to hold them back. "Your profile ought
to be pressed upon a coin."

He bent his blue gaze upon her. "Your body ought to be
pressed upon mine."

Passion's mouth went dry. Her insides went liquid.
"Excuse me," she whispered, backing away.

"No," he said casually. "I do not excuse you."

The low pitch of his voice made a muscle quiver in her
thigh. She moistened her lips and swallowed convulsively
before mustering the strength to turn from him and move
into the milling multitude.

Walking slowly into the main gallery of the Crystal
Palace, she squinted a moment in reaction to the bright
sunlight shining through the towering, vaulted ceiling.
She ought to return to her aunt. She ought to leave. Instead, she glanced behind her.

He was there, leisurely following several paces behind.

One corner of his handsome mouth turned up in a sort of half smile.

Passion veered into another exhibit room, less crowded than the others. Silver pieces, resting upon velvet-covered platforms, lent the room a glow as light reflected off the polished surfaces. Crossing to a corner, she paused before a large tureen decorated with grapes, leaves, and frolicking Pans engaged in bacchanalian pursuits.

She felt him behind her, pressing the protective layers of skirt and petticoats against her legs. She bit her lip. What was she doing? Why didn't she stop him?

His fingers ran up the middle of her back. Gooseflesh lifted on her arms, and her nipples tightened into hard buds. *This* was what she was doing. *This* was what she wanted.

Moving to her side, he seemed to study the tureen. Passion studied him. He was tall, big even, but not coarse. Immaculately dressed, the fine fabric of his coat accentuated his tapering torso. His white shirt showed in sharp contrast to his perfectly tied cravat and dark vest. The long legs of his trousers broke perfectly over his polished boots.

"Do I meet with your approval?"

Passion lifted her gaze. He was looking at her with a hot intensity. People moved about behind them. She didn't care. "Yes."

"Good." Suddenly he pulled her hand to the front of his pants. She gasped to feel his erection huge and hard against her palm. His eyes darkened. "You meet with my approval as well."

Passion's fingers clenched convulsively. His jaw tightened. Lord, she hadn't meant to do that. He felt so big, her fingers had moved of their own accord.

She tried to pull away, but he held her firmly against him. Her eyes widened in silent appeal as a large group of people paused directly behind them. The corner of his mouth lifted a little in that small almost smile, then he

slowly and deliberately rubbed her hand up and down the
thick length of him.

Staring into his eyes, Passion froze, sure that any
movement or sound from her would draw some observant
individual's immediate attention. Her lip trembled, and his
gaze dropped to her mouth.

"Fear or excitement?" he asked quietly.

"Both." The word came out in a soft rush.

"And you simply must see this wondrous tureen," a
woman said loudly behind them.

He released her but let his fingers brush her nipple as
he lifted his hand to once again touch the brim of his hat.
They both stepped back, and a small cluster of ladies, accompanied by a gentleman, moved to crowd around the
gaudy silver piece.

Passion watched them for a moment as they admired
the awful thing. How different she felt from them—how
apart. But then, except in the company of her sisters, she
always felt different. And now, with her whole body tingling with sensation, she felt even more so. It was as if she
were moving in the landscape of a dream.

She looked at him. Yet he was real—he was with her.
Though a stranger, he was somehow a part of her.

His coat was pulled forward, his arms crossed over his
chest. He stood beside a display, watching her watch the
others. His eyes didn't leave her. What must he think?
That she was a strumpet? How odd. She, Passion Elizabeth Dare—dutiful daughter, dedicated sister, respectable
widow, companionable niece, and helpful cousin—a slut?

Her body inclined slightly toward him. Oh, to forget
duty and obligation. Could she not indulge this craving,
this desire? Just this once? It felt dangerous, yet completely necessary.

Passion strode forward, the tips of her gloved fingers
brushing his pant leg as she passed. She knew he followed. She had felt the flex of his thigh as he turned. Her
decision didn't surprise her so much as her boldness. Suddenly she felt like Bathsheba or Delilah. And though she

knew the havoc those women had wrought, she couldn't stop herself—despite a niggling fear.

Passion walked from exhibit to exhibit. He was there, every moment, following. She didn't know what to do or where to go. She just wanted to touch him and be touched by him. She finally stopped in a room of gothic furniture. As with all the exhibits, people roamed throughout.

She strolled to the back of the room, pausing before a huge screen erected in one corner. It was carved to resemble the façade of a medieval castle. Beside it stood a tall *prie-dieu*, an Italian piece made for the purpose of individual prayer, complete with a cushion for the devotee to kneel upon. A Bible lay open upon the broad top. Passion stared at it for a moment before stepping close. She leaned forward tentatively. The words on the page leapt out at her.

Flee fornication. Every sin that a man doeth is without the body; but he that committeth fornication sinneth against his own body.

By God, how many times had her father quoted Corinthians in his homilies? Even miles away, there was no escaping his influence.

She sensed him before he touched her. Not her father. *Him.* Passion shuddered as she felt his hand rest warm on her waist. Why did it feel so comforting, so secure?

He was looking over her shoulder at the Bible. After just a moment, his voice sounded near her ear. "Don't read that." He reached around her. "It's inappropriate for the occasion."

His chest pressed against her shoulder as he flipped the pages. His hands were large and tanned. The subtle scents of lemon verbena, linen, and his skin surrounded her.

"There." He looked into her eyes. He stood so close. "Read this."

Passion tore her gaze from his to see the passage he indicated. The Song of Solomon. A small smile turned the corners of her mouth.

"Beautiful." He said the word as if to himself, but he was looking at her—looking at her so intently.

"Read it to me," he said, his voice low. "I want to hear you say the words."

Passion hesitated.

His eyes flickered over her shoulder, surveying the room. Then he lifted his finger, drew it across her cheek to her chin, and, with gentle pressure, tipped her head to face the page. "Read it," he urged softly.

She didn't need to read. She new the words by heart and spoke them softly. *"As the apple tree among the trees of the wood, so is my beloved among the sons. I sat down under his shadow with great delight, and his fruit was sweet to my taste."* She looked into his fiery gaze, and her voice shook. *"He brought me to the banqueting house"*—his large hand cupped her breast; desire tore through her, wetting her—*"and his banner over me was love."* She gasped.

"I have what you need," he said, his voice rough and urgent. His broad-shouldered frame blocked them from view as his hand slid to her other breast. "And you have what I need."

"Yes."

The word had barely passed her lips when, with one quick glance over his shoulder, he pushed her behind the huge screen.

Passion whirled around and felt the wall against her back. He closed the small distance between them in two strides and braced his hands on either side of her head. Even in the dim light she could see the blueness of his eyes.

His voice came low and quiet. "If you want to say no, say it now." He shook his head. "Not two minutes from now, not five minutes from now." With one hand, he slowly pulled free the ribbons of her bonnet. "Now, or not at all."

Passion stared up at him. Her breathing came fast, yet she was powerless to slow it. The noisy chatter of voices floated over the top of the screen. This was the fork in the road—her last chance to retreat. She had never thought to be with a man again. But here she stood, in the most unbelievable and extraordinary of situations. This man, this day, these circumstances would never happen again. He was a once-in-a-lifetime opportunity. Could she walk away? Everything she was made of—blood, bone, heart, and soul—begged her to stay. She could do nothing else.

Slowly, she reached up and removed his hat. A thick lock of dark brown hair fell forward over his brow. Still, he didn't move.

"You have what I need," Passion breathed. She lifted her other hand to her bonnet and, pushing it back, let it fall to the floor with his hat. She tucked an auburn curl behind her ear. "No reproaches. No regrets." She pulled off her gloves and dropped them. "No repentance."

His mouth was on hers, his body pressed to hers. She had barely had time to draw a breath, but it didn't matter because she had stopped breathing.

His tongue thrust between her parted lips. His hand clasped her breast, and his enormous erection ground against her skirts and prodded her stomach. Passion moaned into his mouth as her body shivered with unfulfilled need.

She tasted and sucked his driving tongue. His nape felt strong and firm beneath her fingers, his chest hard and solid. When had she reached for him? She didn't know. She didn't care. He tasted like desire, and she wanted to feast upon him forever.

His tongue plunged repeatedly to meet hers, and his hands moved in tight, sweeping caresses over her breasts and around her waist. She arched against him. Her thighs were wet.

He tore his mouth from hers, and Passion filled her lungs with a loud, gasping breath. Suddenly, his hand pressed over her mouth, and she stared into eyes that were glittering with lust and potent expectation.

"You must be quiet," he said low, his own breathing short and rapid.

She could hear the voice of the crowd just beyond the screen.

As his fingers moved to lightly trace the outline of her mouth, she felt his other hand working between them. He pulled her hand down, and she curled her fingers around the stiff, thick shaft of his penis.

His jaw clenched, and his hands fell away from her. "Look at it." His words were a demand, but his tone was a plea.

Passion lowered her gaze. Her eyes widened, and she stared hungrily. Protruding from his pants like some giant pagan phallus, his penis jutted massive and heavy in her hand. Threaded with cordlike veins, she watched, entranced, as he thrust it back and forth within her grip. Her hand looked small and her fingers barely closed around him. Her mouth watered, and a heavy throbbing started between her legs. It was beautiful, and she wanted it.

"I told you I had what you needed," he murmured. A clear drop of fluid welled over the swollen head of his penis. "Look, it's crying to be inside you."

Passion gasped softly and licked her lips.

With a finger under her chin, he lifted her face to look at him. "Is your cunt crying, too?"

Something fluttered in Passion's stomach as her womb pulsed with need. She stared into his intense blue gaze, and her legs trembled.

His head dipped and he barely brushed his lips against hers. "Tell me." He kissed her softly, briefly. "Is your cunt weeping for my cock?"

"Yes!" The word came in a whispered rush against his mouth.

And then he was kissing her again—deeply, unrelentingly. His hands pulled at her skirt and petticoats.

Passion's chest heaved, and she opened her mouth wider beneath the force of his kiss. She sucked the air from his mouth in a gasp as she felt his hand between her legs. Yet he kept kissing and kissing, giving her the breath she didn't seem able to draw. Then his fingers pushed through the slit in her pantalets and plunged inside her.

Passion's blood rushed to her center. The tight, throbbing spot pressed to the heel of his palm was like a second heartbeat. She moaned into his mouth as she felt herself clenching around his thrusting fingers. Her legs shook uncontrollably and her arms tightened around him lest she fall.

He broke the kiss abruptly, and his voice came low and raspy in her ear. "My God, has it been so long?"

Passion felt tears well in her eyes. It had been forever. It had been never. Never like this. Her fingers clasped the fabric of his coat. "Please," she begged in a desperate whisper. "Please!"

Something flared in his eyes. One hand slipped over her mouth; the other moved between them. Passion stared into his beautiful eyes and mewled quietly behind his hand as he rubbed the head of his penis against her wet curls and tender flesh. Her hips jerked once, twice.

Groaning, Passion shut her eyes. She had never felt so out of control.

Then he thrust deep inside her, and in one soul-splitting, body-breaking moment, she didn't care. Her eyes flew open, and she cried out behind his hand as a deep groan escaped him.

Passion couldn't move. She was impaled, filled, stretched—pinned to the wall. Her toes barely touched the floor. She didn't want to move. She was held in place by the unrelenting pressure of his cock against the door to her womb. If only she could stay here forever—forever filled, never empty. Her flesh throbbed and clenched around him.

He surged upward, and Passion moaned as she was lifted against the wall. The throbbing pulse between her legs intensified, drowning out her heartbeat.

His eyes blazed into hers and he thrust again. "This is

what you need," he rasped. "You need to be fucked." He thrust. "And fucked."

Yes! It was true. Passion gasped with each driving force, the pressure inside her building, as he seemed to be ever pushing yet never withdrawing.

"Take me inside you," he groaned, thrusting again.

Her muscles drew taught with expectation. She wanted to scream—to spew everything out of her that was not an ally to desire. To rid herself of the woman she was and be only this woman, now, forever. Deep inside her, the pressure built. Was it he trying to get in, or she trying to get out? She felt faint. Her eyes filled with tears of pent-up longing.

Did he see her need? He must have, for she felt his hand tighten on her buttock, and in the next moment, he was bearing down hard upon her hip while he pushed up inside her.

Passion bit back a scream. Her mind reeled. She clenched hungrily, protectively around the thick shaft of his cock, though the swollen head was slowly forcing the tight door of her womb. It was killing her. She writhed wantonly against him. It was the greatest pleasure she had ever known.

"Take me," he rasped. "That's it. Take me." He ground against her.

Passion's whole body began to shake and open. She felt everything inside her was going to shatter. And she wanted it.

His eyes never left her. "Take all of me. Open for me. Open! "

And he bore down so hard upon her and drove up so fiercely that Passion broke. The resisting opening to her womb lifted, moved in some small way. Her heart stopped, and she sucked in air. Then her whole body began to convulse in wracking spasms of hot, quivering desire. The only heart that beat was the one between her legs. Beating so hard, so fast—shaking her with violent jolts of wracking pleasure. Her eyes rolled back, and with a weak, keening cry, warm wetness gushed out of her in a torrential wash of cum and tears.

With a choked groan, he pumped his hips into her, forcing her to give more. Passion sobbed at the exquisite pressure and could do nothing to resist it—she didn't want to resist it.

"That's it." He drew breath through clenched teeth. "Open! I have more to give you." He pushed fiercely into her hot wetness, and Passion choked on a sob—a sob of desire, anguish, and gratitude. "It's all right," he rasped. "It's all right." But he kept pushing, faster and faster, his cock driving into her, lifting her.

Passion saw hunger and supplication in his eyes. Her body answered, and somehow she eased open another small bit.

He gasped, his eyes closing for a moment. Then his hips were driving her into the wall. Passion felt everything drawing up tight inside her. He yanked his hand from her mouth and kissed her, filling her with his tongue.

Her flesh clenched and caressed his thick shaft. The tight opening of her womb rubbed the invading head of his cock. Her arms held him, her fingers twisted in the hair at his nape. Her thighs trembled in willing submission.

Then with a long, guttural groan into her mouth and wrenching thrusts into her body, he spewed hot seed deep inside her. He came and he came, bathing her insides with hot washes of come.

And Passion wept silently between gasps and kisses as the tortured pulse between her legs exploded again and sent a thousand darts of bursting pleasure into her cunt, her womb, and the very organs of her body.

Chapter Two

THE AFTERMATH

"So? What does Miss Charlotte Lawrence look like?"

Outside the Crystal Palace, Mark swung into step beside his brother. "I don't know. I didn't see her."

"Didn't see her? She was supposed to be there, in the china."

Mark shrugged. "She wasn't."

"Where the hell have you been, then?" Matthew flipped open his pocket watch. "I'm going to be late for tea with Rosalind."

"What did we used to say about marriage when we were boys, Matt?"

Matthew raised his brow with a grin as he slipped his watch back in his pocket. " 'Be she alewife, fishmonger, washerwoman, or whore; the woman who fucks my whole cock shall I take to church's door.' "

Mark pushed his hands into his pockets with a smile. "Well, I'm not getting married, but I just got closer than ever."

Matthew laughed incredulously. "What? And how, in

the midst of the spectacle of the Crystal Palace, did you, dear brother, manage to get into a woman?"

They nodded politely at two passing matrons.

"More easily than you might imagine," Mark answered.

"This I've got to hear."

"No. You're late for tea."

Matthew grinned as he raised his arm to hail their coachman. "Damn you. Tell me on the way."

A coach with the Hawkmore coat of arms emblazoned on the door pulled to the curb.

"The Benchley home, Bingham," Matthew directed the driver as the brothers threw their tall frames into the coach.

Sitting across from each other, they propped their boots on each other's seats as the coach started off. They had done so since boyhood, just as soon as their legs had grown long enough to reach. Also in their typical fashion, Mark sat with his arms folded across his chest, while his brother leaned, relaxed, in the corner.

"Well?" Matthew prodded.

Mark shrugged. "What can I say? The day was altogether more delightful than I would ever have expected."

"You can be so very amusing when you choose to be. Now give me the details before I decide to pretend I don't care."

Mark grinned. "I had her behind a large screen in the gothic furniture room. It was very fast and, necessarily, quiet." His grin faded. "And it was very, very good."

"Just good?"

Mark shook his head and gazed out the window. He didn't see the passing view. He saw wide hazel eyes and a perfectly bowed mouth. "No. Better than good. Better than superb. Better than . . . anything." His brows lifted then dropped. "The best." He turned back to his brother. "The best ever."

A light frown furrowed Matthew's brow. He leaned forward. "What's her name? Who is she?"

"I don't know."

The frown deepened. "You have the fucking fuck of your life, and you don't know who she is or how to find her?"

Mark threw his hat on the seat. "No."

"All right. Tell me about her. What does she look like?"

Mark felt his heartbeat quicken. "She looks like desire and hope and . . ." What was it he was going to say?

He leaned his head back against the seat with a sigh. "She has hazel eyes as wide as a doe's. Beautiful, expressive eyes that invite you to look into them." He remembered how she had looked at the group of people admiring the tureen. She was an outsider, like him. He'd seen it in her expression. "Eyes that show her every changing thought and emotion. Eyes that draw you into her.

"She has auburn hair and a mouth made for kissing." Mark closed his eyes and basked in his memories. "She smells of vanilla and orange blossoms. And her smile is too damn beautiful for words." His arms dropped to his sides. "Her voice is low and soft, and there is a tenderness to her speech that makes you want to have her all the more."

Mark opened his eyes and found his brother staring at him with a rapt intensity. When had their coach stopped?

"Young?" Matthew asked, leaning forward.

Mark gazed absently out the window. "A young widow, I'd wager. She was wearing lavender and had a black ribbon tied around her upper arm."

"A young widow in her second year of mourning would be a ripe catch, indeed. Maybe I should look for her and see if I can have a go?"

Mark snapped his head around as hot jealousy roared through him, fierce and undeniable. "Try it, and I'll beat the hell out of you," he growled.

Matthew's sudden smile was wide. "A might possessive of this one, are we brother? I do believe that's a first." He slapped Mark's knee. "I was just joking. I'm in love with Rosalind, remember?"

Mark shrugged and tried to look nonchalant. "What does it matter? I'm not likely to ever see her again."

"No. No, likely not." Matthew paused and then adjusted his hat. "I've got to go. Rosalind will be waiting."

"You're such a slave to that girl."

"It's love, brother," Matthew said as he jumped from the carriage. "True love."

Mark was still rolling his eyes when Matthew poked his head back in.

"What about you?" Matt asked. "Did you give her your name?"

"No. No name." Mark paused as he remembered her tear-filled eyes. "She cried. I gave her my handkerchief."

"She cried? You didn't hurt her?"

"She said no." Mark wished he were back in her arms. "I think they were tears of longing. Tears of passion."

Passion's tears had baptized the fine linen of the handkerchief. She stared at the monogrammed "M" on the corner of the square. Though she sat on a bench in the wide gallery of the Crystal Palace, she saw nothing but that "M." Her thumb moved slowly over the dark blue threads, tracing the lines of the letter. Who was he? Where was he now? Was he thinking of her? Bringing the handkerchief to her nose, her eyes tipped closed as she breathed in its fragrance. Was he wishing for her as she wished for him?

"Oh! Wherever have you been? And where is Charlotte?"

Passion's eyes flew open to find her flustered aunt sitting down beside her. Mathilda Dare's plump cheeks were flushed, and she blew short puffs of air through her nose as if she were preparing to breathe fire upon anyone who might offend her.

Passion's quiet solitude was over. "I'm so sorry, Aunt Matty. Charlotte never arrived and I'm afraid I—well, I became terribly distracted by all the sights."

Her aunt was fishing in her reticule and had barely

looked at her. "Don't say a word. I must get my fan before I faint."

Passion sighed as she slipped the handkerchief—his handkerchief—carefully into her pocket. She didn't want to talk with her aunt. She wanted to think—to think only of him. Alas . . .

Whipping out the small ivory fan she always carried, Aunt Matty closed her eyes and fanned herself energetically. The blue feathers atop her bonnet quivered in the breeze she created. As much as she threatened the event, so far as Passion knew, Mathilda Dare had never fainted in her life. Still, she made a good show of it.

"All right, then. I am recovered," her aunt said dramatically. "Now," she turned to Passion, "what were you— good heavens! What happened to you?"

Passion drew back, startled. Her heart thumped, and she lifted a hand to her cheek. Good God, did her indiscretion show? Was she found out?

Aunt Matty pointed a lace-encased finger toward the corner of Passion's mouth. "You have a red mark there." She leaned forward and, lifting the monocle that hung from a ribbon around her neck, peered through it like a naturalist examining some new flora or fauna. "It looks a bit chafed."

Passion's hand dropped to her chest in relief. It was short lived, however, for she now stared into one hugely magnified gray eye.

"Well?" The gray eye squinted.

Passion paused. She hated lying. "I—when I was in the china exhibit waiting for Charlotte, a potted palm fell right in front of me. I thought it missed me altogether, but I suppose one of the fronds must have brushed my face."

Aunt Matty dropped her monocle and leaned back. "How shocking. You could have lost an eye," she said, fanning herself again. "This exhibition will be a complete failure if there are no provisions for the safety of the spectators and patrons."

His hands had been so firm upon her. She had felt secure in his arms. Safe. "It's perfectly safe, Aunt. The palm wouldn't have fallen if not for the influence of three young boys."

Matty shuddéred. "Odious ruffians." She surveyed the current passersby with disapproval, as if they were all guilty of some offense, and then raised a graying brow at Passion. "I, myself, was jostled by a passing gentleman." She shook her head. "Though I don't know why I credit him with that title. He was in far too great a hurry to get around me." More fanning. "Almost trod upon my toe."

Passion slid her hand into her pocket. Her fingers closed around the handkerchief. *A passing gentleman.* It seemed the place was full of them. A sudden uncertainty overwhelmed her. "We needn't come back," she said, almost to herself.

"Needn't come back?" Her aunt looked at her with surprise and then a quickly manufactured consternation. "Well, *I* wouldn't have minded eschewing the place altogether. It was for *your* sake, Passion—for your love of art—that I made plans with Mary and Agnes Swittly to meet me here all week." More fanning, feathers flying. "Shall I tell them it's all off, then? I will do it, if you say so. Though they've doubtless turned down any number of other invitations in order to join me here. But if *you* wish it . . ."

Passion wasn't duped. Her aunt and the Swittly sisters were inseparable and filled the majority of their social calendars around mutual visits and outings. Besides, what had she to fear? As moving as the experience had been, she and her lover had parted as suddenly as they had met. Once in a lifetime, her mind echoed.

She patted her aunt's hand. "Of course you mustn't change your plans, and certainly not on my account. You just seemed so displeased, what with your toe almost being trod upon."

Matty's expression turned sacrificial. "Yes, my poor toe, and you nearly blinded. But for your happiness, my dear, I shall brave these hordes." Her aunt put her other hand atop Passion's. "Besides, one must take some risks in life, you know. Just because you nearly had your eye poked out, is no reason to shut yourself away from the world. You might as well have just stayed in the country then—at home. No"—Matty shook her head authoritatively—"I won't let you do it."

"You won't?"

"No."

Passion sat speechless for a moment. Her aunt had the most amazing way of turning a situation upside down and inside out. And there was no convincing her that her mind didn't follow natural progressions. "Very well, then," Passion said, humoring her aunt. "Because I was so worried about that—shutting myself away, that is."

"I know. I know, dear." Pat-pat with her hand.

Her aunt seemed to have forgotten the time. Passion smiled. "Don't you think we ought to go? Charlotte has not arrived, and I'm sure she won't at this late hour."

"Oh!" Matty pulled back as if startled then stuffed her fan into her reticule. "That Charlotte Lawrence! I don't know how you have any patience with that cousin of yours. She will never paint flowers upon china as nicely as you do, my dear." She looked up at the sky through the high glass ceiling as Passion helped her to her feet. "And we've missed tea, surely. It's no wonder I'm near fainting!"

As Passion walked quietly beside her chattering aunt, she luxuriated in the heavy soreness that throbbed between her legs and pulsed inside her. She welcomed it, moved with it. With each stride it touched her deeply, conjuring visions of intense blue eyes and the smell of verbena. Her fingers closed possessively around the handkerchief in her pocket. There was no denying it. She wished she could see him again.

He wished he could see her again.
What was she doing now?

Mark quickly ascended the steps to his town house. His butler, Cranford, held open the door for him.

"The countess is in the study, my lord."

Mark's mood immediately darkened. He frowned as he handed over his hat and gloves. "Thank you, Cranford." Damn it. The last person he wanted to see was his mother. He wanted to be alone—alone with thoughts of *her*.

"Shall I have some refreshment brought, my lord?"

"No. My mother won't be staying," Mark said loudly as he crossed to his study.

Lucinda Hawkmore lounged upon the sofa, a glass of brandy suspended between her fingers. "How rude."

Mark sat on the opposite sofa and, crossing his ankles, propped his boots on the table between them. Crossing his arms, he stared at his mother.

Lucinda cast a disdainful glance at his feet and then about the room. "When are you going to sell this tiny house and move into something befitting your station? I'm embarrassed to be seen arriving here."

"Then don't arrive."

Lucinda barely blinked. "You can't even properly entertain here." She gestured at the room with her glass. "It's a matchbox."

"I do not come to London to entertain. I come to work."

"To work," Lucinda scoffed. "How bourgeois. As if you needed to work."

Mark grit his teeth. "I entertain at Hawkmore House. I work because I love architecture. Now, Mother, what do you want?"

Lucinda shrugged. "When you marry, you'll need a proper house here in London, that's all. Build it yourself, I don't care, but this will have to go." She sipped from her glass. "So? What do you think of Miss Lawrence? She's a lovely girl, isn't she?"

"I wouldn't know. I didn't see her."

"What?" Lucinda sat straighter. "Abigail told me she

would be there—in the china. You saw no young lady in a yellow bonnet with a scarlet plume?"

"I told you, she wasn't there." Mark thought of long-lashed hazel eyes. "It doesn't matter anyway."

"Why?"

"Because tomorrow I'm going to offer your dear friend, Abigail Lawrence, a great deal of money in exchange for your letter."

"She doesn't care about money. She wants a title for that simpering little daughter of hers." Lucinda lowered her lashes and sipped from her brandy before asking, "How much money?"

He had been going to offer fifteen thousand pounds. But now he felt an even more urgent need to be free of this entanglement. He didn't want to think about anything or anyone but *her.* "Twenty-five thousand pounds ought to do it."

Lucinda gasped. "You're going to offer that bitch twenty-five thousand pounds? She's blackmailing me, and you're going to offer her a fortune?"

Mark's anger flared. "Blackmailing *you?*" he sneered. "Tell me, Mother, what price are *you* paying in your friend's little scheme?"

"Abigail Lawrence hasn't been my friend for years," Lucinda said haughtily. "She ought never to have been. She was beneath my station. But I was young and didn't recognize that I had no business consorting with a mere merchant's daughter, no matter how rich."

Mark's hands balled into fists beneath his crossed arms. "Oh, but she was your 'dearest and most trusted confidante.' The 'sister of your heart,'" he roared before delivering a furious kick to the table between them.

Lucinda didn't even jump. "When I realized my error in judgment, I jilted her. And when I jilted her, noble society jilted her as well." She shrugged and brushed a bit of lint from her skirt. "She thought she would get a titled husband through me." Lucinda lifted her brows. "I put a stop to that."

Standing, Mark whirled away from his mother and crossed to his desk. Once safely behind it, he leaned on his fists. "Your conceit is unsurpassed, Mother. Though you are the cause, *I* am the one who Abigail Lawrence is attempting to force into marriage with her 'simpering little daughter.' She isn't blackmailing *you*. She's blackmailing *me*—me and Matthew, though I vow he will never know it."

Lucinda stared coolly at him from across the room. "Well, I have a care for my reputation even if you do not."

Mark expelled a bitter bark of laughter. "Your reputation! Madam, you have trod upon your own reputation so often, and with such energy, that it is indistinguishable from the muck that runs in the gutters. I wonder at your believing you have any repute left to protect."

Lucinda downed the rest of her brandy before setting the glass upon the table he had kicked moments before. "How like your father you are," she said, her lip curling. "God help me, you're more like him every day."

"Not so much like him that I'll let you destroy me," Mark bit out. He felt his breath coming fast and forced it to slow. He was not going to let her draw him into an argument about his father. Not today. "I care not for your reputation," he said tightly. "I care not for my own. Matthew's, however, is worth protecting. He is my brother, and I count him as such despite this recent revelation regarding his paternity."

Mark closed his eyes and envisioned his brother having tea at the knee of his beloved fiancée, Rosalind— *Lady* Rosalind. Christ, Matthew was so deeply in love with the girl. Too deeply.

Mark looked at his mother and found her slipping her hands into her gloves. Good, she was leaving. She crossed smoothly to the door.

He spoke to her back. "Lord Benchley will never permit Rosalind to marry Matt if there is even a question surrounding his name. Swear to me that you were only stupid enough to write one letter."

Lucinda turned to gaze across the room at him with cold green eyes—so different from *her* warm hazel ones. What if he never saw those beautiful eyes again? He must.

His mother hadn't answered. His frown deepened. "Tell me now, Mother. Will any more skeletons come knocking?"

Her eyes tipped to the floor. "No," she replied bitterly. "No more skeletons. I was only *'stupid'* once."

Mark let his head drop forward. He could argue that, but didn't want to. He wanted his mother out. A moment later the front door slammed. He slumped into his chair and, resting his elbows atop the architectural drawings scattered across his desk, supported his head in his hands. How he hated her. How he detested her selfish preoccupation—her constant need for attention and preeminence. It was suffocating.

He took a deep breath and strove to shut his mother from his mind. Leaning back in his chair, he let his eyes fall closed and took himself back to the Crystal Palace— to *her*. How had he not noticed her immediately? He'd been so preoccupied with his own thoughts that, had it not been for the falling tree . . . Thank God for mischievous boys. He'd simply reacted, pulling her from harm's way without thought. Then, in the next instant, awareness of her—her body, her scent—had overcome him in a dizzying rush. And then she'd turned and he had stared into the face of desire.

Mark drew a deep breath. He pictured her reciting the words from the Song of Solomon, heard her gentle voice, saw her soft mouth forming the words. Words she knew by heart. That had been surprising.

He remembered the sound of her muffled cries and the feel of her clenching flesh. His cock stirred. He wanted her again. Desperately.

Which was odd. After having her, he had thought to walk away and never see her again. And though he'd never been with a stranger who wasn't a courtesan, walking away had never been difficult, even from women he knew well. But today, he almost hadn't been able to do it. He had forced himself to leave her. Had even denied himself the luxury of looking back. He shouldn't have left her like that.

He'd made a mistake—a terrible mistake.

"M." "M" for mistake? God, she hoped not.

Dressed in her nightgown and bolstered against her bed pillows, Passion stared at the blue letter embroidered in plain block. No flourishes or decorative framing for her mystery man. She fingered the fabric and held it before her bedside candle. The linen was of the best quality. She brought it to her nose and inhaled the fresh scent that clung to the finely woven fibers. Her eyes closed briefly. No, not a mistake. Never.

He had given her a gift—a gift she had longed for. Rapture instead of restraint. Desire instead of disinterest. Freedom and fulfillment instead of duty and obligation.

With a sigh, she pressed the handkerchief to her breast. He had made her feel vital—alive.

How long had she felt numb? The answer came immediately—since her marriage. Over three interminable years, her husband had killed her with indifference. Never cruel, never kind, he had worn away her spirit with aloof disinterest. She might have borne it better had she had a baby to love and be loved by. But no baby had come. And no pleasure or satisfaction had come with the trying. Her husband had always done his "work," as he called it, in less than a minute. At first, her body had yearned for more. But as time passed, the yearning had become a scream. Night after night, year after year, she had clamped the tight hand of suffocating denial over her body— forcing its shrieking pleas for release into strict, unrelenting silence.

She hadn't shed a tear when he died.

But today she had cried.

And *he*—he was the fulfillment of dreams she had forgotten she had. She could almost feel his mouth upon

hers, could almost taste him. She traced her lips with her
fingers. His hands had caressed her and held her with such
unabashed intimacy. She ran her hands firmly across her
breasts and down her sides. There had been no hesitation,
no ambivalence in his touch. He had taken her with passionate ferocity, demanding everything from her in return
for all that he gave. Her hand stole between her legs. His
cock had filled her, stretched her, beyond the boundaries
of mere pleasure and into ecstasy. She could almost feel it
in her hands. So big and so beautiful.

God, what had come over her? Jerking her hand from
between her legs, she clasped the handkerchief to her
chest. She had given herself to a stranger! She could
barely believe she had done so. The memory was amazingly vivid but strangely dreamlike, too.

And it could only have happened with him. She
frowned—only with this man and in this way. He was as
rare and unavoidable as a meteor falling from the sky. And
there she had been, in the Crystal Palace, when he had
fallen upon her. One man, one place. One time?

Of course, it must be one time. Her life was prescribed
and quiet. She had come to find a comfortable satisfaction
in that. Duty and obligation had their own fulfillment.
Duty and obligation had sustained her through her marriage and after. She had found her place.

Passion sighed and lifted the handkerchief to her nose
once again before folding it carefully and tucking it beneath her pillow. She would probably never see him again,
but the smell of lemon verbena would forever bring him
to mind—would forever belong to him.

She turned on her side and stared into the flickering
candle flame. Tomorrow she would return to the Crystal
Palace. An unquenchable thrill ran through her. Deep blue
eyes filled with a beseeching urgency flashed before her
mind's eye. She remembered the curve of his lips—her hand
stole beneath her pillow—the angle of his jaw. Her fingers
closed around the small square of fabric. The feel of his
heavy penis in her hand.

Despite the folly of it, she wanted to see him again.

What would tomorrow bring? Probably the conventional continuation of the life she was accustomed to. But perhaps, just perhaps, she might have the chance to lose herself once again in the dark depths of his blue eyes.

Tomorrow. It seemed forever until tomorrow.

Chapter Three

TOMORROW

Mark strolled once more through the main gallery of the Crystal Palace, scanning the late morning crowd carefully. Where was she? He had been searching for more than half an hour. Discouragement rolled heavily over him. The place seemed more crowded than the day before. Why had he thought it would be so easy? He had been sure she would be here, sure he would find her.

What if he never saw her again? He shoved the question from his mind angrily. Not a consideration. Absolutely *not* a consideration.

He paused beside a tall statue of *Psyche*. Assuming she was there, they could pass each other all day and never know it. He must stay in one place and wait. But where? If she wanted to find him, where would she go first: china, silver, or gothic furniture? He made his decision quickly and headed for the gothic furniture. Yes, she would go there. It was their place.

Mark's shoulders tensed as he strode purposefully forward. She would come. She must come. He need only wait. Damn. He hated waiting.

Crowds of people gathered in tight clusters before every heavy piece of furniture in the exhibit. At the back of the room, a small group stood before the *prie-dieu*. Mark's gaze locked immediately upon a woman in dark blue. The muscles in his gut clenched. Only half revealed through the crowd, he traced the straight line of her shoulder and the tight curve of her waist with his eye. When the rest of the group turned off toward another display, he saw the wide black ribbon tied around her upper arm.

His body relaxed, and his blood coursed again in his veins. He'd found her. Relief flowed over him like a wave—relief and something else. Something indefinable that made him want to smile. Pulling off his gloves and unbuttoning his topcoat, he approached her slowly. It must be desire. He could feel it, even now, stirring in his sac and tingling down his prick.

As he drew closer to her, the feeling intensified. He raised his hand. Her shoulders lifted and fell in a sigh. His fingers reached for her. She bowed her head. Was she praying? And then he touched her—lightly, the tips of his fingers trailing gently down the middle of her silk clad back.

Her body jolted and then visibly relaxed. He stayed behind her, shielding her from the room, as he pressed his hand firmly against her waist and breathed in the fragrance of vanilla and orange blossoms that clung to her.

Feeling her and smelling her exhilarated him. Thank God he had found her. Thank God she had come. The urge to pull her into his arms was almost overwhelming. "Hello," he said, quietly.

She turned, and he let his hand slide around her waist before removing it. Her long lashes fluttered before she met his gaze. "Hello."

Her eyes were even more beautiful than he had remembered. Was it the golden hazel orbs that he found so compelling? Or the expression of gladness reflected there?

He held her gaze as a large group of ladies moved past

them to admire the gothic screen. His cock stirred at the memory of yesterday. Was she thinking of it, too? Was that the reason for the look in her eye?

Mark glanced at the open Bible on the *prie-dieu. Take ye heed, watch and pray: for ye know not when the time is.* Mark 13:33.

"It was open there when I arrived." She nodded toward the Bible. "Mark is my favorite gospel, so I took it as a sign that you might come." Her lips turned in an almost reluctant smile. "So I watched and prayed."

The high-pitched twittering of the ladies faded as they walked away. "And why is Mark your favorite gospel?"

She smoothed her gloved hand over the page in a slow caress, and her words came thoughtfully. "It has a pure, spare quality. In its original, it doesn't offer every answer. And it isn't always pretty." She looked up at him. "But Mark doesn't care. He's honest and unfettered." She shrugged, and her small smile appeared again. "Because it's probably the first, the oldest, I've always believed it's the closest to the word of the Lord."

Mark felt a weighty moment of divine influence before discarding it as ridiculous. He couldn't contain his smile. He actually had a disciple to thank for reuniting him with the woman he wanted to fornicate with. A disciple he shared a name with, no less.

"You're laughing at me."

Mark's smile softened as he studied her beautiful face. Truly, God worked in mysterious ways. "Tell me your name."

She hesitated. "Why?"

"Because," he said quietly, "I like to put a name to the women I fuck." He felt a flicker of regret for his phrasing but then dismissed it. Though crude, it was true, and she should have no misconceptions about what he was there for.

She glanced over her shoulder as a blush darkened the pink of her cheeks, but then she held out her hand. "Passion."

Mark stopped, his hand midway to hers. He shook his head. "No. I want your real name."

She looked at him with those soft, deep eyes. "My name *is* Passion. I was born on Passion Sunday."

Mark paused. The sapphire blue ostrich feather tucked inside the brim of her bonnet framed her face in a soft, sensual arc, the long, darkly iridescent tendrils fluttering gently against her temple. Her beautiful eyes regarded him unblinkingly, and her pink mouth parted with her breath. She *was* Passion. His cock lifted hungrily. He closed his hand around hers. "I'm Mark."

Her eyes widened, and one of her hands pressed to her chest. "Truly?"

He stroked her palm and nodded. "Not always pretty, but honest and unfettered."

She smiled. "Then, perhaps, it really was a sign."

He shrugged. "If you like."

The room was experiencing an ebb. A family stood near the exit with some all too observant children. When they left . . .

Mark turned back to Passion, partly shielding her with his body. "Personally, I don't believe in signs. I believe in what I can see." He pulled off her gloves. "What I can touch." He brought her hand to his stiff erection. God, how he loved her fingers curving around him. "And what I can feel."

She bit her pretty lower lip as she explored him discreetly under the cover of his long topcoat.

The slow shifting of her hand up and down the length of him made him even harder, made him want to have her even more. When he stopped her with the press of his hand firmly over hers, she looked up at him and her eyes moved intently over his features. What did she see? He saw need and desire in her expression. Need and desire softened with something else. What, he didn't know, but she should have no delusions.

He tightened his fingers around hers and thrust against

her palm. "This is the reason I'm here, Passion. For no other reason but this. Do you understand?"

Her lovely lips trembled a little. "Yes. I understand."

He released her hand and returned her gloves. Her voice made him want to fuck her. Damn, everything about her made him want to fuck her. He looked over his shoulder. A few couples milled at the other end of the room. The family was gone. He took a step toward the screen. Passion moved with him. Another large group filed in at the exhibit entrance. Wait—wait. He clasped her hand. No, now. And he pulled her into the shadowed corner that was theirs.

Mark fell back against the wall and brought Passion with him. His arms crushed her close, and he swooped upon her uplifted mouth like a bird of prey, latching onto her tender lips with bruising ferocity. He thrust his tongue into her mouth, tasting her, penetrating her. As he pushed his tongue deeper and drew on her breath, he knew he was being rough. But she brought this out in him. And between her breathy gasps, she didn't pull away, but collapsed more against him, her mouth opening wider to the force of his tongue.

He felt her pulling his hat from his head and, as her fingers threaded through his hair, a soft moan wafted from her mouth to his. He swallowed it and demanded others while he yanked at the fastenings of his trousers. Her body moved wantonly against him, and he felt as if rivers of blood pumped, unabated, into his cock.

He was so fucking hard, he couldn't get out of the opening in his trousers, and each brush against the light wool was torture. Tearing his mouth from hers in a gasp of relief, he finally freed his rampant erection. It jutted up, bigger and harder than he'd ever seen it, and the head bobbed swollen and purple.

Passion pulled back from him and stared, open-mouthed and hungry-looking. She licked her swollen lips. He loved that; she had done the same thing yesterday.

Mark reached down and pulled free his heavy balls so

she could see all of him. As her eyes feasted on his display, he gripped himself firmly and stroked. He clenched his jaw as he squeezed clear fluid from his prick's protuberant head. Then, with his thumb, he smeared the thick drops over the throbbing purple crown until it glistened. "This is what you want, isn't it, Passion?" he murmured low. "If I wanted, I could make you beg for it, couldn't I?"

Passion's whole body seemed to be trembling. The feather at her temple shook, but her eyes hadn't flickered, even for a moment, from his little demonstration. She looked at him now, and the blatant longing in her eyes almost pained him. "Yes." Her voice was a sweet, breathy whisper.

He smoothed the back of his fingers across her cheek. "But I won't." Voices floated over the top of the screen from without. He ignored them and spoke near her ear. "Now take off your bonnet and open the front of your gown."

Passion loosed the bow beneath her chin and let the hat fall to the floor, revealing her dark auburn hair. The straight severity of her center part and braided bun somehow enhanced her beauty and made her eyes look even more doelike. As her hands fluttered at the buttons of her high-necked gown, Mark's breath caught and his cock pulsed painfully. But a shrill laugh from the exhibit room made her pause.

Mark frowned. "Passion, open your damned gown." He sounded harsh, impatient. But damn it, this was what she did to him, and he needed to see more of her—now.

She seemed unperturbed by his tone and quickly released her buttons. As she moved from one to the next, glimpses of her neck and chest were revealed. Finally, she peeled back the two sides, revealing fine pale skin, delicate collarbones, and a deep V of lacy undergarments. Mark's breathing quickened, and he pulled firmly on his tight cods to ease the pressure of his roiling sperm.

Her skin glowed creamy and smooth in the shadowy light. She pulled the pink ribbon tied at her breast, and after undoing the tiny buttons of her batiste corset cover, spread it open. Arching over the neck of her chemise and pushed up by her corset, the high, lush mounds of her breasts rose and fell with her rapid breath. But as beautiful as that sight was, Mark's eyes locked, instead, on the dark shadows of her nipples. Showing just above the curving support of her corset stays, and straining protuberantly against her chemise, in at least the thickness of his little finger, were two of the most succulent-looking buds he'd ever seen.

With a low moan, he pulled her close and brought her hand to his straining cock. As her fingers curled around him, he yanked the layers of her bodice, corset cover, and chemise down from her shoulders. Lifting her against the wall, he braced her with his leg and rubbed his cheek against the hard nub of one nipple while exposing the other with a firm tug at her chemise. Passion gasped, and her back arched.

Mark's cock pumped in her hand, and his mouth watered. Her exposed nipple was dark rose and the bud was thick, distending even farther once released from its confines. He left the other covered. He liked the sight of it pressed to the fabric. They looked positively edible—tits for a man's mouth, not a babe's. How did he get this damned lucky? While he pinched and rolled the bare one between his fingers, he closed his mouth over the one still covered by her chemise. As he sucked and laved it with his tongue, it grew and lengthened even more. When he finally pulled back, he stared hungrily at what he had wrought. The thick little finger of flesh stuck out almost an half an inch from its rosy base, and the wet fabric of her chemise clung to it like a second skin.

Passion's breath came in short heaves as she arched against him, one hand grasping his nape, the other working magic on his aching member.

Even the sound of her breathing inflamed him. He bit down on the covered nipple and flicked the end with his tongue. Passion's body leapt in his arms and as pre-come dripped from his weeping cock, she rubbed it over his now flaming flesh. Mark groaned and latched hungrily onto her naked nipple, sucking it hard and rubbing his tongue over the long, stiff nub until Passion writhed against him.

"Please!"

He heard her urgent whisper even over the growing noise of the crowd without.

"I—I need . . ."

Mark tore his mouth from her juicy nipple and let her slide down his leg. Her hips jerked, and her fingers curled in the fabric of his coat sleeves as if she needed help to remain standing. When she looked up at him, he stopped breathing for a moment. Her beautiful face was the picture of such desperate and poignant longing that a small, answering wash of come actually spilled, thick and creamy, over the head of his prick.

A long red-brown curl had fallen free from her bun, her face was flushed, and her moist lower lip trembled, sweet and pouting. Her heavily lashed eyes begged him better than words ever could. And as he gazed at her, a single tear tumbled down her cheek and splashed upon the heaving rise of her breast. He watched it trickle down the sloping bank and rush to rest upon her rosy nipple.

"Mark, I—I need . . ."

How he loved her voice.

"What do you need?" He spoke low and close as he rubbed his come down the length of his shaft. Her lashes fluttered down for a moment as she watched him. "Tell me what you need, Passion."

A frown wrinkled her brow as she lifted her wet eyes to him. Another tear fell. "You know."

He smoothed the back of his finger down the wet trail on her cheek and then brushed the moisture from her nipple, drawing a gasp from her. "But I want to hear you say it. Just tell me."

Passion bit her lip and her fingers clenched in his coat

again. Two more tears fell down her cheeks. Such lovely tears.

"Many more of those and you'll force me to take pity on you." He pressed a kiss to the path her tear had taken, then pressed another to her trembling mouth. "Come, Passion." He kissed her again. "It pleases me to hear you speak." He bit down briefly on her soft lower lip. "And no one shall know what you say but me."

"I need you," she said breathlessly. Her fingers clenched, and her breast heaved. "I need you, inside me."

"Ah. Well, that's good, because I need to be inside you."

He could drown in her eyes. He brushed the back of his fingers over her thick, bare nipple. "Are your thighs wet?"

"Yes."

"Is your cunt clenching hungrily, even now?"

Her lashes fluttered down, and a blush darkened her cheeks. The noise of the crowd floated over the top of the screen.

Mark tipped her chin up. "Don't look away from me." He slid his thumb across her lower lip. "And never be ashamed. There's no need." He glanced down at himself. "Look at me, standing here with my prick out—so full of spunk that it's spilling out on its own." He pressed his mouth to her moist cheek. "But I don't care, because I'm with you"—he drew her hand to his cock—"and this is what we're here for." Her fingers moved down his shaft and cupped his balls. He bit back a moan. "Now tell me something, before I dump all my come right down the front of your skirt."

She met his gaze; her long, wet lashes spiky. "I am clenching," she whispered. "And right now, I feel that if you don't fill this emptiness in me, I might be driven mad with longing."

Two more tears fell. He loved watching them. He had the power to fulfill her, or not. She needed him.

"Please, Mark."

His breathing quickened.

"You have what I need," she breathed.

"Damn right, I do." He took her lips in a hard, potent kiss. He could taste her tears and pushed his tongue inside, sweeping over her smooth teeth and brushing the roof of her mouth. As he thrust deeper, nudging her wider, he yanked up her skirts and swept his hand between her legs. He moaned into her mouth, and her body almost collapsed in his arms. His blood rushed. Her arms clung to him. He'd never felt anything like it; she was dripping onto his hand.

He broke the kiss and sucked in air as he whirled her around to face the wall. Come was spilling from his prick. The knob was dark purple and distended. Fuck! He crammed it against the slippery mouth of her quim and shoved.

Mark gasped out loud as he slammed the tender head of his cock against the door of Passion's womb. He heard her soft moan beneath the thundering noise of his blood pounding in his ears and the steady hum of the crowd. He could feel sperm, still trickling out of him, as he thrust again, harder. Harder!

His cock felt as stiff as steel, and her cunt was stretched so damn tight around him. He held her hips and thrust again, loving the explosion of mind-numbing pleasure that shot through him with each assault upon her womb. His whole shaft throbbed, and come kept boiling up from his sac and spilling out of him in a slow, constant stream. He thrust again, grinding the swollen head of his penis against the tight opening to her womb, as he bore down forcefully on her hips. He heard Passion gasp. He bit back a groan. The pressure felt so fucking good—and he was so fucking hard—he felt like nothing could keep him from forcing his way into the deepest cavities of her body.

He spoke against her ear, his voice a hoarse whisper, as he kept bearing down on her hips. "This is what you need, isn't it? This is why you came back"—he withdrew and thrust—"to be filled up completely. That's why you need me." He shoved harder. "Isn't it?"

Passion's cunt clenched even tighter around him. "Yes! Yes!"

He squeezed his eyes shut as his hips suddenly pistoned uncontrollably into her, each forward thrust tenderizing the fleshy door of her womb. He heard a choked gasp and, pushing down hard on her hips, crammed his prick with unrelenting force against the barrier.

And with a great inhalation of air, Passion gave, just the smallest degree. An animal-sounding grunt escaped him as he felt the incredible pressure. But he could not withdraw, not now. Her cunt was throbbing with such force—a pulling force that milked exquisite little spurts of come out of him.

Mark's breathing was ragged near her ear. "Passion, your cunt is sucking my prick like a hungry little mouth." He bit her soft lobe as a strong pull leached more from him. "It feels like a plea for more. Is it?" His cock throbbed, and he tilted his hips ever so slightly. "I have more to give you. Tell me you want it."

With one cheek pressed to the wall and the other flushed and moist, her loose lock of hair curled in front of her face and fluttered with each of her short, gasping breaths. Her whisper was so low he had to strain to hear it. "I want all of it. I want to be filled with it. If I could offer my whole body as a sheath for your cock, I would do it."

Mark's legs almost buckled. His prick thumped with a hot surge of blood. "Oh Passion, I would die for that!" He pushed into her with renewed force. "Open for me. Open!" His hips pumped into her in quick, tight, ever-forward thrusts as he bore down harder than ever. She arched her back, and he almost shouted as he felt the head of his cock wedge deeper against the trembling doors to her womb. His balls swelled with more come. "That's it. Open! Let me inside you."

Passion began to shudder. Her hands clawed the wall,

and tears poured down her cheeks. Her voice was a tortured whisper. "Mark! Mark, I'm going to—it's coming! I can't stop it!"

Mark sucked in his breath as her body erupted. He slammed his hand over her mouth just before a long, sobbing moan would have burst from her unhindered. "Yes, yes," he gasped into her ear. "Do it. Come!" He leaned on her hip with his free hand and, as wave after wracking wave of quivering cunt clenched and pulled at his weeping prick, he knew he was going to go with her. He squeezed his eyes shut, his cock throbbed in expectation, and then her clasping cunt actually sucked him deeper. He choked back a groan and bit into her pale shoulder as he thrust against the tight, tilting fingers of flesh that protected Passion's womb. He had never been so deep in a woman.

Sweat broke on his brow. His heart hammered in his chest. "I could give you everything right now," he rasped in her ear. "If I wanted, I could bury my whole cock in you right now. My prick is so bloody hard, and I have the strength to do it." He couldn't stop thrusting. "But I want you to come to me, again and again."

His hips pumped faster and faster. Passion moaned behind his hand. He felt her come dripping down his cods. Her juicy quim was grabbing at him again, and the pressure on the head of his cock was like nothing he'd ever felt. He pumped in a feral fury—wild to push farther, yet denying the urge with the last vestiges of his will. He was on fire, and he wanted to burn forever. Forever!

"Fuck!" he snarled against her shoulder and threw himself into the flames. His cock erupted. Blinding whiteness flashed before his eyes. With explosive force, floods of hot come spewed out of him. He muffled his cries against the pale curve of Passion's shoulder as he pumped more and more and more into her. He couldn't stop it, didn't want to stop it. It kept coming and coming—roaring up from his swollen sac and spurting out in thick washes that only made way for more. He groaned. His legs shook.

With each powerful expulsion, euphoric, blinding bliss tore through his body, wracking it with tremors that felt like they might never end.

Then, just when he thought he'd spent all he had, Passion came again. Her cunt gripped and sucked his half-swollen prick so diligently that she coaxed from it a final glutinous jet of come.

Mark could hear nothing but the sound of his own breathing. He opened his mouth over Passion's shoulder and tasted her skin. It was salty; with her sweat or his, he didn't know. He didn't care. His arms swept around her, and he cupped her luscious breasts.

This was where he belonged. This was ecstasy.

And on the other side of the screen, the crowd moved on. How many people had passed them, unknowing?

After his breathing slowed and he mustered some energy to move, Mark lifted his head and brushed Passion's long curl back from her face. Her eyes were closed. "Are you all right?"

"Yes." The word came on an exhalation of breath. Her eyes stayed closed.

Mark tightened his arm around her. Brushing his finger across her flushed cheek, he pressed a kiss into the soft place behind her ear. "I'm still inside you."

"I know," she said on the wind of another breath.

She smelled of vanilla, orange blossoms, and sex. He kissed her again. "I think I filled you to overflowing. When I pull out, it's going to spill."

"I don't care."

Mark smiled. He liked her answer. Women usually didn't like messes—especially a man's—and certainly not on their person.

"Excellent," he whispered and began to pull out.

Passion moaned and her shoulder lifted. Mark paused as he noticed a darkening bruise on the pale slope. He remembered muffling his cries against her, sucking hard to contain them. He ran his finger over the mark, and his cock jerked almost painfully.

Passion looked back at him.

He met her gaze and throbbed inside her. "I left a mark on you."

"Did you?"

"Yes." He bent and kissed the spot, touching it with his tongue, then slowly pulled out of her.

She gasped softly, and Mark let her skirts fall.

Still half hard, his prick was slick with come. Passion turned and watched him as he wiped it on his shirttail. He looked at her, leaning against the wall, with her auburn hair falling and one beautiful breast half bared, and thought she was the most beautiful thing he'd ever seen. He pushed his reluctant cock down his pant leg and buttoned up before bracing his hands on either side of her. He studied her upturned face, memorizing the curve of her brow, the slant of her nose, and the curl of her lips.

She drew a deep, ragged breath and reached to pull her gown back over her shoulders.

"Let me help you," Mark murmured, carefully arranging the sapphire silk of her bodice over her shoulders.

"Thank you."

"Thank *you*." He let his fingers brush her bare nipple, eliciting a gasp before returning her chemise to its proper place. When she lifted her hands, he brushed them away. "I said, let me." He pressed a kiss to her forehead. "I'll be good."

She smiled at that, and her smile made him smile.

Mark straightened her corset cover. As he slipped the tiny buttons through their eyes, it occurred to him that he'd never, in his entire life, helped a woman dress. Even for his mistresses, with whom he was generally at leisure, he had never lifted a finger of assistance. He tied the little pink bow above the row of buttons. In fact, once he spent himself, he was completely uninterested in exchanging even polite conversation.

He closed the front of her bodice and started the buttons. But then, though paid courtesans all, none of his mistresses had ever given him what Passion had given for free. None had displayed such need. None had given him their tears. And though they all claimed to worship his penis, none had opened their bodies to it. None had wanted to.

Her soft voice drew his attention. "May I ask you something?"

"Yes." He realized he was frowning and eased his brow.

"You said earlier, you like to put a name to the women you fuck."

Christ, that sounded bad even to him.

She blinked and moistened her lips. "I wonder, do you do this often?"

Mark closed her last button. "What do you want to know—if I fuck often, or if I often fuck female strangers in public places?"

She considered that a moment. "I suppose the latter."

Mark held back his smile. His language never seemed to offend her. "No." He bent to drop a kiss at the corner of her mouth. "Never"—he touched her lower lip with his tongue—"until now, with you."

She studied him for a moment, as if gauging the truth of his words. Then: "Thank you for answering."

He lifted his brows. "You're welcome."

He felt her soft auburn curl between his fingers before sweeping it back. She touched him as she took it, then twisted the piece around her braided bun. Lifting her other arm, she pulled a pin and quickly tacked down the heavy tress. She smoothed the sides with her fingers and then pressed her palms to the back, feeling for strands out of place.

He wanted to see her with her hair down.

Bending, he swept up her bonnet. "I want to see you again," he said as he slipped it onto her head. "And I don't like uncertainty." She lifted her chin, staring at him as he pulled the silk ties into a bow. He set it at the same jaunty angle that she'd had it before. "Will you meet me here to-morrow at ten-thirty?"

Passion smiled. "Thank you for putting it where I wanted it."

Her smile dazzled him, and his cock thumped against his thigh. "Putting what where you wanted it?"

Her fingers brushed her bonnet ties. "My bow. Thank you for remembering where I had it and returning it there." Her head tilted to the side. "Thank you for noticing at all."

How could he not notice? "So, will you come?"

She paused only briefly. "Yes."

Mark smiled as he picked up his hat. "Good." He shoved his fingers through his hair and was about to replace his topper.

"Wait," Passion said softly.

Mark's breathing slowed as she stepped close. Reaching up, she smoothed back the recalcitrant wave that always fell over his brow. Then she combed her fingers through the short hair above his ears and smoothed his nape. She was touching him. He wanted her touch.

"All right," she murmured.

Mark settled his hat on his head. Her nimble fingers slid to his cravat, adjusting the intricate folds just so. Why did it matter so much that her hands were upon him? She smoothed the front of his vest and the lapels of his topcoat. Her long lashes fluttered. He rested his hands on her waist. She brushed her palms down his coat sleeves where she had gripped them earlier. He liked the feel of her slim, curving waist.

"There," she breathed, lifting her golden hazel eyes.

Staring into her deep gaze, Mark wished he could make the crowd just beyond the screen disappear. He wished her could have her all over again. Now. "Kiss me."

Passion moistened her lips and then drew her arms up to his shoulders. When he didn't move, she paused.

Mark's fingers tightened on her waist. He waited.

Then her hands slid over his shoulders. One slipped behind his neck. With gentle pressure, she pulled him down.

Her body pressed to his. Her head tilted, her eyes closed, and her mouth parted.

Mark didn't breathe. His eyes closed.

Her mouth pressed upon his with the softest, sweetest urgency. Delicate lips nudged his apart, and her tongue tasted him in slow, luxurious swaths. Her hand tightened on his nape, and her tongue moved more deeply. Mark moaned and swept his arms around her. Passion kissed him and kissed him, sucking his tongue into her mouth and stroking it with her own.

His muscles tightened. A strong pulse throbbed in his groin. A wave of dizziness washed over him. With a low groan, he reluctantly pulled from Passion's embrace and put a steadying hand on the wall.

She supported his shoulder, and a worried frown turned her brow. "Are you all right?"

Mark looked down and expelled a disbelieving snort. His cock was straining, thick and strong against his pant leg, forcing it out at an odd angle. No wonder he felt light-headed. He looked into Passion's concerned frown and felt a hot surge. "Yes, I'm all too well."

Glancing down, her gaze held. "Oh," she whispered, immediately licking her lips.

Mark winced as his erection immediately responded with a hard knock against its confines. Damn it! Where the hell was his control? Sudden anger warred with his lust. He tried to contain it.

Passion lifted her hand toward him.

He clenched his jaw and growled, "I suggest you leave before I won't let you."

She jerked back. A frown furrowed between her brows, then she turned to go. Mark took a step after her. She paused at the narrow exit. His heart thumped. What if . . . ? She tipped her head forward cautiously. What if she didn't return as she had promised? She stepped forward.

"Passion," he breathed, reaching for her.

She was gone.

Chapter Four

FORCED MARRIAGES

Passion painted. A blue hydrangea was her subject. But deep blue eyes, dark slanting brows, and a sensual mouth hovered in her mind. Mark. Her body hummed, as if a low charge of electricity sparked through her.

"I'm sorry I wasn't able to meet you at the exhibition yesterday," Charlotte said as she tried to duplicate the pink rose before her.

"It's all right." Passion's paintbrush swirled on the plate. She could hear his voice, low and urgent—could feel his hands, strong and certain. And his kisses—his deep, hungry kisses, made her weak and breathless.

"Mother kept pressing me to go, but I truly had the very worst of headaches."

"Umm-hmm." Passion dipped her brush into cerulean blue and remembered the feel of Mark's head pressed to her breast, drawing upon her nipple. It made her wet with need. The smell of him, the feel of him in her arms, brought both heady desire and enveloping comfort. How could that be?

"She even had all my clothes laid out. She never does that. I don't know why she was so insistent."

"Hmm, strange." Passion's arm floated, guiding the brush. Behind their screen, she had been in another world. A world made only for the two of them. A world where desire and fulfillment crossed from the realm of dreams into reality.

"If I hadn't begun crying, I think she actually would have forced me to go."

"Really?" Passion applied fresh color to her brush. Mark was all too real. The image of his cock, rising thick and hard against his trouser leg, was ingrained in her brain. If she concentrated hard enough, she could almost feel the incredible sensation of having him inside her. Passion shifted in her chair as a tingling pulse beat between her legs.

"You aren't angry with me, are you? I told Mother you wouldn't be."

"No." But in the end, he'd been angry. Why? He'd asked her to kiss him and then he'd rejected her touch and told her to go. "Go before I won't let you," he'd said. Why would wanting her make him angry? It hadn't before. Did he still want her? Would he want her tomorrow?

She frowned. God help her, she still wanted him. Most urgently.

Charlotte sighed. "You *are* angry with me. I can tell."

Passion finally looked at her cousin. The warm sunlight filtering through Aunt Matty's sunroom windows illuminated Charlotte's chestnut curls. "Charlotte, I'm not angry with you. Your note of apology was here when we arrived home. I wasn't angry with you then. I'm not angry with you now."

Charlotte smiled. "I'm glad." She put a fresh dollop of white paint on the palette.

Passion returned to her painting. How different her day would have been if Charlotte had kept their appointment. Was it possible that the road of one's life could be turned by something as inconsequential as a headache? Surely

she walked a different path today than she had two days
ago. In most ways, it looked much the same—like now,
sitting here painting with Charlotte. But behind the screen
at the Crystal Palace, and in the hidden recesses of her
body, everything seemed changed.

How odd that everything else went on as always.

She paused in her painting. Of course, she wanted
everything to go on as always. This was life. What happened behind the screen at the Crystal Palace was relegated to a realm of dreams and secrecy. Yes, everything
must go on as always.

Passion glanced down at the paint palette. She frowned
at the sight of her steel knife smeared with the white paint.
"Charlotte, did you just mix the Lacroix white with the
steel knife?"

Charlotte glanced up from the china plate before her,
paintbrush gripped tightly in her hand. "Yes, isn't that
right?"

Passion pushed down her frustration. Everything as always. "No, darling. The white and yellows are damaged
by contact with metal. You must use the horn knife. The
steel knife is for the other colors."

"Oh, Passion, I'm sorry. Is it ruined then?" Charlotte's
chagrin showed plainly on her pretty face.

"Well, yes." Passion handed her cousin the turpentine.
"Here. Clean the knife with this."

Passion sighed. She had just purchased that pot of
white, and now half of it was gone. She scraped the con-
taminated paint from the palette and removed the rest with
a turpentine-soaked square of muslin.

When she looked up, she found Charlotte regarding her
with a worried frown. "When next we go for supplies, I'll
purchase them."

Passion's tension eased. At sixteen, Charlotte was so
sweet-tempered and well meaning that Passion could
never stay angry with her for long. She smiled. "Don't
worry, darling. It's just a little paint. But I'm afraid you'll
have to begin anew on your plate."

Charlotte looked dismayed. "And this is the best I've ever done."

Passion glanced at the rather flat-looking rose positioned in the center of the plate. "You *are* improving. The next one will be even better."

Charlotte glanced at Passion's plate, and her eyes widened. "Oh, Passion. That's beautiful. Why, it's magnificent!"

Passion examined the hydrangea she had painted upon the plain china. Though less exacting and more painterly than her usual work, it was alive. It seemed to lie upon the plate, a fluttering remnant from the garden, waiting to be plucked up and saved by a quenching dip into a vase of water. It was the quality of work she always attempted but never achieved. How, in heaven's name, had she accomplished it today, without even thinking?

"Silver," Charlotte said thoughtfully. "You must gild it in silver."

"Yes." Passion nodded as she signed P.E.D. beneath the flower. "Silver will be perfect."

"Passion, why do you sign everything P.E.D.? Shouldn't you use your husband's name?"

She stared at the initials. She would never put her husband's name on her work. It was hers, not his. "To the world, I am Mrs. Passion Elizabeth Redington. But in my heart and in my art, I am Passion Elizabeth Dare. And until I truly give my heart, so shall I remain."

The sound of voices drew their attention.

"I'm so pleased you were able to pay us a visit, Mr. Swittly." Aunt Matty's voice, loud even when she was trying to be discreet, drifted into the sunroom from the adjoining parlor. "Now, when you meet my niece, you mustn't be alarmed by her name. It is absolutely no reflection of her temperament, which is as even and refined as you'll find in a lady. I'll never know why my dear brother permitted the child to be christened with such a name. It was all her mother's doing, I assure you."

As Charlotte giggled behind her hand, Passion rolled

her eyes. She could almost see her aunt shaking her head disapprovingly.

"Please be seated, Mr. Swittly. I'll fetch my niece and her cousin."

Aunt Matty poked her lace-capped head into the sunroom. "Girls, girls," she whispered loudly, "come immediately."

Passion and Charlotte stood and removed their painting smocks.

"Come along, girls," Aunt Matty urged, as she looked them both over carefully. "Charlotte, you have paint on your finger. Passion, my dear, well, you're quite perfect."

Passion waited for Charlotte to wipe her finger and then Aunt Matty ushered them into the parlor.

A tall, corpulent man with a florid complexion and a head of thick, unruly blond hair stood as they entered.

"Ladies, I have the honor of introducing Mr. Alfred Swittly, the nephew of my dear friends, the Misses Eustacia and Arabella Swittly."

Passion felt her aunt's hand pressing her forward. "Mr. Swittly, this is my niece, Mrs. Passion Redington."

Passion nodded as the huge man bowed before her.

"I'm charmed, Mrs. Redington," he said, in a low tone as his green eyes passed quickly up and down her person.

Aunt Matty smiled approvingly. "And this is Miss Charlotte Lawrence, Passion's cousin."

"Charmed again, I'm sure," Alfred Swittly intoned.

Aunt Matty ushered Passion and Charlotte toward the settee as the giant of a man returned to his seat. If furniture could groan, Passion was certain the dainty chair would do so. It creaked dangerously as Alfred Swittly adjusted himself between its curving arms.

"You must forgive me, Miss Lawrence, for interrupting your painting lesson." Alfred looked at Passion. "I have heard, Mrs. Redington, from your aunt, how you are teaching your cousin the finer points of painting botanicals upon china. I must say that I believe such a pursuit to be one of the most proper a lady may occupy herself with.

The hands are kept busy, while the mind is not overtaxed. And the end result is a lovely bit of bric-a-brac with which to decorate the house." He smiled. "Such gentile and domestic accomplishments are a true asset in a lady."

What a boor. Passion lifted her brows and smiled. "I hardly know how to address such praise, sir. I fear it may tax my poor mind to form a fitting reply, so I will sit, instead, in demure acceptance of your superior wisdom."

Aunt Matty sent Passion a suspicious frown from behind her fan, but Alfred Swittly positively puffed up with condescension. "Charming. Charming." He glanced between Passion and Charlotte before turning to Aunt Matty. "You must be very proud, Mistress Dare, to have such lovely nieces."

Aunt Matty smiled. "That I am, Mr. Swittly. My brother's daughters are the apples of my eye. However, Charlotte, dear child that she is, is not my niece. Charlotte's mother"—and here Aunt Matty's voice betrayed her disdain—"a certain Mrs. Abigail Lawrence, was cousin to Passion's mother." Aunt Matty fanned herself vigorously and looked to Passion for help. "What does that make Charlotte? First cousin once removed or second cousin twice removed?"

Passion laid her hand over Charlotte's and managed a small smile for Alfred Swittly. "Charlotte is my second cousin."

Aunt Matty frowned and paused in her fanning. "And what does that make her to me?"

"A distant but dear relation by marriage," Passion offered, squeezing Charlotte's hand.

Aunt Matty shrugged and resumed her fanning. "I can never keep these things straight. Can you, Mr. Swittly? Cousins all, I say."

"Indeed, Mistress. Indeed." Alfred Swittly tapped his hand upon his huge knee. "Though, like you, Mrs. Redington, I, too, have a second cousin whom I have—how shall I say?—taken under my tutorial wing. Though I do not teach painting." He guffawed. "No, far from it. A young man must be brought along to pursue other interests."

Passion could almost swear the hint of a leer flashed briefly in Albert Swittly's green eyes.

"Still," he continued, drawing a handkerchief from his pocket, "you and I, both, in our own ways, are influencing the maturation of our young cousins. How grand."

Passion regarded him carefully as he blotted the sweat from his brow. "Indeed, sir."

He leaned forward, drawing another straining crack from the desperate chair. "You know, Mrs. Redington, you and I have more in common than you might guess. You, alas, are a widow and I, alas, am a widower."

He spoke with such seeming delight at this happy coincidence that Passion felt compelled to behave badly. She crumpled her face into a grimace of despair. "Alas," she gasped, lowering her head and fishing in her pocket for her handkerchief. Drawing it out, she dabbed at her eyes as she spoke. "Forgive me, Mr. Swittly. I'm afraid that at this moment, the very thought of my sorrowful situation has scored my wounded heart afresh."

"Well, I—I . . ." Alfred stammered. "Your aunt assured me . . ."

Passion sniffed loudly and dabbed again. "And *my* sadness is only compounded by your own"—she looked at him, pained—"which, I'm sure, is deep and abiding."

Sweat popped from his brow. "Well, I . . . I mean, yes!" Jolted by her words, his expression changed from open chagrin to affected sorrow. "I still mourn, a little every day, for my dear, departed wife."

His florid face contorted into a frown meant to convey sorrow yet strength. It was really very well done.

He shook his head. "My heart is no less affected than your own, Mrs. Redington."

Passion released a long sigh. "As a compatriot in grief, I know you will excuse me to vent my pain privately, into my pillow." Passion hid her face in her handkerchief.

"Of course, Mrs. Redington."

When Passion stood, Charlotte rose, too, and slipped her arm around Passion's shoulder.

Alfred hoisted himself from the chair, which squeaked in relief. "I hope that when next we meet, we may engage in happier conversation, Mrs. Redington." He bowed. "And that this bond of sorrow we share might grow into a bond of friendship."

Passion smiled weakly. "'Tis more than I would wish for, sir. Good afternoon."

"Good afternoon." Alfred Swittly smiled. Then, seeming to remember that sadness was the emotion of the moment, he quickly reorganized his full face into a somber mien. He bowed to Charlotte. "Good afternoon, Miss Lawrence."

"Good afternoon, Mr. Swittly."

As Passion and Charlotte turned to Aunt Matty, they found her frowning suspiciously. But in the presence of Alfred Swittly, she quickly evinced concern and waved them off. "Go on then, my dears."

Passion and Charlotte walked slowly from the parlor, Passion sniffing loudly a few more times as they went. Once in the hall, they both clamped their hands over their mouths and headed for the stairs.

Halfway up, Aunt Matty's voice floated up from below. ". . . born for marriage."

Passion froze.

"Gracious," Charlotte gasped, bumping into her.

Passion raised her finger to her lips.

". . . are not made to remain widows," said Alfred Swittly. "No indeed. Her beauty, her grace, her feminine demeanor, have all convinced me she would be the perfect addition to my home. Forgive my bluntness, Mistress Dare, but a man is completely unsuited to domestic duties."

"Oh, I know, Mr. Swittly. I know. Were it not for Passion, my brother's house would be a shambles. When she returned home after her husband's death—God rest his soul—she went to no end of trouble to set it back to rights. And since the age of twelve, upon her mother's passing—God rest her soul—Passion has been like a mother to her two sisters. And as you can see, even Miss Lawrence adores her."

Passion and Charlotte shrank back as the downstairs maid crossed into the parlor with a tea tray. "Thank you, Margie, I'll pour. Please have a tray prepared for my niece and her cousin."

When the maid left, Passion and Charlotte pressed forward again.

A belligerent crack sounded from the chair. "Wonderful. Wonderful. For a woman must be more than a wife, Mistress Dare, mustn't she? Forgive me, but what woman's life is truly complete without the role of motherhood to firmly root it in domesticity?"

"I agree, Mr. Swittly, I agree. Even ladies such as myself, never blessed with a husband and children of their own, must find a way to apply their maternal instincts. I have always tried to be a mother figure to my nieces, and I do believe they have benefited from my efforts in that regard."

Passion could almost see Aunt Matty speaking over her teacup.

"And it is well you did so. I just read in the paper that women who remain childless are more likely to experience various degrees of insanity than women who do their maternal duty."

"Really? Well, there you are. *I've* always believed that missing tea could send one to bedlam."

"Missing tea? Well, I . . . I've never thought of it."

"Well, you must, Mr. Swittly. Just yesterday, I missed tea, and do you know what happened? A man trod upon my toe." A brief pause elapsed. Passion imagined her aunt raising her silver brows in her and-what-do-you-think-of-that? expression. "I can barely walk today, Mr. Swittly. And do you know what else? Passion was nearly blinded."

"What?"

"It's true. By a palm frond! I tell you, sir, the lack of

tea at the proper hour causes no end of mischief. Imagine if the whole world were to forgo tea. Mayhem, Mr. Swittly. Chaos!"

Passion shook her head and exchanged a look with Charlotte, who was hiding her grin behind her hand.

"I . . . Then I shall make a point of always observing teatime."

"See that you do." Something clanked onto the tea tray. "Now, about my niece, Mr. Swittly. Though she is not officially here for the season, Passion does come out of mourning next week. And though she only agreed to come to London to spend a holiday with me and to tutor her cousin in painting, Charlotte and I intend to get her out and about."

"Indeed, mistress. Indeed."

"The opening of the Crystal Palace could not have been better timed, for there are so many exciting events planned around it, that I doubt any young woman could resist them—even Passion." Passion could hear the glee in her aunt's voice. "It will be the perfect opportunity for you to begin your courtship. But you must be subtle, Mr. Swittley, subtle."

"I am a model of subtlety, Mistress Dare, a model."

Passion leaned on the banister and covered her face with her hands. God help her. She had told her aunt she didn't want marriage, had told her she was content in her life just as it was. She had agreed to a holiday in London only so she could spend time with her aunt and cousin and perhaps enjoy a little society after she came out of mourning, nothing more.

As Charlotte patted her back, Passion envisioned Alfred Swittly sweating over her as he tried to impregnate her with his progeny. She shuddered. Never! Besides, it wasn't even possible. During three years of marriage, she hadn't conceived—a fact her aunt had neatly avoided.

Passion straightened and gripped the banister. As intimate as the information was, she'd have to tell him. She'd make sure Alfred Swittly knew her body was not fertile ground for a child. Passion grasped Charlotte's hand and hurried up the stairs.

By God, she would not marry again—not now, not ever.

"Madam, I have no intention of marrying. Not now. Not ever," Mark grit out between clenched teeth.

Sitting in her chair like the queen, Abigail Lawrence lifted her formidable chin and glanced briefly toward her closed parlor door before speaking. "I don't see how you can avoid it, my lord."

Mark clenched the arms of his chair. "I might avoid it quite easily if you were to withdraw from this illegal and immoral blackmail."

"Withdraw? Whatever for? When have laws or morality ever kept a dedicated mother from bettering the life of her child?" Abigail sipped from her teacup. "If a mother's child is starving, she shall steal and lie to feed that child."

Mark leveled his gaze on the stout woman. "Neither you, nor your daughter, are starving, madam."

"Well, that's relative isn't it, my lord?" Abigail Lawrence returned her cup to the table. "Besides, I'm merely taking advantage of an opportunity." She shrugged. "When opportunity knocks . . ."

"The devil often disguises himself as opportunity, madam. Don't you feel the heat of his breath upon your neck, even now?"

Not a glimmer of uncertainty showed in the matron's cold gray eyes. "Why don't you ask your mother that question? She bedded down with the devil years ago."

It was a well-aimed dart, but Mark was immune. He drew his wallet from his breast pocket. "If she is his old whore, then you are his new one."

"I beg your pardon!"

He tossed the bank draft on the table in front of her.

Her eyes widened and her hand reached forward before she snapped it back. She glared at him. "What is this?"

"Payment. Now give me the letter."

Abigail Lawrence leaned back in her chair, almost as if to get as far as possible from the 25,000-pound note that stared up at her. She raised her brows haughtily. "I'm afraid the devil's new whore is more expensive than that, my lord."

Mark's fury coursed through him. "How much?" he managed.

She smiled. "Your earldom, of course. Money can be frittered away, my lord. A title is forever. And my Charlotte deserves a title."

Mark could barely keep his calm. "And what of my brother? Doesn't he deserve his life—deserve marriage to the lady he loves? Expose his paternity, and he will lose all."

Abigail shrugged. "You have the power to save your brother, my lord. The title I want is yours to give."

"With enough money, you can buy a title."

Abigail shook her head. "That takes far too much time and energy. Besides, everyone knows when you are doing it. It has no honor."

Mark laughed harshly. "Madam, blackmailers are not permitted to use the word *honor*." He stood and moved behind his chair to get away from her. "You have rescinded all rights to honor." His hands gripped the chair back till his knuckles turned white. "Don't use the word in my presence. Hearing you speak it offends me."

Abigail leaned forward. The tight ringlets on either side of her face barely moved. "You *will* keep a civil tongue in your head, my lord, or I'll publish your mother's sordid little letter," she snapped.

"No, you won't," Mark snarled. "You want my title too badly." He leaned forward. "Understand me well, madam. I *never* offer civility to uncivil people." He leaned even closer. *"So don't threaten me,"* he sneered, enunciating each word.

Abigail Lawrence pulled back in her chair, and Mark saw a flicker of uncertainty flash in her eyes. He turned and strode across the room without another word. Before he reached the parlor door, she spoke.

"I have forwarded a marriage contract to your solicitor, my lord, with a wedding date of June tenth."

Mark turned and felt his blood boiling. "One month? What are you about, madam?" He needed time. Time to figure a way out of this. "It will be assumed I've fucked your daughter and put a babe in her belly."

"What I am about, my lord, is ensuring that my daughter's future is secured as soon as possible. I'm taking no chances. I want to see an announcement in the paper this week."

Mark felt hot with impotent fury. "Go to hell!"

Without pausing, he yanked open the door and slammed it behind him. He almost ran over a servant who scurried out of his way and hurried off toward the rear of the house. Frowning and furious, he looked after her. Had she been listening?

Later that evening, Passion closed her bedroom door and turned the key. Alone at last—alone with her thoughts of Mark. She hadn't been able to put him from her mind all day. Every other thought or consideration, every other duty or obligation, was an irritating interruption to her reflections upon him.

Per her aunt's plans, Passion only had two more days at the Crystal Palace. Only two more days and then everything would return to the way it was before—as it must. She had a life.

Oh, she could insist upon returning there over and over, but to what end? What Mark and she had together wasn't a part of real life. What they had could only exist in the small, dreamlike world behind their screen. Their brief relationship had been born there and, in two days, must die there. But until then, she wanted to bask in her experience, to remember every little bit of it, every little bit of him.

Wrapping her arms around herself, she crossed to the

window and threw up the sash. The night air touched her with its cool, comfortable breath. She leaned on the sill and gazed up at the stars. Tonight they seemed to shine brighter than they had in a long time. Aunt Matty's walled garden was dark, but the scent from the flowering jasmine below floated up to fill Passion's senses.

She closed her eyes and pictured Mark as he had looked buttoning her gown, his intense blue eyes suddenly soft and languid, his full mouth unsmiling yet relaxed. A warm chill ran down her spine. He was so amazingly handsome.

Passion pulled back from the window and moved to her dressing table. Tugging pins from her hair, she put them in a neat pile as she remembered the texture of his hair and the feel of his nape against her fingers. She remembered the solid strength of his broad shoulders and the flexing muscles in his arms.

Her bun uncoiled, and she sighed as the heavy weight of her hair fell down her back. Shaking her head a little, she ran her fingers through the thick strands and massaged her scalp. Catching a glimpse of herself in the mirror, she suddenly wondered how he saw her. Moving into the full reflection, she cocked her head to the side. Her wavy auburn hair fell forward around her face. Her large hazel eyes blinked back at her. She knew she was pretty. But beautiful? Had he said so that first day they met? She had been so nervous, she couldn't remember. She flipped her hair back and began unbuttoning her bodice. It didn't matter. He made her feel beautiful.

After removing her gown, Passion untied her petticoats and shimmied out of five layers of flounced cotton, plus one stiffened with horsehair. She laid them across the arms of a chair.

As she unbuttoned her corset cover, she remembered Mark's large hands carefully working the tiny buttons. She remembered how greedily he had latched upon her nipples. Parting her corset cover, she looked down at them, sticking straight out at the mere thought of him. She pulled down her chemise and brushed the tips of her fingers over the bare nubs. She sighed as they hardened and lengthened even more. She remembered how he had pinched and nibbled them, remembered the sight of his cheek pressed to her breast. She formed the vision over and over in her mind. She must burn every detail of him into her memory, so that when time drew her ever further away from these days, she would remember—always.

Pulling up her chemise, Passion dropped her corset cover with her petticoats and, in naught but pantalets and corset, hurried to her desk. She stared down at her sketchbook. Could she capture him on paper? She had drawn her sisters before, and even her father, but she knew them so well. How could she draw a man she knew intimately and yet not at all? Sitting, she opened the sketchbook and flipped through pages of floral renderings before finding a blank sheet. Perhaps just his eyes. Those beautiful, intelligent eyes that seemed to look into her very soul. Eyes in which she caught glimpses of need and hope through the dark shadow of cynicism that veiled them. She picked up her pencil and began to draw.

Two more days at the Crystal Palace. Two more days in which to experience enough bliss to last her for a lifetime. Two more days in which to store away enough memories to console her when the inevitable emptiness returned.

"You've returned."

Mark pulled his eyes away from his architectural drawing to look at his brother.

"About time," Matthew remarked, crossing the study. "Where were you all afternoon? I came to hear about your mystery woman. Waited around for almost two hours, but you never showed."

Mark threw down his pencil and leaned back in chair. "Yes, Cranford informed me you were prowling around here for an eon."

"Well, where were you?"

How he wished he could tell Matt about the thieving

Abigail Lawrence. He shrugged. "I had some business to see to."

Matt half sat on the corner of the desk. "Fine, don't tell me."

Mark smiled.

"But I insist on knowing if you found your fair damsel of the Crystal Palace."

Mark's smile widened. "I did."

"Damn, I knew she would be there." Matt leaned forward. "Now don't be a boor and make me pull it out of you. What happened? Who is she?"

"I had her again, and her name is Passion."

Matt grinned. "It is not."

"It is. She was born on Passion Sunday."

Matt shook his head. "Oh, this is too good. Go on. Go on."

"Guess what her favorite gospel is?"

"She has a favorite gospel? Christ, you're doing a woman who's named after a religious holiday and has a favorite gospel?"

"Mark. Her favorite gospel is Mark."

"This is getting a little too theological for me. Get to the fucking part."

Mark leaned forward and examined his drawing as he picked up his pencil again. "We fucked," he said dismissively.

"Well, was it as good as yesterday?"

"Better."

Matt snatched the pencil out of Mark's hand and tossed it on the desk. "How the hell does it get better than yesterday?"

Mark remembered the relief that washed through him when he saw Passion. "It was better because I wanted her to be there and she was. It was better because we had more time together."

"Really?" Matt said in a slow, *is-that-so* tone.

Mark frowned, irritated. "What?"

Matt shrugged. "I just don't recall you ever wanting to

spend 'more time' with a woman—even one you're sleeping with. Fuck and flee, remember? You used to say that."

Mark's frown deepened. He didn't like the lack of control he had demonstrated upon parting with Passion. He should have been sated and ready to leave her. Instead, his body had betrayed his true desire: to stay and have her again. "Well, this woman makes staying worthwhile."

"Why? What about her makes staying worthwhile?"

"When did you become such a damned pain in the ass?" Mark sat back and crossed his arms over his chest. "You know why it was better? It was better because she let me get deeper inside her. It was better because she has the hottest, tightest, sweetest cunt I've ever had. It was better because I know I could have pushed my whole cock in her, but I didn't because I'm going to have her again tomorrow, at which time, I plan to get my whole prick, once and for all, into a woman."

"Ah"—Matt nodded—"a worthy goal."

Mark expected to see sarcasm in his brother's expression but found none.

"Did she cry again?" Matt asked.

Mark felt his shoulders relax and almost smiled. His brother had a penchant for tears. "Yes. She wept lovely, quiet tears."

"Mmm." Matt looked rapt. "Does she have a nice wide mouth?"

Now Mark laughed. "You letch! Does Rosalind know about your passion for tears and fellatio?"

Matt grinned slyly. "No, but she will."

Mark leaned forward and picked up his pencil again. "Good thing you like giving it as much as getting it."

"So, does she? Does Passion have a mouth for—"

Mark gave his brother a warning look, but beneath the desk his cock pulsed as he remembered her licking her lips. "I'm *not* discussing this with you." He glanced down at the thick bulge in his brother's pants and felt a spark of anger. "And save your damned erections for Rosalind."

Matt chuckled as he stood and adjusted himself. "This *is* for Rosalind. But a tempting story is a tempting story." He pulled his gloves from his pocket. "Say, why don't you come to the Benchleys with me? I'm going to play this evening."

Mark thought about it. Matt played the cello magnificently. "Is Rosalind going to ruin your performance with that bashing about she does on the piano?"

Matt smiled. "Probably."

"I'll pass." Mark bent over his drawings. "I have work to do, anyway."

Matt came around the desk and looked over Mark's shoulder. "Are these the plans for the library?"

"Yes." He showed his brother his drawing of the coffered dome that would arc over the library's main rotunda. An oculus of leaded glass would illuminate the space with natural light.

Matt nodded. "It's superb, brother." He smiled down at Mark and squeezed his shoulder. "Lord Fitzgerald would be crazy to give the commission to anyone else. Despite his Crystal Palace, Joseph Paxton doesn't have a chance."

Mark looked into his brother's brown eyes—eyes inherited from a gardener. It hurt that Matt wasn't his full brother. Ultimately, it didn't change anything, but it hurt. Matt was the only person he cared about in the world. It meant something that they were brothers, that they were close not only in name but in blood. Now they were less so. Goddamn his mother!

Matt's brow furrowed quizzically. "What? Don't you think you deserve the commission?"

Mark forced a grin. "Hell, yes, I think I deserve the commission. And he better damn well give it to me, too, or I'll stab him through the heart with my compass."

Matt laughed and slapped Mark's shoulder. "And you'd do it, too." He walked back around the desk but then turned as if just remembering something. "You know, Mother told me she thought you went to call upon the Lawrences today. Did you?"

Mother should keep her mouth shut. "Yes," Mark said casually. "I stopped there."

"So did you meet this Charlotte Lawrence?"

Mark erased a smudge from the architectural drawing. "No. She was not at home."

"Hmm. This lady is becoming rather mysterious. Are you sure she really exists?"

"Alas, yes."

"Aha!"

Mark looked up to find his brother pointing a long finger at him. "Aha, what?"

"I knew you weren't interested in this girl," Matt continued. "What's going on? You've always sworn you wouldn't marry. While I've never fully believed you, the idea that you would consider a girl without title, whom you've never met, *and* upon our *mother's* suggestion, makes no sense at all."

Mark thought fast. "I'm thinking that while I have no desire whatsoever to be a husband, I might like to be a father." There was truth to that. It was the one aspect of his decision not to marry that caused him some regret.

Matt looked at him nonplussed. "You don't even like children."

"Not in general. But I'm sure I'd feel differently about my own. So," Mark continued quickly, "because I can't have the child without the wife, and because I have no regard for the putrid ideals of our class, I am merely giving this Miss Lawrence some consideration." Mark squeezed his eraser between his fingers and cursed his mother for making him a liar. "As for our mother, her association with the Lawrences bears *no* weight upon my decision, which, at this moment, is still entirely undecided."

Matt shook his head. "You're horrid. Absolutely horrid. I pity this poor Miss Lawrence if you actually deign to court her. What will you do—send your proposal by messenger?"

"That's an excellent plan." Mark smiled as his brother rolled his eyes heavenward. "But it's not likely things will go that far. I'm already losing interest in the idea." Mark tossed down his eraser. He'd find a way to get that damn letter. He wasn't marrying anybody, least of all Charlotte Lawrence.

Matt pulled on his gloves. "I've got to go. Sure you won't come? Rosalind would love to see you."

"But I would not love to *hear* her. How can you, a superior musician, be affianced to a woman who butchers Beethoven whenever she sits at the piano?"

Matt grinned. "Well, she does have that nice wide mouth . . ."

Mark raised his brow. "I guess that's as good a reason to marry as any."

Matt shook his head with a small smile. "Love is a wonderful thing, my hard-hearted brother. You should try it sometime."

An old memory flashed clearly in Mark's mind. *"I don't love you!"* his mother had shouted at his father. *"I never did!"* Mark frowned. How old had he been as he had watched from the open doorway? Seven? Eight? And then his mother had looked at him. Actually, she had grimaced at him. *"Nor you either, you little brat."*

He had cried—more than once. He vaguely remembered the feel of his pillow, wet beneath his cheek. Today, he felt only disgust. Love! Love, indeed.

"Just because it didn't work for Father doesn't mean it can't work for you," Matt offered.

"Enough!" Mark resisted the urge to slam his fist into his desk. He was being blackmailed into marriage by a thieving bitch, his brother wasn't his full brother, and his slut of a mother was, as usual, at the heart of all his problems. This was not the time for a damned lecture on the merits of love. "Our mother has slept with half of London and the adjoining counties, which only proves that love isn't really 'working' for anyone," he said tightly.

Matt held up his hands in resignation and backed toward the door. "I'll say no more." He turned to go but then paused. "Passion. Tomorrow I want to hear all about your adventure with her. She intrigues me."

"Aren't you late for some bad Beethoven?"

Matt left with a smile.

Mark released a deep breath and rested his head in his hands. He rubbed his scalp. His brother was a fool. Love led to lies. One day his beloved Rosalind would betray him and he would be ruined, just as their father had been. No, not *their* father—Mark's father. Damn women. Damn them all.

Lifting his head, he stared into the flames that leapt in the fireplace across the room. His meeting with Abigail Lawrence played over in his mind. He had been so sure she would take the money. It galled him that she hadn't. If she thought he was going to just roll over and let her dictate his life, she was wrong.

He twirled his pencil between his fingers as he allowed himself brief fantasies of murder and arson. Unfortunately, he did have some morals.

He stopped twirling. A little thievery, however, would not be out of the question. And he knew just the young pickpocket to pull it off. He tapped his pencil idly. The question was, did Abigail Lawrence have the letter in her home? Mark remembered her haughty arrogance and the fact that she had kept this letter for years, waiting for the time to use it.

Yes. A woman such as she would never let that letter out of her keeping. It must be there. It would take time to search the house without being discovered, but it could be done. He had until June 9th. Of course, he'd have to go along with Abigail Lawrence's demands in the interim. He threw down his pencil. He wouldn't do it amicably, but he'd do it. Tomorrow he'd send for his thief.

He gazed again at the fire. Tomorrow he'd see Passion. Anticipation coursed through him. Why did he want her so much? He didn't really know anything about her. Was she as false as most women? No, she didn't seem anything like most women.

His shoulders relaxed. Everything about her seemed genuine and real. Even courtesans were as much actresses as prostitutes. But with Passion, there was no artifice, no pretension . . . no exchange of anything except honest, mutual pleasure.

Mark remembered her amazing breasts and the long tendril of her auburn hair falling forward across her cheek. His cock stirred. He thought of his brother's words and imagined Passion with her lovely mouth open around his prick. He moaned as his blood rushed and his erection grew. Yes. He had stumbled upon the ideal situation—a beautiful woman with whom to share sexual satisfaction, without the loathsome pretense of love or affection.

He smiled as he adjusted himself. Tomorrow they would enjoy each other in a wholly different manner. Tomorrow . . . anxiety suddenly plagued him as he remembered the way they had parted. *If* she showed up tomorrow.

Chapter Five

DONE

Therefore I say unto you, What things soever ye desire, when ye pray, believe that ye receive them, and ye shall have them—Mark 11:24.

Passion sighed. She knew her prayers were not the sort Jesus referred to. Yet, she couldn't help herself. She prayed God grant her another hour in Mark's arms. She prayed for his firm touch. She prayed for his breath upon her ear. A warm tingle tumbled down her spine. Why had God given her a body if she was not to experience the joy it was capable of? Why had God given her emotions if she was not to plumb their depths?

"Excuse me," a low voice sounded beside her.

Passion's heart thumped as she turned. Disappointment washed through her. A handsome man in a plaid waistcoat smiled at her. "I apologize for intruding. You were so still and so intent in the midst of this throng. Are you all right?"

Something in his smile reminded her of Mark's. Passion glanced around the crowded room. It *was* a throng today, a throng without Mark.

Passion turned back to the gentleman. Even the angle of his jaw looked a bit like Mark's.

His brows furrowed a little over his dark eyes. Not Mark's eyes. "Are you well?" His voice was gentle. He was being kind.

Passion smiled. "Yes. Thank you. I'm completely well." She gestured to the Bible. "I was just reading."

He glanced at the book and then returned her smile. "St. Mark, is it?"

"Yes."

He studied her intently for a moment. Then he glanced at the Bible and seemed to consider before speaking. "Mark is difficult, but he's worth the effort."

Passion lifted her brows. "Do you think so?"

"I do." The man smiled at her. "He can be downright boorish, but beneath the hard exterior is gold."

Passion returned his smile. "It's rare to find one who speaks of the gospel so personally. Are you a theologian, sir?"

"No, madam." He regarded her steadily. "I just know Mark very well."

"Ah."

The man glanced over her shoulder, and the look in his eyes told her someone approached.

Passion shivered as she felt a hand slide around her waist. A hint of lemon verbena flirted with her senses. She looked up. Excitement sparked through her. Mark!

He was frowning hard at the gentleman. "Is this man bothering you, darling?"

Passion blanched. They were supposed to be strangers. No one should know they knew each other. Yet, her heart responded to his endearment with a pleased flutter. Just as quickly as the blood had drained from her face, she now felt it rushing back in a hot flush. "I—no. This gentleman and I were just discussing the gospel."

"Really," Mark drawled, his tone dripping sarcasm.

Glancing quickly at the other man, Passion was surprised to find him smiling. Her thoughts scattered, though, as Mark pulled her closer.

"Yes, really," the man replied. He turned to her, and his smile softened. "Now that your escort has arrived, madam, I shall bid you good day."

Passion smiled. "Good day, sir."

The man nodded at Mark before melting into the crowd.

Mark's gaze followed the retreating gentleman. His arm was still around her, and she could feel the warmth of his hand on her waist. Why did his mere touch make her giddy? A shiver of delight tingled over her skin.

He looked down at her, and the frown eased from his brow. His mouth softened, and the hard look in his piercing eyes fell away as he regarded her. "Hello, Passion."

The use of her name was like an intimate touch. Her nipples tightened. "Hello, Mark."

Something dark flared in his eyes. "Your voice makes me hard."

Passion took a deep breath. A large group of spectators passed near. Mark's hand tightened on her waist before releasing her. They faced the *prie-dieu*.

He seemed to study the page. "I'm sorry I'm late. I was detained twice by parties of people I know."

Passion nodded. She suddenly wondered what it would be like to be among the people he knew. Was he a good friend? Her instincts told her yes, despite his outward demeanor, for she remembered his tender dressing of her and how he had put her bow just so. Yet, she would never really know. For they only knew each other in the secret world behind the screen. In the real world, they were strangers.

"What's wrong?" He was looking down at her.

Passion realized a frown had crept between her brows. She smiled to ease it. "I was just wondering what sort of man you are. I realize I'll never know, of course. But that's odd, isn't it?" Passion felt heat rise to her cheeks. "I mean, under the circumstances."

Mark regarded her intently. Another large group of people moved behind them, waiting to view the huge screen. His eyes passed over each of her features. The crowd pressed nearer. He was not going to answer. Passion's cheeks flamed hotter. The chatter of the crowd intensified.

Then Mark was behind her. His hands gripped her waist, and his voice sounded low near her ear. "I'm not the sort of man you would like to know, Passion. I live my life for myself. I do what I want, and I couldn't care less what people think about it. If something pleases me"—his hands stroked her sides—"then I'll pursue it for as long as my interest lasts."

Passion tensed as a tingling started between her legs.

"But when I'm done"—his hands fell slowly away— "I'm done."

Passion felt bereft of his touch. Despite his words, she wanted him. She wanted him because tomorrow would be their last day together—tomorrow *she* would be "done." That was fortunate, for she knew she couldn't bear being cast away yet again.

He moved back to her side.

She met his serious blue gaze. "I'll miss your touch when we part. I miss it now."

A sudden smile softened his mouth as, within the folds of her skirt, he clasped her hand and threaded his fingers between hers. "Aren't you going to try to convince me that I must be wrong? Aren't you going to try to imbue me with all sorts of noble qualities that I don't have?"

Passion smiled. "Why would I do that?" Even the feel of his gloved hand around hers was heaven.

Mark shrugged. "I don't know. Most women do."

"Do they?" Passion flipped a page of the Bible idly as she suppressed a brief twinge of jealousy. "It must be nice to be obliged to no one. I don't know what that's like."

His thumb stroked her palm. "No, I don't imagine you do." He nodded toward her left hand, resting upon the page. "Tell me about him."

Passion looked down. Her gold wedding band could be seen through her black crocheted gloves. She didn't want to talk about him. "What do you want to know?"

"Everything you want to tell me."

Passion searched for something to say. "I was married to my husband for three years before he died. He was killed in a riding accident. It was very unexpected."

Mark's blue gaze pinned her, seeming to look into her thoughts. Passion drew a deep breath. Was the room less full? Or did everything, even sound, fade in his presence?

"Did you love him?"

Passion's chest constricted. No one had ever asked that question. Her sisters hadn't needed to. Nor had her father. They had known the answer. "No." The word came in a whisper.

His gaze imprisoned her. "Did he love you?"

Tears suddenly welled in Passion's eyes. Turning away, she blinked them back as she stared down at the band of gold around her finger. Was the lack of love so painful? Or was it acknowledging it aloud that hurt so?

Mark moved even closer. "Answer me, Passion," he urged softly. He pressed her toward the screen. "Did he love you?"

She swallowed her tears.

His hand tightened around hers. "Did he?"

"No," she gasped. "No!"

And then they were behind the shadow of the screen. Gloves flew to the floor. Mark's arms came around her. His mouth swooped down upon hers. His scent enveloped her.

Passion moaned into his mouth and clasped him close. Beneath the force of his deep kiss, her tension melted away. Everything melted away: the pain, the lost years, the desperate longing. The only thing that mattered now was this kiss, this moment.

She gave herself to it completely. Arching against him, her hand crept around his nape whilst her other cupped the firm angle of his clean-shaven jaw. Her mouth opened for the sweeping stroke of his tongue. She breathed in short gasps around the thrust and withdrawal, luxuriating in the firm press of his lips and the heady taste of him.

His hands moved around her waist and up her back. He captured her mouth again and again. His fingers brushed her hardened nipple and pinched it. Passion shuddered. Her head spun. She could feel the hard length of his cock between them. It throbbed heavily and, between her legs, her cunt responded with a strong pulse. She gasped as a warm rush wet her thighs.

When Mark finally released her mouth, a regretful moan escaped her as she opened her eyes. Her heart pounded.

"Your kisses make me faint," she breathed, reaching to remove his hat.

The heavy lock of brown hair fell forward over his brow.

"You were made for sex," he said low. "Do you know that, Passion? You don't just want it." He flexed his hips, eliciting a sharp indrawn breath from her. "You *need* it." His fingers rubbed her nipples through her gown. "And your body is made for it."

Passion bit her lip. Was it true? She remembered the playful yet sensual conversations she and her sisters had engaged in as girls, their avid enjoyment of the Song of Solomon, memorized after so many times read aloud. But she had sublimated her own wants and needs for so long that those memories had faded. She had faded.

She traced his curving mouth with the tip of her finger. It didn't matter. Tomorrow was their last day together. Then everything would be as before. And memories would be her consolation—memories she would not allow to dim.

He nipped her finger between his teeth and touched it with his tongue. A hot tremor tightened her nipples and quickened the pulse between her legs. Then, as his tongue stroked her finger, he began to move rhythmically against her.

Passion gasped, and her cunt cried. Voices sounded from beyond the screen. Yet the feel of his tongue moving on her finger, combined with the thrust of his cock, made her suddenly wild with need. Reaching down, she curled both hands around the stiff length of him and stroked.

He sucked in his breath and, yanking the ribbons beneath her chin, sent her bonnet flying to the floor. "That's good," he encouraged, as he leaned against the wall. "In the future, don't wait so long to touch me."

Future? No, they had only today and the brief future of tomorrow.

Passion moved her hands all over him, even cupping his heavy sac through the fine wool of his trousers. The feel of him, the sight of him with his trousers tented over the throbbing force of his huge erection, made her hot and flushed with desire.

"Do you want me to take it out?" he asked.

Her cunt clenched. "Yes!"

"Very well." Mark slowly released the fastenings of his trousers, revealing the long, marblelike column of flesh for which she yearned so much. The head, swollen and large, bobbed toward her eagerly.

Passion's mouth watered. It was too beautiful, too powerful. She reached for it, but Mark's hand stayed her.

He smiled. "What say you we strike a bargain?"

Passion hesitated. "A bargain? What do you mean?"

"Well," he murmured, "you've gotten a good look at my prick. But I haven't seen you at all."

The little heart at the mouth of her cunt pulsed anxiously. "You saw my breasts."

"True." Mark licked his lips. "And two more perfect breasts I've not seen. But I was referring to that juicy little place between your legs."

Passion's brows shot up with surprise. "You *want* to see me? Down there?"

"God, yes," he breathed, tracing her parted lips with his finger. "I want to see you, smell you, and touch you."

The noise from the exhibit room escalated.

An old memory filled Passion's mind—she and her sisters at their pond after a swim. Clad only in wet chemises, with much laughter and giggles, they had ended up comparing each other's quims. That had been before her marriage, when she had still believed in the joy of love and life.

Now Mark wanted to see her. Passion felt her cheeks flush and her legs quiver with excitement. The tip of his finger was hot against her swollen lips. As he had done, she touched it with her tongue. His smile faded as he slid his finger farther into her mouth.

A searing wave of sensuality sluiced through Passion's body, igniting her nerves and heating her blood. Her eyes tipped shut as she closed her lips around his finger and sucked it. Moisture dripped down her thigh as he slid his long finger in and out of her mouth.

"Ah, that's very pretty," Mark whispered tightly.

Passion moaned. She knew why this simple act titillated her so—remembered the many times she and her sisters had spied upon Wilson, their butler, during his daily two o'clock ejaculation into the mouth of Mary, the upstairs maid. Country life and, perhaps, too much freedom had given her sisters and her a well-rounded education.

Her heart raced at the distant memory, suddenly vivid. She wanted to taste Mark, to feel his beautiful cock against her tongue. Unable to resist any longer, she reached for it. Her fingers brushed the veiny length, but he pulled back, slipping his finger from her mouth.

With a frustrated groan, Passion met Mark's hard stare. All levity had left him, and his sensual mouth was drawn in a firm line.

"What a delicious little wanton you are," he murmured. "But what of our bargain?"

Passion shook with need. Her lips trembled. She glanced longingly at his pulsing penis. The big head glistened.

Mark lifted her chin with his finger. "I won't give it to you until you give me what I want."

Could he really deny himself? The head of his prick was already darkening with desire. "So, if I refuse," she said softly, "you'll bid me good day and we'll both leave here unsatisfied?"

His mouth lifted in the predatory half-smile of their first meeting. "Are you calling my bluff, Passion?"

She wanted to know the extent of his craving for her. Did it equal hers for him? "Yes, Mark."

His smile faded. "Truth is, I have no intention of letting you out of here without gaining satisfaction—both yours and mine." His hands went to her skirts, lifting them. "So, if you refuse, I'll take you any way I can have you. But"— his hand stole between her legs, cupping her, as he dropped a soft kiss upon her lips—"I see no reason for you to refuse such an innocent request."

Passion shuddered as he turned her to lean against the wall. He rained kisses across her face as he slid the hard length of his penis between her pantalet-covered thighs. "Come, Passion," he breathed. "Let me see that sweet little quim."

Her muscles quivered in delicious anticipation as she luxuriated in the feel of his heavy member sliding in and out between her tightly clenched legs.

His hand rested on her breast. "You're so wet and warm." He nuzzled her neck as he unbuttoned her bodice. "Say you won't say no. Say you won't refuse me."

Passion gasped as he pulled open her gown.

His fingers worked fast at her corset cover. "Say you'll give me everything I want. Say you won't ever hide your body from me."

She arched her back when he opened her corset cover and ran his hands over her distended nipples. Still contained by her chemise, they poked out over the top of her corset.

Mark dropped a wet kiss upon the high mound of her breast. "Now, pull down your chemise for me."

Passion lifted shaking hands. The noise from the exhibit room grew even louder. But she could not refuse
him. She didn't want to. And when she pushed down the
fabric covering her breasts, he actually moaned at the
sight of her.

He latched, voraciously, onto one thick nipple and
rolled the other between his fingers. Passion bit back a cry
at the hard pull of his mouth. Yet she arched against him,
offering herself as she threaded her fingers through his
hair and held him close. He fed upon her longer and more
insatiably than he had the day before. And every swath of
his tongue, every hungry suck, sent a spiraling bolt of
pleasure straight to her womb.

Her breast heaved and her heart raced as he released
her aching nipple and moved to the other. She gazed down
at it, amazed to see it so inflamed and erect. Mark's fingers plied it continuously, pinching and pulling it, while
he coaxed the other into a like state of swollen excitement.

Passion held him close and squeezed her thighs around
his thumping cock. She could stay here forever while he
kissed, sucked, bit, and . . . If only he would fuck her!

She wasn't sure when her hips began to rock. She only
noticed when he released her nipple and pulled back to
watch her. She reached for him and winced at her own
need. "Mark, please . . ."

"Please, what?"

Passion squirmed. "Please . . . Help me . . ."

He frowned and slid in and out from between her
tightly pressed thighs. "Please help me come," he said,
finding the words she could not. "Say it, Passion. Please
help me come."

Her voice shook. "Please, Mark, help me come . . . I
beg you . . ."

"That's it." His mouth softened. "How I love to hear
your beautiful voice speak the words. Now, hold up your
skirts for me."

She did as he asked and sucked in her breath as he
dropped to his knees before her. *This* she had never seen.

"Spread your legs."

Barely breathing, she planted her feet wide. She squeezed her eyes shut as he reached to open the slit of her pantalets. But in the next instant, her eyes flew open as he ripped the fragile fabric open to her waist. She bent to see past her gathered skirts and stared wide-eyed at her exposed mount. Thank the Lord for the high volume of chatter in the room.

Mark gazed at the site before him intently. His eyes never shifted as he raked his fingers through her auburn curls. And then he was parting her flesh, opening her.

Passion was transfixed. Her late husband had never looked at her, let alone explored her. Everything had occurred between quickly lifted nightclothes, which had been just as quickly replaced.

Mark's fingers slid between her wet folds. Then he slid one long finger inside her. She gasped and her eyes fluttered. He slid in another, and she felt a trickle of moisture seep out of her. His thumb pressed against the spot that pulsed and ached.

Passion sighed with relief, for the pressure eased the terrible throbbing somewhat. But his fingers continued to slide in and out of her, feeding her desire for fulfillment.

"God, you're wet, " he said, more to himself than her.

He slid a third finger into her, and she canted her hips forward. Lewd though it seemed, she couldn't help it. She was trembling with need, and he wasn't giving her enough.

"Very nice. But I want to see more," he murmured. "Bring your hands down and hold yourself open for me."

When she faltered, he looked up at her. "Do it, Passion. You won't be sorry."

Her heart racing, she reached down and pulled herself open.

"More," Mark crooned. "Open it wide."

A choked gasp escaped Passion. She felt completely exposed. She should cover herself. But instead, she opened herself wider.

"Ah . . . that's so beautiful." He tapped his thumb a couple times. "Clitoris all swollen and red."

He tucked in his thumb and pumped his fingers into her. Passion's hips bucked forward, and she froze, suspended, as he thrust in his fourth finger and continued to pump her tender flesh. Passion bit her lip. The friction built and built, until each thrust brought a squish of moisture.

That's when he pulled his fingers out. Her body clenched, and she thought she might scream if he didn't grant her satisfaction.

"There," he growled, "that's how I like it."

And then his mouth was on her. Lips and tongue all over her gaping flesh. Passion bit back a sharp cry at the same time her hips jerked forward. His open mouth slid all over her. She felt his tongue lapping moisture from her sheath, felt his teeth nibbling her swollen nether lips, and felt the sandy scrape of his clean-shaven jaw.

Such a feeling! Passion's thighs flexed and her knees quivered as she jutted her hips out even farther. He drank from her body, sucking the moisture right out of her. His tongue laved her slick skin and throbbing clitoris, driving her wild with an almost torturous pleasure.

Her hips jutted forward and back uncontrollably. Her head spun. She closed her eyes to block out everything but the intense sensation driving her. It mounted and mounted. Everything else faded. Nothing mattered but her satisfaction. Nothing mattered but that his mouth bring her release. She wanted it. She needed it. She must have it. Now!

With a great gasping breath, Passion thrust her fingers through Mark's hair and rubbed her burning clitoris frantically against his wet tongue. Faster and faster she stroked. A low hum droned in her ears. Floods of molten sensation kept pouring into the straining bud. Filling it and filling it . . . Until it burst.

Choking on her own cry, Passion's whole body stiffened. But she could not contain the explosion. Hot shards of stabbing pleasure shot through every part of her, wracking her with uncontrollable shuddering as they ricocheted from nerve ending to nerve ending.

Passion struggled to remain silent under the fierce onslaught. And just when she thought she couldn't bear it another moment, just when she thought she couldn't quiet her body's ecstatic shaking, everything coalesced back between her legs in a final dying burst.

With a soft moan, she fell to her knees and landed in Mark's enveloping embrace.

She wasn't sure how long she sat there, leaning against his solid frame and breathing in the fresh scent of his neck. The noise from without seemed to grow loud again.

If only she could stay here with him. If only . . .

A sigh escaped her.

She felt his chin brush her cheek. Then a kiss warmed her brow. "Passion?" His hand cupped the high swell of her breast pushed up by her corset.

She drew a deep breath and tipped her face up to look at him. His hair was tousled, and his blue eyes blazed with an inner fire. She followed the straight line of his nose to his full, sensual mouth. A mouth that, moments before, had been latched between her legs with a fervent hunger. Her chest tightened as she lifted her mouth to his.

The kiss began softly but quickly deepened as Mark surged against her. Passion tasted herself upon his lips. She had never known that a man could bring a woman pleasure with his mouth. Wilson had never done so with Mary. Or if he had, he had done so at some time other than two o'clock.

Passion closed her hands around Mark's jutting penis. He moaned into her mouth, and his hips flexed forward. She stroked him as she kissed him, knowing what she wanted to do yet embarrassed to say it.

But she didn't have time for embarrassment. Her time was short, and if she wanted to have him as he had her, she needed to say so. He was, after all, always urging her to say what she wanted.

She broke their kiss and then pressed a few more to his full lips. "Mark," she whispered against his cheek, "I want to—I want to taste you." Her fingers tightened briefly around him so he would get her meaning.

His tongue touched the corner of her mouth before he pulled back, forcing her to meet his gaze. "Do you, now?"

Passion's lashes fluttered briefly. "Yes."

"And have you ever 'tasted' a man before?"

"No."

"Ah," he traced the tip of his finger across her lower lip, "a virgin mouth."

He slipped his finger between her parted lips, and Passion sighed as she brushed her tongue along it and sucked it more deeply into her mouth.

"That's good," he breathed, "just like that, Passion." He coaxed a second finger between her lips. "All tongue and mouth. No teeth, all right?"

Passion acknowledged him with a slow blink.

He stood slowly before her, letting his fingers slip free from her mouth.

Passion's heart pounded excitedly. Mark's penis curved huge and heavy before her. The thick veins throbbed, and the swollen head was shiny with moisture. She licked her lips in anticipation.

Cupping her chin, Mark tilted her face up as he bent to her. His eyes were like blue glass. "Just how much of me do you want to taste?"

"All of you."

His thumb brushed her jaw. "You may not like me coming in your mouth."

Mary had always seemed quite hungry for Wilson. And now, Passion felt that same hunger. "Why? I came in your mouth."

"It's not the same. You've never done this before, and I'm going to come hard."

She wasn't going to let this experience go half-met. "Say you won't refuse me," she whispered, quoting his very words. "Say you'll give me everything I want."

Mark's eyes darkened, and an odd frown furrowed his brow. "By God. Your voice is a siren's call." He slowly unfolded to his full height. "Very well." His hand released her chin in a caress. "Don't say I didn't warn you."

Sitting on her heels, Passion faced the object of her desire. It protruded, thick and strong, from a patch of dark brown hair. The contrast between the dark bed of hair, the marblelike pillar of flesh, and the moist, enflamed head fascinated her. Her clitoris throbbed in acknowledgment, as if to say, yes, isn't it magnificent!

Passion combed her fingers through the coarse hair and then, with both hands, trailed a feather-light touch over the hard length of him.

He flinched and she glanced up. "No?"

His jaw clenched. "Yes."

She drew her fingers back down and watched a clear drop of fluid pool in the opening at the tip of his prick. Her own body moistened at the sight. As she closed her hands around him and squeezed, it spilled down the swollen head like a tear.

Passion's nipples hardened, and her quim tightened. Without further pause, she wrapped her hungry lips around the weeping head. She barely heard Mark's choked grunt over her own moan, for the sensation of him in her mouth was an exhilarating aphrodisiac. She swept her tongue all over the smooth, tender head, eagerly sucking up the moisture that leaked in earnest now. It tasted salty, just like tears.

Pushing her lips just past the throbbing head, she ran her tongue around the rim as she stroked the shaft with her hands. He was the most perfect combination of hard and soft. His skin, fine and smooth, felt like heaven against her tongue. Yet beneath that silky sheath pulsed a hard, thrusting core—a core that forced heavy veins to ripple the smooth surface, a core that ripened the tender knob until it dripped moisture from its dilated orifice.

Passion swirled her tongue over the head, sucking it firmly while she scooped one hand beneath his heavy sac.

Mark groaned as she fondled and stroked his balls, all the while keeping her mouth tight around the desperately swollen head of his cock.

Then his fingers were twisting in her hair, holding her as his hips jerked forward once, twice, a third time, each thrust a little deeper than the one before.

He froze. And as a guttural exhalation sounded above her, Passion felt him grow even more in her mouth. In small, pulsing increments, his swelling member forced her mouth wider. She opened for him, wishing she could take all of him.

Then he was thrusting again. Her mouth was full of him, and each thrust sent his eager knob deeper into her. She stroked and sucked him in rhythm with his movements, luxuriating in the urgent push and withdrawal that drew his hot, thick flesh in and out of her hungry mouth.

His hands tightened in her hair. He drew in a ragged breath. And suddenly he was pumping into her faster and faster. He held her as she had held him, immobile, while he found the pace that would bring his release. Grasping himself with one hand, he sent deep, rapid strokes into her mouth.

Passion felt a hot wash of sensual power flood through her as he stiffened, thrust hard, and froze. She felt the boiling surge of his come as it rushed up his straining shaft. It jetted into her mouth, hot, thick, and creamy, and each eager swallow, followed by the urgent downstroke of his hand, brought more—and more and more. Held in a rapture of erotic gluttony, she drank with open, full-throated pleasure, taking everything that poured out of him and, finally, sucking up the last salty drops he squeezed into her mouth.

Feeling almost a drunken light-headedness, she rolled her tongue around his softening member before he eased from her and dropped to his knees. His breathing came fast, and he cradled her face in his hands. His gaze was intense. Did he see her passionate pride at bringing his release?

"You've done this before," he said, his voice taut.

"No," Passion denied softly. "I never have." She stared into his eyes. It was important that he believe her. They only had tomorrow left. She wanted him to know the depth of the gift he gave her. "I've never . . . I mean, my husband never . . ." Tears suddenly stung her eyes. Why could she cry so easily in front of him when she hadn't cried for years? She blinked and willed her tears not to fall.

Mark pressed his mouth to hers. "You've never what?" he whispered between kisses.

"I've never experienced anything like what you've given me these past three days." Passion sighed against his warm lips. "I believed pleasure existed—knew it existed—but I didn't think it existed for me. I didn't know the depth of my need—didn't know what I held inside myself."

"You were married for three years." He trailed kisses across her brow. "Pleasure can exist without love." His hands swept over her breasts.

Passion shut her eyes. During her whole marriage, she had never felt a bodily pleasure that was not brought by her own hand. And even that small indulgence she had forgone long ago. It was too lonely, too empty. Better to bury her need entirely than keep it alive, half starved and craving.

"My husband afforded me no pleasure," she managed. "Nor was he interested in doing so."

Mark's gaze moved over her features, dropped to her bared breasts, and then returned to her face. "Then he was a bastard."

Passion couldn't stop the smile that turned her lips.

Mark nodded, and his eyes held her. "A stupid, blind bastard who wouldn't know Passion if she laid herself, naked, at his feet."

Passion's smile deepened. "Especially since he never saw me naked."

Mark shook his head and touched his finger to her

cheek. "Beautiful dimple." He slid the same finger beneath her chin and tipped her mouth to meet his in a long, leisurely kiss.

Passion's chest tightened. How she would miss him!

"I'm glad he never saw you naked," he said, brushing his lips against hers. "Because I *do* intend to see you naked. And when I do, I'll have something of you he never had."

He kept alluding to the future. She would love to be naked with him. Oh, to feel him, flesh against flesh. But that couldn't happen. Tomorrow would arrive all too soon. Passion sighed. "You already have more of me than he ever did. And you've already given me more than he ever did." She brushed her fingers across his jaw. "Thank you."

His brow furrowed for a moment. "No, thank *you*."

"You're welcome," she said with a small smile.

He sat on his heels, his knees resting on either side of her curled legs. His cock, half-hard, lay on her skirts. As satisfying as their encounter had been, she suddenly wished they could fuck. She wanted him deep inside her. She wanted him again and in the future that couldn't be.

He stared at her, his arms at his sides. "What is it?"

Passion felt her cheeks warm. She shook her head.

He glanced down at himself and then back at her. "Dress me." His voice sounded rough, but his gaze was soft.

She clasped his softened member in her hands. Before putting it back into his trousers, she took a moment to feel it. That moment proved a mistake.

His gaze never left her face as she struggled to contain his quickly hardening flesh. Her cheeks flamed hotter. The head of his cock defied her attempts to cover it. His stare felt like the heat from a fire. She bit her lower lip and pressed one hand against him as she tried to pull the opening of his trousers closed with the other. She couldn't manage the buttons one-handed.

Distressed, Passion finally lifted her eyes to his. She

was surprised by the tenderness with which he regarded her. Her heart fluttered beneath her breast.

"I can't do it," she said softly.

"No, you can't," he murmured. "Because this is what you do to me. I just had you, yet I want you again." His gaze held hers, and his voice remained gentle and even. "Your husband was a damned fool. Do you hear me? He didn't deserve you. Whatever his problem was—and I assure you, he had one—it wasn't you." He drew her hand to his erection. "*This* is what you inspire. *This* is what you deserve."

Something in Passion snapped. She wasn't sure if whatever it was snapped open or snapped closed, but her blood surged and her eyes stung.

Her sisters had insisted she wasn't responsible for her passionless marriage. But they were prejudiced by their love for her and, as women, couldn't truly speak to her desirability. Mark had no such prejudice, and he clearly desired her. But even more meaningful than his words was the fact that he had uttered them, and with such vehemence. That had been a great kindness.

She lifted shaking hands to his lean cheeks. "Thank you," she breathed. "Thank you for knowing me so little, yet still taking my side." She brushed her thumb across his lower lip and her finger over his dark eyebrow. "I think I will miss you more desperately than I know."

Beautiful blue eyes held her. "Let's not speak of that now. There is so much more we have yet to share." His mouth curved up ever so slightly as he adjusted himself and closed his trousers. "I'm not done with you yet."

Passion let her hands fall to her lap. She couldn't put the truth off any longer. "Mark, I—I'm afraid tomorrow will be our last day."

In a blink, his warm gaze turned to ice. "What?"

Chapter Six

PROPOSALS

Mark's body went rigid. "Why is tomorrow our last day?"

"I'm just visiting London," Passion replied. "And tomorrow is my last day coming to the Crystal Palace."

His gut twisted. "You're leaving London?"

"No, not yet." Her long lashes fluttered. "But I'm staying with my aunt, and I can't keep coming here day after day."

"How long? How long before you leave?"

"A little less than two months."

Would he fall out of lust with her in two months? Possible, but with the way he'd been feeling, not probable. "And then?"

"Home."

"Where is home?"

Passion paused.

Mark gripped her hands. "Passion, where is home?"

She looked up at him, her hazel eyes urgent. "Mark, you have to understand. I have never done anything like this before. Besides my husband, you are the only man I've ever had intimate relations with. My father is a vicar.

At home, I'm a respectable widow. I cannot continue with you like this forever—and certainly not after I return home."

Glancing at her beautiful breasts, pushed high by her corset, Mark thought she looked completely respectable just as she was. "I'm not interested in forever. I'm interested in as long as it takes for one of us to lose interest. And while I don't have a lot of respect for what passes for respectability, I have no intention of damaging your reputation." A sudden thought came to him. "I will take precautions to insure that I do not get you with child."

"I cannot bear children." A hint of sadness tinged her voice.

Mark paused. Why was her admission so surprising? Why should he care? All the better for him. "Then we need only concern ourselves with discretion. As a widow, you have a degree of freedom. I've already considered the ways and means of getting you in my bed, Passion. It can be done." His prick throbbed at the thought. "It *will* be done."

Passion paled with shock. It seemed she hadn't even considered such thoughts. "Your bed?" She shook her head. "When I was speaking with that man earlier, you put your arm around me and called me darling. Had he been someone I knew, you would have ruined me right there. And you want me to come to your bed?"

"He *wasn't* someone you knew."

"But he could have been."

"I *knew* you didn't know him."

"How could you know that?"

"Because *I* know him, damn it!"

Passion's eyes widened, and a long silence drew out between them.

Mark grit his teeth. The hum of the crowd suddenly seemed loud.

Finally, she spoke. "You know him?"

"He's my brother."

Her cheeks turned pink. "Obviously, he knows all

about me." Her flush tinted even the high mounds of her breasts.

Mark felt a twinge of discomfort but then quashed it. "He's my brother, for Christ's sake. He's the only person in the world I tell anything personal. And meeting you was a rather extraordinary event."

Passion regarded him for a long moment and then moved to pull her chemise up over her breasts. "Well, he being your brother explains much." She shrugged her corset cover and gown back onto her shoulders.

"My brother is a gentleman, Passion. Your reputation is safe with him."

Her slim fingers briefly stopped working the tiny buttons of her corset cover and then began again. "I believe you. In fact, I rather like him."

A hot flash of inexplicable jealousy flared just beneath Mark's skin. "You like him? You barely spoke." His voice sounded angry, even to himself.

Passion glanced up. "You and I have spoken little, yet I like you very much."

He glared at her. "That is an ill-spoken comparison."

She smoothed her soft palm across his temple. "You're right. There is no comparison. None at all." Her finger traced the edge of his ear, sending a warm tremor through his body. "I think your brother cares deeply for you." Her large eyes delved into his. "And that's why I like him."

Something warm and comfortable coursed through him.

"Besides," she began buttoning her bodice, "I'm going to tell my sisters about you. So I can't very well resent your telling your brother about me, can I?"

Mark watched the pale skin of her décolletage disappear beneath the dark brown silk of her gown. "And where do these sisters reside?"

She tipped back on her heels and got to her feet in a soft swish of silk. "My aunt will be waiting. I must go."

Mark stood and grabbed her arm as she bent to pick up her bonnet. "Damn it, Passion!" His voice was a barely contained whisper. "I don't want this to end yet. It's—it's too soon."

She glanced at his hand on her arm. "Would you force me? Expose me, if I refuse you?"

"Of course not." He released her, and she put on her bonnet as she moved toward the edge of the screen. . . . If I refuse you. She had said "if." He followed. "You don't want this to end yet either. I know you don't."

She lifted her beautiful eyes to his. "No, I don't. Not even remotely."

Relief rushed through him. About time she came to her senses.

She smoothed back the hair from his brow. "However, I am accustomed to not having what I want."

In the moment it took for her words to register, she slipped away.

"Oh, no you don't!" he growled. And scooping up his hat, he followed.

Beneath the shade of a pear tree in Aunt Matty's garden, Passion stared down at her sketchbook. Mark's face stared back at her. She had captured the cynical curve of his mouth so well that she almost expected the rendering to smile at her. She smoothed her finger over the charcoal line of his brow, softening it.

Her heart fluttered with both gladness and trepidation. It was the best drawing she'd done in a long time. It was as good as some of the long-ago sketches she had done of her sisters and father. How long had it been since she'd accomplished a drawing so fine? Years? But one successful portrayal didn't mean she could count upon another.

Besides—she studied her drawing—Mark was the perfect model. His classical features would beg the hand of any artist. How she would love to paint him. Images flashed before her mind's eye: his head pressed to her breast; his hands working her buttons; his face, that morning, as he had looked up at her from his knees.

Her body warmed at the memory. The vulnerability she

had felt and then the sensual power she had exerted, thrilled her. Yet as gratifying as their encounter had been, she yearned for more. Her release had been incredibly intense, yet not sustaining. She closed her eyes and tried to conjure the feeling of him inside her. There was nothing like being filled by him. Her body craved the aching fullness that joining with him gave her. It satisfied her in ways that today's experience hadn't.

Today's experience . . . His resistance to their parting had surprised her. His admission that he had been thinking of ways to get her into his bed had been both tempting and shocking. It hadn't even occurred to her that their relationship could exist outside the Crystal Palace. It was one thing to give herself over to this incredible, impossible experience. It was quite another to actively contrive its occurrence.

And why was he so unwilling to part? With everything he'd said, she had expected easy acceptance. A man such as he could surely find any number of willing women to please him. He didn't need her for that. So what was it? Why the reluctance to let her go? Could it be that he wanted her for something more than physical satisfaction? Though a tempting thought, she discarded it quickly. Mark had been abundantly clear as to the nature of their relationship. It was best to take him at his word. It would be all too easy to fall into the trap of believing she was more important to him than she was.

She had, after all, been duped by her own hope before. Her husband had courted her with some urgency and charm. He had wooed her with pretty phrases and fine speech. And though he had exhibited moments of seeming disinterest, she had come to believe that he wanted her, that he cared for her. Though she hadn't loved him, she had entered into her marriage with the expectation that love would grow. She had believed that her marriage could be fulfilling and that it would turn, in time, into something wonderful. Instead, it had been an empty husk of an existence.

With a frustrated sigh, she stood. No warm wash of semen moistened her thighs as it had the days before. She was empty. Empty as always. How familiar empty was. Her chest tightened painfully. She yearned for Mark. Would it not have been better to never experience such pleasure, than to suffer this new and terrible yearning? A yearning not just for his body, but for his hands that tied her bonnet just so, for his eyes that seemed to never leave her, for his embrace that somehow reassured her.

She swept her fingers along the edge of his image. And his words . . . *Your husband was a damned fool . . . He didn't deserve you. Whatever his problem was . . . it wasn't you.* When she thought of his kind words to her, words he needn't have said, her heart seemed to swell, pushing against her lungs and quickening her breath.

By God, if she felt this way now, how would she feel if she were to spend more time with him? No, she was right to end their relationship. But she must never regret it. Never!

"Passion, there you are," Aunt Matty called. "Look who has come to call."

Snapping her sketchbook shut, Passion whirled around and inwardly groaned. Alfred Swittly and another, younger, man flanked her aunt and were making their way quickly across the garden.

"Mrs. Redington," Alfred Swittly bellowed as he approached, "how grand to see you again. I see you have your pad in hand. I hope you do not mind our little intrusion upon your foray into the artistic realm."

Passion nodded and managed a smile.

"I'm sure my niece welcomes the diversion of some company. She has been sitting here alone for far longer than is good for her." Aunt Matty shook her head. "Too much quiet gives me a headache. Doesn't it you, Mr. Swittly?"

"Indeed, Mistress Dare. Indeed," Alfred said. "But please, Mrs. Redington, allow me to introduce my cousin, Mr. John Crossman, of whom I spoke yesterday."

Passion exchanged greetings with the man. Though tall, blond, and green eyed, John Crossman somehow managed to look nothing like his cousin. Handsome, and with a quick and easy smile, he had a breadth of shoulder that seemed a bit wide for his lean, well-dressed frame. Passion guessed him to be only slightly older than she.

"Mr. Crossman is the heir to Crossman Shipping, my dear." Aunt Matty raised her brows meaningfully.

"Crossman Shipping?"

"A modest family business, Mrs. Redington," the young man acknowledged.

"Modest family business." Alfred chuckled. "Bosh! My cousin is the modest one, Mrs. Redington."

"You must forgive my niece, Mr. Crossman. Passion is from the country and has no knowledge of who the important people of our fair city are."

"No forgiveness is necessary. It is a pleasure to be unknown."

Alfred laughed and slapped his cousin on the shoulder.

"You must stay for tea, Mr. Crossman. You will, won't you? Of course you will." Aunt Matty turned, only to turn back again. "Do you know, that just the other day I was almost crippled for life? And my dearest Passion barely escaped blindness?" She raised her finger. "All due to the lack of tea. Tea, Mr. Crossman! *Never* underestimate its importance."

John Crossman kept a serious demeanor. "As I wish to suffer neither crippling nor blindness, I shall stay, Mistress Dare, for tea."

"Wisdom and fine features are rarely seen together, Mr. Crossman. You, however, appear to be blessed with both. Come, Mr. Swittly." Aunt Matty took Alfred's arm and pulled the reluctant man with her. "I would have a word with you in private."

When they were a little away, John Crossman turned to Passion. "She's wonderful."

Passion formed an instant liking for the man and smiled. "She is. Truly." They glanced over at her aunt. She was batting an insect from Alfred Swittly's arm with her handkerchief. "Most people think her an odd fish, but really she's kind and loving. And loyal as well."

Passion turned to find John Crossman regarding her intently. "Characteristics that run in the family, I see."

She smiled at his flattery. "I see graciousness is one of your traits, Mr. Crossman."

He grinned. "I merely acknowledge the obvious. This morning, I was in the company of a young lady who felt it necessary to make several excuses for her younger sister, who is not blessed with a large measure of beauty. Would that she could have shown the girl some kindness, love, and loyalty instead." He looked pensive and then nodded. "Had she, we would have got on much better." He glanced at her and raised one golden eyebrow. "After all, Mrs. Redington, when I grow fat and bald, I wouldn't want her making excuses for me."

Passion laughed. "And I can see you're in so much danger of that, Mr. Crossman—fat and baldness, that is."

He laughed with her and indicated the bench. "Shall we sit, Mrs. Redington?"

Passion glanced over at her aunt and Alfred Swittly as they sat. "I hear from Mr. Swittly that you and he are very close. Is he mentoring you in some way, Mr. Crossman?"

John Crossman's golden brows lifted and then he chuckled. "I've only just become reacquainted with my cousin last week, Mrs. Redington. We happened to meet at the glove-makers', where he introduced himself to me."

Passion frowned. "Oh . . ."

John shrugged. "My father recently passed away, Mrs. Redington. I'm finding that all sorts of past friends and relations are interested in renewing a relationship now that I am at the helm of Crossman Shipping."

"Oh, I see," Passion said. "Well, I'm very sorry for your loss. I'm sure this is a terribly difficult time for you."

John nodded. "My father prepared me well, Mrs. Redington. But I miss him."

Passion leaned forward in the way that her father did

when consoling one of his parishioners. "Of course you do, Mr. Crossman."

She curled her fingers around the binding of her sketchbook. Though they had just met, something in the man's demeanor made her believe he might welcome some words of comfort. "So many emotions attend death," she offered. "When my mother died, I was sad and angry, and frightened, too. My father mourned terribly; yet, as vicar, he had duties he could not put aside. So as the eldest, many responsibilities fell upon me."

He was staring at her, his green eyes serious and unwavering.

She continued. "It was difficult at first. But as time passed, I became comfortable in my new role, even taking pride in it. I find there can be great satisfaction in the fulfillment of duty."

Passion paused. Though she had told herself this a thousand times, today her words felt like an echo of the truth, not the whole truth. She frowned, suddenly unsure of what the whole truth was. Unsettled, she shook her head. "Forgive me, Mr. Crossman. I don't know that I'm making any sense. Anyway, I'm sure you have no need of my counsel."

John regarded her a moment. Then said, "No, forgive me for disturbing the peace of your thoughts with my problems." He smiled. "And I do appreciate your counsel."

Passion managed a smile but, at the same moment, desperately wished he would go. She needed to be alone with her thoughts.

"Tea!" Aunt Matty called as she approached with Alfred. The giant of a man held his hand out. "May I escort you inside, Mrs. Redington?" he bellowed.

Passion glanced at John Crossman, who she found looking at her intently, and then back at Alfred and Aunt Matty.

There was no escape, no excuse.

Tension shot down her back. She was obligated to remain.

She wanted to scream.

She wanted Mark.

He wanted Passion.

He *didn't* want the syrupy-sweet-looking Charlotte Lawrence who sat across from him. He didn't even want to be in the same room with her. He glanced toward the door that the contemptuous butler had slammed on leaving the room. How Mark wished that he, too, could stalk out and slam the door on this parlor of viciousness, schemes, and lies.

Mark grit his teeth as he listened to Abigail Lawrence.

"I've only just informed my daughter this very morning of your proposal, my lord. I explained how you saw her at the Italian Opera—how you found her beauty beyond compare and her grace unparalleled."

Mark slid his gaze to Charlotte. Light brown curls fell over her shoulders. Under his regard, she lowered nervous gray eyes. Pretty, perhaps. Beautiful, no.

"Charlotte is honored and will, of course, be proud to be your bride," Abigail continued. "And what a happy coincidence, that you and I should know each other, countess. How long has it been since last we saw each other?"

Mark glanced at his mother and was glad to catch the glint of dislike in her eyes. Good. He hoped she hated every moment of this.

"Well, I'm sure it's been years, Mrs. Lawrence," Lucinda said in a cool tone. "I had quite forgotten about our acquaintance. It was Lady Rimstock who brought you to mind when she asked me whatever had happened to my *old* friend, Abigail Lawrence." Lucinda's eyes raked the other woman as she emphasized the word *old*. "I told her I had no idea what had become of you."

Abigail's lips thinned into a tight line. "Well, it seems we'll be seeing quite a bit more of each other now, doesn't it? And *my* Charlotte will be the new countess." The woman's voice was almost a snarl.

Mark's shoulders tightened. Christ, but they were birds of a feather.

His mother lifted one eyebrow. "As you don't circulate in our society, Mrs. Lawrence, you can't know that my son has a reputation for eschewing the noble values of his own class. He has always felt comfortable moving in lesser circles." The slightest of smiles turned his mother's mouth. "And though I understand the unfortunate allure of friendships with those of the lower classes, such relationships never last, for their vulgarity always becomes so tiresome." She paused, and Abigail Lawrence's cheeks reddened with suppressed anger. "However, my headstrong son is his own master and will not be swayed by me."

Mark lifted his brows. Finally, some words of truth.

Lucinda glanced at Charlotte. "I hope your daughter has the grace and intelligence it will take to overcome her breeding. Countess of Langley is no small title."

"I daresay, countess, that my daughter will bring more grace and beauty to the title than it has heretofore seen," Abigail Lawrence spat.

Lucinda cast her eyes briefly in Charlotte's direction. "Not in that frock, she won't."

Abigail Lawrence's hands actually balled into fists. "Perhaps you have forgotten the financial stature of my late husband, countess. My daughter is more richly dressed than many a noblewoman. That lace"—she thrust a finger in the direction of her daughter's fichu—"is from Brussels!"

His mother shrugged dismissively.

Mark halted all talk when he stood and pulled out his watch. He'd had enough of the catfight. He wanted out. "I'm leaving."

"Leaving?" Abigail Lawrence rose from her seat and glanced at her daughter. "Did you not wish to speak with Charlotte, my lord?"

Mark raised his brows. "Speak with her? I was not aware that she could speak, Madam. You have spoken for her the entire time I have been here." His mother snickered as he turned to Charlotte. The girl was just hiding a smile, but her expression turned serious in the face of his frowning regard. What was her role in this scheme? Could she be opposed to marriage with him? Was his way out standing right in front of him? "Do you, in fact, accept this proposal, Miss Lawrence? Surely, a girl such as you with such lofty—how did you put it, Mrs. Lawrence?—'financial stature,' has many gentlemen prospects."

The girl glanced nervously at her mother and then back at him. "I—well, I—I don't know about prospects, my lord." She wrung her hands. "But I—I do accept your proposal."

Mark's frown deepened. He had no respect for simpleminded little girls. They did things they lived to regret and then made the world sorry for it. He felt his anger flaring. "Are you really ready to become engaged to a man you don't even know, Miss Lawrence? When my mother was your age, she married a man she didn't know." He heard his mother's gasp but went on undeterred. "She grew to hate him for stealing her precious youth and for making her fat with child. Though he tried to love her, she made his life a misery. Nothing he ever did was good enough for her."

"That's enough!" his mother snapped.

"Shut up!" he shot at her. His voice had grown harsher and harsher. He glared at Charlotte. "Is that what you want, Miss Lawrence? To be a bitter old shrew who rues the day she let another decide her fate?"

The girl stared at him, her eyes wide with shock and confusion. "I—I . . ."

"*My* daughter is not *your* mother, my lord," Abigail Lawrence said icily. "What right do you have to assume she will behave in such a way?"

"She's *your* daughter, isn't she? I have the right to assume whatever I like, madam."

"Speaking of assumptions, my lord," Abigail Lawrence sneered, "my daughter is under the assumption that you desire her hand. Is she mistaken in this regard?" She narrowed her eyes. "If so, tell us now, so that I may know what course to take."

Bitch! He wanted to tell her to go to hell and rot there. He grit his teeth to keep the words back. Matt. He must remember Matt. His mother was staring at him and must have sensed that he tottered on the edge of indecision.

"Of course he desires her hand," she said. "My son is angry with me and, like all men, confuses his feelings at this important crossroads in his life."

Mark wanted to rage at them all. He wasn't confused. He knew exactly how he felt. He clenched his jaw shut.

His mother turned to the bewildered-looking Charlotte. "My son has chosen you, Miss Lawrence. Now we must determine the best way to proceed so that society accepts you as willingly as he." She looked up. "Sit down, Abigail. This will take some time."

Good. Mark crossed the room. Let them take a very long time to work out all the social machinations. The more time they took, the better for him. He needed time to get that letter.

At the door, he paused and found them all looking at him. In his mother's eyes he saw loathing. Abigail Lawrence looked at him with haughty insolence. Charlotte looked confused. He felt no pity for her. She was the knife in his side. Ignorance did not excuse weak character, and it was her weak character that made her so easily used. He hated weakness.

Passion left her dream reluctantly. She had been lying in the embrace of a huge lion. Yet she had not been afraid. She blinked sleepily. What had awakened her? She wanted to return to the dream, to the warm, enveloping presence of the lion. She turned and closed her eyes again.

Then she heard it, a sound at her window. Instantly wide awake, she sat up in bed. Moonlight illuminated the window, which she had left ajar so the fragrance of the jasmine could waft into her room. There was nothing there. She waited and listened. Then she gasped as a light tap, followed by another, sounded against the window. Something landed on the floor with a small ping.

Sliding cautiously out of bed, she went and, kneeling beside the tiny pebble, picked it up. It was one of the smooth little stones that decorated the ground around the garden birdbath.

A deep but nervous thrill ran through her body. There was only one person who had the reason and daring to be pitching pebbles at her window. But that was impossible. It couldn't be. He didn't even know where she lived.

But who else? A vision of Alfred Swittly's rotund face filled her mind. Oh, heavens no! She glanced up as another tap sounded against the window.

Unsure, she slowly unfolded and moved to the side of the window. Hiding in the shadow of the lace curtains, she peeked around the edge. Her heart leapt. With arm drawn back to pitch another pebble, Mark stood just below her window! Mark, in Aunt Matty's garden! Her whole body grew hot.

She must have made some movement, for he suddenly looked right at where she was and dropped his arm. Passion froze, her blood coursing in her veins and her legs trembling beneath her. She tried to still her breathing. Oh, God! It was exhilaration that filled her, not alarm. She ought to be alarmed, but as he stood, staring up, she felt only joy.

She found herself moving to the sash and lifting it. As she leaned out, her braid swinging over her shoulder, he didn't move at all. They stared at each other for a long moment, neither speaking.

Then his voice lifted to her, low and rough. "The house is asleep. Let me in."

Her body shook with need and apprehension at the tenor of his voice. How could she let him in? She couldn't do that. Her nerves stretched. Her breast heaved. That would be too much. There would be no going back.

She shook her head. "I can't."

He immediately strode forward and, grabbing the lattice, began to climb.

Passion jerked back with a gasp and backed into her room. Her knees shook so badly that she held onto the bedpost for support. The silhouette of his head and broad shoulders appeared and then his long legs swept over the sill.

He seated himself there. "The stairs would have been easier," he said softly.

She could smell him.

"I need to speak with you," he said. "May I come in?"

"You are in," she whispered.

"Passion, I didn't intend to come here tonight."

"Yet here you are. How did you know where to find me?"

"After our conversation today, I thought I might never see you again, that you might disappear." He paused. "I had an appointment I couldn't break, so I had my brother follow you when you left the Crystal Palace."

"Did you?" Why didn't that frighten her? She ought to be frightened.

"Yes. He prowled the alley for more than an hour before you appeared at this window." He paused again. "If you didn't arrive tomorrow, then I would know how to find you."

"But you're here now."

"Yes."

He hadn't moved. He thought she was afraid.

"I need to speak with you, Passion."

A tingle tripped down her spine. He spoke her name like an endearment. "We haven't proved capable of mere talking."

Did he smile? She couldn't see him well enough in the dim light.

"What if I promise not to touch you?" There was no mirth in his voice. In fact, it sounded tight.

"That's very well. But you're not the only one I'm worried about."

A long silence drew out between them.

Then: "Just a few moments, Passion." His voice was soft again. "That's all I ask."

Passion pressed her forehead to the bedpost. This was dangerous. She should ask him to leave. But how could she do it when she yearned for him so? When the very smell of him made her want to press herself against him?

She pushed away from the bedpost. "Let me light a lamp."

Crossing to her desk, she swept up her robe along the way and put it on before striking the match. When she ignited the wick of the oil lamp, its warm glow still left shadows in the corners of the room. But she could see him, and her heart beat faster.

He wore no hat, and his hair was tousled. Without a cravat, his shirt fell open at the neck, unbuttoned. He seemed to have no vest or jacket beneath his long topcoat. And he was staring at her—staring at her as hard as she was staring at him.

"Why don't you move away from the window?" Her dry throat made her words catch. She swallowed. "There are warm coals in the grate."

When he stood and crossed to the chair by the hearth, he overpowered her dainty room. Everything seemed small in his presence.

Once settled in the chair, his eyes returned to her. "Won't you sit with me?"

Passion looked at the empty chair across from his. His long legs almost touched it. "I think I had best not."

"Passion, plea—" He cut himself off and pulled back his booted feet. "I've promised not to touch you."

Had he ever said *please* to her before?

No.

"Please—that's a difficult word for you to say, isn't it?"

He frowned and stared into the hearth. Something in his expression, a shadow of pain, perhaps, made her relent. As she sat in the chair, his gaze returned to her. The dim light made his eyes appear dark. They moved all over her. She jerked her bare feet back beneath the cover of her dark green robe when he looked at them.

"You're beautiful," he finally said.

Passion's heart skipped a beat. "Thank you."

"I want to see more of you. I don't want to part yet."

"I know. Nor do I."

"But you will. Why?" He leaned forward. "Because tomorrow is your last day visiting the Crystal Palace? What difference if we meet there or somewhere else? What difference a week of stolen pleasure or a month?"

"What difference?" Passion was incredulous. She shook her head. "Once, one of the boys from my father's parish was seen picking up an apple that had fallen from an apple cart. The boy was poor and had no money. After a brief moment, he ate the apple. The fruit monger wanted him punished. But my father, who knew the boy, understood that he never would have actually gone up to the cart and stolen the apple. The apple fell, and the boy was hungry. Though an error in judgment, it was not as great a one as the fruit monger tried to insist." Passion tipped her head to the side. "Can a starving person be blamed for eating when food falls into her lap?"

Mark leaned back and rested his temple against his fist. "So, I'm the apple in your little parable."

Passion pressed her hand over her heart. "And I was so hungry, Mark. Too hungry to resist you."

His eyes darkened. "You're still hungry."

Passion tried to ignore the warmth that flooded her body. "I know. But I cannot let my culpability escalate."

"Culpability?" Mark pushed his hand through his hair. "You can placate yourself with degrees of culpability if you like. But do you want to know the truth, Passion? The boy ate the apple. Whether it fell into his hand, he stole it, or he bought it with solid silver, the end result is the same—he ate the damned apple." His eyes bored into hers. "Just like you did."

Passion's heart pounded. Her chagrin must have shown clearly on her face, for his voice softened. "Just like I did." He leaned closer. "And is that so horrible? Have we hurt anyone? Have we altered the course of history? Has any dire circumstance been brought to bear by our being together?"

No. She had to admit that the answer was no, but she couldn't say it. She squeezed her eyes shut and quoted her father. "When God's laws are broken, the world suffers."

"Passion."

Her eyes flew open.

"The only suffering here is the suffering you are inflicting. Needless suffering, I might add." He braced his elbows on his knees, and his hands almost touched her. "Now, I know this can't go on forever. These things never do. But I also know it can't be wrong to partake of a pleasure so mutually fulfilling. What we have between us is right. That's why it happened in the first place—because it was right."

Was it true? It felt true. Or was that her desire speaking?

His eyes delved into hers. "You said I had given you a gift. I took you at your word."

"Of course!" she breathed.

"Then how can you throw it away? I still offer it to you."

Passion's resolve was crumbling. He had eroded her justifications and called into question her reasons for having them in the first place. His assertion that what they had was right had the feel of truth. And yet, didn't secrets breed trouble?

With her body as taut as a bowstring, tears welled. She stared down at her hands. Her certainty was gone, and all that remained was a driving need to be with him and a niggling voice that whispered, no.

"Passion, listen to me. I have a proposal."

She lifted her eyes to his. He was so close. She ached to touch him.

"In two months, you leave London. If you agree to continue our relationship, I'll agree to say good-bye at the end of those two months."

A flicker of worry touched Passion's heart. How difficult would good-bye be after another two months? "You don't want to say good-bye now. What makes you think you will want to then?"

"I may *not* want to. But I will."

"Are you sure?" Passion whispered.

He glanced down at their hands, so close but not touching. "Today, when you said tomorrow was our last day, you surprised me. I don't like surprises. If I'm prepared, I can deal with anything."

"Can you, really?"

A frown twisted his brow. "Damned right I can. Do you agree or not? And before you answer, know that I will want you as often as possible—in your bed, in my bed, wherever it's feasible. In return, I promise the utmost discretion. No one will ever know."

He held her gaze. "When the two months are at an end, we will part forever. You will return to your life. All will be as it was.

"Now, Passion, what is your answer?"

Chapter Seven

RAPTURE

Mark sat rigid. Anxiety stretched his nerves as she continued to sit, silently staring at her hands folded in her lap. He thought he might snap if he moved. What was her answer, damn it?

Finally, she raised her eyes and took a breath to speak. His shoulders twitched, and a pain shot up his neck.

"You're very persuasive," she said, her voice just above a whisper. "Nonetheless, a part of me still urges that I refuse you."

A heavy weight pressed down upon him.

Her eyes glittered with unshed tears. "But your arguments, coupled with the desire I feel for you in my heart and body, are too powerful to overcome. Despite my fears, I tremble at your nearness and long for your embrace." Her lip trembled. "I accept your proposal, Mark."

He filled his lungs with a deep breath. Her words washed over him like a soothing balm. His tension melted away, and an array of emotions welled—relief, satisfaction, comfort, and . . . what? Desire? Yes, of course, desire. Always, desire.

God, but he wanted her. Loose hair framed one side of her face while the rest hung twisted into the thick braid that lay against her breast. Her cheeks were flushed and her lips moist. But it was her eyes that held him. Open yearning and supplication glowed in their depths. Was that what called to him, what compelled him to pursue her?

"Done," Mark murmured.

Her hand was warm in his.

"Done," she breathed.

He stroked his fingers against her palm as he leaned back in his chair. "Come, Passion."

She rose at his urging and came to stand between his open knees. His coat fell open and revealed his erection bulging beneath his trousers. No need to hide.

"Is the door locked?"

"Yes," she said softly, her eyes moving over him.

"Where does your aunt sleep?"

"On the other side of the house. She snores loudly."

"How fortuitous. Maids?"

"The attic rooms face the street."

"Take off your robe."

Pausing only a moment, she opened the row of buttons and shrugged out of the green silk. It fell behind her with a soft swoosh.

She stood in a batiste sleeping gown with a high neck and long sleeves. She might have looked the picture of modesty were it not for her nipples eagerly protruding against the fine fabric. That, paired with the expression on her face, made his blood race.

She moistened her lips, and he thought of how she had looked with his cock in her mouth—remembered the heady feeling of milking his come into her. That had been marvelous. But tonight he wanted her body.

His erection throbbed. "Open your gown."

This time she didn't move. "Open your trousers."

Mark's heart beat a little faster. Her low, soft voice affected his body like a touch. Unbuttoning his trousers, he freed his rampant erection and heavy cods, wincing as he did so. He wore no undergarments, having come straight from his bed, and he was already swollen.

Passion stared, and he felt himself growing even more under her regard. Her eyes darkened, and her tongue flicked out to lick her lips.

What was she thinking? "Tell me something," he murmured.

As she seemed to consider her words, her eyes delved into his. "I crave the feel of you inside me. I crave the more lasting fullness that having you inside me imparts." Her hands smoothed across her abdomen. "As satisfying as today was, it wasn't long before I was missing the aching tenderness I feel after you've fucked me."

She was the only woman he knew who made the word *fuck* sound like it ought to be written into poetry. His chest felt tight. She spoke his very desire. To be inside her—to be enveloped by her. To be allowed, completely, into her woman's body.

His cock pulsed almost painfully. He took a deep, calming breath. There was time. He would have her. No need to rush. No need to worry about a crowd without. "Remove your gown, Passion."

Her long, graceful fingers freed each small button swiftly, yet not swiftly enough. His breathing quickened as the expanse of skin slowly grew, until a deep but narrow swath showed between the parted gown.

"I've never undressed in front of a man before," she whispered.

"Good." His throat felt dry.

Her hands lifted, pushing the thin fabric from one shoulder and then the other.

Was he holding his breath?

With a small shrug, the white gown fell to the floor and billowed around her ankles in a whispering cloud.

Shifting ash fluttered in the hearth.

Light and shadow played across her skin, illuminating the convex curves of cheek, breast, and hip in the golden glow of the oil lamp, whilst darkness chased into the beckoning hollows of elbow, waist, and inner thigh.

He wanted to touch her, to feel the texture of her skin and the slope of her hip, yet his hands were too heavy to lift. Perhaps it was enough just to look at her. To follow the lush under-swell of her breast, to the firm line of her ribs . . . To look into the shallow valley of her navel and to trace the slant of her pelvic bone . . . To stare at her long legs and the dark auburn curls at their juncture—to stare for as long as he liked.

"Tell me something." She echoed his earlier request.

The fine fabric of her gown lay around her ankles like thin foam upon sand. "You are Aphrodite."

How odd his voice sounded. Those words weren't his. He had said them before thinking. He *never* said such ridiculous things.

He frowned. He should tell her something true, something real. "I couldn't sleep for wanting you—couldn't sleep for the uncertainty of whether I would be with you again. I had to see you tonight." His gaze moved over her lithe body. "I had to have you tonight."

"Touch me, then."

He slid his hands around her slim waist, molding his palms to the shape of her and pressing his fingers into her soft skin. She was both firm and yielding. His breathing quickened as his hands roamed. Pulling her close, he pressed his cheek to one full breast and kneaded the other while he caressed her buttock. His urgency mounted as her arms came around him. He wanted to touch her everywhere at once. He opened his mouth and felt the full flesh of her breast against his tongue. He squeezed her nipple while he slipped his fingers beneath the curve of her bottom to touch the downy folds of her cunt from behind.

She gasped and moved against him. He nipped the side of her breast as he pushed his fingers just inside her. Her hands moved through his hair and around his shoulders. She pulled at his coat, but he couldn't bring himself to let go of her. She filled his arms and senses with everything he needed.

She expelled a small breath and tightened her hold on him as he pulled her into his lap. He moaned, both for her embrace and the feel of her naked body in his arms.

Her hip rested against his erection. The gentle pressure tempted and relieved him at the same time. His hands roamed, feeling the long line of her leg and the curve of her back. He pressed his nose into her neck and, tasting her tender skin, felt the rapid beat of her pulse against his tongue. Just the smell of her made his blood race and his prick pulse with eager expectation.

Her hands were touching him—smoothing his nape, slipping into the open neck of his shirt—while she pressed her lips to his brow. Her soft kisses warmed and beckoned him. He twisted his hand in her braid and pulled her lips to his for a kiss that both fed and fueled his hunger. The more deeply he drew upon her, the more he wanted of her, until they were both breathless and gasping.

His head spun as Passion drew back. Her hands cupped the sides of his face, and her eyes looked soft as velvet in the dim light. Her breath came in small bursts from her moist, swollen lips. "Shall I be alone in my nakedness, Mark?" Her hands dropped to his coat lapels, then moved to his shirt buttons. "I would see and feel you, as you see and feel me."

His balls tightened. "Don't ask. Take."

Mark watched as she worked the buttons of his shirt and parted the white silk. Bared from neck to balls, she stared for a moment without touching. Then she smoothed her hands across his chest, slipping her fingers through his light furring of hair. He sucked in his breath, and his cock throbbed as the tips of her fingers barely touched his nipples and then trailed down his stomach.

"Let me up, Passion."

She stood almost reluctantly but then backed away from him as he rose from the chair. While he shrugged out of his coat, she moved to her bed and took refuge behind the bedpost. He almost smiled. *No escaping now.*

His shirt followed, then his boots. He saw her fingers tighten on the carved wood before he pushed down his trousers and stepped out of them.

Her lips parted and her eyes moved over him with rapt attention.

Freed from the confines of his trousers, his cock swelled to its full size. Ten and a half inches of hard flesh rose up in turgid readiness.

He stayed where he was and let her look. He knew he could be intimidating without the civilizing influence of his clothing. Yet he also knew most women found him desirable. In fact, most women were wild for him—until he tried to get into them more deeply than they liked.

His gaze dropped to the spot where her long leg curved beside the bedpost.

But Passion knew his need to breach the deepest recesses of her body. She knew it, and she wanted him anyway. In fact, she seemed to need all of what he had to give.

She finally lifted her eyes to his. "You are splendid."

Pleasure flickered in his belly.

Her head tipped against the bedpost. "You are Laocoon made flesh."

Mark knew the sculpture of Laocoon battling the serpents. He flexed his arm and smiled. "If I recall, things didn't go well for Laocoon."

Passion returned his smile. "That's true. But it was an epic struggle," her dimple deepened as her eyes tipped to his erection, "for a hero of classical proportions."

Mark choked back a surprised laugh. "My, aren't you a saucy girl."

Even in the dim light, he could see her cheeks darken with a deep blush. Something warm tugged at him. Such a lovely blush. He admired the delicacy of her features as he crossed to her. Her smile faded, and she looked up at him with hesitancy.

"I like you saucy," he murmured. "And Laocoon's

struggle was nothing compared to standing here without touching you." He slowly lowered his head and took her uplifted mouth in a soft, unhurried kiss that was potent with promise.

And then she was in his arms. Everywhere she touched, her skin caressed his, warming him, both without and within, while her hungry kisses stoked a new fire in his gut.

He thrust his hands into her hair and drank so deeply from her mouth that he almost forgot to breathe. Tearing his mouth from hers, he took a gasping breath and stared into her uplifted face. Her eyes were luminous; her cheeks flushed, and her lips, red and swollen.

A fierce, possessive intensity, such as he'd never felt before, flashed through him. His hands fisted in her hair. "You're mine," he growled.

Passion tightened her arms around him. "Yes."

He ground his cock against her firm belly. "Say it. Say you're mine." Why the hell did he suddenly feel angry? "Say I'm the only one who fucks you."

She stared at him for a moment, seeming to look into him. Did she wonder at his anger? He couldn't hide it.

She reached for his wrists and guided one hand to her waist and the other to her breast. "I *am* yours—only yours. Completely and without reservation." Her eyes fluttered and her hips pressed against him. "You know you're the only one."

As quickly as his anger had sparked, it disappeared. He took a deep, calming breath. The hard bud of her nipple pressed into his palm. He brushed his fingers against it, eliciting a soft sigh from her.

Her braid hung over her shoulder like a thick rope. He grasped it and ran his hand down the soft length to the ribbon tied at the end. With a light tug, it slipped off. Threading his fingers through the thick strands, he unraveled her long hair.

Vanilla and orange blossoms wafted from the supple auburn waves as they fell across her shoulder and breast.

Scooping up the heavy tresses, he breathed in deeply. "You smell of sweetness and desire."

Her lips turned in a small smile, and her hands swept in soft caresses over his waist and lower back. Such hands.

Taking a step back, he let her hair slip through his fingers. The curling ends brushed the slope of her hip, some clinging in tender regard, as though it had been too long since they had last hugged such gentle curves. She *was* Aphrodite.

His blood coursed and his cock throbbed painfully. So painfully, that he glanced down. Christ! His prick was so big; it looked frightening even to him. The head rose dark and purple from the top of his reddened shaft, yet no moisture escaped to soothe his stretched skin. He was dry, dry and hard as steel.

"Does it hurt?"

His sac felt heavy. "Yes. Does it frighten you?"

"A little. But it excites me more."

His muscles jumped. "Show me how much it excites you."

Passion's head tipped to the side. "Show you?"

His balls tightened. "Sit down and open your legs. Put your heels on the edge of the bed."

She only paused a moment before lifting her pretty feet and letting her long limbs fall open.

The soft folds of her beautiful cunt parted and, as he stared, a pearly stream of moisture trickled from her rosy sheath. Hot desire flooded Mark's body. He wanted inside her. He needed inside her.

He moved so quickly, he startled her. Grabbing around her knees, he rubbed the whole length of his cock and balls against her wet slit. Her hips jerked, and she pushed her warm, wet quim hard against him.

He pulled her to him and crushed her lips beneath his. Grinding against her, he pushed his tongue deeply into her sweet mouth.

She opened for him, and her arms and legs held him with a strength that begged fulfillment.

He tightened his hand in her hair and pulled her back so he could look into her beautiful face. "I want to throw you down and get inside you. I want to push and push and push," he growled, "until I'm so deep inside you that my cock becomes another organ of your body, as necessary to you as lungs, liver, or heart."

A soft moan escaped her, and she quivered in his arms. Her eyes were full of the urgent yearning and sensuality that he loved to see there. But tonight, everything was magnified. She exuded sex—and desire for it.

He felt as if he stood on a precipice with no knowledge of what lay below, yet knowing he must leap. His hand tightened in her hair. "I need to be a part of you. Tell me you'll let me. Tell me you won't say hold." Every muscle in his body wanted to drive into her. "Because once I start fucking you, I swear to God, I'm not stopping."

She regarded him with such desperate need. "I want that. Please, Mark." Her eyes welled with tears. "I *need* to be broken, remolded. I crave it. If I could do it myself, I would." Her lips trembled. "Spare me no quarter. Please . . ."

The last dregs of his reserve scattered. He tossed her back on the bed. Her breasts bounced, and some of her hair fanned against the white sheets. He fell upon her, and canting his hips high, he grabbed his cock just below the head and squeezed the knob between the moist lips of her quim. With one strong thrust and a groan, he pushed his straining member into the hot wetness of her cunt, slamming the too-eager head against the barrier of her womb.

Recoiling beneath the force of his entry, Passion gasped.

Mark leaned on his elbows and cupped his hands around her head. "I'm sorry, Passion." He kissed her full, tender lips. "But you have the sweetest—" He thrust, bouncing her again. "The tightest—" He shoved harder, bouncing her harder. "Most *fuckable*—" He slammed his rock-hard cock into her with all the force he could muster and wrenched a cry from her as she jolted beneath him. "Most fuckable cunt I've ever been in."

Her eyes sparkled and her lips trembled as her thighs eased farther open.

He kissed her softly. "Besides, this is what you asked for." He rammed hard. "Isn't it?"

"Yes!" Her face was all tender entreaty. "I yearn to be full of you, to have you so deeply inside me that I cannot tell where you begin and I end."

Mark's gut tightened. "Fuck!" He sent three body-jolting attacks against her womb, choked back a moan, and then sent three more.

Her cunt clenched around him. Her chest heaved.

When he paused, she lifted trembling hands to his face. "If I am Aphrodite, then be my Hephestus. Be the hammer, and mold me to your purpose." She bit down on her lip and tilted her hips in offering. "Please, Mark."

Something potent and indefinable seared his heart with a branding heat. It pained him and empowered him. It made his sperm boil with rutting force. His fingers clenched in Passion's hair, and with his cock as hard as steel, he battered the door to her womb with unrelenting ferocity.

Each strike sent courses of pleasure down his shaft and into his cods. The harder he fucked her, the harder he wanted to fuck her. And all the while, her breasts bounced wildly and her cunt squeezed and sucked his invading prick with tender rigor.

Rearing back on his heels, Mark watched the progress of his assault.

Her beautiful quim was stretched tightly around him, but about four inches of his cock, the thickest four inches, had yet to feel the sucking caress of her sweet cunt.

Grabbing her hips with a muttered oath, he held her fixed as he sent a barrage of shattering blows against her defiant flesh. He would fuck and fuck until her resistant womb moved and turned.

Passion moaned. Her head fell back. Her eyes closed.

"This is what you need," he gasped. "You need me for this."

Her whole body tensed.

He tightened his grip on her. "Look at me, Passion."

Her eyes opened and her hips bucked.

"I'll *be* the hammer, but never stay me. From this night forward you're mine to break whenever I choose."

He saw the nearness of her orgasm and thrust fiercely against her three more times. He wanted her come. He needed it.

Passion's eyes darkened. Her cunt clenched.

He thrust again. "Do you hear me, Passion? You're mine. You're the sheath for my cock, and I'll work you as hard as it takes until you fit me like a glove."

Her body began to shake. Her back arched. Her fingers grasped the sheets so tightly that her knuckles turned white.

Mark held his breath, waiting for the perfect moment. Waiting.

On a low moan, her cunt began to draw. With the first strong, sucking pull, Mark bore down with all his strength, grinding the swollen head of his cock against the opening to her womb.

Sweat beaded on his brow, and he thought he heard Passion gasp. But he held her writhing body to him and kept his eyes on his goal. A juicy wash of come lubricated his shaft, and when her cunt pulled again, he bore down anew, lending the weight of his body to his efforts.

Suddenly, half an inch of his exposed flesh disappeared into Passion's body. Mark gasped for breath and groaned. He could feel the tight fingers of her cervix move slightly against his knob.

Passion froze, but her hungry little cunt kept pulling.

With fresh strength, Mark pushed and pushed, forcing the head of his prick against the door to her womb. He could feel her giving way, could feel her cervix tilting.

Passion began to pant, and in the next moment, she

started to convulse beneath him. More wetness bathed his shaft.

Mark grit his teeth and, chancing a slight withdrawal, heaved a final, mighty thrust against her resisting flesh.

Passion bit back a sharp cry.

And with a tiny pop that he wasn't sure if he heard or felt, he watched the remaining length of his cock slide into Passion's quivering cunt.

A low, guttural moan escaped him, and his head spun as unbelievable excitement and pure heart-stopping joy washed over him all at once.

Looking at Passion, he found her pale and still beneath him. Yet her eyes were fixed on him and burning with something he'd never seen—something raw and untouched. He tried to decipher what it was, but his thoughts were numbed by the pure physical sensation of being completely inside her.

For the first time in his life, he was up to his cods in a woman—not just any woman—Passion. He could still feel the tight nub of her cervix, but now it was below, rubbing the thick, distended passage that brought his spunk. The pulsing head of his cock was in a deep pocket of flesh above her womb. It was pure heaven, and he was desperate to move. "Are you all right?"

"Yes." The word came on a breath. "I feel . . . I feel full." Her hand lay over her navel. "I can feel you here." She slipped her hand lower, touching the stretched opening of her cunt. "I can feel you here." Her velvety eyes delved into his. "It's the most exquisite sensation I've ever felt."

His body was trembling, and his cock throbbed mercilessly, demanding satisfaction. He had only moments before he would lose himself altogether.

Bending over her, he braced himself on his elbows and spoke against her mouth. "I've got to move, Passion. I've got to fuck." She smelled so sweet and her arms were around him. He rocked forward again. "I don't know if I can be careful."

"Then don't be." Her fingers pressed into his shoulders. "There is too much of 'careful' in my life."

The muscles in Mark's legs leapt. Still, with every last vestige of his will, he drew back as slowly as he could.

Fuck! His arms shook and his eyes closed. The sensation was like nothing he'd ever experienced. The firm press of Passion's cervix worked the underside of his shaft with delicious pressure. He pulled back enough so he could feel the rim of his knob against it and then slid back in.

"Oh, God . . ." Passion moaned low and deep, and her eyes glowed with that indefinable emotion. "If I could have only one pleasure, one purpose, it would be this."

Her words blew through him like a hot and sudden wind. The flame he had been keeping at bay exploded and sent a torrent of fire roaring through his body.

His hips pumped wildly. His hands twisted in her hair. "This *is* your purpose," he gasped. "You were made for me."

Passion's body leapt beneath him. "Yes," she gasped. "I know."

Mark groaned and began thrusting in a gluttony of sensation. The deep pocket he had made in her cunt was like nothing he had ever felt before. Her cervix worked the tender underside of his cock while her cunt squeezed the shaft and thick root. On each withdrawal, he pulled the swollen head of his prick all the way to the firm press of her tilted cervix before thrusting back in. It was the sweetest torture, and he couldn't stop. He wanted to fuck and fuck.

Passion gasped with each forceful intrusion. A sheen of perspiration gleamed on her brow. Yet, still, her tight, hungry cunt lifted and clenched.

"You're so good," Mark groaned, never pausing. "So damned good." He dropped his mouth to hers, pushing his tongue deep, as he kept withdrawing and thrusting, withdrawing and thrusting. He bit her lip before breaking the kiss.

Passion's swollen mouth trembled, and the pulse in her neck beat wildly.

His hips pumped and pumped. He could tell her orgasm was rising. He wanted to feel the luscious pull of it. He wanted to see it in her beautiful face. "Pull back your knees with your hands." His cock throbbed in knowing anticipation. "I don't want to feel anything but cunt."

Passion did as he asked, and suddenly her wide-open quim sat at a completely unobstructed angle. She drew in a deep breath as he sank even deeper.

"Oh, God, that's good." Mark groaned, and his cock wept come at the deliciousness of her.

He pulled the sperm-moistened head of his prick to her tilted cervix. But this time he pulled back farther, dragging his engorged knob over the firm flesh.

Passion froze. Her eyes grew glassy. Her breath came in short pants.

Mark thought he might die from pure pleasure. His breach had been so fast, but this long, slow withdrawal exacted the most succulent pressure on the head of his inflamed prick. Then, with his eyes on Passion, he pushed back in, stopping just as he rubbed over the firm opening that sheltered her womb.

Her body curled and her panting increased. Without pause, he retreated and drove back in, this time harder and faster.

She strained beneath him, every muscle taut and quaking. Again and again he thrust over her tight cervix, finding the short, perfect rhythm. His heart pounded. Passion's head tossed. His cock strained, driving her, driving her to climax.

Then, with a great intake of breath, her head lifted from the bed and slammed back down. Her neck stretched, fine veins and tendons distending. Her cunt clamped around him, and her body went rigid.

Still thrusting relentlessly, Mark stared, transfixed.

In the most beautiful display he'd ever seen, she found rapture.

With a heart-wrenching gasp, her head lifted again. He stared into her radiant eyes. And then, with a low, fierce cry, they squeezed shut as a violent shudder radiated from her clenching cunt. It wracked her taut body. Her head flew back, and her knees drew up even farther. The walls of her quim pulled, gripped, and pulled again.

Her eyes flew open and then rolled back as her ravenous cunt sucked and sucked, drawing him into her as deeply as ever. She jerked uncontrollably. Her pelvis lifted. And with a final, great heave and a muffled cry, she let down a hot wash of cock-soothing come.

Mark lay still in her juicy sheath. Her body was limp beneath him, and her lip bled from where she must have bit back her cries. A deep flush tinted her skin.

"You are magnificent," he breathed.

Her eyes fluttered open, and the look in them was soft as down. "No. You are." Her trembling arms lifted and curved around him. Her legs pressed against his sides. "Come," she whispered, "take from me what you need. Until you have your satisfaction, I am unfulfilled."

Mark's gut wrenched, and a choked gasp escaped him as his cock pulsed eagerly. "What I need?" He thrust deeply. "This is what I need." He thrust again, pulling his knob nearly halfway out then shoving all the way in to the root. "I need to be inside you."

Passion moaned weakly.

He kissed her bruised lips, and the taste of her blood fired his own. Pressing his stomach to hers, he scooped his hands beneath her back and gripped her shoulders. With each driving push into her body, he felt the powerful knock of his prick within her.

"I can feel my prick fucking you," he growled. His head pounded with exhilaration. "It's so deep inside you."

He slammed into her over and over, luxuriating in each pounding assault.

Passion's eyes glittered. "Fuck me," she whispered. Her arms tightened around him. "Fuck me."

Mark's sperm churned in his balls. His vision narrowed. Everything disappeared from sight but Passion. She was the only thing that mattered. She was the sole object of his desire. She was the cup into which he would pour his seed—and his hope.

He fucked with a wild ferocity. His hips pistoned hard and high, and with every deep stroke, his heavy, sperm-laden sac slapped her firm bottom. The sound and feel of each smack drove him mad with excitement.

His muscles strained. Blood pounded in his head. He pummeled her cunt with his cock and, pressing his body against hers, he touched her everywhere—arms, torso, cheek.

Dots of light skittered across his vision. His balls tightened. His cock jerked. The smell of her filled his brain.

Suddenly, sound receded.

He pressed his face into the curve of her neck.

Held in a silent cocoon of splendor, fiery bliss consumed him whole as molten-hot sperm roared from his cock in a heart-sundering purge. It poured out of him, burning away layers of pain and sorrow in its powerful wake. He felt the hot wash of it, spilling back upon him, as deluge after deluge spewed from his enraptured prick.

And within the fire, his heart beat with a fierce joy, throbbing exuberantly with each potent ejaculation. The more seed flooded from his pulsing shaft, the more full his heart became. He felt as if it might burst as he filled the deepest cavities of Passion's womb with himself.

If his heart exploded into a thousand pieces, he wouldn't care. Passion held him in the paradise of her bodily embrace.

He'd never been to paradise.

Chapter Eight

TROUBLESOME RELATIVES

The gray-blue light of pre-dawn filtered through Passion's lashes as she blinked sleepily. Had she ever felt this warm and secure? She pressed herself more tightly against the strong body curved around hers. Mark! Her eyes flew open, and she looked over her shoulder.

He was awake and propped on his elbow with his head braced in his hand. His hair was tousled, and his blue eyes regarded her seriously. Only God could have conceived eyes so beautiful.

"Good morning," he murmured.

Passion felt herself blushing. "Good morning."

"I've never slept the night with a woman."

Surprise and a warm tingle of pleasure tumbled through her. "Really?"

A brief frown creased his brow. "During your marriage, did you share a bed with your husband?"

Taken aback, Passion paused. "Well, yes." Why did he have to keep asking about her late husband? "But never like this," she said, glancing at Mark's bare chest. "And, but for the times when—well, you know—he never touched me. He slept on his side of the bed, and I slept on mine."

Mark's frown deepened and his arm tightened around her waist. "I'm glad he never had you like this."

Passion smiled. "As am I." She wished he would kiss her, but he didn't. She glanced back at the window and then at the clock beside the bed. "Heavens, it's almost five o'clock." She pulled away from Mark's embrace and, grabbing the light throw at the foot of the bed, held it to herself before standing up.

A deep soreness in her inner thighs made her gasp.

Mark sat up and reached for her. "Are you all right?"

She glanced over her shoulder and saw his concerned frown. "I'm fine. Just sore."

"But can you walk?"

She took a few tentative steps. Her legs ached, but it was the tender soreness of her cunt and womb that both pained and pleasured her most. She savored the raw pull of her muscles as she moved to the end of the bed. As the day passed, the feeling would mellow to a barely notice-able throb. She would miss it. Pausing at the foot of the bed, she smiled reassuringly. "I've been well and truly fucked, that's for certain."

Mark laughed and shook his head as he leaned back against the pillows. "I love to hear you say that word." Propping up one knee beneath the sheets, he tipped his gaze to the satin throw she clutched to her breast. "A little late for modesty, isn't it?"

Her cheeks warmed and she nodded toward the clock. "You must go. The maids rise at five-thirty."

When he didn't seem inclined to move, she frowned re-provingly. "If we're caught here together, it would send my aunt into an apoplectic fit—not to mention the scan-dal."

Lifting his arms, he laced his fingers behind his head in an all-too-relaxed fashion. "Kiss me and I'll go."

Lord, a kiss could lead her astray. She raised her brow. "Promise?"

His large sculpted shoulders lifted in a small shrug. "Of course."

Gripping the satin throw, she went to the side of the bed and, bending quickly, gave him a peck on the lips.

He looked at her reprovingly. "*That* is not a kiss."

"Oh, for heaven's sake . . ." Passion sat down beside him and, gripping his nape, pulled him to her for a warm, moist kiss. She had meant to keep it brief, but the taste and smell of him—and the ardor with which he responded—made her linger.

Deepening the kiss, Mark drew her other hand beneath the sheet. She moaned at the feel of his penis, large and firm.

God, even sore she wanted him.

Her fingers curled around him, and her quim moistened as she felt the brush of his fingers across her nipples. Gasping as he nipped her lower lip, she stroked his shaft and lifted her chest.

"You have the most beautiful breasts I've ever seen," he murmured against her mouth. She sucked in her breath and tightened her hand around him as he delivered a firm pinch to both of her distended nipples. "Shall we have a quick fuck?" he whispered, kneading her breasts.

"Oh, very well." She sighed.

Mark kissed her and she felt his smile. "I'm sorry, I can't stay. I've promised to go."

Passion snapped her eyes open and frowned into his smiling face. "Beast." She realized she had let the throw drop and yanked it up as she stood.

Mark chuckled as he slung his legs over the side of the bed. "I'm only letting you go because I'll see you later at the Palace. I will see you there, won't I?"

She picked up her robe from the floor and shrugged into it quickly. "Yes, I'll be there."

As she worked her buttons, he stood and stretched. She couldn't help looking. He had a glorious body—large, yet beautifully sculpted. Broad shoulders flexed above a firm chest and tapering torso. She admired the musculature of his pelvis, the jutting power of his penis, and the strength of his thigh.

He let his arms drop with a contented grunt and, shoving back his hair, crossed to where he had left his clothes. His cock, not quite fully hard, bobbed before him.

Passion's mouth watered and she swallowed. There was no denying he was huge. Beautiful and arousing, the potent masculinity of him made her wet.

Glancing at her as he pulled on his trousers, Mark smiled his half smile. "You have that come-fuck-me look in your eye. Sure I shouldn't stay?"

Blushing, she swept his shirt from the chair and held it for him to slip into.

He paused briefly before turning and sliding his arms into his shirt. Turning back to face her, he pressed a kiss on her brow. "Thank you."

As he closed the buttons of his shirt, he examined the things decorating her mantel. He paused at her hydrangea plate, leaning closer as he examined it. He glanced back at her. "P.E.D.? Did you do this?"

"Yes."

He looked at it again then back at her. "It's very good."

She smiled at the admiring-surprised frown on his face. "Thank you."

"Actually, it's better than good, it's wonderful. Do you paint on canvas as well, or solely porcelain?"

Her heart fluttered with pride. "I have painted on canvas, but mostly I work on porcelain."

He studied her plate again and shook his head. "You're very talented."

Passion could barely contain her smile. His praise made her incredibly happy. By what she knew of him, he wouldn't say one word he didn't mean. *Not always pretty, but honest and unfettered.*

"P.E.D." He lightly touched her scrolling initials and then turned back to her. "Are you going to tell me what they stand for?"

How easy it would be to tell him. How easy to become

more than they ought. "I think it best we just remain Passion and Mark."

He sat in the chair and pulled on his boots. "I know where you live. I could find out your name if I wanted."

She frowned. "But you won't because I've asked you not to."

He studied her for a moment and then shrugged. "I already know anyway."

Passion tensed. "You do?"

"Yes." He stood and picked up his coat. "It's Passion Ermintrude Dittsnapper."

Passion widened her eyes and let her mouth fall open. "How did you know?"

He stared at her for a split second and then a deep chuckle rumbled out of him. "All right, then. I see how it's going to be."

She grinned and batted her lashes at him over her shoulder as she crossed to the window. Served him right for tempting her earlier. She swept aside the curtains and bowed. "Your coach, my lord."

An odd look passed over his features and just as quickly disappeared. He paused beside her, his handsome mouth turned in a small smile. "My, what a lovely footman." He threaded his hands through her hair and pressed a soft, languorous kiss to her lips.

Passion sighed and gripped the lapels of his coat as she savored the taste and closeness of him. Lord, but he felt good.

He pulled back, kissing the corner of her mouth, before he cupped her face in his hands. She gazed at him and knew she'd never seen a more handsome man.

"Last night," he murmured. His blue eyes held hers. "I've never felt such pleasure."

Her blood surged. "Nor have I."

He seemed as if he might say more, but then he just smiled and dropped another kiss upon her lips. After a surveying glance out the window, he climbed out.

Passion gripped the sleeve of his coat. Her hair fell for-

ward, and her hands slid to his wrist as he moved down
the trellis. He looked up at her, and his eyes reflected the
blue of the day to come.

"I'll see you at the Crystal Palace," he whispered.

"I'll be there."

With a soft caress, his fingers slid through hers as he
climbed down. Leaping the final few feet to the ground,
he turned and ran across the garden, his long coat kicking
up behind him. She didn't think he would look back, but
as he topped the garden wall, he paused.

They stared at each other across the distance. Passion
trembled. Her insides quivered. Her blood quickened in
her veins, rushing to fill her swelling heart. She gasped
and clenched her fingers on the sill.

How would she ever give him up?

He disappeared over the wall.

Tears welled.

God, what had she done?

Mark tossed his coat over the chair beside the foyer
table. Despite his late night and the earliness of the hour,
he was wide awake and invigorated. During the walk
home, his mind had been so filled with thoughts of Passion that he'd barely noticed his surroundings. Shoving
back his hair, he grinned. That's what a great fuck could
do to a man.

He walked to his study. He could get in a couple hours
of work on the library plans before he would need to clean
up and go to the Crystal Palace.

Opening the door, he stopped short. Matt sat by the
window, a tray of breakfast sitting on the table beside him.

Matt looked him over. "Good morning, brother."

Mark lifted one brow as he crossed the room. "Do
make yourself at home," he quipped as he fell into the
other chair.

"You always said I should," Matt replied over the rim
of his coffee cup.

"Mmm." Mark frowned. "I did, didn't I?" Looking over the tray of food, he picked up a slice of toast.

"So." Matt put down his cup. "I take it by your unkempt appearance, and the fact that you had me follow a certain lady home yesterday, that you have just come from the bed of Passion."

"Yes. And that's very well said, by the way." Mark bit into his toast and glanced at his brother. Matt hadn't smiled once. "What's wrong?"

His brother picked up the other slice of toast. "It seems to me that you have an avid attraction for this woman. Am I wrong?"

"So what if I do?"

"I thought I knew you, that's what."

Mark frowned. "What the hell's the matter with you?"

"I'll tell you what the matter is." Matt tossed his toast back on the plate. "I'm having dinner with Mother last night. She keeps going on and on about this Miss Charlotte Lawrence—how beautiful she is, how charming, how perfect for you." Matt leaned closer. "I'm thinking to myself, *Mark isn't interested in Charlotte Lawrence. He told me so himself. Besides, I happen to know he's on fire for a beauty by the name of Passion. And when it comes to women, my brother* never *splits his attentions.*"

Mark's shoulders tensed. He had a feeling he knew where his brother was going.

"So," Matt continued, "I, thinking to save my dear brother from unwanted aggravation, mention to Mother that she ought to drop the subject of Miss Lawrence. That you are currently interested in quite a different woman and that she should leave you the hell alone."

Mark's frown deepened. That was information his mother didn't need to know.

"Imagine my surprise when she informs me that I must be entirely mistaken." Matt slammed his hand on the table. "Because the fact is, you've become engaged to Miss Lawrence that very afternoon!"

"Temper, temper," Mark growled.

"You're my brother," Matt said, lowering his voice. "We tell each other everything. How the hell could you make this decision without informing me? Something this fucking important?" His expression read disbelief. "I have to hear it from *Mother*? In that damned condescending tone she likes to use when she feels she has the upper hand."

Shit. Passion filled his thoughts so much that he wasn't considering all the factors involved in extricating himself from Abigail Lawrence's blackmail. If he was going to keep his brother in the dark, his plans needed to be passed through the what-to-tell-Matt filter.

Mark tossed the remainder of his toast on the tray. He wasn't handling things well.

His jaw clenched. Fucking lies. He hated them.

Even more, he hated the conniving women who forced him to tell them.

He looked at his brother. "I apologize for not telling you." Christ, he hated this! "I didn't know I was going to make the decision until I'd made it." He shrugged. "I want children."

A sudden vision of Passion with her stomach swollen filled his mind. He took a deep breath and focused on his brother. "She's pretty. Seems fairly even-tempered. And you know I've never cared about a title. In fact, I prefer to have a common wife."

Matt stared hard at him. "Commoners commit adultery, too. I thought you never wanted to suffer Father's fate."

Mark swallowed the distaste that rose up in his throat. "Unlike Father, I'm not marrying with any expectation of fidelity. Unlike Father, I don't intend to languish in a hell of abstinence. Unlike Father, I'll fuck anyone I like, whenever I like."

"Just like our mother did."

Mark's blood began to boil. "Go to hell."

Undeterred, Matt sat back in his chair and seemed to be considering. "What about Passion?"

"That's temporary."

"Temporary?" Matt frowned. "Why?"

Mark's body tightened with anger and frustration. "Because *everything* is temporary, Matt. Everything beautiful dies. Everything sweet turns sour. It's just a matter of time."

"I don't believe that."

"More's the pity."

Mark heaved himself from the chair and went to his desk. The drawings for the library were stacked neatly beside his drafting tools. He had absolutely no desire to work.

Matt strolled over and held out his hand. "Congratulations on your engagement."

Mark shook reluctantly. "Thank you."

"When shall I meet her?"

"Soon, I'm sure."

Matt nodded. "Don't forget you're coming to dinner at the Benchley's tonight."

Mark groaned inwardly. "Right."

"And be charming, if you please. You make Rosalind nervous when you're morose."

"I'm sure I told you to go to hell. What are you still doing here?"

"Waiting for you to show me the way."

Mark glared into his brother's smug grin.

As Matt picked up his hat from the desk, a light knock sounded on the door. At Mark's call, Cranford stepped in.

"My young relation has arrived, my lord."

"Excellent. Send him in, Cranford."

"If you insist, my lord."

Mark almost smiled. Cranford had worked hard to elevate himself. He hated the fact that he had ne'er-do-well relatives.

Mickey Wilkes sauntered in. Cranford gave the boy what was meant to serve as a warning frown before bowing out.

Matt smiled. "What's this young knave doing here?"

"Sent for, I was," Mickey offered. He looked at the two men and then pulled off his hat.

Matt shook his head. "I thought you gave this light-fingered little thief a position at Hawkmore House. I hardly think the city is the place to break him of his old habits."

"Oh, I be entirely broke o'.me old habits, Mr. 'Awkmore." Mickey jingled the coins in his pocket. "I's a new man, I am. Completely habilitated from me old ways."

Mark doubted it. Though only seventeen, Mickey had the easygoing confidence of someone who had been through a few scrapes in his life yet somehow escaped serious consequences. He'd bet the boy wasn't as "habilitated" as he claimed.

"I need an errand boy," Mark said to his brother.

Matt spoke over his shoulder as he left. "You'll be lucky if he isn't arrested on his first errand."

The study door closed with a light slam.

Mark turned to Mickey. "Sit down. I have a job for you."

"You'll never guess who's here, my dear," Aunt Matty called from below.

Passion smoothed her gray silk skirts as she rounded the upper landing. The smile froze on her face as she stared down into the beaming visage of Alfred Swittly.

"Good morrow, Mrs. Redington." With one hand on the banister post and one foot braced on the bottom stair, he posed. "It is the east, and Juliet is the sun!"

Passion moved down the stairs slowly, an embarrassed flush heating her cheeks. "Good morning, Mr. Swittly. What a surprise to see you."

"Yes, isn't it though." He took her hand when she reached the bottom step. Passion quickly withdrew it once in the foyer. "May I observe, Mrs. Redington, that in your gray silk, you are like a flower about to bloom. Like a tropical bird about to take flight."

"Like a lizard about to shed its skin," Aunt Matty offered.

Passion clenched her jaw to keep from laughing.

"Well, not quite like that," Alfred said. "More like a butterfly about to shed its chrysalis."

"Yes, well, butterflies are lovely," Aunt Matty agreed. "But you know, Mr. Swittly, at a recent meeting of the Nature Society, I observed a lizard shedding its skin. It was very beautiful."

"Really, Mistress Dare?"

Passion felt as though she were at a tennis match, her eye moving from Alfred to her aunt and back again.

"Why, yes. I even wrote an essay on the subject. Passion said it was 'very well phrased,' and your aunts are going to submit it for publication in the Society newsletter." Matty beamed. "Of course, there are no guarantees, but I'm certain that soon I shall be an authoress."

"How grand, Mistress Dare. You must sign a copy for me."

Leisurely fanning herself, Aunt Matty seemed to grow taller. "I should be delighted, Mr. Swittly."

Passion's fingers twitched with impatience. How the two of them could go on!

The next moment, she felt ashamed for the thought. Was she becoming a salacious wanton, thinking of nothing but her own satisfaction? She mustn't let her carnal desires take precedence over the needs of others or impede upon the normal occurrences of life.

She must be as patient and controlled as ever.

"Of course, one never knows how these things shall go," Aunt Matty continued. "I once read a brilliant essay on the contrary aspects of the garden snail—contrary because it has such a delicate and beautiful spiral shell and yet it's a voracious villain in the garden, isn't it?"

Passion's neck stiffened with her efforts.

Aunt Matty shrugged. "When I find one, I never know whether to leave it where it is or heave it over the garden wall. But if I did that, I would be infecting my neighbor's roses, wouldn't I? That is, if the poor thing survived. Because I might just have dashed it all to pieces, mightn't I?"

Passion's shoulders tensed. She pursed her lips shut.

Aunt Matty sighed and shook her head. "What a quandary."

Passion drew a deep breath as she observed Alfred Swittly's confused frown. Poor man. He was unused to her aunt's meandering mind.

"I confess, mistress, that I've never given such consideration to the common garden snail. However, from this day forward, I shall view them with a new sympathy."

Passion grit her teeth and drove her nails into the palms of her hands.

"Very good, sir. Very good." Aunt Matty touched his arm. "Would you care to see it now?"

He bent nearer. "See what, mistress?"

"My essay on the beauty of the shedding lizard, of course. Would you care to read it now?"

"But Aunt!" The words fairly burst from Passion's lips. Alfred and Aunt Matty looked at her with surprise. "Are we not going to the Crystal Palace?" she asked more calmly. "It's our last day, and there are so many things I still want to see."

Aunt Matty nodded. "Of course, my dear, of course. Mr. Swittly, I must decline your request to read my essay. Now just isn't the time, sir."

"Uh, yes. I understand completely, mistress. Another time."

Passion slipped her arm through her aunt's. "I regret that we must bid you adieu so soon, Mr. Swittly. I know you only just arrived, but my aunt and I have spent all week surveying the Crystal Palace, and today is our last day."

He frowned. "But . . ."

"Darling, I have invited Mr. Swittly to join us today."

"What?" Passion's heart fell into her stomach.

Aunt Matty pattered her arm and winked meaningfully. "Of course, I'll leave you two to explore on your own. I'm sure you'll have so much to talk about."

No! She wanted to scream her protest.

But she didn't.

She walked to the cab, a stunned prisoner of disappointment. Her aunt and Alfred Swittly flanked her. They bumped and jostled her on the narrow path.

It took every ounce of her will not to shove them both aside and run.

If she ran now, she could probably escape through the crowd. But she couldn't do it. It would be rude and a terrible embarrassment to her aunt—even if she did try to make it seem as if she and Alfred were separated by accident. Besides, she glanced up at him, she just couldn't be that mean-spirited.

"I say, what a throng," Alfred commented jovially. "Personally, Mrs. Redington, I love a crowd. So many people to see and be seen by."

And he was seen! He cut a wide path with his massive size, easily bumping aside those who failed to move out of his way.

She needed to let Mark see why she couldn't meet him. "May I show you the gothic furniture room, Mr. Swittly? There are some lovely pieces there."

"Certainly, Mrs. Redington. Certainly. Today," he leaned down and winked at her, "I am entirely at your disposal."

Passion drew back slightly. "How delightful."

He beamed. "Yes, isn't it? We are among the fortunate few, Mrs. Redington, who have the means to afford leisure and the wit to use it for our personal edification. Think, Mrs. Redington, of all the vile wretches who slave away their lives in menial jobs and then spend what little free time and money they have in the desperate pursuit of drink. Horrid existence. I pity them, really."

The man spoke in a voice that could be heard by all who passed. Indeed, he seemed more interested in the reaction of others to his words than he did hers.

Passion blushed with embarrassment. *"But many that are first shall be last; and the last first."*

"What's that, Mrs. Redington?" He harrumphed. "I certainly don't intend to be last. I rather fancy being first, if you must know." He guffawed. "First shall be last—last first? Wherever did you come up with such a thing?"

Passion lifted her brows reproachfully. "The Gospel according to St. Mark, chapter ten, verse thirty-one."

"Oh!" His forehead wrinkled as he nodded thoughtfully. "Yes, I knew the words sounded familiar. I say, look at this astounding screen, Mrs. Redington. Have you ever seen such a thing?"

Passion looked up at the screen. Her body relaxed. She reached out to touch the carved wood. It was *their* screen. Turning her head slowly, she looked over her shoulder.

From a short distance away, deep blue eyes captured hers. Passion's heart lifted joyfully. A pulse beat once between her legs. She took a quiet breath.

He stayed where he was, in the center of the room yet apart from the crowd, and bent a frown upon Alfred Swittly.

Passion glanced at the big man, who was still delivering his critical opinion of the screen, then returned her gaze to Mark.

She hated that he was here, yet so far from her. He was supposed to be near. He was supposed to be touching her. She let her gaze wander over his immaculate form. Her breasts tingled, and her tender womb quivered in memory of their night together. God, how she wanted him!

When she lifted her eyes to his, she found the blue orbs full of fire. With slow deliberation, he slid one hand into his pocket. As his arm moved up and down in a leisurely caress, moisture filled Passion's mouth.

Her sore muscles convulsed, and her cunt clenched.

"After all, something this huge would never fit, would it?"

Passion yanked her attention to Alfred. He was looking at her expectantly.

Passion swallowed. "I'm sorry?"

"I said, a screen this large would never fit in a house."

Alfred looked at it dismissively. "Completely impractical, if you ask me."

Passion shifted her gaze to Mark. His hand was still in his pocket, but now he was moving closer.

"Entirely ridiculous, really," Alfred scoffed.

Her body trembled. "Actually, I'm quite fond of it. Sometimes you need something large to cover emptiness."

Lemon verbena titillated her senses.

Alfred looked back at the screen. "Well, I see why you might like it."

Passion shivered as Mark's fingers trailed down her back. He stood right next to her, seeming to examine the screen.

"But could you really accommodate something this massive?" Alfred asked.

Passion turned to him as Mark pulled her hand behind her skirts. She curled her fingers around his stiff erection. Her heart pounded. "I'm sure nothing smaller would do."

She froze and released Mark as Alfred raised his thick blond brows at her. "Really? I must see the place where you would put such a thing." He smiled. "Perhaps we might visit your home someday soon. I'm sure your family would like to meet me, and I so admire the country, with its large, sprawling homes."

Gripping her elbow, he led her away from the screen. "Your aunt informs me that your father supports her. He must have quite a rich vicarage to be able to support a spinster sister so comfortably."

Passion pulled her arm free of Alfred's thick fingers.

"And," he put his hand on his chest, "he must be rich in generosity as well."

"My father is rich in many regards, sir. Not least of all in the love of his daughters."

As they entered the busy main gallery, she glanced behind her. Mark followed with a dark scowl leveled on the back of Alfred Swittly.

Passion fairly leapt out of her skin when, suddenly, Alfred's voice boomed and he threw his arms wide. *"Tell me, my daughters, which of you shall we say doth love us most? That we our largest bounty may extend where nature doth merit . . ."* Alfred's hand came to rest in the small of her back.

Passion turned away from the curious stares of those around them. Mark was near, his gaze fixed on her. Why couldn't she be walking with him? Why must she be with this pompous, conceited man?

Frowning, Passion pulled away from Alfred's grasping hand. "Unlike the obtuse King Lear, sir, my father loves each of his daughters for themselves and would never bestow unequal favors."

"But of course, of course," Alfred blustered. Lowering his voice, he leaned close as he led her down the gallery. "I must tell you, Mrs. Redington, that I am very impressed by your knowledge of Shakespeare. It so happens that I am a scholar of the great man. Tell me, did you recognize the line by my kingly delivery?"

Once again Alfred's heavy hand dropped to her waist. Once again, Passion sidestepped. "And I must tell *you*, Mr. Swittly, that I merely guessed—by the context of the line and the fact that you quoted Shakespeare earlier."

"Then what of this, Mrs. Redington?" He scooped up her hand, clutching it in both his own. *"O, she doth teach the torches to burn bright! It seems she hangs upon the cheek of night, as a rich jewel in an Ethiop's ear: Beauty too rich for use, for earth too dear!"*

Passion realized he had led her to a very quiet section at the end of the gallery. "Mr. Swittly, please!"

Trying to pull her hand away, she looked for Mark. He stood at a distance, engaged in conversation with a small group of people.

She gasped as Alfred pulled her behind a large statue, her hand still captive in his grip. "Forgive me, Mrs. Redington, but I could not help but notice the way you have been looking at me." He grabbed her to him, forcing a whoosh of air from her compressed lungs. "I recognize the look of desire in your eyes, Mrs. Redington. You cannot imagine my delight at knowing your passion, forgive the pun, is equal to my own."

Passion's eyes widened with shock, and she squirmed against him. "Let me go this instant, Mr. Swittly!"

"I cannot, dear girl. *In truth . . . I am too fond . . .*"

The man was as immovable as a tree! Her tension mounted. "This instant, Mr. Swittly!"

His head lowered. A drop of sweat trickled down his temple. *"O, wilt thou leave me so unsatisfied?"*

Passion shrunk back. She couldn't take a deep breath. A frantic urge to scream was building in her. "Please, Mr. Swittly! Let me go! Let me go, or I shall scream!"

He held her tighter, and his wet lips got closer and closer. *"Methinks the lady doth protest too much."*

Just as she opened her mouth to scream, a startled woof and a grunt escaped Alfred. In the next instant, she was free as the big man slithered to the floor, holding his side.

Passion looked into Mark's fury-filled eyes.

"Are you all right?" he growled, his hands still fisted at his sides.

She wanted to run into his arms. "Yes."

Wheezing, Alfred rolled up onto his elbow. He raised reddened eyes to Mark and pointed at Passion. "I am courting this woman, sir! We are here together. I am her escort."

"I'll escort you right onto your ass if I see you mauling this woman again. She has no need of your attentions."

Alfred struggled to his knees. "You, sir, have no right to intrude upon us."

Mark's fist tightened, so Passion stepped forward. "Thank you, sir, for your assistance." She touched his arm and looked at him meaningfully. "I'm afraid this man mistook a sentiment he thought he saw in my face."

"That's right, sir." Blowing, Alfred heaved himself to his feet. He yanked down his vest with a huff. "And despite how it might appear, my intentions toward this woman are completely honorable."

An odd expression passed over Mark's features. He stared at Alfred for a moment before looking at Passion. What was he thinking?

His blue eyes delved into hers. "This man doesn't deserve you, madam." He touched the brim of his hat and turned on his heel. "Good day."

"I say! You are entirely wrong, sir. I am completely deserving of her!" Alfred called after Mark's back.

Passion stepped out from behind the statue and watched him until he disappeared into the crowd.

Suddenly she felt bereft.

When would she see him again?

Chapter Nine

ARGUMENTS, ANNOUNCEMENTS, AND LIES

Mark drew a careful detail of the festoon that was to curve around the outer saucer dome of the library. It would bear an open book and a globe joined by an acanthus swag.

He tried to concentrate, but the image of Passion in the embrace of that giant ass kept intruding. Was she considering marrying such a lout? Was she considering marrying at all?

He repaired an uneven line.

She wouldn't be in mourning forever. How many men wanted her?

A hot tide of anger and jealousy welled in him. His hand clenched on his paper, crumpling it. He threw it on the floor with an oath.

Whatever her plans, she was his for the next two months. He was of no damned inclination to share her with slobbering, enterprising oafs!

A light knock sounded upon the door. Yanking another sheet of paper before him, Mark called for admittance.

Cranford opened the door. "The countess, my lord."

Mark's shoulders tensed as his mother sauntered in.

"Close the door, Cranford," Lucinda ordered.

Mark nodded at his butler and then bent his head to his work.

His mother poured herself a drink before crossing to his desk. Turning to a pile of his drawings, she leafed through them.

Mark glared up at her from beneath his brows. "Do you mind taking a step back? I'll have to wring your neck if you spill that drink on my work, and I have no desire to be hung for matricide."

Lucinda tossed down the sheet in her hand and retreated a step. "Don't you think that classical style is a bit outmoded? It looks too plain."

Mark kept working, shading the detail carefully.

"You know, I saw one of Mr. Paxton's preliminary drawings in Lord Fitzgerald's office. It was neo-Gothic and completely modern. You might consider doing something more in that vein."

"Joseph Paxton builds spectacles, not buildings," Mark said tightly. "This is to be a National Library, not a Crystal Palace."

Lucinda shrugged. "Suit yourself. I'm just trying to help."

He snorted. "What do you want, Mother?"

"Fine, I'll get right to the point. Matt tells me you're fucking someone new."

Hell, that didn't take long. He put aside the detail and pulled out his sketch of the rear edifice.

"He told me you're quite intrigued by whomever it is and that I should stop pushing Charlotte Lawrence on you. Of course, that was all before I told him you'd become engaged to Charlotte."

A muscle pulled across his upper back.

Lucinda sipped from her brandy. "By the way, he was quite peeved that you hadn't told him. He can't stand to feel as if your brotherly confidence is suffering in any way. So, since you're going to have to tell a lot more lies, I suggest that you consider what you will say to your brother and when. This must all come off with as few questions as possible."

He hated hearing from her what he already knew. He lifted his shoulder to ease the cramping muscle.

"Which brings me back to this affair of yours. You've got to put her aside."

His whole body tensed. "No."

His mother slammed down her brandy snifter. "Do you realize that your brother's future is at stake here? Fortunately, your complete disdain and disregard for the standards of our class make it believable that you would take a commoner. But Abigail Lawrence and I are trying to paint a credible picture of romantic love between you and Charlotte. Society's acceptance of this marriage depends upon it, and Abigail will have it no other way. If it gets out that you're fucking someone else, no one will believe it."

He shrugged.

Lucinda balled her hands on her waist. "You think you're still getting out of this, don't you? Well, you're not! And too much is at stake for you to be fucking around with some slut!"

He grit his teeth. "Watch your mouth."

"You *will* end this."

Mark forced himself to relax. "I said, no."

Lucinda paced to the window. "What does it matter if you leave her now or later? Eventually, you will tire of her and she of you."

Two months. They only had two months. "I don't care." He could almost feel Passion's skin, taste her lips. He looked at his mother. "This is different. She's different."

Lucinda stared hard at him, and suddenly her eyes narrowed. "This isn't any different, and neither is she."

It pleased him to disturb her. He returned to his work.

She crossed to his desk, her skirts swishing. "What? You think she'll be your loyal little mistress forever? It won't happen!"

No, not forever. His gut clenched. Would she marry after they parted?

"And if you think you're going to hold her with that monster cock of yours, you're wrong."

Mark's hand jerked the pencil. A crooked line marred the perfection of the architectural drawing.

"What? You think just because I didn't nurse you, I don't know," she scoffed. "You're my son."

Mark swept his pencil across the page, correcting the arch and continuing the columns. Calm. He must remain calm.

"And you're your father's son." Lucinda steepled her long fingers on the desk. "As I know you are aware, his big lance didn't keep me."

Mark frowned. His muscles quivered. *Don't let her draw you in. Don't let her!* He sketched Corinthian details on the columns.

Lucinda leaned forward. "Do you want to know the truth? You're nothing but a novelty to her. She doesn't care about you; she just cares about that big thing between your legs. Until she gets bored with it, that is. Then she'll leave you for some other big penis."

The tip of Mark's pencil snapped off. He threw it aside and picked up another. "Stop."

Lucinda smiled. "You're not the only one around, you know. World's full of big cocks. I should know; I had quite a fondness for them at one time." She tilted her head. "But do you know what happened? I discovered that size wasn't everything, and I abandoned men like you all together. You watch, so will your little lovely."

Mark's pencil snapped in his hand. "Stop. Now."

Lucinda leaned even closer, her voice sharp. "You have the same problem as a beautiful woman, my son—always in demand for your physical endowments, but never for yourself."

His hand balled into a fist. "Shut up!"

She drew back. "Fidelity is not for the likes of us.

We're too smart. We have too many advantages. For us, relationships are fleeting and ever changing."

Lucinda lifted her chin disdainfully. "Monogamous, everlasting bondage is for ugly, uneducated peasants who know no better and have no choices." She raised her brows. "And even they stray. Just ask your brother's father. He had a sweet little wife when he was fucking me."

Mark's chair crashed to the floor, and he rounded the desk in a fury, his voice a roar. "Tell me, Mother, which was my father? Ugly or stupid?"

Lucinda flinched as he ripped the diamond necklace from her neck and held it up in her face. "He certainly wasn't poor. Yet even after you had abandoned his big cock for another, he remained faithful to you. True to you. Smiling into the faces of your lovers in public, even while he knew you were fucking them the moment he turned his back."

He leaned nearer, his rage barely contained. "Hmm, and he wasn't ugly either. In fact, after you abandoned his big cock, he was offered consolation by a great number of lovely ladies. But he turned them all away. Not because he was stupid, but because he believed in honor and loyalty. Because despite the fact that he was married to a lying, conniving, self-absorbed, self-serving bitch, he loved you!" His eyes stung. "Until you killed that as well."

He sneered into her face. "Now, I'll tell *you* the truth. You're nothing but a pathetic, worn-out, used-up whore, who finds solace in making sure everyone around you lives in as much misery as possible. And soon, though you may not know who he is, your last lover will tire of you for the last time, and *you* will be abandoned. Forever!"

Mark shook his head. "Do not come to me on that day. For I will not pity you." He stared into his mother's cold green eyes. "Now get out!"

Lucinda whirled around and strode across the room. She turned at the door and paused. "I never asked your father to waste away for me. And the fact remains that marriage is a business arrangement between families. You *will* marry Charlotte Lawrence, despite your current entanglement with this other woman. You'll do it, or see Matthew shamed as a bastard."

She stared at him, and her eyes glittered. "I wish it were you. If Matthew were my firstborn, I'd be tempted to tell Abigail Lawrence to go hang herself."

"Don't think I don't know it. And don't think I don't know your first concern is not for Matthew, but for yourself. Society has never liked its nose rubbed in its own gutter, and that's truer now than ever. If this got out, no one would receive you. No one! You would be ostracized—given the cut direct, every day of your life, if you dared even appear on the street! You'd lose everything that matters to you." He steeled his voice. "So let's not pretend that I don't know exactly what is at stake here!"

He sent the diamond necklace crashing against the door near her head. "Now get the fuck out. And don't bring your moldy presence into my house ever again."

Lucinda bent, picked up the necklace, and left.

Passion glanced up at Charlotte as she entered the sunroom. "Charlotte, darling, will you move that vase a little to the left?"

"Hello to you, too," Charlotte teased as she shifted the vase.

Passion smiled at her cousin. "I'm sorry."

"Charlotte, sit down and have a cup of tea," Aunt Matty directed. "The scones will be here soon."

"In a moment, Aunt Matty. First, I have an announcement to make." Charlotte clasped her hands. "Do I have your complete attention?"

Laying down her pencil, Passion noticed a paper tucked beneath her cousin's arm. She exchanged an inquiring glance with Aunt Matty.

"Are you ready?" Charlotte asked excitedly.

"Oh, for heaven's sake, child, spit it out," Aunt Matty urged.

Charlotte took a deep breath. "I'm engaged to be married!"

Passion's eyes widened with amazement as she smiled. "What?"

Aunt Matty's jaw fell open.

Charlotte nodded happily. "It's true!"

"Gracious, congratulations!" Passion exclaimed. Standing, she gave Charlotte a firm hug. Lord, why did she suddenly feel sorry for herself? She pushed the uncharitable feelings away and pulled her cousin to a chair. "Sit down and tell us everything. Who is the man?"

"Yes." Aunt Matty had managed to pick up her jaw. "Who?"

Charlotte sat a little straighter and lifted her chin. "I, Charlotte Rebecca Lawrence, am engaged to be married to Randolph Hawkmore, Eighth Earl of Langley."

"Eigh-Eigh-Eighth Earl of Langley!" Aunt Matty stuttered.

"*I* am going to be a countess," Charlotte proclaimed.

"But this is incredible." Passion grinned. "How did you ever keep something like this a secret?"

Charlotte shrugged innocently. "Because I didn't know it myself."

Aunt Matty huffed. "Heavens, Charlotte! How do you get courted by an earl and not know it?"

Charlotte took the paper from beneath her arm. "Apparently, the earl observed me one evening at the Italian Opera." She blushed. "Though he didn't make his feelings known at the time, he thought me the most lovely woman there. As the days passed, he thought of me continually."

Did Mark think of her continually?

"Yesterday, he offered marriage."

Would Mark ever marry? Passion's chest tightened.

Her cousin held out the paper. "The whole story is in today's society pages."

Passion swallowed the uncomfortable feelings welling in her. "Oh, Charlotte, how romantic."

She took the paper and, clearing her throat, read aloud:

*"It is announced that Randolph Hawkmore, Eighth
Earl of Langley, is engaged to Miss Charlotte Rebecca
Lawrence. Nuptials shall take place on the tenth of June,
in a private ceremony, at Hawkmore House Chapel."*

Passion paused.

"(Contract pending)."

"Mother says that's just because everything is going so
rapidly," Charlotte said. "The contract will be signed
soon."

Aunt Matty raised her brows in a we'll-see-about-that
manner.

"Oh, Aunt Matty, really," Passion chastised. "This is
absolutely wonderful for Charlotte."

"I know. I know." Aunt Matty looked at Charlotte. "I'm
happy for you, child. Really, I am. But now, your mother
will be beyond impossible. She always did think she was
better than our side of the family. The day Passion's
mother married my dear brother, your mother snubbed us.
Why, she barely acknowledges us. I'm sure, now, we shall
cease to exist." Aunt Matty lifted her chin. "Not that I'll
miss her, mind you."

"Aunt Matty!" Passion exclaimed.

Charlotte shook her head. "It's all right, Passion. I
know my mother better than most." She sighed. "But she
is my mother."

Passion squeezed Charlotte's hand. "Of course she is.
And you needn't defend her to us." Passion sent her aunt
a look.

Aunt Matty sent one back. But then she heaved a re-
signed sigh. "Oh, very well, I shan't think at all about
Abigail Lawrence." She pointed to the paper. "Does it say
anything else?"

Passion read the commentary below the announcement:

*"As the Earl of Langley has long eschewed the conven-
tions and ideals of his noble class, it can hardly be a surprise to those in society that he has become engaged to a
mere Miss. However, what will set tongues wagging is the
extraordinary fact that the earl is in love with the girl!
Who could have guessed that the cynical and worldly
Langley would ever fall in love? Yet it's true! It seems the
earl became completely enamored of the lovely Miss
Lawrence when he saw her at the Italian Opera. And according to those who know, he is entirely impatient to
make her the Countess of Langley!*

*"Parlors and drawing rooms are already abuzz. What
will happen, dear readers? Will this Miss Lawrence be
embraced or snubbed? Will romantic love flourish or
flounder? Who shall be the first to invite the charming
couple to their soirée? And WHO shall be invited to the
blessed event at Hawkmore House?"*

Passion smiled to chase away the nervous look in her
cousin's face. "Without doubt, you will be embraced.
Don't you worry about that."

"Or course you will, child," Aunt Matty agreed.

How wonderful that her cousin would have a loving
husband. Another pang of sorrow accompanied the
thought. What was the matter with her? She must think of
her happiness for Charlotte, not her sorrow for herself.
"Oh, Charlotte, I'm so pleased for you. And June is so
near. Heavens, you must have a thousand things to do."

"Yes. My fiancé's mother, the countess, and my mother
have taken things completely in hand. The countess says
everything must be done perfectly so the nobility accepts
me. I must go *where* she says and do *what* she says. She
must approve all my gowns before I appear in public."
Charlotte frowned. "I'm afraid I will not be able to continue my painting lessons just now, Passion. There will be
so much to do . . ."

"Good heavens, Charlotte, painting will wait."

Charlotte's frown deepened. "And I shan't be able to

accompany you to the events we had planned. I'm afraid my social schedule is no longer in my hands." Her brows lifted. "But you must go to everything. Your mourning is over, and I want you to have a marvelous time. Promise me you'll still get out."

"I promise." Passion looked at her aunt. "Besides, you won't let me stay at home, will you?"

"Certainly not." Aunt Matty put down her teacup and glanced toward the door. "Where are those scones?" She turned her attention back to Charlotte. "In fact, I'm quite convinced that Passion will be announcing her own engagement before her time with me is over."

"I'm not marrying again, Aunt Matty."

"What nonsense." Her aunt handed Charlotte a cup of tea. "Now, tell us about your fiancé, Charlotte. What sort of man is this earl?"

Charlotte grew a bit flustered. "Well, I must confess that our first meeting was not what I expected."

Aunt Matty leaned forward in her chair with interest. "Why? Is he ugly? Crippled? Impoverished?"

Charlotte's curls swayed as she shook her head. "No, nothing like that. In fact, he's one of the handsomest men I've ever seen. And he's one of the richest men in the realm."

"Oh." Aunt Matty looked a little disappointed.

"Then, what's the matter?" Passion asked.

Charlotte looked pensive. "It's just that he didn't seem particularly enamored of me. In fact, he barely looked at me."

Passion frowned in confusion.

"He was extremely rude to the countess and my mother," Charlotte continued. "And when he left—the expression on his face—well, he seemed furious with us all."

"Who could be furious with you?" Passion offered. "Perhaps he was burdened with other troubles that were weighing upon him."

"Perhaps his toe was paining him," Aunt Matty suggested. "When my toe was trod upon, it put me in a terrible temper."

Passion shared a tiny smile with her cousin. "There you are, Charlotte. It must have been his toe."

"I'm sure you're both right." Charlotte put down the cup she had been sipping from. "His mother did say that he was angry with her. I suppose they must have been arguing."

Aunt Matty excused herself to see what was keeping the scones.

As soon as she left, Charlotte leaned forward. "I tell you, cousin, he gave his mother and my own such a dressing-down! You would not have believed it, had you seen it. He was in such a rage." Charlotte clasped her hands. "I have to confess, I found it wonderfully thrilling. Oh, Passion, I have bit my tongue and held my peace so often with my mother . . . Why, I have never dared to speak to her as he did. But I have wanted to a thousand times." Charlotte lowered her eyes. "Please don't think I'm horrid, but for that alone, I could love this man."

Passion didn't know what to say. Abigail Lawrence wasn't known for her kindness and charm, but still, a child must honor her mother. "I'm sure you will grow to love the earl for many reasons, darling. Not least of all because he loves you."

Charlotte lifted her gaze. "If he does still love me. I think, after meeting Mother, he believes I may be like her. I think that's why he was so cold."

"Well, then you'll prove to him that isn't true."

"Oh, I hope so." Charlotte's gray eyes turned dreamy. "I can see him in his bridegroom's garb."

A vision of Mark standing beside her, speaking vows, flashed in Passion's mind. She quickly pushed it away. That was a covenant they would not share.

"He is so handsome, Passion. Wait till you meet him. He's like a god."

Passion smiled and couldn't help her heart beating faster. Would Mark come to her that night?

Charlotte sighed. "He has the most extraordinary blue eyes I've ever seen. Even full of anger, they were captivating."

Passion remembered the tenderness she had seen in Mark's eyes that morning—remembered the hot gaze he had raked over her the night before. No man could have eyes more beautiful than his.

Mark looked into Rosalind Benchley's brown eyes and forced a smile as she offered him another chocolate from a cut-glass candy dish. "No, thank you, Lady Rosalind."

The low notes from Matt's cello hummed in the background.

She put down the dish. "Aunt says you may rely upon us, in any way, to help forward the social acclimation of your fiancée, my lord."

Mark clenched his jaw. He could kill his mother for placing that damned announcement.

"Isn't that right, Aunt?"

Rosalind's aunt looked up from her hand of cards. "Who could refuse true love?"

Christ. He exchanged a look with Matt.

Lord Benchley snorted. "True love. What a bunch of rot. Marriages are made for the purposes of increasing one's status or wealth, preferably both." He looked over the top of his glasses at Mark. "The only reason you'll pull this off, my lord, is because your own status and wealth needs no bolstering." He played a card. "I suppose you can afford love."

Matthew put aside his cello and joined Rosalind on the couch. "Your daughter and I are in love, my lord."

"A happy but unimportant circumstance," Lord Benchley commented. "You will marry my daughter, dear boy, because you are a Hawkmore and, of course, because you have a great deal of money."

Rosalind's aunt frowned at her brother. "Really, my lord."

Matt grinned at Rosalind and kissed the tips of her fingers. "Would you still love me if I were poor?"

"Of course." Rosalind giggled.

Mark crossed his arms over his chest. "Would you love him if he weren't a Hawkmore?"

Matt's brows lifted with surprise. But then he turned to Rosalind. "Yes, would you?"

"Well, of course." She laughed again. "But you are a Hawkmore, my darling, and you do have money."

Matt nibbled her finger discreetly. "Mmm, good thing, that."

Mark looked at the two of them. He felt a sudden surge of animosity toward Rosalind Benchley. She was lying. At least her father was honest.

But then, what else was she to say? *No, Matt darling, actually I would cease to love you if you were poor and not a Hawkmore.*

She only said what Matt wanted to hear. And in truth, they weren't fair questions to begin with.

Still, he hated all the lies. He closed his eyes and rubbed his brow. Why did it suddenly seem as if he were surrounded by lies? Lying to Matt, lying to the Benchleys. Now, with the announcement in the paper, lying to the world. It made him feel ill.

Passion. Passion was his tonic. With her, there were no lies. The tension in his shoulders eased. When he was with her, everything bad faded and everything good magnified.

At the Crystal Palace, he'd been so irritated that she wasn't alone. But when she saw him, the expression that came over her face had made him breathless. Every emotion showed clearly. Yearning, desire, tenderness. And that indefinable something that heightened them all to . . . to something wonderful.

"You all right, brother?"

He needed her. He needed her now.

Mark nodded. "Yes. Just tired." He stood and felt his cock pulse. "I should take my leave."

Something in Matt's expression told him he knew

where he was going. "Have a good evening, then. Send the carriage back around, will you?" He nodded toward Lord Benchley. "I'm going to play a few hands before I go."

Mark made the hastiest exit he could. His body knew his destination, and by the time he leaned back in his carriage, his prick was full and straining against his trousers.

He had his coachman drop him a few blocks from Passion's house, then sent him back to the Benchleys. But the short walk only served to heighten his need. He was still hard as he scaled her trellis. A dim glow lit her room. Was she still awake? He smiled when he found the window ajar. Sliding up the sash, he quickly entered and let the curtain fall behind him.

Though his heart raced, he stood still for a moment. Passion rested on her side, eyes closed. She faced the window, as if she might have been waiting for him. An oil lamp burned low on the side table, illuminating her in its soft circle of light.

Mark doffed his hat. Slipping off his topcoat and tailcoat, he moved to her bedside. Her lips were parted in slumber, and her lashes, under the influence of some dream, fluttered gently. Her auburn hair lay in waves across her pillow like a silken pennant.

God, but she was beautiful.

Carefully, so as not to wake her, he braced his hands on the side of the bed and, leaning close, breathed in the sweet smell of her. Vanilla and orange blossoms assailed his senses. She murmured something in her sleep and turned onto her back with a sigh.

Her lips were too close to resist. He brushed his mouth against hers and then tasted her with a gentle kiss. Her lips were soft and warm beneath his, and it seemed only moments before he felt the beginnings of her response. Then her hand curved around his nape and the other slid against his cheek as she pulled him closer, deepening their kiss.

Mark moaned into her mouth and forced himself to pull back.

Her hazel eyes blinked up at him.

"Hello," he said.

Her lips turned in a small smile. "Hello. I didn't know if you'd come."

"I told you I would be with you as often as possible."

"Yes." She slowly pulled loose his cravat. "You did say that."

Mark sat beside her on the bed. "Open your gown."

Slowly, she sat up. He couldn't take his eyes off her as she undid each tiny button.

"From now on, you must sleep without your gown." He pulled off his cravat and loosened his collar. "You won't be needing it."

A blush turned her cheeks to roses. Her hair fell around her shoulders, and her gown lay open to her waist.

Mark's prick thumped eagerly. He slipped off his shoes. Damn it, he'd never been this hot for any other woman. She watched him as he took off his vest and worked the mother-of-pearl studs free from his shirt. He wanted her desperately.

"I kept some hot chocolate on the grate for you," she said quietly.

Mark paused, and something trembled deep inside him. "What?"

"Some hot chocolate." She reached for his wrist and easily freed the stud from his cuff. "I thought you might like something warm."

He stared at her as she freed his other cuff. His various mistresses had offered him innumerable drinks: brandy, scotch, port. But he'd never been offered hot chocolate. He'd never been offered anything that was not a stimulant to sex.

She put the stud on the table and lifted her lovely eyes to his. Even as a boy, he'd never been given something like this. Oh, he'd had more things than he needed, but nothing that wasn't part of a purchasing list. Nothing purely and especially for his comfort. Nothing thoughtfully offered in anticipation of his need.

His eyes stung.

Nothing warm and reassuring had ever been given to him without his having to ask for it.

He had stopped asking long ago.

A frown wrinkled Passion's brow. "You don't care for hot chocolate?"

His hand shook as he slipped it through her hair. He drew her close and pressed his lips between her brows.

"I would love a cup of hot chocolate."

Chapter Ten

DREAMS, WISHES, AND JUSTIFICATIONS

Passion dreamt of the lion. He reared and roared at her and bared his teeth. Even though she was frightened, she moved closer. With each step she took, he grew more fearsome. She paused, wanting to throw herself against him, yet afraid to do so.

Why? Why did she tempt him? Did she think he would protect her? How could he, when he was wounded himself? Blood leaked from a gash over his heart.

He tossed back his head and roared angrily at the sky. Would he tear her to shreds? No, he could have done that already. No. No, he would never harm her.

With sudden determination, she went to him.

Passion opened her eyes. The oil lamp still burned. But no warm body touched hers. She sat up in bed and then breathed a happy sigh.

Wearing only his trousers, Mark reclined in one of the chairs by the hearth. He was looking at her.

"I thought you'd gone," she said.

"No."

Passion glanced at the clock. Almost three in the morning. Slipping out of bed, she grabbed the throw for modesty.

"I should have hidden that thing while you slept."

Passion smiled as she crossed to him. He took her hand and pulled her into his lap.

She pushed back the hair that had fallen over his brow. "Why aren't you in bed?"

"I couldn't sleep." His gaze flickered to the bit of breast that was revealed above the throw. "I would have been too tempted to wake you had I stayed."

Passion traced the curve of his ear. "That would have been all right."

"I thought you might still be sore." His voice sounded hoarse.

She shook her head. "That is long gone. The only soreness I feel now is the aching need to have you inside me."

"By God," he murmured. "You are my temptress. I cannot resist you."

She rocked her hip against his erection. "Then don't," she breathed before taking his lips in a soft, searching kiss. She felt the throw being pulled away and let it go.

Earlier, he had brought her to a trembling climax just with the use of his fingers. Propped on his elbow, he had watched her every gasp and shudder. He had encouraged her between the tender kisses he plied upon her lips. Now she wanted to give to him.

She slid around so she straddled him and, sitting on his legs, she unbuttoned his trousers. He was already hard. Yet as she watched, he grew larger.

He brushed her nipples with the palms of his hands before cupping her breasts around each full side.

Her breathing quickened. She adored his touch— adored the power and strength of him. She stroked the whole length of his smooth flesh with the tips of her fingers.

Mark sucked in his breath, and his hips tilted beneath her as his hands came to rest on her hips. He lifted his eyes to hers. They reflected a raw, aching need. And burning brightly behind the need was pain.

Her heart skipped a beat in her breast.

For a moment she didn't know what to say or do.

So she gave him the only thing she could think of—herself. She pressed close to him and held him tightly.

"I'm here," she whispered. She kissed the soft lobe of his ear. "You're safe with me."

She didn't know where the words came from, only that he seemed to need them.

His arms tightened around her, and his hands held her to him.

She pressed kisses to the strong column of his neck, breathing in lemon verbena, while she rubbed the moist folds of her quim along his shaft.

She would lead the way. She would take him to bliss.

He moaned into her shoulder, and one of his hands curved around the fullness of her breast.

Passion surged against him and captured his mouth in a kiss that offered him all she had. He latched upon her with an open-mouthed hunger that revealed the true depth of his craving. And while her wet quim massaged his shaft, she let him feast upon her for as long as he needed. The more he took, the more she gave, until finally he released her with a broken gasp.

Light-headed and panting, she moved higher against him, sliding the swollen bud of her clitoris up to the engorged head of his penis. And there she remained, rubbing one to the other, while he sucked her nipple into his mouth. He drew upon her voraciously. She wrapped her arms around him and held him to her.

He shook beneath her, and her own body trembled with suppressed need. But she wanted to take him further. She wanted to make him forget everything that hurt, if only for a moment.

She moved a touch higher and pressed the wet opening of her body over the head of his cock.

A deep groan escaped him as she pushed down just slightly and then withdrew.

His body leapt beneath her as she did it again and again and again. His arms crushed her, his hands clawed in her hair. Yet still, she drove them on—each brief taste promising the banquet.

His hips began to jerk.

Sweat broke on her brow.

"I—I need you," he gasped.

Passion gazed down at him, emotions and physical sensation tangled together inside her. Fulfillment was hers to give.

He pressed his cheek to her breast. His hips lifted. "God, Passion! I need you," he repeated hoarsely.

Her body tightened and throbbed.

"I'm here," she breathed and slid down over him all the way.

He crushed her in his embrace, one hand gripping her buttock as his mouth drew upon her nipple so strongly that she felt a tiny pull high in her breast.

As she held him to her, without even moving, the powerful throbbing that signaled his release brought her own. She gasped her pleasure.

His hips lifted.

Her fingers clenched in his hair. She shuddered and shook around him.

His tongue laved her swollen nipple.

Her heart pounded. She bit back a cry.

He trembled and clutched her as she let down a warm, sucking rush of moisture.

Her arms tightened around him. "Come, Mark. Come," she breathed.

He groaned and bucked beneath her and then bathed her womb with a thick torrent of seed.

She didn't want to let him go, but all her strength left her limbs at once. She collapsed upon him, resting her head on his shoulder.

He held her for a long time, stroking her hair and pressing kisses to her brow. Finally he said, "Thank you. I think I can sleep now."

Passion smiled and forced herself to clamber off him. Crossing to the bed, she slipped beneath the sheet and tossed herself back on the pillow. She watched him as he stepped out of his trousers. He joined her, but he didn't lie down.

Leaning over her, he swept a stray tendril of hair back from her face. "You are beyond beautiful," he whispered.

A warm tingle tickled her insides. "It pleases me you think so."

His striking eyes moved over her features as he sat back against the pillows. A frown puckered his brow. "Who was that man with you today?"

Passion sat up. "I'm sorry about that. I've only just met him." She turned to face him and crossed her legs. "He is the nephew of one of my aunts' good friends."

"Is he really courting you?"

She lifted her brows. "I suppose. But I don't think he will be for long."

"The man is an ass." Mark scowled. "And a lecher as well. I could have broken his arms for grabbing you like that."

Passion refrained from commenting on the fact that he had done far more than try to kiss her when they first met.

He looked at her, and she knew he had guessed her thoughts. "There is no comparison. You wanted me."

She took his hand. "Yes."

His gaze locked with hers. "I have you for two months. The last thing I will tolerate is some lecherous lout getting in my way. Get rid of him."

That he felt the irritation of Alfred Swittly as much as she did surprised her. "I shall. In fact, after you left, we came upon a couple with a rather large group of children in tow. Mr. Swittly commented upon them, so I let drop the regrettable fact that I shall never have such a family." She lowered her eyes. "That should deter him. But still, I must consider my aunt. I cannot embarrass her by being rude."

"What's embarrassing is the suggestion that that man is appropriate for you. Christ, he's an opportunist of the worst sort. He'll marry you, children or no, then take everything." Mark suddenly frowned. "Just what is your situation, Passion? You said you were a vicar's daughter, yet the cut and quality of your clothing suggests greater wealth than that profession affords. Was your husband rich?"

Passion shifted uncomfortably. Thoughts of her husband were always an unwelcome intrusion. "My husband was prosperous—a gentleman farmer. But upon his death, I turned the whole estate over to my father. I take only a small allowance from it." She shrugged. "I also receive some money from a trust. My mother brought a comfortable income with her when she married my father. Of course, according to her side of the family, she squandered her worth by marrying down. They hardly acknowledge us." Passion met Mark's blue gaze. "But my mother was happy. She married my father for love and was never sorry for it."

Mark didn't look away. "That pompous oaf will not make you happy."

Passion smiled. "I know." She traced the lines on his palm. "It's just that I'm coming out of mourning, and my aunt loves to play matchmaker. She's usually very good at it."

Mark looked tense. "Is that why you came to London? To find a new husband?"

Why was he on edge? What did he think? Lord, did he think she was trying to entrap him? "I came to London for a much-needed holiday—to see my aunt and cousin, to see the sights, and to attend some events." She looked into his eyes. "That's all."

His expression didn't ease. What could she say, and why was this starting to hurt?

"Mark, in two months I shall return home. I shall return

to the same life I left. You will be free—I mean, you *are* free to do whatever you please."

His frown deepened. "And how many men are at home? How many are waiting for you to shed your mourning so they can start chasing after you?"

Both relief and confusion welled in her. Why was he acting jealous? Just what was his concern? "Mark, I have very few admirers." She shook her head and smiled. "My sisters are the ones. I think, between them, they own every heart in the county."

He didn't smile with her. "No offense, my sweet, but you are oblivious."

Passion tipped her head to the side with a perplexed grin. "What?"

"I noticed today, at the Crystal Palace. You're completely unaware of all the eyes that roam over you."

Now she frowned. "What eyes? Whose?"

"Plenty," he grunted. "And I'll wager you have at least a dozen randy neighbors sniffing after your skirts at home."

Passion thought about it. "Really, I can only think of three gentlemen that might have thoughts in that regard." She looked at him. "But I'm not interested in any of them."

He twirled a piece of her hair around his finger as his blue eyes met hers. "In whom *are* you interested?"

This was the oddest conversation. He had said the day would come when he would be done. They had a finite time together. So why did he care what she did after that? "I have no marital interest in anyone."

His eyes didn't waver from her. "But one day, do you hope to remarry?"

Why did he want to know? What did he expect her answer to be? The image of them she had pushed away earlier blossomed in her mind, where he had held her hand and spoken vows she would only hear him utter in her dreams.

His blue gaze held her. Her heart hurt.

"I don't know," she admitted softly. "I used to think not. But now"—she looked down at his hand clasped in hers—"I might dream of it."

He was silent for a long time. When she finally lifted her eyes, he was still regarding her. "I don't believe in lasting relationships. Nonetheless, if you ever remarry and I discover it, I think I will hate that man."

He lay down and pulled her to him as he spooned his body around hers.

Sadness edged down Passion's spine. But what justification did she have for sadness? From the beginning, she had understood the transient nature of their relationship. When she had accepted his proposal, she had known there would be consequences. This sorrow was the unavoidable consequence of her decision to be with him. To want a man who didn't believe in lasting relationships. To yearn for what he would never give. To crave a future that would never be hers.

These impossible desires were proof of her wrongdoing—covetousness born of fornication, sin begetting sin.

Her emotions were wrong, indefensible. Her chest tightened.

When we break God's laws, the world suffers.

Passion drew the sheet beneath her chin. At least this suffering was all her own. She would have to bear it. She must bear it.

She could do nothing else, for she could not resist him.

Mark's arm tightened around her, and his hand moved to hold her breast.

She sighed, and her body warmed with comfort.

The whole truth was that she couldn't resist her own feelings for him. She felt physically fulfilled. She felt stronger and more appreciative. She had renewed interested in her art.

She felt *alive*.

How could all these good things come from wrong? Were they her "Judas price" for the betrayal of herself?

No! *This* was her true self. Lord, had she forgotten the

girl she was before her marriage? Had she forgotten the lightheartedness and laughter that had filled her days? Had she forgotten her hopes and dreams?

She had betrayed her true self long ago. She had turned her back on the pain of her barren marriage and allowed her natural tendency toward duty and obligation to become both her shield and her defining attributes. It had been easier to constantly do for others than to face the neglect of herself.

Her fingers curled in the sheet. As long as she wasn't hurting anyone else, how wrong could it be to indulge her need for a short time? How wrong could it be to find her old self—the self who had loved and laughed, the self who had entered her marriage with happiness and hope?

Soon enough, their relationship would end. Until then, she would abide the suffering and embrace the joys of being with him. Though she didn't know where the road would lead her, as long as the consequences of her journey were her own to bear, what harm? What harm . . . ?

Mark woke slowly.

The room was lit with the dim overture to morning. Somewhere, just outside the window, a dove cooed to her mate.

In his arms, Passion sighed and snuggled more closely against him. Her cheek lay against his chest, and her hair blanketed his arm.

He didn't want to move. He wanted to sleep beside her into the late hours of the morning. He wanted to rise with her and share breakfast with her. He wanted to talk with her. He wanted to watch her dress. Then he wanted to undress her.

He trailed his finger down the bridge of her slim nose. He wanted to stay—just to stay—with her.

He sighed. But he'd promised discretion. Shoving back his hair and ignoring his morning erection, he forced himself to look at the clock. Almost five o'clock. Time to rise and depart.

Slowly, so as not to wake her, he slid his arm out from beneath her head and slipped from beneath the sheets. He picked up his clothes from where they lay, putting them on as he found them.

While he dressed, he studied her. Though a little taller than most women, she had a delicacy of feature and form that gave her a refined appearance. Yet there was no fragility to her. Softness and yearning, yes—even supplication. But intelligence and strength as well.

When dressed, her elegant appearance didn't even hint at the intimate details of her body. He never would have guessed that her lovely breasts would have been graced with such thick, edible nipples. He never would have guessed that the tight little cunt he first felt with his fingers would have accommodated him so completely. He *never* would have guessed that her sweet mouth would suck him so deliciously.

He swore under his breath at the curving bulge in his trousers and turned away from her.

On the desk, he noticed a paint palette and an open sketchbook. As he tied his cravat, he stared down at a beautiful iris rendered in watercolor. It looked as delicate as the original, which stood in a vase beside the pallet. Intrigued, he flipped the pages. Three more botanicals followed, each one as lovely as the one before.

On the forth page, he stopped and stared. Two young women sat together in a room that was only vaguely depicted. But the women themselves were magnificent. One, with a head full of riotous curls, played the cello. Her arms curved around the instrument with the grace of a dancer, and her beautiful face wore an almost rhapsodic concentration. The other sat facing the first. With her cheek supported upon her hand, she read a book. Her lovely profile, the curve of her neck, the slant of her shoulders, all bespoke peace and calm contentment.

Beneath the picture were inscribed the words "Patience and Prim." No, not words. Names. They must be Passion's sisters, for he could see reflections of her beauty in their faces.

He shook his head. She was more talented than he had thought. It was one thing to capture the essence of a flower. It was quite another to capture the individual and complex spirit of a person.

He stared at the drawing, reluctant to turn the page. This was a small peek into Passion's life, a tiny hint of what he would never be a part.

He suddenly wished he had a drawing of her. He flipped more pages, hoping to find a self-portrait. He found only blank pages.

Then, at the very back of the book, he found something he never would have expected—himself.

Awestruck, his throat constricted. Was this what he looked like? He recognized his features and the expression on his face, but there was something else in the drawing he didn't recognize. Something in his eyes he didn't know he showed the world—something, perhaps, that could only be viewed from the angle she had drawn him. What was it?

He stared hard at the picture, simultaneously studying it and marveling at it. Whatever it was, it was in more than his eyes. It was in the curve of his mouth and the set of his jaw as well.

He shook his head. For the life of him, he couldn't figure it out. But every picture was a reflection of the artist's vision. If she saw him as this handsome, then fine. It gave him a warm feeling deep in his gut.

He glanced over at her. She still slept, breathing deeply and evenly. He penned her a quick note.

Even sleeping, you're beautiful. I'll come again tonight.
M.
P.S. Passion Ermagine Diddlemot?

He left it on her bedside table, where she'd be sure to see it.

He wanted to crawl back into bed with her.

But he couldn't.

He sat in the chair by the hearth to put on his socks and shoes. He looked at her again and noted her fine-fingered hand lying palm up. Such soft, pleasure-giving, talented hands. He shook his head as he stood. He never would have guessed.

The chocolate pot still sat on the grate in the hearth. He stared at it and then glanced over his shoulder at her. That had been the biggest surprise of all—the offer of hot chocolate.

Suddenly and unexpectedly, his mother's words loomed before him. *What? You think she'll be your loyal little mistress forever? You're nothing but a novelty to her.*

His neck stiffened painfully. The words infuriated him. The thought that Passion might tire of what they had— might tire of *him*—was more disturbing than he could explain. He hated the thought.

Yet who was he to harbor such feelings? No one had ever held his interest for more than four months. And even that had been stretching his regard.

He would have to give up Passion in two.

He picked up her gown from the end of the bed and breathed in the fragrance that clung to it. His eyes closed.

But when would this craving for her fade?

When would he stop yearning for every next moment he could be with her?

He let the gown slip through his fingers.

Why did he wish two months could be two years?

"Forgive me, Mrs. Redington," Alfred Swittly intoned, "but you look just like I have imagined Hermia might appear as she runs into the forest after her beloved Lysander."

Alfred Swittly waltzed her around the crowded dance floor of the pavilion. Situated in the Crystal Palace Park, the pavilion was modeled after the Crystal Palace itself. The long dance floor, which had been divided that evening for a private party, could accommodate nearly a thousand couples. Couches lined the walls, and six separate refreshment halls branched off the main room.

"Thank you, Mr. Swittly." Passion forced a smile.

Though he seemed to want to behave as if nothing whatsoever had occurred at the Crystal Palace, she felt uncomfortable in his embrace, and his rotund stomach kept bumping her. Also, though his attentions had cooled slightly when she informed him she couldn't have children, his enthusiasm was immediately renewed when he learned Passion's cousin was engaged to an earl.

As they came back around to where her aunt and the Swittly sisters were sitting, Passion saw John Crossman with them. Perfect! "Oh look, Mr. Swittly, your cousin. Perhaps we should go greet him."

"Quite right, Mrs. Redington. Quite right."

John Crossman looked at her twice as she approached, then a slow smile spread across his handsome features. He didn't even seem to see his cousin, but held his hand out to her as she approached. "By God, Mrs. Redington, you are beautiful this evening." He kissed her hand. "I take it you are officially out of mourning."

She smiled and began to answer, but Aunt Matty spoke first. "She certainly is, and about time, too. What young widow stays in mourning for two full years, I ask you?" She looked at the Swittly sisters, who sat on either side of her. "A year, certainly. Eighteen months, perhaps. But two years! Ridiculous! Am I not right, ladies?"

The Swittly sisters nodded vigorously, as they most always did. Alfred joined in.

"Aunt Matty, please," Passion begged.

John Crossman smiled sympathetically at her before turning to her aunt. "I cannot agree, Mistress Dare. For then I would have missed seeing her astounding transformation."

"Well, that's true, Mr. Crossman." Aunt Matty fanned herself and smiled proudly at Passion. "Passion has the rarest coloring," she offered. "There isn't another lady I know who could wear that color. She, however, is perfection in it."

"I couldn't agree more, Mistress Dare," Alfred said. "Couldn't agree more."

John Crossman shook hands with Alfred but quickly returned his attention to her.

Passion smoothed the copper silk of her gown. She wished Aunt Matty wouldn't speak as if she weren't present. But she was pleased her aunt thought well of her appearance. The gown was austerely, yet elegantly, cut. A fine gold lace banded the neckline, shoulders, and back, and a verdigris sash swept diagonally across the bodice. It wrapped once around her waist before falling, off center, down the back of her skirt. Would that Mark could see her.

"Passion has a particular affection for fine clothing," Aunt Matty continued. "The past two years, she has been relegated to mourning colors. I loathe them on her. But tonight, she looks like a princess." She beamed.

"A queen. An empress!" Alfred upped her.

The Swittly sisters beamed and nodded.

Passion felt herself blushing. Still, she felt an almost giddy delight at being swathed in copper silk and verdigris trim.

It was good of her father not to have balked at her expenditure upon a new wardrobe. She wished he could have seen her tonight. She missed him.

John bowed and offered his arm as the first notes of another waltz began. "Will you allow me this dance, Mrs. Redington?" He glanced at Alfred, who looked like he was going to protest. "Can't have her all night, cousin."

Passion took his arm with pleasure, and they whirled onto the dance floor.

The swaying chords of a waltz filled the huge pavilion. They stepped and twirled past couple after couple, until they became lost in the crowd of dancers. Passion fully enjoyed herself. She hadn't danced in so long and, though she couldn't help wishing he were Mark, John Crossman proved an able partner. He turned her in wide arcs that threaded through the other dancers without a bump. The music swelled; she spun.

"Do you captain the ships you build, Mr. Crossman? You navigate the dance floor with the sure step of a seaman."

John smiled. "Interesting you should say that. In fact, I have never captained a ship. My father wouldn't allow it." He shrugged. "I was his only heir. He worried."

Passion waited for the next series of turns to pass. "So when do you embark?"

John laughed. "I haven't decided yet. Care for a glass of punch?"

"Yes, please."

He smiled and twirled her right to the entrance of the refreshment hall.

As they entered, Passion heard a startled gasp beside her. "Passion!"

Passion turned at the sound of Charlotte's voice. Her cousin rushed into her arms and then stepped back immediately. "Oh, Passion, I snuck over here in hopes of seeing you. You're stunning!"

Passion laughed. "So are you!"

Charlotte stepped around and looked at Passion's hair and the back of her gown. "Oh, Passion, it thrills me to see you like this. Leave it to you to pick the very most perfect color." She gently touched the coppery-gold roses and verdigris leaves in Passion's hair. "Where did you find these?"

"Charlotte! What do you mean leaving our party?" Abigail Lawrence's stern voice came low. "Stop gawking at her as if she were the blue ribbon pig at a country fair." She forced a smile at a passing couple and then fixed a fast glare upon Charlotte. "You're making a spectacle."

The smile faded from Charlotte's face.

"But madam"—John Crossman stepped forward—"it was a charming spectacle." He smiled at Charlotte. "It is rare to see such a spontaneous show of happy admiration from one woman to another." He fixed his gaze on Abigail. "Would that more women could be so gracious and confident."

Abigail held her tongue. Passion knew it was only because she didn't know who was addressing her.

"Well, Passion," Abigail said authoritatively. "Aren't you going to introduce your escort?"

Since her arrival in London, it was the first time she had seen Abigail Lawrence. Not once had she been invited to the Lawrence home. Charlotte always came to Aunt Matty's. "A pleasure to see you again, Mrs. Lawrence. My family sends their regards and prayers for your well-being."

Abigail lifted her chin. "You may send them my regards as well. And I suppose I should thank you for trying to teach Charlotte to paint. It was a valiant effort, I'm sure. But she has more important things to do now. And I'm afraid I shall not have the opportunity to entertain you and your aunt at my home."

Passion nodded. All the better, as long as she still had a chance to see Charlotte now and then.

She turned to John. "Mr. Crossman, allow me to introduce my mother's cousin, Mrs. Abigail Lawrence, and her daughter, Miss Charlotte Lawrence."

As John took Charlotte's hand, Abigail stepped closer. "Are you any relation to the Crossmans of Crossman Shipping, sir?"

John nodded but kept his eyes on Charlotte. "Yes, madam."

Abigail raised her brows haughtily at Passion, as if to say, "My aren't we doing well for ourselves—and isn't that surprising?"

"Well"—Abigail smiled as warmly as she could manage—"it's very nice to have met you, Mr. Crossman. I hope you will excuse us, though. We are engaged this evening for a private party at the other end of the pavilion—it is my daughter's first evening out with her fiancé." Abigail took Charlotte's arm. "Come, Charlotte, we don't want to keep the earl waiting."

Charlotte dared to stay Abigail for a moment while she paused to give Passion a parting kiss on the cheek. "You look beautiful, and I'm sorry about Mother," she whispered before Abigail managed to pull her away.

Passion sighed.

"Do you suppose her broom is in the cloakroom?" John asked.

"Her what?"

"Her broom." John drew Passion's arm through his. "Isn't that how Mrs. Lawrence arrived this evening, upon a broom?"

Passion laughed as he led her to the refreshment table.

"We're late," Matt remarked. "Mother will be peeved."

Mark shrugged as they entered the pavilion. "The less amount of time I have to spend on display, the better."

Matt smiled. "You really hate this, don't you?" They paused just inside the entrance. "This isn't just for Mother's sake. It's for your fiancée as well. Wedding invitations are being delivered. If we don't put the right face on this, the nobility will ostracize her."

Mark raised his brows. Invitations? As soon as he got that letter, he'd be delivering notes of cancellation. "So what. Who needs their acceptance?" He gestured to the tall screens and silken ropes that segregated the nobility from the gentry and well-to-do middle class that filled the rest of the pavilion. "Look at them, all clustered here together. They're no better than the people on the other side of those screens, yet heaven forbid they should deign to mix."

Matt gripped his shoulder. "Climb off that high horse, will you? Lord Fitzgerald has had this event planned for weeks. And while a bit unconventional for you and your fiancée's first public appearance, it's actually perfect. Most everyone will be here. Even Prince Albert may show." Matt cocked his brow. "And since I don't see you becoming a doting husband, the least you can do is make a good show of it and insure that your future wife has some society."

Mark frowned. His future wife was being forced upon him and could go to the devil as far as he was concerned. But Matt didn't know that. Matt was good and decent and wanted Mark to be, too.

Damn, he hated lying to him.

He nodded at his brother. "I suppose I can bear it for a minute or two."

Matt grinned. "Excellent."

But it turned out that his tolerance didn't last even that long. The moment he saw his mother and Abigail Lawrence standing together, his anger mounted. Charlotte was there, too, standing at her mother's side.

It took iron will to keep his face relatively blank as he moved through the crowd. Everyone who wasn't dancing, and many who were, seemed to be looking at him. He was forced to nod greetings, shake hands, and bow over and over again before reaching the three women who awaited him.

They smiled as he bowed before them. "Mrs. Lawrence. Mother." He bowed to Charlotte. "Miss Lawrence."

At an almost imperceptible nudge from her mother, Charlotte lifted her hand to him. Christ, she was nothing but a damned puppet, moving on the commands of the marionette master at her side.

He took her hand and restrained himself from crushing her white-gloved fingers in his as he bowed low and touched his lips to the kid leather.

Releasing her quickly, he introduced Matthew. His brother was as charming as ever, and Lucinda smiled proudly upon her favorite son.

As Matt requested the second dance with Charlotte, Abigail Lawrence stepped close to Mark. She smiled broadly, but her tone was ice. "Don't you ever keep my daughter and me waiting like that again. Do you hear me?"

"Fuck you," he murmured.

Tense with suppressed fury, he looked to his mother. She just stared at him.

And what the hell did he expect? That she would come to his defense, that she would say something to buffer the odious Lawrence—that she would, in some infinitesimal way, demonstrate that she was *his* mother as well as Matthew's?

That would never happen. It never had.

His head pounded. He hated himself for these moments of weakness. They only occurred when he was forced into the presence of his mother and Matt together—which he usually managed to avoid.

At least, after their argument the day before, she had the wit to remain silent.

He turned to Charlotte. She smiled sweetly. He hated it, her sugary grin. He wanted to slap it right off her face. Maybe that would knock some small sense into the girl. Her smile faded.

He held out his arm. "Shall we dance, Miss Lawrence?"

And so it went for the next interminable two hours. As he was forced to bear the constant control of his mother and Abigail Lawrence, who continually lashed him to the stone of Charlotte, he alternated between varying degrees of frustrated fury and rage.

He bore their machinations, and Abigail Lawrence's nasty directives, by thinking about Passion. If he had to smile, he thought of her. If he had to speak amicably, he thought of her. If he had to dance with any of the three women he hated, he dreamed of her.

But now, he felt near to breaking. He had momentarily escaped and stood with the Benchleys, yet his mother was making her way over to him. Abigail Lawrence, with Charlotte in tow, was trying to stroll over in a casual manner.

He had to get out. Without a word to Matt or the Benchleys, he exited the screened area and made his way into the milling crowd. He breathed easier. Indeed, the farther he got from that end of the room, the better he felt.

Soon, he would leave and go to Passion. Then he could forget the night's misery. Taking a deep calming breath, he paused at the side of the dance floor to watch the dancers.

She caught his attention immediately.

He stared at her from the back as she danced with the man. Her thick auburn hair, decorated with burnished gold roses, was twisted and braided into an intricate style that just hid her nape. As she moved, he noted the set of her bare shoulders and the curve of her trim waist encircled by a verdigris sash. He knew the feel of that waist.

But how could it be? He frowned at the lustrous glow of her copper-colored gown. Gold lace glittered across the low back and shoulders. Her partner was a tall, handsome young man, not the big oaf. It couldn't be her—not here, not in that gown, and not with that man.

His stomach dropped as she twirled gracefully.

It was Passion, looking like he'd never seen her.

She didn't see him. She smiled graciously at her partner as they talked. She was enjoying herself.

A hot flare of jealousy burned through him. He was envious, not only of her happiness, but of being excluded from that happiness. While he had been suffering fury and misery, she had been having fun.

His heart pounded in his chest. God, she was beautiful. He wanted her. She was his, damn it!

Matt strolled up beside him and looked over the dance floor. Mark knew, by his brother's low whistle, the moment he'd spotted Passion.

"Christ, she looks beautiful," Matt commented.

"You haven't seen her at her most beautiful," Mark replied.

Matt glanced at him, but Mark kept his eyes on Passion. There seemed to be a certain easiness between her and her partner. He hated that. But most of all, he hated the man for being able to dance with her at all. How readily he supported her through the steps.

Drawing a deep breath, he glanced toward the other end of the pavilion. The tops of the tall screens were so distant. Could he get away with it?

"I wouldn't, were I you," Matt said under his breath. "The way you look at her—the way she looks at you—anyone who sees will know."

Mark frowned. "Just one dance."

Matt gripped his arm. "Do you want to ruin her? You have a reputation, my brother. And as much as you'd like to think everyone at the other end of the room is holed up behind those screens, I assure you, I've seen many walking about." His grip tightened. "Anyone who knows you will assume you're fucking her—which you are. There'll be questions about who she is. Do you really want that?"

Mark's frown deepened as he watched Passion. "No."

Matt released his arm. "Besides, you're an engaged man now. You can't just dance with whomever you please. At least not when your fiancée is at the other end of the room."

Mark's shoulders tensed. He hated being told what he couldn't do.

The music ended. Passion's partner led her off the floor and then departed after a brief exchange of words.

Ah, there was the great oaf. He cornered Passion and began expounding upon something. Though she smiled, Passion looked tired. She pressed the back of her hand to her brow, as the elderly woman beside her peered at her through a monocle.

Damn it, he wanted to take her in his arms and carry her to his carriage. He would take her home with him, remove her copper gown, and lay her in his bed. There, she could sleep for as long as she needed—and he would keep her for himself.

She said something to the woman and the oaf, then turned to face the dance floor. Her eyes swept slowly across the dancing couples, moving ever closer to him.

His gut clenched. *Find me, Passion. See me.*

She was close, so close. Her perusal paused somewhere to the left of him.

If he couldn't go to her, at least let her see him—let her know he was there—wishing he could be with her.

Her gaze continued on its path. His hands fisted at his sides.

There—so near. *Now!*

Oh, God . . . Her chin lifted and her lips parted, as if she took a deep breath. The quiet disinterest faded from her eyes, and they filled with the tenderest joy and longing. She held him in the embrace of her gaze and touched him with a beseeching caress.

His blood surged, and his heart soared.

"Jesus Christ," Matt breathed.

Passion's hands lifted, one to her side, the other to her stomach. Her breast heaved and, with a quick word to the woman with her, she turned and fled.

Yes! Go.

Mark stepped forward. *I'll find you.*

Matt grabbed his arm.

He looked back at his brother. "Let me go."

Chapter Eleven

WALTZES AND WOUNDS

Passion barely heard Aunt Matty's protestations as she
fled. After she was out of the pavilion, she turned in the
opposite direction of the crowd, which was converging to
watch the fireworks. Picking up her skirts, she hurried
down one of the statuary-lined paths. She didn't look
back, but kept hurrying farther and farther away.

Did he follow? She hoped he did.

But then why did she run?

She was the only one on the path. The music from the
pavilion was distant. She threw herself behind a huge
statue of a lion.

Why did she hide?

She pressed her palms and her forehead against the
smooth marble base of the statue. It was cool and soothing against her warm skin.

After a moment, a shadow moved around the corner of
the statue. She closed her eyes as the faintest hint of
lemon verbena touched her senses.

"I've been longing for you all evening," she said softly.

"And I for you," he replied.

Her body hummed. She pushed away from the statue.

He closed the distance between them. He was so amazingly handsome.

"You didn't tell me you were coming out of mourning," he said.

"No."

He paused before her. "You should have told me."

"Why?"

He traced her collarbone with his finger. "Because I want to know such things."

A shiver shimmied beneath her skin.

"Because I want to know you," he said quietly.

Passion gazed up at him. What were they embarking upon? Another level of intimacy would only make it more difficult to part.

I don't believe in lasting relationships, he'd said.

She shouldn't allow it.

But how could she resist what she wanted so desperately herself?

She shut out cold logic and followed her heart. "I want to know you, too."

She leaned into him, and he took her in his arms. Why was his embrace such heaven?

"I was so tired before," she said. "I haven't danced in a long time. I enjoyed myself. But after a while, I got tired of wishing my dance partner were you. I wanted to leave." She slipped her hand around his nape and looked up at him. "I was thinking of you and then there you were."

He held her in his intense gaze. The heavy lock of his hair had fallen forward. He shook his head. "You're unlike any woman I've ever known."

"I think that must be good."

His head lowered. "It is."

He kissed her tenderly and deeply.

And when he began to yield, she took the lead, luxuriating in his responses—the press of his body, the tightening of his arms, the deep moan he breathed into her mouth.

The strains of another waltz lilted through the air.

"Dance with me," he murmured against her lips. "Dance with me."

They started slowly, but as the distant music swelled, he whirled and turned her over the dampened grass.

Her heart raced exuberantly.

His white collar glowed in the moonlight. His body pressed against her. His smile flashed.

She laughed, and her skirt flew out behind her.

A great explosion burst above them. Sparkling fire rained from the night sky.

Still, they waltzed, on and on, as boom after boom of colored light illuminated the heavens.

Passion's heart took flight.

Surely, this happiness was a gift from God, for only He could devise a night this perfect.

Mark breathed the cold morning air and smiled as he let himself into his house. The night before had been torture until he'd found Passion. After that, it had been bliss.

He crossed to his study. He'd get a drink and then go to bed. Where was Cranford?

He paused in the doorway and groaned. Matt stood by the window.

"Shit. I guess you're still an early riser." Shoving back his hair, Mark crossed to the couch and threw himself onto it. "I know I said you could come here whenever you want, but you're starting to wear out your welcome."

Matt stayed by the window. "Did you have a nice evening?"

Mark stiffened at the tone of his brother's voice. He couldn't see him clearly as he was silhouetted by the light behind him. "You know I did."

"Good morning, my lord." Cranford came in with a steaming tray of breakfast.

"Morning, Cranford. Bring that tray over here, will you?"

His butler didn't miss a step. "Certainly, my lord."

Mark waited for Cranford to place the tray. As his butler poured the coffee, the silence in the room grew profound beneath the light clink of china and silver. "Will there be anything else, my lord?"

Mark kept his eyes leveled on his brother. "No, thank you, Cranford."

His butler closed the study door with a quiet click.

"Now"—he frowned at Matt—"if I know you, which I do, you're famished for breakfast. You want it, you'll have to come over here for it. And I'm in no humor for your peevishness. So if you can't say whatever the hell you have to say directly, don't bother."

Matt paused only a moment before coming to sit on the opposing couch. Piling a plate with eggs, sausage, buttered toast, and berries, he rested his elbows on his spread knees and ate. "Damned uncomfortable way to have breakfast," he muttered.

Mark picked up his coffee and, resting his heels on the table, lounged back on the couch. He let his brother eat. Since boyhood, Matt had had a voracious morning appetite. Mark was convinced the reason his brother woke so early was because his growling stomach prodded him into consciousness.

"Remember at school how you used to hide part of your dinner in your jacket so you could eat it the next morning?"

Matt grinned around his sausage and nodded. He put down his plate and sipped his coffee. "Remember how you used to sneak out and get me hot rolls when that wasn't enough?"

"Yes."

Mark had a vision of his mother wagging her finger at him. *You make sure Matthew wants for nothing, do you hear me? I expect you to take care of him.*

He had done as she asked.

She never thanked him for it—never praised him for it. His brows lifted and fell. It didn't matter. He would have done it anyway. Those had been good times. Just the two of them—away from her.

Matt's voice pulled him from his memories. "Why don't you tell me what the hell you're doing."

"What do you mean?"

"I mean this whole Charlotte Lawrence business." Matt braced his elbows on his knees and leaned forward. "Why are you engaged to her?"

Tension crept across Mark's shoulders. He took his feet from the table. "Because I want heirs."

"Is that the only reason?"

Bloody hell! "As a commoner, she's pleased enough about becoming a countess that I can forgo the lengthy courtship necessitated by our class. Nor must I abide loathsome marital negotiations with some status- and money-hungry aristocrat, like your future father-in-law."

He winced. That had been a shot. But damn it, at least it was true.

"And this Miss Lawrence isn't status- and money-hungry? You said yourself she was just happy to become a countess. And what of the mother? Christ, you could see her avarice at sixty paces." He scowled. "I don't like her. Despite all her smiles and flattery, she rubs me wrong." Matt pointed at him. "And I know you feel it, too."

Thank God, a moment of truth. "No. I don't like her. Not at all."

"Then forget this engagement. Find a way to call it off. This whole damn thing feels wrong."

"I'm marrying the daughter, not the mother."

"Oh, right. I'm sorry—I forget that you know her so well," Matt said, his voice dripping sarcasm. "And I could see how much you adore her, how excited you are to make these heirs you speak of. Christ, you were dying to get out of there. Which brings me to my real point," he continued.

Mark sat up and rubbed the aching spot between his brows. "I thought you'd already given me the 'real point.' There's another? I asked you to be bloody direct."

"Shut up and look at me," Matt growled.

What the hell? Tight with anger, Mark dropped his hand and lifted his eyes to his brother.

Why did Matt look as tense as he?

"Did you see how Passion looked at you last night?" His brother's voice was hard. "I mean, did you really see?"

"Of course I did," Mark snapped.

He didn't like Matthew talking about her. She belonged to him, and he didn't want his brother tainting her with whatever he was going to say.

"That's all you have to say? *Of course I did?*" Matt shoved back his hair, shook his head, then looked back at Mark. "I'm going to give you some advice. And I want you to take it." He leaned farther forward. "Marry Passion. Make your heirs with her. She meets your requirements for a common wife. And from what little I know of her, I can't help but think her family will be a sight less repugnant than Mrs. Lawrence, who, I am fairly certain, is a damned bitch!"

Mark stared at his brother. Marry Passion? How could he marry Passion? He had no intention of marrying anyone.

Did he?

Marry Passion.

"I can't," he finally said.

"Why the hell not?"

"Passion cannot bear children."

It wasn't the real reason for not marrying her, but it was true, and it would do.

Matt's face fell, only to fill with tentative hope. "Does that really matter? Rosalind and I will surely have a son— a son we'll christen Mark. As long as the boy has Hawkmore blood in his veins, what matter if he's yours or mine?"

Jesus fucking Christ! Mark shoved the heels of his palms against his eyes. His throat felt tight. This was too goddamned much.

"She's right for you, Mark. She's the one. Don't let her go. Don't do it."

Mark stood and crossed to the window. He stared out but saw nothing. Everything was wrong! Everything was completely, entirely wrong!

The brother he loved, who was only his half-brother, was desperately trying to give him happiness. The problem was, Matt didn't know everything. The problem was, Matt was being lied to. The problem was, Matt didn't have any fucking idea about anything and yet, somehow, was right about everything.

The problem was, it hurt like hell to admit he didn't want to pass his title to the grandson of a gardener.

His eyes blurred with shame. He was no better than those he castigated.

"I appreciate what you're trying to do," he said between clenched teeth. "But I've made my decision for now."

Silence hung heavy in the room.

"Then let Passion go."

Mark's heart sunk into his stomach. "I will not."

"You have to."

Mark whirled and crossed to his brother. "I—said—no."

Matt stood, his brow furrowed in a deep frown. "You're going to hurt her. I know you are."

Mark shook and his fists clenched at his sides. "You have overstayed your welcome."

Matt stared at him a moment longer, then stepped around him.

Mark heard the door open and then Matt's voice. "I'll forgive you for this. Passion may even forgive you. But I don't know how you'll ever forgive yourself."

The soft click of the closing door exploded in his ears like thunder.

"Honestly, Aunt Matty!" Passion half smiled, half frowned. "You make it very difficult for me to draw you when you keep fidgeting."

"Oh, for heaven's sake, you know how desperately dif-

ficult it is for me to sit still. How long does it take to do a
portrait anyway?"

"Hours. Days even."

"Hours! Days!"

Charlotte entered the sunroom.

"Oh, Charlotte. Thank heavens you're here." Aunt
Matty leapt to her feet. "Sit here a while for me, won't
you? There's a good girl. I've simply got to move about
for a bit or else suffer some sort of attack!"

Passion smiled at Charlotte as Aunt Matty fairly ran
from the sunroom. "This was to be my first attempt at a
portrait in oil, and I've already lost my model."

Charlotte tipped her head to the side. "You always used
to say you were going to be a portrait painter." She came
around to see what Passion had accomplished. "But that
was so long ago. I thought you had given up the idea."

"I had."

Charlotte gazed at the preliminary drawing. "What
changed your mind?"

Mark had changed her mind.

She blushed and shrugged. "It wasn't any one thing,
really. I remembered that I had wanted to. Then someone
told me I was very talented—someone who always tells
the truth. Suddenly, I remembered my faith in myself."

Charlotte examined the drawing. "You *are* talented."

Passion looked at her cousin. Her voice lacked its usual
lightness, and her lovely features were drawn and serious.
Come to think of it, she hadn't smiled with Passion when
Aunt Matty had fled the room.

"What's the matter, darling?"

Charlotte dropped into the chair. "Oh, Passion, last
night was so awful."

Passion put aside her canvas and drew her own chair
close. "Why? What happened?"

"I don't know. It was everything. The earl arrived late,
and Mother was furious about it. You know how she is.
She picks on everything when she's angry, most of all
me."

"Darling, you mustn't take that to heart. You're a good and kind person. And you looked beautiful last night. I didn't really have an opportunity to tell you, but you looked like an angel." She smiled. "My word, John Crossman could hardly take his eyes off you."

Charlotte's mouth trembled. "Then perhaps I should be engaged to John Crossman, because I think my fiancé hates me."

"What?" Passion swept her arms around Charlotte. "You must be mistaken. Why would you think such a thing?"

"I saw it in his face, Passion, just after he arrived. He looked at me as if I were some vile thing."

"Did you suffer this all evening?"

"No. Most of the time he didn't even seem to see me."

Passion pulled back and held Charlotte's hands in hers. "Well, did he talk with you? Dance with you?"

"He only spoke a little. We did dance." Charlotte looked down at their clasped hands. "I suppose that was the best part of the evening. There were a few moments when I felt, perhaps, he might like me." Charlotte lifted her gray eyes, and they held some hope. "Moments when he held me closer and his eyes softened. But they were only moments."

Passion thought of Mark and their dance under the fireworks. She wished Charlotte could have even a portion of that happiness.

"A moment is something," she offered. "I know I wasn't there, but it was only your first public outing together. You hardly know him, Charlotte. Perhaps your fiancé dislikes social situations. Perhaps he is merely a quiet, stoic man of serious nature."

Charlotte shook her head. "His smiles never seemed to reach his eyes, Passion."

"Ah, but he *did* smile. You know, before they were married, my mother thought my father didn't like her. She used to tell us how he barely spoke and rarely smiled. The truth was that my father was so in love with her and, as a

result, so nervous around her, that he couldn't demonstrate how he felt. It took almost losing her to another man
to bring him out of himself."

Charlotte's brow twisted. "Do you think that could be
it?"

"It's a distinct possibility. Remember, Charlotte, he
asked for you. Why would he have done that if he didn't
want you?"

"That's what I keep asking myself."

Passion thought for a moment as she remembered her
exchange with Abigail Lawrence. "There's another thing,
Charlotte. You said before you thought he disliked your
mother, and that he even seemed angry with his own
mother. Weren't both of those women there last night?"

"Yes."

"Then perhaps his demeanor had more to do with them
than you. Or perhaps . . ." Passion considered how to tell
her cousin that she needed to be less cowardly. "Perhaps
he believes you are too much under your mother's thumb.
Perhaps he believes your mother will be too much in your
lives, or, as you suggested, that you may be like her or become like her."

Charlotte was staring at her with wide eyes. "If she
weren't my mother, that would frighten me, too. She *is* my
mother, and it frightens me."

Passion held back her smile. "As a daughter, you must
be dutiful and respectful, as God commands. But if you
were to allow a little more of Charlotte to show herself,
perhaps he would have faith that, when the time comes,
you will cleave unto him. And that's the only way he's
going to know you aren't like her."

Charlotte nodded. "I know I must be stronger." She
tightened her hands around Passion's. "I *shall* be
stronger."

"We have a visitor, my dears." Aunt Matty ushered in
John Crossman. "Please sit down, Mr. Crossman, and I
shall arrange for tea."

"Good afternoon, Mr. Crossman." Passion smiled as

she moved her chair back from Charlotte's. "You know my cousin, Miss Lawrence."

John bowed over Charlotte's hand. "Have I interrupted something? I can come another time."

"No, please, join us. We were just discussing the events of last evening. Isn't the park a wonder?"

"It is." John took a seat beside Charlotte and turned to her. "I didn't have the opportunity to extend my best wishes to you upon your engagement, Miss Lawrence. Your mother made reference to an earl. Just who is your future husband?"

"Thank you, Mr. Crossman. I'm engaged to Randolph Hawkmore, Earl of Langley."

"Really?" John's brows lifted. "I'm familiar with his lordship."

Charlotte leaned forward. "You know him?"

John shook his head. "Only by reputation. But he's a large investor in Crossman Shipping. My father knew him."

Passion glanced at Charlotte. "If you don't mind, Mr. Crossman, just what is his reputation, and did your father ever tell you what he thought of him?"

"Unlike many of his class, he's a man of good business sense. Therefore, my father liked him very much. As for his reputation—" He paused and looked at Charlotte. "He's known for his honesty and integrity. And unlike most of his class, he won't often be found at the gaming tables or the racetrack." He hesitated. "Some do see him as dour and somewhat of a misanthrope. But his friends are few and close, so who really knows?"

Charlotte's whole demeanor lifted.

Passion smiled with relief. "There, Charlotte, you see?"

"Tea? Did someone say tea?" Aunt Matty said as she entered. "God bless the Queen, and God bless tea! It's on the way!"

Passion and John exchanged smiles.

Charlotte laughed.

•   •   •

Mark stood behind his desk and looked down on the drawings spread across the top. Work usually made him feel good, but not today. Since his breakfast with Matt, he had been trying to reconcile his emotions.

Though he had always had a small measure of regret over the idea of not having children of his own, he had become comfortable with the notion of passing his earldom to a son of Matthew's. Now, that meant killing a bloodline—and he kept seeing his father's face.

With a grunt of frustration, he tossed his pencil on the desk and crossed to the window. His garden was in full bloom. He had designed the well-manicured space. But it, too, failed to please.

Passion occupied his thoughts as well. He wondered how much she was influencing his feelings. Not because he wished she could give him an heir, which she couldn't, but because she made him want more for himself.

Before her, he had believed his life was, for the most part, set. He would go on as he was, take what pleasure he could from being an uncle, and his work would be the most important thing in his life.

But Passion had inspired a whole new range of emotions and desires in him. His previous life felt empty and cold to him now.

He frowned. He wasn't sure what he wanted, but he knew it wasn't what he had before.

A knock sounded on the door, and Cranford poked his head in. "Pardon me, my lord, but Mr. Wilkes is here to see you."

Good Christ, let him have found it! "Send him in."

Mickey sauntered past Cranford in a superior fashion, and Cranford closed the door behind him a bit louder than usual.

"Have you got it?"

Mickey pulled off his hat. "No, milord. Not as yet, I 'aven't. But I thought I'd keep ye informed o' me progress, as it were."

Mark crossed his arms over his chest. "She was at the

pavilion all evening. I assume you searched her room first?"

"That I did, milord. That I did. Found lots o' letters, too. But not a one from the coun'ess, I's afraid. Howe'er"—he held up a slim finger—"I 'ave ingratiated meself wit' th' upstairs maid. And, on me first day on the job, I's a position o' sorts in the Lawrence 'ouse as a go-fetch-it boy."

"Really?"

He nodded his head proudly. "'At's right, milord. 'Cause there be more'in one way to skin a cat, as they say. The 'elp a'ways knows what's what. And I'll tell ye some'in." He leaned indolently against the back of the couch.

Mark let him.

"Turns out, 'at Mrs. Lawrence is a real narsty type bitch. E'eryone 'ates 'er." Mickey squinted his eyes. "Which works real swell for us, milord. 'Cause when the 'elp 'ates ya, theys'll do jus' 'bout anythin' t'put the screws t'ya. So"—he winked—"I's thinkin' we got our-selfes a whole 'ouse full o' 'elpers."

Mark recalled noticing the butler's sneer when he visited the Lawrences. He nodded. "Very impressive. Use them however you can. But in case you're wrong, they can't know your true purpose."

"O' course not. 'At's the trick, ain't it? 'Owe'er, I's a professional, I am. I's a fly on the wall, I am. I's as inno-cent as a babe, I is. No need t'think Mickey's up to nothin'. 'E's a good boy, 'at Mickey is." He grinned. "''At's what they says 'bout me, milord."

Mark nodded. "Excellent, Mickey. Excellent." He crossed to the boy and hauled him off the back of the couch by his lapels. Setting him down, he patted the rum-pled fabric with his hand. "Now, listen to me. I want that letter. And I want it soon." He turned his mouth in a small smile. "So you use all the means at those deft fingertips of yours to get it. Understand?"

"Perfec'ly, milord. Perfec'ly."

"Good. Get back to work then."

Mickey tossed his hat on his head with a grin. "Good'ay, milord."

Mark went back to his desk as the boy left. He felt better than he had all day. Despite his youth and bravado, Mickey Wilkes was as smart as a whip. And the truth was, he'd managed to accomplish a lot in one day's work.

Mark picked up his pencil.

Mickey would find the letter.

He bent and darkened the shading on a column.

He had to.

Chapter Twelve

LOVE

Passion leaned back in the cab and adjusted the dark mourning veil she had donned. Excitement coursed through her veins. It was more than a week since she had come out of mourning. Though her nights had been spent with Mark, her days and evenings had been occupied with almost constant visits and outings. Charlotte came almost every day, even if only for a short while, mostly for reassurance about her fiancé and wedding. In the evenings, Aunt Matty accompanied her to social events, and they were usually joined by Alfred Swittly and John Crossman, who, thankfully, buffered Alfred's overzealous behavior.

But today, she had told her aunt she was going out to do some shopping. When Aunt Matty protested, Passion reminded her that it was perfectly acceptable for a widow to go about a bit on her own during the day.

Of course, she wasn't going shopping. She was going to Mark's home. A shiver of anxiety shot through her at the risk she took. And a rivulet of remorse trickled through her for lying to her aunt. Though she knew it did not excuse her behavior, she decided she would stop at some shops on the way home, so as not to be completely false.

A light rain began to fall on the roof of the cab as it slowed to a halt. Passion peeked out the window. There were only a few people farther down on the street. It looked safe. After paying the driver, she stepped out and pushed open her umbrella. As the cab clip-clopped away, she gazed up at the front of the house. Situated on the corner, it rose two stories above the ground level. The pediments bore crisp white paint, and the front door was dark green with a large lion's head door knocker. She stared at it for a moment. Of course, she wasn't going in the front door.

Hurrying around the side of the house, she ducked her head and held her umbrella more tightly as a cold breeze buffeted her. She had known that the lion of her dreams was Mark, but how odd that it should appear at his home.

Quickly and without looking around, she pushed open a gate and entered a small side yard. There was the servant's entrance. Just as she reached it, the door opened and she was pulled inside, umbrella and all. The door slammed, and Mark's arms came around her.

He flipped back her veil and smiled. "What took you so long?"

She held her umbrella over them and water dripped onto the floor. "Am I late?"

He took her mouth in a brief intense kiss. "No, what took you so long to walk from the front to the side?"

"Oh, well I—"

He kissed her again, taking her breath away with his urgency.

She gasped and then smiled as he pulled back.

His blue eyes sparkled. "God, you're beautiful." He took her umbrella and, snapping it closed, put it in the umbrella stand.

"Don't worry. I gave everyone the day off." He held out his hand. "Your cloak and bonnet, madam. Or should I address you as Miss Passion Elvira Dartpoof?"

Passion laughed. "Oh, yes, that's the one!" As she removed the articles, she said, "I have to leave by three. I have an important dinner engagement this evening."

She discreetly admired Mark. He wore a dark blue dressing gown over a pair of buff trousers.

A brief frown puckered his brow. "I do, too. However, it isn't at all important. In fact, I'd rather miss it."

Though she'd seen him naked plenty of times, she'd never seen him dressed as if he were readying to bathe. She blushed as she handed him her bonnet and cloak.

Holding her things, he stared at her. "That gown is the color of buttercups," he said, his voice a little rough.

Passion smiled. The gown was one of her favorites, and she'd worn it hoping he would notice.

He took her hand. "Come with me."

She followed him through the back hallway to the front of the house, where they came out in a lofty vestibule with an elegant curving staircase to one side.

"You have a beautiful home," she commented as he pulled her up the stairs.

"Thank you. It's a Robert Adam house." He looked over his shoulder as they started up a second flight. "I like how he varies the shapes of rooms."

"He is an architect, I presume."

Mark smiled. "Yes—of the last century."

At the landing, he turned toward the back of the house. Pushing open a door, he ushered her into his bedroom. It was large and expansive, taking up most of the width of the rear of the house. A huge bed, draped in dark green silk and gold trim, anchored one end of the room. At the other end, a cheerful blaze burned in the fireplace and a comfortable seating area beckoned her.

A large desk was well placed by the light of the windows. As she passed it, she saw that it was covered with drawings. She paused and drew closer. Precise and intricate architectural renderings covered every page.

She looked at him as he crossed to her. "You're an architect."

He came to stand beside her. "Yes."

She shook her head at the amazing detail drawn into a classical dome. "This is beautiful."

"Thank you. These are my plans for the new National Library. That is, if I get the appointment."

Passion gazed at four drawings depicting different sections of the library. The design was clean and elegant. It was Mark. "I think you're right to have chosen a classical style. Everything is neo-Gothic now, but this—this is perfect."

"I'm glad you like it." He paused. "I chose it because I believe a building should be representative more of its purpose than its time. A library ought to be free of extraneous ornament and full of light to promote the pursuit of knowledge. I wanted a building that would reflect enlightenment and learning . . ."

Passion listened to Mark as he shared his vision. She looked at his drawings as he pointed out important details. Her heart warmed. This was what moved him. This was what mattered to him. She felt privileged that he was sharing something so important to him.

She smiled. "You'll get the commission."

"I hope you're right." He turned her toward the windows. "Look down there."

Through the raindrop-splashed glass, Passion looked down at a garden. A fountain was situated in the center, and incredible islands of color broke the green, softening the formality of the space. "What a beautiful garden," she commented softly.

Mark rested his hands on her shoulders. "The fountain is new."

Passion looked at it, and a slow smile turned her lips. "Is it Aphrodite?"

He kissed the sensitive spot behind her ear. "Who else?" His arms came around her, and he pulled her close. "It isn't running yet, but it will soon."

She leaned against him. "Your home is beautiful, Mark. Just beautiful."

"I'm glad you like it," he breathed into her neck.

Passion shivered and then sighed as his hands lifted to cup and squeeze her breasts.

He turned her in his arms and began to unbutton her bodice. "As much as I admire you in this gown, I think I'd like to see a little more of you."

Passion's heart beat faster, and she helped him by loosening her skirt and crinoline while he made quick work of her corset cover.

His eyes roamed over her, and Passion trembled beneath the sudden intensity of his gaze.

"Don't move," he said as he stepped to his desk.

Passion's eyes widened as he picked up a pair of scissors. She watched, frozen, as he cut into her drawers and then ripped the fabric off her.

Nostrils flaring, he cut away the fabric of her chemise that showed above her corset, baring the high mounds of her breasts.

Passion's heart pounded and her cunt throbbed as a sensual vulnerability came over her. She was alone with Mark, in his house. She trusted him, but she was also completely at his mercy.

"That's better." He tossed the scissors on the desk and removed his robe as he went to stand beside his bed.

When he turned, Passion felt herself moisten at the sight of his huge erection bulging beneath his close-fitting trousers.

"Lift your breasts higher," he said huskily. "I want to see your nipples."

Passion blushed but did as he said. Her nipples hardened and swelled at the light touch of her own hand and, between her legs, her clitoris pulsed anxiously.

"Take your hair down," he said softly.

Passion lifted her arms and carefully removed all the pins from her hair. It fell, finally, in a heavy coil down her back.

He held out his hand. "Give the pins to me."

His eyes never left her as she walked to him. Her low-heeled boots were silent against the thick carpet beneath her feet.

She looked at his large hand as she turned over her pins. He had strong, capable hands. Hands she gave herself over to completely.

He put the pins in a box on the bedside table and then circled slowly behind her.

Passion held her breath. Gooseflesh rose on her skin as he stroked his fingers across her shoulder blades. His hands moved down and rested around her waist. She heard his breathing quicken.

"I like you this way." His fingers pressed against her. "The curve of your waist draws me." He trailed his hand across her bottom and softly stroked the folds of her cunt from behind.

Her back arched, tilting her bottom.

"That's nice." His fingers touched more of her. "God, you're wet with wanting," he said as he slid two fingers inside her.

She arched more and reached back to curve her hand around his nape.

"I think my cock is in love with you," he murmured into her neck.

Passion shivered as he slipped another finger inside her. "Is it?" she whispered.

He pressed his hips fully against her, and she felt the hard, stiff length of him against her buttocks. Her cunt clenched hungrily as her other hand slipped back to hold him to her.

He stroked her breast. "Whenever you enter the room, it stands at attention." He pinched and rolled her nipple, encouraging it to swell even more as he plunged his fingers deeper into her cunt. "It's completely slovenly and lackadaisical the rest of the time."

Good! Let him be hard only for her.

Passion drew a deep breath as his hand moved from her breast to her clitoris. He knew just how to touch her.

"You're getting hotter and wetter," he said near her ear. "You want me now, don't you?"

She gasped and her knees trembled. "I want you always."

He paused for the briefest of moments. His fingers slid from her cunt. He walked around in front of her, still stroking her throbbing clit while his other hand squeezed her bottom.

Her hands went to his trousers immediately. She couldn't get the buttons undone fast enough. But as soon as she was able, she curved both hands around his shaft and stroked the whole heavy length of him.

His eyes were dark and intense as he lowered his mouth to hers. He kissed her hard and deep, and Passion opened to receive his thrusting tongue. His hand slipped past her clitoris, and his fingers thrust into her quim.

Her hands tightened around his throbbing prick. She wanted him so badly.

Suddenly, he pulled back and crouched in front of her.

She watched, breathless, as he unlaced and removed her boots. The ribbon of her garter shook as a muscle in her thigh trembled.

His hands swept from her ankle to her thigh, smoothing her stocking as he went. He did the same with the other but paused to kiss her thigh as he let his hands wander up the back of her legs.

Passion moaned as he gripped her from behind and slid his fingers along her wet folds. And while he stroked her, his chin tickled the tender skin of her inner thigh as he kissed and licked the moisture from her. And the longer he stayed there, the wetter she became.

Passion shook with tension. Her clit throbbed mercilessly, and she thought she might die from need. Her hands clenched at her sides and then in his hair.

"Please," she begged.

Slowly, he stood before her, pausing to suck hard upon one of her nipples as he pushed free of his trousers.

Saliva filled her mouth and her quim wept as she saw

that the head of his cock was dark red and dripping pre-come.

He saw the direction of her gaze and traced her quivering lower lip. "Are you hungry for it?"

"Yes," she breathed. "Yes!"

He sat on the side of the bed. "Come then."

Light-headed with desire, she dropped to her knees and ran her tongue from the base of his prick all the way up to the head. Mark's hips jerked forward. She stroked him with both hands as she wrapped her lips around the wet head of his prick.

Famished and shaking, she sucked the salty fluid from his swollen knob, running her tongue around the rim and into the weeping duct over and over. And all the while, she drew her hands up his shaft, squeezing more drops into her hungry mouth.

Mark's hands settled in her hair, and his hips began to thrust. It made her wild with need, and she pushed her lips farther down his shaft, pressing her tongue against the distended passage that brought his come.

He moaned and thrust, inching a little farther into her. Her cunt clenched and released, begging its own fulfillment.

Passion moaned as she sunk deeper. His thighs went rigid around her.

He jerked her from him and, picking her up, tossed her on the bed. Passion gasped as he fairly leapt upon her.

He held her head in his hands as he bruised her lips with a penetrating kiss. She opened her mouth and her legs. Her hips arched.

"This is my house, Passion," he said against her mouth, "and I say how it goes."

Her heart pounded with both desire and submission. "I know."

With a choked oath, he flipped her onto her stomach. She tilted up her hips as she felt the push of his knob against the wet folds of her cunt. His hands settled around her waist, she sucked in her breath, and with one long, hard thrust, he pushed into her.

Passion exhaled on a deep moan as she stretched around him. Her cunt pulsed ecstatically at finally being filled.

Each and every time he entered her was heaven, but today she felt fuller and more vulnerable than ever. Her clit throbbed, and her hips tilted.

"Yes, Passion," he murmured. "That's it, my sweet." He lifted her hips. "That's it."

She gasped as he rocked forward, pressing against her womb with more direct pressure than he ever had before. A hot rush of moisture flooded her at the exquisite sensation.

When he drew back, she moaned for the loss. "No, don't stop," she breathed. He had found the deep pocket in her cunt three times since that first night in her room, and each time he had done it on the tide of her orgasm. Today, she wanted the experience undiluted. She wanted Mark undiluted. "Please . . ."

He shuddered behind her but didn't move. "I may not be able to stop once I start." His voice was tight. "I don't want to hurt you."

"Take me now," she entreated softly. "I want to feel all of you—every inch of you inside me."

His hands gripped her tightly corseted waist. He took a deep breath.

Passion closed her eyes and released a sigh.

He withdrew slowly and then thrust hard into her, bringing a cry from her parted lips. His hold on her waist was so firm that her body bowed to the full force of his strength.

He didn't pause, but thrust again. Passion gasped. The reverberation inside her was so deep and strong that she shook and softened with its power.

He withdrew only once more before delivering a final and demanding thrust against the door to her womb.

She must submit. No more doubts. No more resistance. She belonged to him.

And then he was pushing and pushing, bearing down upon her hard and with direct pressure. "Open," he gasped. "Open for me, Passion."

Her back arched, and she gave her body to his command. He took what she offered and pressed the full weight of his body upon her. "Good," he grunted. "That's good."

Passion shuddered and panted. Her cunt clenched, and her clit throbbed.

"Oh, God," he growled. "It's going, it's going."

Passion gasped then bit back a cry as the pressure built and built.

Mark groaned behind her.

Her hands clutched at the coverlet. She felt like she was breaking, and yet the sensation was exquisite. As the pressure built, so did her fullness. Her body was opening and her cunt was stretching. And just when she thought she might split in two, something inside her gave. The pressure eased. She cried out as he filled her with all he had.

She moaned and panted and felt him throb inside her. Her heart pounded. This was what she was meant for. This was where she belonged.

"Oh, God! You must always give yourself like this," he rasped, his hands clenching on her waist. "Don't resist me, and I can fill you like this every time." He rocked against her. "You'd like that, wouldn't you?"

She sucked in her breath as the tip of his cock touched her somewhere high in her body. "Yes," she panted. Let him breach her forever and always!

He drew back, and suddenly the pressure grew again as she felt his swollen knob pulling back down over the firm opening of her tilted womb.

She whimpered and shook. Her cunt clenched fiercely.

He stayed there, neither withdrawing fully nor entering fully, but thrusting between that tight, trembling spot.

"Feel that," he gasped. "Feel how good it is. Don't come. Just feel it."

Passion couldn't move as she endured the torturous pleasure he inflicted upon her. Though she was dying for release, she held it at bay. And as he kept thrusting and thrusting, the pressure seemed to grow. She whimpered again.

"That's good," he panted. "That's good. God, I'm getting biggcr."

He surged inside her, the pressure eased, her cunt stretched. She groaned, and perspiration broke on her brow as she felt the head of his cock press firmly against some unknown organ of her body.

"Oh, God," he moaned. He rocked against her, nudging it gently.

Passion sobbed and pushed against the headboard, helping him plumb her depths. Her body began to shake uncontrollably.

Grabbing her waist with a low grunt, Mark began to thrust wildly.

Passion cried out. She gasped for air. With each powerful thrust, he pulled back enough to rub against the firm flesh of her cervix before driving in to touch the unresisting organ of her body. And with each thrust, his heavy cods spanked the stretched and swollen lips of her cunt.

Her heart pounded and her head swam. Everything she was or had been coalesced between her legs.

Her cunt clenched and sucked his magnificent cock with the fervor of a starving supplicant. Her clit throbbed and pulsed, pulling the blood from her heart into its tender bud.

And still he drove her on, unrelenting in his determination to bring her bliss. She need only submit. Her back eased and arched even more. Her vision narrowed to a single point of clarity.

She need only surrender.

With a fierce, unrestrained cry, she let every inhibition of thought and emotion fall away from her. Her heart filled with the love for him she had refused to acknowledge. Her cunt pulled and clasped around him. Her clit pounded exuberantly. And as he moaned above her and poured hot rivers of seed into her body, she burst into a thousand scintillating sparks of ecstasy and joy.

Spurred by love, her release went on and on. She still shivered and clenched around him long after he had collapsed upon her.

He pressed soft, moist kisses along her shoulder, and she reveled in the tender touch of his lips. Would that she could stay with him forever.

Forever . . .

"I have a gift for you," he murmured.

Her heart fluttered. "You are my gift."

He smoothed her hair back from her brow and kissed the corner of her mouth. "And you're mine."

She moaned softly as he withdrew from her. He passed a soft caress over her bottom before he levered himself from the bed.

Turning onto her elbow, she watched him as he crossed the room. She loved his large, tall form. She loved his confident stride.

She loved him.

When had it happened? It wasn't new. She knew that now. It had called to her at the pavilion. It had beckoned her the night he first came to her room.

He returned to her with a picnic basket and a black box tied with burgundy satin ribbon. He paused to look at her. "I love to see you in my bed. When you're there, you're mine."

If he only knew. "I'm yours wherever I am."

His eyes held her for a moment and then he sat beside her. She pushed herself to a sitting position, and he placed the box in her lap.

"For you," he said quietly.

Passion's chest tightened. She stroked the black moiré that encased the box and ran the burgundy satin ribbon between her fingers.

"I've never bought a gift for a woman before," he said, his voice rough. "But this, this seemed like it ought to be yours."

She lowered her face to hide the tears that threatened. Carefully, she loosened the wide ribbon and lifted the lid. Black tissue paper hid the contents. She folded it back and revealed swirling paisleys in red, green, blue, and black on a golden ground. Lifting it reverently, she pulled out a full-length cashmere shawl. Its beauty and quality was fit for the queen, who was said to have several.

Her tears spilled as she admired it. But far more wonderful than that, he had chosen it for her, and it was perfect.

She drew it around her shoulders and dared to lift her eyes to his. "Thank you, Mark. I love it."

He kissed her softly. "For that reaction, I would have bought you a hundred."

And then she knew. Love had whispered to her the first day they met.

Mark let his hand wander over Passion's knee.

"I do wish you would try to be still." Passion smiled at him and yanked the sheet back over her crossed legs.

They had eaten from the picnic basket and were sitting, naked, on his bed.

She was trying to draw his profile. Her shawl was draped around her shoulders, but he couldn't keep himself from stroking her thigh and lightly touching the soft folds of her cunt beneath the linens.

"I'm keeping my head completely still," he said.

Her smile deepened. "If you want this to be any good, you won't distract me."

He sighed and took a sip of wine.

"You reminded me of the impatient Sunday school children I've drawn. Why don't you tell me a story," she suggested.

"A story?"

"Mm-hmm. Something about your youth, perhaps."

His jaw tightened. "I don't have any stories about my youth."

She glanced at him. Her gaze was so tender. "Anything then," she said.

He met her eyes over the top of her sketchbook. "When I was at Oxford, I held the record for the biggest penis."

Passion laughed. She reached out and turned him back to profile. "I had no idea such lofty credentials could be earned at Oxford."

"Most people have no idea. I also held the record for the most volume of ejaculate. I can fill a shot glass."

Passion lowered the sketchbook, her eyes disbelieving. "You're teasing, aren't you? There aren't really such competitions."

He looked at her benignly and pushed the sketchbook up for her to keep working. "Actually, Matt and I held that record together. As for distance covered by ejaculate, that record belonged to Sir Peter Wells. He had the smallest penis, but his come could really fly." Mark shrugged. "Matt and I couldn't figure it. We finally determined that our sperm was just too weighty to make the distance Wells' could."

Passion dropped the sketchbook into her lap. "I cannot believe this is what goes on at Oxford. I cannot believe that young men go about partaking in these sorts of contests."

"We did some studying as well."

Passion rolled her eyes. "Oh, well that's good."

"What, you've never done anything the least little bit outrageous—before me, that is?"

Passion's cheeks flushed pink.

"Aha!" Mark turned and leaned on his elbow. "You tell *me* a story. And make it a good one."

Passion's blush deepened. "In the summertime, my sisters and I used to bathe in a small lake near our home. We'd leave our clothes on the bank and swim in our chemises."

Mark's brows lifted. "Really?"

Passion grinned. "Yes, really. Now do you want to hear or not?"

Beneath the sheets, his cock nodded. "Oh, most definitely. How old were you when you did this?"

"Oh, we did it for years. But I was about fifteen at the time I'm referring to."

"Excellent. Go on."

"Well, on one particularly warm day, we were lying on the grass after our swim, when Prim leapt up with a shriek, pulled up her chemise, and started batting at her thighs. Patience and I went to her, but it turned out to be nothing more than a ladybug. Anyway, as I took it from her thigh, Patience said, 'You have a beauty mark on your cunny, Prim.'" Passion's blush deepened. "So before we really knew what we were about, we were sitting there, examining each other's quims by the side of the lake."

Mark's breathing shortened. "Did you touch each other?"

Her regard was so warm. "A little."

His cock came to a full stand. The image of Passion with her legs open and her chemise around her waist, touching herself and being touched by her sisters was more erotic than he'd expected. Not because he wanted her sisters, but because he wanted her, and it was innocent yet sensual proof of the woman she would become.

Though they had looked at each other with interest and curiosity and their exploration had been between them, not for the excitement of an observer, he couldn't help wishing he could have been there. He would have dragged Passion away from her sisters and had his way with her in the grass. "Christ, I wish I'd known you then. I would have followed you to that damned lake every day." He pulled her hand to his rampant erection. "And early on, my sweet, you would have known the pleasure of a good fuck."

Passion smiled but then grew serious. "Would that I had known you." She looked at him. "If you had been in my life, I never would have married my husband."

The thought of her enduring life with some cold son-of-a-bitch angered him. He frowned. "No. I wouldn't have let you."

"You wouldn't?"

"No."

"But how would you have prevented it?"

The answer came immediately. "I would have married you myself."

The words hung in the air between them.

Mark knew they were true. And strangely, he felt no surprise or discomfort at their utterance.

"But you said you don't believe in lasting relationships," Passion whispered. "You said, when you're done, you're done."

He had said that. He'd said it because that's what always happened. He'd said it because that's what life had shown him.

But when he was with her, everything felt different. With her, his life seemed full of happiness and possibility. With her, he had faith in forever.

"Yes," he answered. "But if I'd met you as a boy, I think I would have wholly different ideas about that."

"But you met me now."

"Yes." He traced his finger between her breasts. "Thank God."

He let his finger slide down to her pretty navel and then he remembered. He frowned. "You know, just because you didn't bear a child with your husband, doesn't mean you can't."

Passion stared at him. "What do you mean?"

"I mean the problem could very well have lain with your husband."

"It didn't."

"How do you know?"

Her eyes sparkled with unshed tears. "My husband was fucking one of the dairymaids. I saw him do it more than once, with more enthusiasm and vigor than he ever fucked me." Her tears spilled and she swiped them away.

"Shortly, she got with child. She came to my husband, and he gave her money. She went away."

"Christ, I'm sorry." Mark pulled her into his arms. He never should have raised the subject. "I'm sorry, Passion."

Bloody bastard! If her husband weren't already dead, he'd kill him.

He smoothed her hair from her wet cheek and kissed her trembling lips. They were salty with tears. "You're the most beautiful, desirable woman I've ever known," he murmured. He took her mouth in another deep kiss to punctuate his point. Her clinging response and sweet embrace evoked a selfish exaltation that her husband had never known what she had to give.

He pulled back and took away a tear with the pad of his thumb. Her eyes looked like wet leaves of brown, green, and gold. He wanted them to sparkle with happiness, not sadness. He wanted to tell her that just because her husband had been fucking the dairymaid didn't mean the baby was his. The damned dairymaid could have been fucking any number of men.

But he couldn't tell her that. He could be wrong, and false hope would be a misery.

So he tried to speak to her other pain. "Some men lose their desire for their wives the moment they step out of church," he said softly. "It has nothing to do with the wife; it's merely that a wife is too available, too permitted. Their zeal is for all the women they can't have."

Passion seemed to consider his words. She looked at him after a moment. "Is that why you want me so much? Because I'm not too available, not too permitted?"

He frowned. His feelings were so far from that, he hadn't even thought of the comparison. "You know that's not why I want you."

"I know." Her eyes delved into his. "I just wanted to hear you say it wasn't so."

He held her chin and kissed her gently. "I want you because you give me your whole self. I want you because you ask me for nothing, yet take everything I offer you."

He frowned. "Which only makes me wish you *would* ask me for something—makes me wish you would ask me for something no one else can give you."

Her eyes glowed with that indefinable emotion. Did she know it was there? He stared and recognized it was the same intangible something he'd seen in her drawing of him. What was it? Realization seemed so close, but somehow, still, it hovered just beyond his sight—just beyond his grasp.

His voice shook. "I want you because you're everything I never ever dreamed could be."

Passion smoothed the soft fringe of her shawl. It was beautiful against the dark red silk of her gown. She drew it more closely around her as John Crossman escorted her up the walk to the Lawrence home.

The windows were full of light. All the Lawrence clan would be in attendance for Charlotte's engagement dinner, along with Abigail's Netherton relatives.

She mounted the steps on John's arm. She would be the only representative of the unfortunate country cousins—those Dare relations that were never spoken of. Charlotte had made sure that Passion and her family would be invited to the wedding. The formal invitation had arrived that day. She must be responsible for this evening's invitation as well. Aunt Matty had been pointedly excluded, while Abigail had had the gall to suggest that Mr. Crossman would be a suitable escort for Passion.

Passion had wanted to send her regrets based on that slight, but Aunt Matty had insisted she go for Charlotte's sake.

John paused before ringing. "Do you suppose Mrs. Lawrence will be riding her broom this evening?"

Passion laughed. He was good company, and nothing, not even Abigail Lawrence, could dim her happiness this evening. "In my experience, which is obviously limited, she is never without it."

John smiled and shrugged. "Then let's stay well out of her way."

Passion grinned. "Agreed."

He rang the bell, and they were admitted by the butler. The buzz of voices came from the upstairs salons. Abigail swept down the stairs to meet them. As she descended, her eyes moved over Passion with an assessing look.

She greeted John Crossman first. "How kind of you to join us this evening, Mr. Crossman. I didn't know if your social schedule would permit you to come."

Passion realized that if John hadn't been able to attend, she wouldn't have either. She could have come un-escorted, but knowing so few of the guests, she likely wouldn't have. Abigail had probably hoped for that.

"It is no kindness, madam. I am always privileged to be in Mrs. Redington's company. I would cancel the queen to be with her."

Passion glanced at him with a grateful smile, but he was regarding Abigail with a completely serious expression.

"Yes, well." Abigail turned to her. "Charlotte will be pleased to see you, Passion. But do not monopolize her. When you're present, she clings to you like a limpet. After you're introduced to her fiancé, see that you keep your distance."

Passion nodded and, taking John's arm, followed Abigail up the stairs.

"Would the front steps be distance enough, do you think?" John murmured.

Passion grinned and nudged him in the ribs. "Thank you, by the way, for defending the worthiness of my company."

He looked at her. "I meant what I said."

Passion challenged him with a smile. "As if you'd really toss off the queen."

He chuckled. "For you, I just might."

The volume of the party grew as they crossed the landing. Abigail must have invited everyone she knew.

They followed her into the noisy parlor. Passion smiled and nodded to the few faces she recognized. Then, as she crossed the room, her eyes fixed on a familiar tall, broad-shouldered back.

Chapter Thirteen

WHEN GOD'S LAWS
ARE BROKEN . . .

A small frown puckered Passion's brow. She stared at the broad shoulders and tapering torso. She knew that physique, even completely covered by immaculate evening attire. She knew the feel of his nape and the texture of his dark brown hair.

Her body hummed and her heart thumped wildly in her breast. But how could he be there? And how would she get through a whole evening without throwing herself into his arms? Lord, they seemed to be moving directly toward him. She reined her love in close and hid her smile.

"My lord," Abigail said.

My lord? People stood all around them.

"Allow me to introduce Charlotte's second cousin, Mrs. Redington, and her escort, Mr. John Crossman of Crossman Shipping."

For a moment, no one moved. Then, finally, the tall back she had been admiring turned.

Mark's blue eyes landed upon her directly. His mouth parted, and a dark shadow fell over his gaze.

Passion tried to smile. Wasn't he happy to see her?

"Passion!" Charlotte rushed forward to hug her.

She returned Charlotte's embrace. She hadn't even seen her cousin until that moment. She saw, now, that Mark's brother was there as well, and another woman who must be their mother.

Mark was shaking John Crossman's hand. His brother was staring at her with the oddest expression. He stepped forward and took her hand in his. His dark eyes were full of compassion.

Passion's heart trembled. Hadn't Charlotte said her fiancé had blue eyes? She blinked. What was happening?

"I'm so pleased to meet you, Mrs. Redington," he said softly. His hand seemed to support her.

Charlotte was greeting John Crossman.

Passion's stomach tightened painfully. She grasped at hope. "Do I have the pleasure of meeting the Earl of Langley, my lord?" Her voice quavered. "You are Randolph Hawkmore, are you not?"

He frowned and bent his head.

Mark took her hand from his brother's. His fingers stroked her palm. She looked into his beautiful blue eyes.

"I am the Earl of Langley, Mrs. Redington. Mark Randolph Hawkmore, at your service."

No! God, no!

"All the earls of Langley are christened Mark, Mrs. Redington, so we acquired the habit of going by our middle names to distinguish ourselves." His gaze was so soft. "Only those who are closest to me use my given name."

Passion's head spun, and her stomach twisted into a tortured knot. She tried to draw a breath and couldn't.

Mark frowned and put his other hand atop hers.

She began to shake uncontrollably.

"Passion." Charlotte hurried to her side. "You're white as a sheet."

Perspiration broke across her brow. "I—I feel unwell," she gasped. She couldn't look at Mark, though he still held her hand. She turned to John. "Mr. Crossman, please." Black dots flashed before her eyes. "I am ill."

He gripped her elbow. "Do you need a physician?"

"I—no, I . . ." She had to get out of there before she fainted. She looked up at him and barely kept back her tears. "Please, I need to go home."

"I can take her to a room above," Mark said.

"No!" Her stomach wrenched. As she tried to take a step, her knee buckled.

Mark reached out to her, but John Crossman caught her around her waist.

Mark stepped forward, his face tight with tension, but his brother grabbed his arm as John led her away.

Charlotte hovered at Passion's side as they hurried through the parlor. "My cousin is unwell," Charlotte offered as explanation to the gawking faces they passed.

Passion pressed her hand against her stomach and fought the urge to retch. She couldn't bear Charlotte's presence, couldn't abide her touch. "Please, Charlotte," she begged as they reached the landing. She tried to smile. "Go back to your party, darling."

Mark came out of the parlor, his brother on his heels.

Passion swallowed bile and, turning quickly, hurried to the stairs. Fearing Mark's pursuit, she raced down the long flight. The steps blurred before her tear-filled eyes. She couldn't see, but she couldn't stop. Sobs hiccupped in her throat.

Mark, her love—*her* love—was Charlotte's fiancé! With a cry, she stumbled, but John was there to catch her. She went where he led her, for she could see little through her tears and pain.

Where was Mark?

She couldn't think.

John said something to someone about his carriage as he pulled her outside.

Mark's words reared up from her memory. *I'm not the sort of man you would like to know . . . I live my life for myself. I do what I want, and I couldn't care less what people think about it.*

She swayed on her feet.

All the time he'd been touching her, kissing her, laying with her, he'd been lying to her!

She shivered violently, and the rush down the front steps proved more than she could stand. At the curb, she bent and vomited her misery into the gutter.

"Let her go," Matt growled in his ear. "He can comfort her. You cannot."

But he could comfort her. He would comfort her. He needed to tell her everything.

Abigail and Lucinda strolled from the parlor.

"My guests are awaiting your return, my lord," Abigail said stiffly.

"We were just seeing to Passion, Mother," Charlotte said in a diminutive voice.

"Passion." Abigail snorted. "I hope you see now why I didn't want her here, Charlotte. She has ruined my party with her ill-timed sickness and her ill-bred flight. Now everyone will be talking about how your cousin took sick, rather than talking about you."

Mark wanted to hit her. He kept seeing Passion's face as he told her who he was. "Shut up, or I'll leave, too, and then they'll really have something to talk about."

Charlotte's eyes widened in dismay, and Matt grabbed his arm discreetly.

Abigail's eyes narrowed. "If you leave, I swear I'll make you sorry for it."

Mark grit his teeth with suppressed fury. Right now Passion was thinking every terrible thought possible. She was suffering, while he stood there in a bloody catfight. Goddamn it!

Just as he took a step back, Matt stepped forward, glaring venomously at Abigail. "Just what the hell do you mean, threatening my brother? Frankly, madam, you ought to be on your fat knees in gratitude that the Earl of Langley has stooped to encumber himself with your daughter."

Lucinda snickered and stroked Matt's arm. She always

seemed to take particular pleasure in her son's rare but fierce loss of temper.

"I don't know what you think you're about, but you will remember whom you are addressing," Matt growled. "Or I will make *you* sorry for it."

"Oh, really?" Abigail replied, her voice dripping with superiority and rage.

Mark's heart pounded. The huddle was close, and shots were flying. The whole thing was going to blow.

And he would be free—free to convince Passion to stay with him for as long as he wanted.

Matt whirled to him. "Let's go. This woman is unbearable."

Mark took a step. Passion needed him. Matt could survive the scandal. He could.

"Matt, darling, there you are." Rosalind stepped from the parlor. "Is everything all right? I heard someone took ill while I was in the music room."

Mark's shoulders tensed, and his hands fisted at his sides in helpless frustration as he saw Matt's expression soften.

"Everything is fine, darling," Matt said. "But why don't you get your parents. I believe we're leaving."

Lord Benchley's words to Matt rang in Mark's ears: *You will marry my daughter, dear boy, because you are a Hawkmore.*

Matt could survive the scandal, but his engagement—his love—never would.

Mark's brief elation died. And with its death, a cold, impotent fury settled over him. A fury that held everyone in its frozen scope—even Matt.

"No."

Matt turned back to him. "What?"

"You don't have to stay, but I do."

Lucinda took a deep breath. Abigail smiled disdainfully and, turning on her heel, returned to the parlor.

"What the hell for?" Matt asked irritably.

Mark looked over Matt's shoulder at Charlotte. How

he hated her. She imprisoned him with her mere existence. She held him while Passion needed him.

"For her." He nodded toward Charlotte.

Matt turned, and a layer of irritation lifted from his face. He frowned. "I hope you know my anger was not directed at you, Miss Lawrence. I have come to know you a little in this past week, and I have seen that you are as soft as your mother is hard. But I cannot stand by while she makes empty threats against my brother." He bowed his head. "Forgive me. I bear you no ill will."

Charlotte nodded but seemed unsure if she should stay or go. Her gray eyes were hesitant as she raised them to Mark. "If I were you, I would think my mother horrid, too. But I am nothing like her. I will be a kind and loyal wife to you, my lord."

Mark stared at her. How he loathed her if-ing and but-ing. How he despised the pathetic attempts she'd made all week to rebuff her mother. They amounted to nothing. She ought not bother.

"I shall join you in the parlor," he said.

Charlotte bowed her head and left with Rosalind.

Matt glanced at Lucinda and then turned to him and raised a finger. "I told you. I told you, you would hurt her." He turned away only to turn right back. "That, I must admit, was a whole lot worse than anything I could have imagined. But leave it to you to do it in the worst way possible."

Mark shook with his effort to keep his fists at his sides. "Fuck you. I had no idea they even knew each other."

"And you're going to throw her away—so you can attach yourself to that vile bitch in there. You know what, brother mine, you must *need* misery in your life."

Rage ricocheted through Mark's tense muscles. He walked away from Matt and his mother and the open parlor doors.

But Matt followed. "Yes, that's it. You can't abide happiness. No. No, you don't even recognize happiness."

Mark whirled and slammed his fist right into his

brother's jaw. Matt reeled back, holding his chin. Lucinda gasped and hurried to them.

Mark closed on him and shoved his finger in his face. "By God, if you say one more fucking word, I'll hurl you down those stairs so fast and so hard, your loving Rosalind"—he sneered the words—"will have to come pick up your pieces and sew you back together."

Lucinda yanked at Mark's arm. "Don't you ever touch my son!" she hissed. "Do you hear me? You leave him alone."

Mark jerked his arm from Lucinda's grasp and stepped back from Matt.

His mother turned to her favorite. Matt wrenched away from her and then, faster than Mark could react, his brother slapped their mother across the face.

Lucinda gasped with shock and held her hand to her cheek.

"This is all your fault," Matt growled. "*He* is your son, too. If you could have found it in yourself to show him even the smallest bit of motherly regard, maybe he wouldn't be marrying himself to misery. But thanks to you, he knows nothing else." Matt turned and, testing his jaw, strode back to the parlor.

Lucinda whirled on Mark. "This is all *your* fault. Why do you have to make everything so difficult? Why can't you be as agreeable as—"

"As Matthew?" Mark finished for her. How many times had he heard that as a boy?

He looked at her reddened cheek. "If I'd only known what 'agreeable' truly meant to you, I'd have obliged you long ago."

He pushed past her and looked at his watch. It was too damned early. He wouldn't be able to go to Passion for hours.

God, what was she thinking? What was she doing?

Drained and exhausted, Passion clutched her sheets beneath her chin and curled in a tight ball. The hours had ticked away since Aunt Matty and John Crossman had left her to her to sob into her pillow. Her throat still stung with bile and her eyes with tears. The pain tearing at her heart suffocated her with the weight of betrayal, sin, and loss.

She drew only the shallowest of breaths. She was both betrayed and betrayer, sin and sinner. Worst, her love, her hope for love, was nothing but a desperate illusion laid on a foundation of deceit and wrongdoing.

Her heart tightened painfully. She gasped and pressed the heel of her palm against the shrinking organ. No. Not an illusion. Her love was deep and true—and unrequited.

And undeserved. How could he have given her so much of himself, brought her into his home, when all along he was taking steps toward his future with Charlotte?

A dry sob rose in her throat. With Charlotte! God, with her cousin! Her cousin, who was a commoner like herself.

Why Charlotte?

Why not her?

She squeezed her eyes shut in shame at the thought. But she couldn't keep the questions at bay.

The answers were all too simple. Charlotte was rich; Charlotte was young. Tears welled in her sore eyes. And an earl needed heirs, which he knew Passion could not provide.

He had proposed to Charlotte after he knew she was barren. Might he have asked her, if she weren't? Such a futile question. But at his home, he had said things— things that made her believe he cared for her.

She bit her lip and turned her face into her pillow. Her thoughts were pathetic, and she hated herself for having them. But how would she survive the marriage of her cousin to the man she loved? God save her, she could not help loving him.

Fresh tears fell. Would her love fade? Would the pain ease over time? What malevolent twist of fate had conspired to bring this about?

"I was sure I would find the window barred."

Passion gasped at the sound of Mark's low voice and turned her face from her pillow.

When he saw her, his concerned frown deepened. "Oh, Passion."

He stepped toward her, but she threw up her hand as she sat up. "No. Don't come any closer."

She had been expecting him. But now that he was here, holding her in his blue gaze, she questioned her decision to speak with him. "I locked and unlocked the window a dozen times," she said, her voice uneven. "But finally, I realized that we . . . That I needed to say good-bye."

"There's no need to say good-bye, Passion."

Her head spun. How could he say such a thing? Her hands clenched around her sheet. "Very soon, you will be my cousin's husband." The words made her stomach turn and her heart rip. "How can you tell me there is no need for good-bye?" Her voice quavered. "We ought to have said good-bye long ago. We ought never to have been."

He frowned. "Don't ever say that. That's a lie." He stared at her. "You're the most perfect part of my life— the only perfect part. That's not a mistake. That's not wrong."

Passion pressed her hand upon her pounding heart as tears welled painfully. "It's all wrong. How can you not see that? You belong to my cousin."

"She's your second cousin, and I don't belong to her," he snapped. "I don't even like her." He shoved his hand through his hair. "You want to know what's wrong, Passion? Everything."

He dragged the chair to the side of her bed and sat down, his body rigid. He looked at his clenched fists for a moment before lifting his eyes to hers. They were cold as ice. "I was recently informed by my mother, whom I despise, that my brother is a bastard. Now, that was rather disturbing news in and of itself. However, there was more. It turns out she wrote a letter to a friend in which she bragged about her adulterous pregnancy."

Mark's jaw was a hard line. "This so-called friend, a

very rich woman with no title but with aspirations to the
aristocracy, retained the letter for years, waiting until her
own daughter was of marriageable age."

Passion's head hurt. Could it be?

Mark's face was granite. "Then, just a month ago, she
sent my mother a copy of the original letter along with a
demand."

"No," Passion whispered.

"Yes," Mark hissed. "Either I marry her daughter and
make her Countess of Langley, or she publishes my
mother's nasty little news in the paper. And as my brother
has no idea that he is illegitimate, and is currently engaged
to a lady of some stature, you can imagine what such news
might do to him."

Passion didn't want to believe it, but it was just the sort
of vile thing Abigail would do. She dropped her pounding
head into her hands. No wonder Charlotte had complained
of her fiancé seeming so cold and withdrawn. "I'm sorry,"
she said softly.

"You're sorry?" He sounded so bitter. "I offered her a
fortune for that bloody letter, but she wants my title and
my heirs."

Passion looked up and sucked in her breath at the fury
etched in his features. "That's right, Passion. I'm not only
required to marry your cousin, I'm required to bear children with her. Only after she is delivered of a minimum of
three healthy children, with at least two being boys, will
that bitch, Abigail Lawrence, give the letter into my
hands."

His teeth ground together. "Of course, that's what she
says, but I don't believe she will ever give it to me."

Passion struggled with her emotions. They all piled
upon her in unrelenting succession. He didn't want Charlotte. She was being forced upon him. She felt relief, then
shame for that relief. And how must it be for Mark? He
was not a man who could tolerate submission. Horror,
grief, heartache, and love all bore down upon her with an
unbearable weight.

"You must love your brother very much," she whispered.

"Matt's the *only* reason I haven't told Lawrence to do whatever she wants with that damned letter."

Passion nodded. Would that he loved her. She stared at her hands twisted in the sheets. No. No, that was wrong. Thank the Lord he didn't. She tried to swallow her sorrow, but it caught around the lump in her throat. "This is the last time we shall see each other like this, Mark." Tears filled her eyes. "For all Abigail's evil, Charlotte is innocent. You must be a kind husband to her."

"No!" He shook his head. "No, I will not give you up. I have no intention of marrying Charlotte Lawrence." His frown deepened. "And she's far from innocent. She's a weak, simpering, mealymouthed nitwit who bows to her mother's every command. You think I would give you up for her?"

Passion frowned. "But what do you mean, you have no intention of marrying her?"

"I mean I have someone searching for that letter. And as soon as he finds it, which he will, I will tell Abigail Lawrence to go to hell and to take her daughter with her."

She stared at him through the blur of her tears. "But you can't do that. If you abandon my cousin, she will be ruined."

"Perhaps you didn't understand—I'm being blackmailed, Passion. I'm being fucking blackmailed," Mark growled. "Do you expect me to just roll over and take it—as if it were nothing? Do you expect that I won't do everything in my power to free myself from this loathsome tyranny? Do you expect that I will give you up for anything or anyone? Because, if so, you are sorely mistaken."

Passion's tears fell. His words were a joy and a torture. Oh, terrible pride, terrible love! "I expect you to be the man I know you are—a man of nobility and honor."

"Do not speak to me of nobility and honor," he spat. "Nobility and honor destroyed my father. I have no aspirations to either of those characteristics."

Could he know himself so little? God, how she longed to take him in her arms. "You cannot help who you are," she murmured. "And I cannot stay with you. You belong to my cousin."

"I belong to no one but you," he answered, his voice cracking.

Passion sucked in her breath as her heart wrenched fiercely in her breast. "Would that were true."

Mark leaned closer. "It *is* true. That first day I went to the Crystal Palace, I was supposed to go to the china exhibit and view your cousin. But I had decided I wouldn't. Matt and I roamed the place for an hour and were preparing to leave when I changed my mind. At the time, I had no idea why." He held her in his gaze. "Now I know I went there to find you. You are the woman I was supposed to meet that day. You, Passion Elizabeth Dare, not your cousin."

Passion's eyes brimmed with tears of anguish. She shouldn't hear this, not now. But she couldn't bring herself to stop him.

"You know what I say is true." Mark's voice grew urgent. "When I pulled you out of the way of that falling tree, I smelled you and felt you and you filled my embrace. Then, when I looked into your beautiful eyes, I saw something that made my heart beat faster and my blood race. I had to force myself to release you. But when I walked away, it felt wrong. And the farther I walked away from you, the more wrong it felt." He leaned forward in the chair. "I told myself I would take one last look, and as I turned, I was afraid you would be gone. But you weren't. You were there, looking right at me. I knew then I wanted you more than I'd ever wanted anything."

"Stop!" Passion cried on a whisper. "Stop! You are more than an architect, you are an earl. Earls require heirs." She pressed her hands against her stomach. "Today, as we spoke, I let myself dream of what it might be like to have a life with you. But that is impossible. We both know it is."

He stared at her, his eyes full of unreadable emotions. "I won't give you up," he repeated. "I won't."

"It isn't only up to you. This has moved beyond our secret." Secrets breed trouble. She had told herself that. "In the eyes of society, you belong to Charlotte."

"I do not."

"You do!"

His eyes glittered. "I don't love her!"

"But *I* love her!"

Mark's face became a mask.

Passion's tears spilled down her cheeks. *I love you!* "And I will not betray her!"

Mark didn't move.

"Don't you see? Everything I feared, and more, has come to pass. I knew it was wrong to be with you. I knew I risked my heart and more. But I put my own needs before propriety, before duty. I ignored my morals and gave myself, willingly, to the temptation you offered. Your touch, your kiss, your mere presence called to me so strongly. I reveled in my fall. And now I'm paying a greater price than I dreamed imaginable." She swallowed and choked on her tears. "This is no longer just between the two of us. My father is right. The world does suffer when God's laws are broken."

Mark's expression was a portrait of rage. "What of the laws Abigail Lawrence is breaking? Where are her morals? Where is her propriety and duty? Or is it now proper and moral to pander one's daughter?" His eyes flashed with fury. "And what of my suffering? Suffering, in the face of which, you expect me to be noble and honorable. Suffering I'm supposed to bear over a lifetime with equanimity and grace." His voice grew harder with every word. "I'm not the bloody Savior, Passion. I'm a man. And I will not crucify myself on the altar of your morality!"

"Charlotte is innocent!"

Mark leapt to his feet and bent toward her. "Abigail Lawrence holds a knife at my throat, and that knife is

Charlotte. She is the tool of my torture, the prison I am confined to. I am enslaved by her pathetic existence."

Passion's misery streamed down her face.

"Don't you tell me she is innocent. She is as much a participant in this disgusting scheme as her mother and mine. I do *not* excuse her ignorance!"

Passion gasped as he grabbed her chin.

His eyes flashed. "And I will *not* give you up for her. Do you hear me? You are mine."

She stared up at him through her tears. "I am yours only when I give myself. You cannot take me."

"Can't I? I could do it now."

Oh, God! "You won't."

He spun away from her, and she closed her eyes with a sob.

His voice reached out to her. "Don't ever refer to what we've had together as a 'fall.' To do so is a greater sin than any other you believe we've committed."

Her insides twisted with regret. But when she looked for him, he was gone.

Her heart broke into a thousand pieces.

How would she ever find them? How would she gather them back together?

How would she ever be whole again?

Chapter Fourteen

INSISTENT RELATIVES

Mark rolled his completed plans for the new National Library and tied them with two dark green ribbons. Between them, he carefully dripped green sealing wax and then affixed the Hawkmore seal. With a brush and bit of gold paint, he put the finishing touches on his escutcheon. He stared down at the gold lion rampant upon a field of hunter green.

He was like the lion—forever rearing and raging. He'd been doing it his whole life. When would it end? When would his life finally cease to be a battle?

When Passion gave up her ludicrous ideals and accepted that they still belonged together. When she realized that she couldn't keep him away. When she understood that *they* were more important than the life of treachery and lies she would have him live.

She had to understand. She must!

He picked up the plans. Three weeks ago, they had meant more to him than anything. Yesterday, as Passion had admired the design and details he pointed out, her interest had made him feel proud and accomplished. He had believed her when she'd said he would get the commission.

Today, he didn't care.

He put the plans on a shelf.

"Are they finished?"

Mark turned to face his brother. "Yes." He pointed to the covered tray on the table by the window. "Your breakfast is over there."

Rubbing his hands together, Matt sat down and served himself a heaping plate of food.

"Mother doesn't rise till eleven," Matt commented, "and I hate to eat alone."

Mark took a seat opposite his brother and leaned on his fist. Matt's chin was varying shades of red, black, and blue. He'd told everyone at the dinner party he'd run into a door.

"Does that mean I should expect you every day? Your presence is becoming a habit."

Matt shrugged. "Your cook *is* excellent." He looked at Mark as he chewed and swallowed his bacon. "I'm sorry about last night. I spoke in anger. Your life is your own. You have responsibilities to your title, not the least of which are heirs. It is not my place to question you."

"Yes it is."

Matt smiled briefly, fingering his chin. "Well, perhaps not so vehemently." His face grew serious. "You're my brother, Mark, and I stand by you, whatever you do. If I step over the line, it's only because I care about you."

Mark's chest tightened. "I know."

Matt took a bite of his poached egg. "I apologized to Mother as well."

"She forgave you, of course."

"Yes."

"If I'd slapped her, she would have had me arrested for assault."

Matt nodded. "Probably." He put down his fork. "I'm sorry about it, Mark. It's that she sees so much of Father in you." Matt shook his head. "You know, when we were boys, that used to make me jealous."

Mark rubbed his temple. "What did you have to be jealous about? You had all her love."

"How she always used to say you were just like Father. Christ, she still says it. But she never said that about me." His dark eyes held Mark's. "I wanted to be like Father, too." He paused. "There was something between you and Father. As hard as I tried, I could never be a part of it."

Mark frowned. "What are you talking about? Father was good to you. Kind. He loved you."

"Did he? He never told me so."

Mark's frown deepened. His head was beginning to hurt. "I'm sure he did. You were only ten when he died. You probably just don't remember."

Matt shook his head. "No, I remember very well. He'd say, 'You're a good lad, Matt,' or 'Well done, Matt,' but never 'I love you, Matt.' "

His brother's thoughts looked far away.

"Once," he continued, "when I was practicing the cello, he stopped in the doorway to listen. He stayed for the whole piece. I was in heaven because you were in the next room, but he'd stopped to listen to me. I even played past the end so he would stay longer. When I finally finished, he came over and ruffled my hair. 'You've talent, lad,' he said. 'Don't ever quit. I love to hear you.' " Matt's focus returned to Mark. "So I haven't. I'll always play. Because if he didn't love me, then at least he loved my music."

Mark stared at his brother. He'd never felt his father's preference, never been aware of it. "He wasn't a man to voice his love, Matt, especially as things worsened between he and Mother. I remember that he said it only a few times to me."

"But he said it. Always when he thought I wasn't around. 'I love you, son,' he'd say to you. Then he'd put his arm around your shoulder. I observed it more than once, Mark. And there must have been times I didn't witness."

Jesus Christ! Under the circumstances, his father had been a paragon of fairness. "Maybe he told me because I didn't have a mother who would tell me. Maybe he told me because I didn't have a mother who would ever stop to watch me do anything, let alone ruffle my hair and offer me some kind words of encouragement. Forgive me, but I could recount a thousand worse ways that Mother slighted me while she poured her undying love upon you."

Matt regarded him for a long moment. "I only meant for you to know that Father belonged to you. I didn't think you realized it. I thought it might be a comfort to you in the face of Mother's favoritism."

Mark shoved his hands through his hair. Why did they keep having these disturbing conversations? "You think it comforts me to know that Father disappointed you? It doesn't. He was a good man, Matt. He tried to be fair. You'll just have to believe that."

"I do believe that, and I know he was a good man. That's why I wanted to be like him."

"You *are* like him. That's the irony, Matt. Mother always says I'm the one, but I'm not. You are. You're a reflection of all his best qualities. You're a man of honor, strength, and nobility."

"And you're not? You may not wear the qualities on your sleeve, but they're all in you."

Mark shook his head. "You believe in love and you'll fight for it. That's a trait of Father's I do not have."

Matt took a bite from his toast and looked at Mark as he chewed. "May I ask you? How is Passion?"

"Sick, crying, and unreasonable."

His brother shook his head. "Last night was a shock, even for me. I can only imagine what it was for the two of you."

Mark frowned. "Who could have guessed she would be related to those people?"

"What are you going to do now?"

"Convince her it doesn't matter."

Matt lifted his brows. "What?"

"I've explained the situation to her," Mark said. "She has only to accept my viewpoint."

"Ah, so you want her to remain your mistress while you marry and impregnate her cousin." Matt's fingers were white on his coffee cup. "Have I got it right?"

"Not exactly," Mark ground out.

"Oh, good. For a moment there, you had me concerned for your sanity."

"What's happened? Not three minutes ago, you said, 'I stand by you, whatever you do.'"

"I *am* on your side, which is why I have to convince you to do the bloody right thing." Matt leaned forward. "I would have walked out of the Lawrences' with you last night. But you chose to stay. You chose Charlotte. Fine. Then live with your decision."

"I won't let Passion go."

"You must!"

Mark leapt to his feet and walked away from the table. "This refrain is becoming tiresome."

"If you care at all for her, you'll release her."

Mark threw open his study door, but Matt followed. "Enough!"

"For Christ's sake, you're marrying her cousin!"

Mark started up the steps. If his brother followed, he'd be sorry.

There was a brief silence.

"You won't let her go, because you can't."

Mark paused with his foot on the next step.

"You can't stand the thought of living without her." The clock in the vestibule ticked. "Only it's too late for that."

Mark gripped the stair rail and felt his knees quake beneath him.

"Well, it isn't all up to you, is it? You think you can convince her to stay with you? I saw her. I saw her face. She's going to lock you out of her life."

Mark's body stiffened. Matt was wrong! Matt didn't know what they had. Passion would never abandon him. She was his. He would never let her go. Never!

"It's early for a call," Abigail said as Passion entered her fashionable parlor.

"Yes, forgive me."

"Be seated, Passion."

The sage green silk of her skirt sighed softly as she took a seat across from Abigail.

The woman's cold blue eyes moved over her slowly as a maid entered bearing a tray of punch and two glasses. Abigail frowned as the maid placed the tray. "Can't you get anything right? I asked for lemonade, not punch."

Before her mistress could observe it, the maid shot Abigail a brief but furious glance. "There were no lemons at the market, madam."

"I don't believe that, Anna. Pour the punch and leave. I will attend to you later."

Passion had never liked Charlotte's mother, but now slivers of loathing pierced the broken fragments of her heart. Abigail was horrible to absolutely everyone. And she was forcing Mark's hand into Charlotte's. It was a despicable, reprehensible act.

"You look like you barely slept," Abigail commented after the maid took her leave. "Really, Passion, it would have been better if you had stayed at home last night. I had to have the gutter washed down after you left."

Passion wished she could hold back her blush of embarrassment, but she couldn't. "My apologies, ma'am. My illness came upon me very suddenly. I never would have come had I felt unwell."

"Well, I hope you are completely recovered. It would be very rude of you to come calling if there were any chance of your infecting my house. Charlotte cannot afford to be sick right now."

The woman was rudeness personified. How did Charlotte tolerate her day after day? "I am entirely well, I assure you. I came to apologize for any disruption I caused last eve, and to speak with Charlotte."

"I'm glad you recognize the necessity for an apology, Passion. The whole evening was tainted by your hasty departure. My cousin kept worrying, all evening, that she might fall ill. Charlotte's fiancé, the earl, asked an inordinate number of questions about you. It was very distressing."

Now he knew her name and her relation to Charlotte. What else had he inquired about?

"May I speak with Charlotte, Mrs. Lawrence?"

Abigail shrugged. "Charlotte has begun taking her breakfast in her room. You may join her there, but do not stay long."

Passion stood. She wanted away from Abigail. "Very well, thank you."

The woman's hard voice held her at the entrance to the parlor. "Where is the shawl you wore last night? You should wear it with such a plain gown."

Passion turned. "It's a special piece, reserved for special occasions. And I prefer my gowns simple."

"Yes, well, you always wear the best fabrics. But you skimp on the trimmings, which is all too clear. However did you afford such a shawl? For a vicar, your father must be doing very well, indeed."

The woman was disgusting. "Father *is* doing very well. How gracious of you to enquire. His health is as hearty as ever, and he recently finished a wonderful essay on the merits of humility. Now, if you'll excuse me . . ."

Passion didn't wait for the woman's leave, but hurried up the stairs. She seethed as she climbed, and her eyes prickled with the tears she blinked back. How dare Abigail Lawrence behave as if she had a right to know anything and everything? Did her sense of entitlement spur her to engage in something as monstrous as blackmail? Did she think Mark's freedom and title were her due? Did she care that she was marrying Charlotte to a man who didn't want her?

Passion's stomach cramped. She knew all too well the sorrow of an indifferent marriage. The repercussions could be terrible.

As she stepped onto the landing, Passion drew up short. Just down the hall, one of the upstairs maids stood in the tight embrace of a tall lad with black hair. The young man's hand wandered down the maid's back and then cupped her bottom.

Passion sighed, and terrible pain and loss welled in her. She knew what it was to lean into Mark's firm embrace and feel the touch of his searching hand. But the sweetness of that embrace was closed to her forever.

Did the girl love the boy? Did he love her?

The maid pulled away with a giggle but then jumped when she saw Passion. Sudden fear filled her face. The lad looked unconcerned.

Passion forced a shaky smile to ease the poor girl. "It's all right," she said. "I'm just going to Miss Lawrence's room. If memory serves, it's at the end of the hall?"

The maid bobbed a curtsey and nervously straightened her cap. "Yes, miss."

The young man just leaned against the wall and hooked his thumbs in his pockets with a grin.

Passion turned her back on the couple and walked down the hall. She would never feel that breathless excitement again. She would never feel Mark again.

Pausing at Charlotte's door, she took a deep, steadying breath before she knocked.

Charlotte's call for admittance was slow in coming. Passion eased open the door only to find her cousin huddled in the middle of her bed, her breakfast untouched on a tray.

"Oh, thank God it's you!" Charlotte exclaimed. "I was afraid it was a summons from Mother."

Passion frowned as she closed the door. Dark circles shadowed Charlotte's gray eyes, and her cheeks and lips were pale. "Are you all right, darling?"

Charlotte smiled briefly. "Now that you're here, I'm

better. Oh, Passion, I'm so glad to see you. Come and sit."
Charlotte shoved aside the tray to make room for her.

Passion felt her cousin's forehead as she sat on the side
of the bed. "You don't feel feverish. But you look like you
need sleep."

"So do you," Charlotte observed. "I was so concerned
for you last night. Are you well?"

Passion lowered her eyes for a moment. When would
she feel well again? "You mustn't worry, darling. I'm
completely well." She lifted her eyes to Charlotte—sweet
Charlotte, who was innocent and knew nothing.

Sorrow, envy, remorse, and shame all boiled up in Passion. She would be facing none of this if she had behaved
as a proper, moral woman. It was her self-indulgence, her
defiant rejection of what she knew to be right, that had
brought her to this moment.

"I'm so sorry about everything, Charlotte. I hope you
know I would never knowingly hurt you."

Charlotte frowned. "Mother spoke to you, didn't she?
You mustn't mind her, Passion. She believes every unin-
tended accident, including illness, is a personal affront to
her. Every little thing that doesn't go as she plans infuri-
ates her." She shook her head. "You should have heard her
last night. She enraged the earl and his brother so much
that they almost left." Her eyes filled with tears. "I don't
know what would have happened had they gone, Passion.
If the earl backs out of our engagement, I'll be ruined. I
don't have the social status or birth to weather a scandal
unscathed, and there's no doubt that an earl breaking off
with a commoner after a shockingly brief courtship and
engagement period would cause a huge scandal. People
will assume I proved unsuitable. I'll be a social exile—
cast-off goods, interesting only to those who are in desperate need of my money."

Passion wrapped her arms around her cousin. It was
true. Mark couldn't break off this engagement. But could
she really blame him for trying? What of his life? She
rubbed Charlotte's back. "But he didn't leave, darling,"

she offered. "He stayed. He stayed when he could have left."

"Yes," Charlotte said as she drew back from Passion's embrace. "And he did say that he was staying for me. I think he, and his brother, too, understand that I'm not like Mother. I told them I wasn't. And in this last week, I have been trying to stand up to her more."

Passion pushed a chestnut curl back from Charlotte's face. "There, you see."

Charlotte's face fell. "But Passion, he hasn't shown me one shred of warmth since the evening at the pavilion. The countess treats me with utter disdain, unless we're in public, where she puts on a show of adoring me. And Mother is just getting worse and worse. She finds fault with everything and berates the household staff constantly." Her gray eyes filled with tears. "She and the countess snap at each other like vipers. And the earl's brother, who is one of the kindest men I've ever met, looked like he might strike her last night." Charlotte hid her face in her hands. "Oh, Passion, I wanted him to do it. I wanted him to hit my mother. I'm awful, I know, but I can't help it."

Passion closed her eyes. She would have wanted it, too. "You are not awful, Charlotte. Sometimes situations arise that make it almost impossible to keep charitable thoughts. At those times, we can only ask God's forgiveness and resolve to be better."

Charlotte clasped Passion's hands. "You always have charitable thoughts. You always do the right thing. I wish I could be more like you."

Passion's stomach hurt. She squeezed her cousin's fingers. "Nothing could be further from the truth. I've had many an ill thought, and I've made decisions that have led me down the wrong path."

Charlotte shook her head. "I think terrible thoughts every day, Passion. You don't know what it's like. Mother has always been difficult and critical, but since the earl's proposal, she's unbearable. Just last night, she fired a servant who has been with our household for ten years!

That's why I escape to you and Aunt Matty whenever I can. Do you know how many times I've thought of packing my things and coming to you?" Her gaze grew sadder. "Even as a girl, I used to dream of coming to live with you at the vicarage. I would be another sister to you, and your father would talk to me in his quiet, firm voice. And no one would yell at me anymore or think everything I did was wrong."

"Oh, Charlotte . . ." Passion said softly.

Her cousin looked at her with such sorrow. "I hate her, Passion. I do. Some days, I wish she were dead."

Passion pulled Charlotte back into her embrace. What could she say to such an admission? Nothing. "It's all right, darling," she whispered. "It's all right."

Charlotte clung to her for a long time.

How vicious a circle was hate. And now she was drawn into it as well. Finally, Charlotte spoke. "I'm so glad you came today. Do you know, if it weren't for you, I don't know what I would do. You are always such a comfort to me. Come again tomorrow, won't you? Please, Passion."

Passion squeezed her eyes shut and took a deep breath. "Charlotte, darling, I came here today to say good-bye."

Charlotte pulled back, dismay written across her face. "What? No! No, please, you can't go." She grabbed Passion's hands. "I need you now. You're my only solace. There's no one I can turn to but you."

Passion's stomach lurched. She couldn't stay, she couldn't! "Darling, I—I'm just so homesick. And you know how Aunt Matty is. She believes the remedy for everything is more activity." She struggled to smile. "And try as I might, I can't seem to rid myself of Alfred Swittly."

Tears spilled down Charlotte's face. "I beg you to stay, Passion! In one week, it will be time to go to Hawkmore House. I must be presented to my new household and all the local gentry before the wedding." Her pretty mouth twisted into a grimace. "I need you there. With a fiancé who hardly acknowledges me, the countess who barely tolerates me, and my mother who constantly humiliates me, I won't survive it—not without you. Please, come with me!"

Passion frowned as pain stabbed her temples. Ten days in Mark's house. Ten days of Mark's powerful insistence that they remain together. How would *she* ever survive?

She would need to protect herself. She would need her sisters. And she would have to talk with Mark—he needed to understand that her decision was final. It all seemed too difficult.

Yet how could she abandon Charlotte? And what if Mark found the letter? Then *he* would abandon Charlotte. Might she prevent that?

"Please, Passion," Charlotte pleaded. "Your family is already invited to the wedding. Send for Patience and Prim early. Have them meet us at Hawkmore House. Your father, too, if you want. Many people are arriving early. Two or three more will be nothing. But to have you there, to have all of you there, would be everything to me." Her gray eyes swam with tears. "Please, Passion. Please."

Passion lowered her gaze. Could she do it? Could she convince him? Mark cared for her, that much she knew. Could she persuade him to stay with Charlotte? Was *her* influence powerful enough?

Her chest hurt with the weight of the burden.

She blinked back her own tears before lifting her eyes to Charlotte. "Very well, darling. If you need me, if I can be of some help to you, then I must stay, mustn't I?"

Charlotte threw herself against Passion. "Thank you! Thank you!"

Passion shuddered at the uncertainty of her new resolve. "I must write to Patience and Prim right away," she murmured. "Right away."

She would need her sisters. They would buffer her in the storm to come.

Anxiety and doubt strummed her nerves painfully.

She clung to Charlotte.

Was she strong enough to push the man she loved into the arms of her cousin?

She closed her eyes.

And would he hate her for it?

"Where the hell is it?" Mark growled.

He stood up from behind his desk as Mickey Wilkes entered the room.

The boy shook his head. "She's hid it right well, she 'as. But you knows me, milord. If'n it can be found, I's'll find it."

"Then why haven't you?"

"Truth is, milord, I 'spected to by now. But she's a clever ol' bitch, she is." He scratched his chin. "Ain't in any o' the usual places."

Mark leaned forward and ground his knuckles into the desktop. "Then you must look in the unusual places."

"Yeah." Mickey nodded. "I know." The boy squinted his eyes thoughtfully. "'Ere's the thing, milord. There be a lot o' whisperin' and gossipin' 'mongst the ser'ants. A'-most seems like they got themsel'es some sort o' secret. An I's won'erin' if'n it don't 'ave some'in t'do wit yer let-ter."

Mark's heart pounded. "If so, then they must know where it is."

Mickey nodded. "They might. I just won me way under the skirts o' the upstairs maid. She be a sweet girl, but not real smart. So if'n she knows some'in, I should know it, too, in a few fucks."

Mark opened his desk drawer and, picking up a leather purse, heaved it at Mickey. "What are you waiting for? Get back to work."

The coins clinked, and Mickey grinned as he weighed the purse in his hand. "My thanks to ye, milord."

"Don't thank me yet. If you don't find that letter, I'll have to kill you."

Mickey looked speculatively at Mark and then smiled. "You wouldn'a do that, milord."

Mark shoved back his hair. "Perhaps not. But if I kill myself, you won't get paid. So get that bloody letter."

Mickey grinned. "Righto, milord."

Flipping his cap onto his head, the boy turned to go.

"And Mickey," Mark called. "The unusual places—look in all the unusual places."

Mickey winked. "I's the king o' unusual, milord. The emperor o' unusual, I am. The—"

"Go!" Mark ordered.

After the boy had sauntered from the room, Mark collapsed back into his chair.

He needed that letter.

It was time for this farce to end. He was sick of the lies. And if he had to endure another lecture from his brother, he was in danger of breaking something. He didn't want that something to be Matthew's jaw.

Mark rubbed his forehead. When he had the letter, he would be free. Free to pursue Passion—free to convince her to stay with him. She was all he wanted. He knew that now. Her presence magnified everything wonderful and diminished everything terrible. With her he felt happy, alive. He would never give her up. *Never!*

But what of heirs?

He pushed away the thought.

His head hurt. And he was so tired.

Although his bed had always been a place of peaceful slumber in the past, last night, it had been a rack of torture upon which he had tossed and turned restlessly until dawn.

It was the first night he hadn't slept with Passion since coming to her room. He missed the warmth of her curled beside him. He missed the smell of her. He missed her touch and the feel of her in his arms.

He missed *her.*

His eyes stung, so he closed them.

Everything was amiss.

Everything.

Chapter Fifteen

PUNISHING MARK

"Were I directing this production, Mrs. Redington, I would cast you in the role of Bianca, so sweet is your disposition," Alfred Swittly declared as the lights went up for intermission on *The Taming of the Shrew*.

He mopped his brow with his handkerchief, and Passion wondered if his theater seat wasn't pinching him terribly.

"Yet the shrewish Kate turns out to be the better wife," John Crossman interjected.

"Oh, Mr. Crossman, don't tell the end!" Aunt Matty exclaimed.

"A thousand pardons, Mistress Dare."

Aunt Matty looked at the crowd as people rose from their seats. "I simply must move about," she said. "However, my poor toe is sure to be trod upon, and I simply couldn't bear that again. Perhaps I might lean upon your arm, Mr. Swittly. A man of your stature will surely prevent my being bumped and jostled."

Alfred glanced reluctantly at Passion. "Well, I—"

Aunt Matty took Alfred's arm. "Mr. Crossman, do take

Passion beneath your protective wing, won't you?" She turned, pulling Alfred with her. "Oh!" She glanced back. "There's one of those treacherous palm trees just at the exit, here. So, everyone, mind your eyes." She turned to Alfred as they stepped into the aisle. "Did I mention, Mr. Swittly, that Passion was nearly blinded by a palm frond? They are really very dangerous. I think they ought to be banned from all public places. Don't you?"

Passion shared a small smile with John Crossman as they, too, moved into the crowded aisle.

He looked at her for a moment. "How are you feeling?" he asked softly.

"I'm well, thank you."

A small frown puckered his brow, but he nodded. "Mrs. Redington, if there is any way I may be of service to you, I hope you will allow me."

Passion looked into his vivid green eyes. The night before, in his coach, he had held her while she wept upon his shoulder. "Thank you, Mr. Crossman. But you have already been of the greatest help to me. Had you not been there last night, I don't know what I would have done. I'm so grateful to you for your graciousness." She lowered her eyes. "I'm afraid you've seen me at my worst."

"I would rather be with you at your worst, than with some people at their best."

Passion smiled. "You are a kind man."

He looked down at her. "Kind, gracious, grateful. Those aren't exactly the words I was hoping for."

She frowned. Did he think her insincere? "You have become a good friend to me." She put her hand atop his arm. "I hope you know I honor our friendship by speaking only from my heart."

He looked at her hand upon his arm. "I know." His smile did not reach his eyes as it usually did. He nodded. "I know."

Aunt Matty and Alfred had turned and awaited them.

Alfred put his huge hand over his heart. "Forgive me,

Mrs. Redington, but you look like a rare flower in that rose-colored gown."

"I wasn't aware that a rose could claim rarity as one of its attributes, Mr. Swittly." She smiled to soften the sting of her words.

"Your lovely face rarifies the color, Mrs. Redington."

The man was quick with a response, that was certain.

"Tell us, what do you think of the play?" Alfred inquired. "I have a particular fondness for Petruchio. Such a jolly and wily fellow. I do believe I could play his role splendidly."

Passion looked at Alfred. He probably would be perfect for the role. She frowned as a thought came to her. "Have you never considered taking the stage, Mr. Swittly? You seem so well suited to it."

The man's eyes lit up. "Do you think so, Mrs. Redington? The truth is, I have considered it."

"I happen to know that his aunts are not in agreement with such a pursuit," Aunt Matty said, shaking her head.

A little of the light faded from Alfred's expression. "Unfortunately, it is not a profession that affords a stable living. A man must make his fortune in the world."

"Some men are destined for fame, not fortune," John offered.

Alfred puffed up and stood a little taller.

"Besides," John continued, "fortune often follows fame."

Passion nodded. Let him pursue the stage rather than her.

Aunt Matty frowned and wagged her finger. "Your aunts would not approve of this, Mr. Swittly."

Alfred's face was all excitement. "I am merely giving the idea some thought, Mistress Dare. A man must, after all, follow his destiny."

"Destiny is a powerful force." The low voice came from behind Passion.

Her stomach flipped, and her legs trembled as she turned.

Mark held her in his blue gaze. "Some things are meant to be—and ought not be resisted." His eyes moved over her. "Do you agree, Mrs. Redington?"

Passion could hear her blood rushing in her ears and, God help her, her nipples tingled and tightened. "I—I do not pretend to understand the complexities of destiny, my lord. I can only say that people must follow their hearts, their minds, and their morals and hope that what they do is right."

"I couldn't agree more," Mark said. He turned and moved between Passion and John. "Good evening, Mr. Crossman."

John bowed his head. "Good evening, my lord."

Passion made the introductions for the rest of the group. Mark stood so close she could smell him. She longed to touch him.

He bowed to Aunt Matty, who was aflutter with excitement, and nodded to Alfred, who had turned red from collar to hairline.

"I—I—that is to say, forgive me, my lord," Alfred stammered. "Had I—had I known who you were at the Crystal Palace, I would not have addressed you so harshly." Alfred dabbed his brow with his handkerchief. "I should tell you that I came to regret my actions that day and wished that I might have the opportunity to meet you again, so that I might convey those regrets." Alfred smiled. "But I despaired of the opportunity ever occurring." He held his handkerchief to his chest and bowed his head. "I'm just grateful that it has."

"I do not require your apology, sir," Mark said stiffly. "Mrs. Redington is the one who merits your regrets." Mark arched a brow. "As I'm certain you have already voiced them to her, I have no further quarrel with you."

Alfred glanced worriedly at Passion while Aunt Matty looked confused.

John stepped forward and frowned at his cousin. "To what is the earl referring?"

"If I may?" Passion interjected. "It was an unfortunate misunderstanding that does not bear repeating."

Alfred nodded vigorously. "Mrs. Redington is correct. And in the words of the bard, *all's well that ends well.*"

While John engaged Mark about a measure coming before the House of Lords and Aunt Matty and Alfred listened attentively, Passion tried to calm her nerves and quiet her heart.

She stared at the relaxed curve of his gloved hand. Yesterday, she might have briefly slipped her hand into the warmth of his. He would have stroked her palm with his long fingers.

And if they had been alone, she would have stepped into his embrace and lay her head against his chest—closing her eyes as she listened to the steady beat of his heart. He would have held her close while he pressed his lips to her brow and then to her mouth. And she might have breathed, *I love you,* because her heart was so full and the words would no longer be contained.

She swallowed the lump in her throat.

But that was yesterday.

Now it was going to be like this. Near, but never touching. Wanting, but never having. Feeling, but never acknowledging.

"Passion, Aunt Matty!"

Turning with a smile, to hide the shine of unshed tears, Passion faced Charlotte and Mark's brother. She quickly hugged her cousin. "Hello, darling."

"I'm so glad you're here," Charlotte whispered before withdrawing.

Passion forced her smile to remain as everyone was introduced. She could feel both Mark's and Matthew's gaze upon her.

"We're here with the countess and Mother," Charlotte said. "We're going to the Pavillion after the play. A new orchestra from Austria will be playing this evening." She looked quickly and nervously at Mark and then said, "Why don't all of you join us there?"

Passion sucked in her breath. *Dear God, no!*

Mark looked at her.

Matthew looked at Mark.

Aunt Matty and Alfred spoke over each other in their eagerness to accept.

John looked at her with a hopeful smile. "Would you like to, Mrs. Redington?"

"Please, Passion," Charlotte begged.

Passion's head pounded. She wanted to run.

"Have you forgotten that your cousin was ill last night?" Mark said icily. "Do not press her."

An uncomfortable silence fell over the group, but it gave Passion a brief moment to gather her wits. "Thank you, my lord, for your concern." She smiled. "Charlotte knows, however, that I am quite recovered. We would be delighted to join you."

Only after the bells had summoned the guests back into the theater—and she had taken her seat between Alfred and John, the lights had dimmed, and the play had begun—did Passion let herself fall apart.

She fell silently and internally, with barely the flutter of an eyelash or the twitch of a finger.

Just as during her marriage, no one would see, no one would know.

But inside, she fell as she had never fallen before. She wailed and groveled beneath the weight of her emotions—emotions that were a hundred times more devastating than those she had suffered while she was married.

That experience had numbed her.

What would this do?

How long could she stand the pain?

How long before the scream inside became too loud to contain?

Mark watched Passion whirl across the dance floor with John Crossman. He hated the sight of the other man's hand on her waist. He hated the easy familiarity they seemed to share.

Most of all, he hated having to pretend that Passion didn't mean anything to him. He was dying to take her in his arms, dying to shout to the world that she was his. To stand there passively, acting as though they were no more than mere acquaintances, was almost more than he could endure.

Somehow, it was the worst lie of all.

"You mustn't stare at her so much," Matt said quietly. "Mother is watching you."

Mark frowned but kept his eyes on Passion.

His mother and Lawrence had been appalled that Charlotte had invited such lowly guests into their company—guests of whom they would never have approved. However, Charlotte had remained surprisingly resolute in her insistence and, for once, he had supported her. Since arriving, his mother and Lawrence had remained unsurprisingly rude and dismissive, though it was clear they both took particular notice of Passion. Lawrence's snide comments indicated jealousy, his mother's, suspicion.

He just wanted her—desperately.

"In about two weeks, she is going to be related to you by marriage," Matt continued. "You're going to have to learn to see her as nothing more than a distant cousin."

A chill moved down Mark's spine. He turned to his brother and spoke in a low, tight voice. "And how shall I do that, Matt? How shall I teach my body not to yearn for her, when the very scent of her makes me hard? How shall I force her from my mind when every memory of her is a joy? How shall I treat her as some inconsequential relation, when every fiber of my being cries out for her?" Mark tried to slow his heart. "How, Matt? How shall I do that?"

Matt just stared at him. "I don't know," he murmured. "I don't either."

The music ended, and Mark crossed the dance floor before John Crossman could lead Passion off.

She lowered her eyes as she saw him approaching. He hated that. He wanted her to look at him as she had before.

"May I have the next dance, Mrs. Redington?"

She paused for a moment, and his shoulders tensed as he thought she might actually refuse him.

But then she nodded. "Yes, my lord."

John Crossman bowed and put Passion's gloved hand into Mark's.

He drew a deep breath as he closed his fingers around hers. It was right. He remembered the first time he had held her hand at the Crystal Palace. It had been right then and it still was.

As the music began, he swept her into the curve of his arm and pulled her close. She kept her eyes lowered, but he was ecstatic just to hold her.

He breathed vanilla and orange blossoms and, beneath that sweet fragrance, he breathed the sweeter smell of her—Passion's skin, Passion's hair—the scent that still clung, in traces, to the pillow he had clutched during the previous night.

He danced with her to the far side of the dance floor. He wanted to look at her and touch her in a way that was the truth—no pretense, no lies.

He splayed his hand across the gentle curve of her lower back. "You can look at me now," he said softly. "They can't see us."

"Other people can. We are on public display. Besides, it no longer matters if they are near or far," she replied. "There is no screen that can shield us anymore."

He frowned as he turned her. "What do you mean?"

She finally raised her eyes to his. Such beautiful eyes. "I mean that we cannot hide from ourselves."

"I have no desire to do so."

"Yes, you do." She implored him with her eyes as they moved blindly to the waltz. "Oh, Mark, don't you see?" Her voice shook. "We can never be together again. Never."

Stunned and brittle with tension, he felt his chest constrict. "I explained everything to you last night. I came to you and I explained everything."

"Yes"—her fingers tightened on his shoulder and her eyes closed briefly—"and I loathe the horrible circumstances that are forcing us apart. With all my heart, I do. But, Mark, knowing them changes nothing."

She's going to lock you out of her life. Terrible foreboding crept across Mark's skin. It made him want to claw out of it. "How can you say that? How can you say that when you know I only want to be with you?"

"Do you think I don't want to be with you?" Her eyes welled with tears. "Do you think this isn't destroying me?"

He clung to a shred of hope. "Then don't throw us away. I'm going to have the letter soon. I can feel it, Passion. And then this whole charade of lies can end." The music played on. "I want you. I need you."

She lowered her eyes again. "What we want is no longer relevant. Despite what we want, despite the letter, my cousin will be ruined if you leave her. I cannot be part of that."

Mark tried to breathe. His chest was so tight. "I told you everything. I told you everything, trusting that you would understand. Trusting that you would want to thwart Lawrence's vile evil as much as I. Trusting that you would not abandon us."

"I can do nothing else," she whispered.

"And when I get the letter? What then? You will still refuse me?"

She looked at him. "Get the letter if you can. You should have it, Mark. But your having the letter will change nothing for me. The die was cast when the engagement was announced." She shook her head. "If you abandon my cousin to shame, I will never see you again."

The music swelled. His head was aching. If he could just breathe. "You say that now, in my arms. But how will you bear the nights and days?" He drew her closer as he whirled her across the floor. "What will you do when your body cries out for satisfaction? Now that you have found pleasure, it will pursue you, burning and relentless."

Anger and anxiety pumped in his veins. "What will you do? Find someone else? No one can satisfy you as I do. No one."

"I know," Passion gasped. "I know." Her eyes were full of anguish. "But shall I weep for joy and cry out my pleasure in your arms while my cousin sobs into her pillow in shame because the Earl of Langley has thrown her away?"

Mark's heart pounded with fury and fear. He grasped at a final, weak straw. "I'll send it out that she left me."

"Stop!" The word came on a choked whisper. Passion's lip trembled as she looked at him. "No one will believe that, Mark. And what of Charlotte? There is no excuse you can give her that would not be the worst rejection." Tender misery dimmed her eyes, yet her body leaned into his. "There is nothing to be done. Nothing."

He stared into her tormented gaze, and a sharp pain cracked inside him. He winced as it sundered his gut and fissured down his limbs. His head throbbed and Passion blurred for a moment before his stinging eyes. "Why did you come here tonight?" he managed. "Why?"

"To tell you these things."

"Here?" His voice caught. "On a goddamn dance floor?"

"Where else, Mark?" Her eyes implored him for understanding. "Where else? My window is locked. And so it must remain." Her fingers tightened around his. "I thought it best . . ."

He squeezed her hand—her hand, which belonged in his. How could she do this? How could she? "You thought it best? I do not. I thought when you heard the circumstances, when you had time to consider them, you would recognize the injustice of what you demand of me. I thought you would realize the impossibility of parting." He blinked. "Instead, you denounce us. And you sentence me to as horrid and indifferent a marriage as your own. Why don't you tell me how to live with that, Passion? Because I don't know how."

Her frown was pained. "Charlotte will care for you, if you let her. She wants to care for you."

The music was ebbing. "I do not want her care." He felt sick—sick and angry as something horrible and inexorable washed over him. "I do not want any of this."

"Mark, I—"

"Say nothing more." He shook his head. "You have punished me enough. I beg you, say nothing more."

As the music came to an end, Mark held Passion a moment longer, felt her a moment longer, before bowing over her hand. He didn't want to let her go, didn't want to release his hold on her. If he did, something calamitous would occur.

Tucking her arm in his, he walked slowly back to their party. He moved as a mourner in a funeral procession, briefly holding back the inevitability of looking into the cavernous depth that is the final farewell. But with each step he took, he felt more and more as if he were marching toward his own tomb.

He saw their faces—his mother, Lawrence, Charlotte, his brother—participants all, knowing or unknowing, in his demise.

And yet he kept walking, deeper and deeper into the shadow they cast, until it covered him completely. Cold gloom seeped through him as Passion's arm slipped from his, and as her fingers slid from his sleeve, happiness and hope were extinguished.

Everything went dark.

The funeral was his own.

Passion stared at the unfinished image of her cousin upon the canvas. The late morning light in Aunt Matty's sunroom was dimmer than usual, and rain splashed the windows. She could hear the drops hitting the glass with an ebbing and flowing intensity.

Perhaps it was the gray light of the day that seemed to bring Charlotte's gray eyes to life. Perhaps it was the dim mood of the weather that enhanced the subtle sweetness, sorrow, and uncertainty that they reflected.

Passion looked at the brush in her fingers. Or was the credit all her own? Had the pain of her shattered heart moved her hand and guided her strokes to a new depth? Was it her own sorrow and uncertainty that allowed her to capture her cousin's poignancy so well?

She closed her eyes.

Or was it love?

"Passion, darling, you have a visitor," her aunt called.

Passion's eyes flew open at the tone of her aunt's voice. It was someone unexpected.

Mark?

As she stared at the entrance to the sunroom, Aunt Matty stepped in, followed by none other than the Countess of Langley.

Passion stiffened with dislike. She'd seen enough of the countess the night before to form an ill opinion of her. Still, she stood and met the countess's chilly gaze. The woman strode past Aunt Matty, who remained near the door with a cool expression of her own.

"The countess would like to speak with you privately, my dear. Shall I have some refreshment brought?"

Passion looked at Mark's mother. "That depends upon how long the countess will be staying."

"Not long" came the cold reply.

Passion nodded to her aunt, who scowled at the countess's back. "Then we shall require nothing. Thank you, Aunt Matty."

Passion waited for her aunt to close the double doors of the sunroom before removing her painting smock. Then she indicated a chair. "May I offer you a seat, Countess?"

Mark's mother sat with an elegant swish of violet satin.

Smoothing her own gown of pink, black, and cream-striped silk, Passion took the chair beside her. "To what do I owe this surprising visit, my lady?"

The countess's beautiful but cold green eyes held her. "I came to warn you."

Passion folded her hands in her lap. "Warn me? About what?"

"We are women who take our pleasure, Mrs. Redington. Let's not pretend that we don't understand each other."

A pang of genuine loathing reverberated through Passion, but she kept her expression blank.

The countess looked incredulous. "I saw your face when you were introduced to my son at the Lawrences'. Fortunately, Matthew and I were the only ones who saw you. And then there was last night. Do you think it isn't obvious to me?" She raised her perfectly arched brows. "You're my son's latest fuck."

Passion's stomach clenched at the woman's words, but she remained impassive. "You said you were here to warn me, my lady. Are you going to do so?"

The countess smiled. "Don't try to act unaffected, Mrs. Redington." She leaned forward. "I told you. I saw your face."

Passion couldn't quite manage a smile of her own.

"Really, Mrs. Redington, I admire your gumption in embarking upon an affair with a man about whom you obviously knew little. But in the end, it wasn't very smart, was it?"

"I'm going to ask you to leave," Passion said, "so if you have anything of purpose to say, I suggest you do so now."

The countess leaned back in her chair. "Stay away from my son and your cousin."

"I will not."

"What do you mean, you will not?" She frowned. "He's having a difficult enough time accepting the loss of bachelorhood without your stirring the pot. And I am trying to do you a service as well, Mrs. Redington. You don't know my son the way I do."

Passion shook her head. "No. I do not. And you do not know him the way I do."

The countess leaned forward again. "You listen to me,

you little tart. My son has never fucked one woman for more than a few months. Soon he will lose interest in you completely. Your time is short." She lifted her chin. "You mean nothing to him."

No. The word echoed in Passion's head. Though he, himself, had said similar words when they first met, now they sounded hollow and false.

She remembered the way he looked at her, the way he touched her, the things he had said to her on their final day together. She remembered the tears that had welled in his eyes the night before.

He cared about her.

Deeply.

"Let's not pretend that we don't understand each other, Countess," Passion said with sudden strength. "You're here because you're worried that Mark will *not* lose interest in me. You're here because you have no idea what is between your son and me." Passion nodded with clear conviction. "You're here because you are afraid of what you cannot understand."

The countess laughed, but Passion could hear the strain.

"Really, Mrs. Redington, you're very amusing. I'm here to save us all, your nitwit cousin included, from the public humiliation that would befall us should your nasty little affair with my son get out."

Passion stared. How incredibly staggering that she could speak of nasty little affairs when she had embroiled them all in the consequences of her own.

"I feared that you would not see reason, Mrs. Redington," the countess continued. She opened her purse. "So I am prepared to pay you." She held out a cheque written for five thousand pounds.

Passion did not move a finger. "Do you know, Countess, you remind me a great deal of Abigail Lawrence."

The cheque fluttered in her hand. "What?"

Why did she feel so serene in the face of this bribery? "Yes, it's true. You and she both try to bend people to your will. Doesn't it become tiresome, always forcing people's arms behind their backs?" Passion's frown deepened. "And what will happen when you no longer have the strength, or the beauty, or the power to get what you want? How will you live?"

The countess snatched back her hand and stuffed the note into her bag. "I see you cannot be reasoned with."

"On the contrary, I can be reasoned with. I just cannot be bought."

The countess's face twisted into an unattractive sneer. "If you don't stay away, I'll tell your simpering little cousin you've been fucking her fiancé."

Passion felt no fear. "Blackmail, Countess?" She shook her head. "Oh, you really are another Abigail Lawrence."

The woman's eyes narrowed. "Just what do you know?"

Passion ignored her question and kept her voice even. "Now you listen to me, Countess. I have promised my cousin that I will stay by her, so she might better tolerate your loathsome presence. I have promised *myself* that I will help your son, in any way I can, to accept my cousin." She leaned forward. "So, if you want this marriage to proceed as planned, then you stay out of my way."

The countess stared at her incredulously for a moment. Then a smile spread across her face and she burst into laughter. "You've left him!" she exclaimed. "That's why he was so incredibly awful last night!"

Passion's pain flared anew.

The countess leaned back in her chair and held her hand to her chest as she chuckled. "You know, he left right after you. But not before laying into all of us. I was sure you had begged him to dissolve his engagement." She shook her head and looked gleeful. "Well, if this isn't the perfect turnabout. It's high time he was the one walked out upon."

How could a woman, a mother, be this hateful?

She smiled at Passion. "In a way, I actually predicted

this. Though I didn't really believe it at the time, I told him you would tire of him."

Passion wanted to slap the smile right off her face. "Why would you say something you didn't believe?"

The countess leveled her eyes on Passion. "To punish him, of course."

"And why must you punish him?"

"Because he is his father's son, and he has been punishing me for a lifetime."

"Really?" Passion's throat tightened. "A lifetime? How does a babe punish his mother?"

"I'll tell you how," she snapped. "By stealing her youth. By making her grotesque with fat and discomfort until she is forced into confinement. By making her shriek with pain while he forces his overlarge body from hers. And then, by crying, and crying, and crying." Her voice rose with each repetition. "By clinging to you and clawing at you, when all you want is to get away." Her gaze grew distant. "When he could walk, he began to chase after me. I would run away. And then, when Matthew was born—my darling, easy Matthew—he tried to get between us. Hold *me,* Mummy. Carry *me,* Mummy. Kiss *me,* Mummy. Me! Me! Me! The brat. I sent him away and told him that until he learned to say 'please,' I would do nothing for him." She closed her eyes and her frown deepened. "Then it was please, please, please—all the time please. I came to hate the word."

Passion blinked back her tears. "It must gratify you, then, that he never says it now."

"Doesn't he?" The countess looked at her. "You weep for him. But you should weep for me. A woman's youth is fleeting, Mrs. Redington, her beauty brief. Once it is gone, it cannot be reclaimed."

"Neither can childhood."

"I tell you, I was not ready to be a mother!" the countess snapped. She squared her shoulders and took a deep breath. "Besides, he doesn't even remember his infancy. I, however, remember the theft of my youth—only too well."

"He doesn't need to remember. Your dislike and disdain for him is clear. In one evening, I could see that you favor Matthew over him."

"And what of his dislike and disdain for me, Mrs. Redington? He is rude and insufferable, yet you say nothing of that."

"You began it, Countess. You are his mother." Passion's voice caught in her throat. "All a child ever wants is love."

"You weren't there. You don't know how it was—his father always trying to foist him upon me, when I had my hands full with Matthew. My dear, Matthew, who was easy and sweet-natured from the beginning." The countess raised her chin. "Matthew is *my* son. The son *I* chose by my own decisions. For that alone, I will always favor him."

Passion shook her head. "Would that Mark had been able to chose a mother as you chose a son."

The countess's face became a cold mask. "I must be going."

"Yes, you must."

She stood, but Passion did not stand with her. The countess left without another word.

Passion broke into sobs.

Why? God, why?

Why must she be the one to punish Mark yet again?

In the wet stillness of his garden, Mark stood by the fountain and blinked back the cold rain that drenched him. He stared at the statue of Aphrodite. He had chosen her for the loveliness of her face, the grace of her figure, and for the way her hair fell down her back in waves.

The workmen had come that morning to begin digging the pipes. He had sent them away. He no longer wanted it connected.

But rain had filled the shallow tiers and so it appeared

to run nonetheless. Water fell from the top to the middle and then from the middle into the bottom. Would it overflow?

It didn't matter.

Lifting his hand, he looked down at the brass hairpin that lay in his palm. Water splashed upon the small seed-pearl flower that decorated the top.

He had handed Passion the pins, one by one, as she had coiled her beautiful hair at her nape. He had watched her place each one, had smoothed an errant strand.

He had laughed with her. He had detained her with kisses and caresses.

That day had been the happiest of his life.

Water fell from his palm into the fountain.

Every man ought to have one truly happy day. Just one.

His hand trembled.

It was over. Done. Finished.

He closed his fingers around the pin.

A murky chill ran through his veins.

He had lived without happiness before. He could do it again.

He could.

He blinked back the rain and let the small bit of bent brass fall into the fountain.

He turned and forced himself down the path. He watched the rain spatter the ground before him.

He had lived without her before. He could live without her again.

The pain would pass, and all would be as it was.

Rain ran into his eyes. His legs shook and slowly stopped moving.

The heavy drops pelted him. Thunder rolled somewhere far away.

Lies! All lies!

Nothing would ever be as it was before.

He turned and hurried back to the fountain. The rain fell so hard upon the water that he couldn't see anything beneath. Where was it? He thrust his hands into the chilly pool and felt for the pin.

Nothing. Where was it? Where?

His heart pounded, and a choked grunt escaped him as he felt across the smooth bottom. What if it had fallen into one of the drains?

Anxiety coursed through him.

Where was it? He needed it!

Then his fingers brushed something. The pearl flower!

With a relieved moan he closed his hand over the small piece of bent metal and drew it from the water.

He looked at it anxiously. So lovely, so delicate.

Closing his hand protectively around it, he kissed the top of his clenched fist.

His shaking legs would not hold him. He dropped to the wide ledge of the fountain and sat.

His breath came in heaves.

No. Nothing would *ever* be as it was before—because he loved her.

Chapter Sixteen

DECLARATIONS

From beneath the shade of her wide-brimmed straw hat, Passion gazed across the smooth lake at a lovely rotunda. A place where one might enjoy tea or a little music, it was one of the focal points of the grounds at Hawkmore House. Trees in graduated heights framed the view.

A Romanesque bridge had brought her to the place she now stood. It was quiet and peaceful, the only sound being the occasional twitter of birds. The sky hung clear and blue above her, and the air was still.

The grounds were the most beautiful she had ever seen, grounds to inspire joy and serenity. In the next few days, the sound of voices and laughter would filter across the lake and sprawling lawns, as wedding guests explored the many views, monuments, and outbuildings that made up the circuit around the main house.

And the house itself, a huge Palladian manor with extended wings, would fill with excited guests—guests who knew nothing of the misery, dishonor, and hatefulness that infected the main players of the event they had come to witness—guests who knew nothing of the secrets and lies that drove everything toward some inevitable finale.

Passion turned and walked slowly along the edge of the lake. She had seen Mark almost every evening during their last week in London. But she had had no opportunity to plead Charlotte's case. Exchanging only the briefest, most trivial dialogue, they had always been in the presence of others.

They acted as mere acquaintances, and Mark might as well have been just that, for Passion came to barely recognize him. As the week progressed, the dark shadows had deepened beneath his eyes. Morose, and with a constant frown etched deeply between his brows, he seemed to have thrown off even the slightest pretense of civility to those he despised.

His mother and Abigail Lawrence bore the brunt of his wrath, but Charlotte did not entirely escape him. He avoided and ignored them in front of others. Privately, he cut them at every turn.

Passion felt no pity for the countess and Abigail, but Charlotte was suffering. Withdrawing from the engagement was out of the question—she could not bear that scandal. Yet she cried every day on Passion's shoulder as she disclosed her feelings. Charlotte secretly gloried in Mark's furious retorts to Abigail, but she cringed and wept when he sent a dart at her. She was exhibiting an ever-increasing independence from her mother, and most painful, she was trying so hard to win Mark's regard. But nothing she did affected any change in him.

Passion watched a pair of swans land on the lake.

It had been a harrowing and horrible week. If she hadn't been comforting Charlotte, she'd been trying to comfort herself. She had slept little, for at night she missed Mark most. Painting had become her main solace.

She sat down on a low bench and observed the lovely birds glide across the surface of the glassy water.

She was exhausted.

She closed her eyes and summoned images from their last day together.

At first she had denied herself her memories, but now she basked in them. They were all she had—and they were hers.

She saw him laughing, his beautiful eyes crinkling at the corners. She saw him gazing at her with rapt attention as he cut away her undergarments. She saw his tender uncertainty as she had opened his gift, and his reluctance to let her go as he had slowly tied the ribbons of her bonnet beneath her chin.

Her chest tightened, and she tried to take a deep breath.

"Passion!"

"Passion!"

The remnants of her broken heart leapt. Her eyes flew open, and she jumped to her feet as she heard the familiar cries.

Patience! Prim!

She sobbed and began to run to the two young women who waved at her from the bridge. Patience's bright red curls bounced, and Prim's hat flew back on her shoulders as they both ran to meet her.

Tears streamed down Passion's face.

They were here!

Sobs racked her. She gasped for breath, but still she ran.

Just a moment more. Just a moment more, and she would feel their comforting arms around her.

"Patience! Prim!" Her voice cracked and her call had no power. But she could see them through her tears—could see their pace quicken even as hers slowed.

She opened her arms. And they were there.

"Thank God!" she sobbed as she felt the familiar feel of them, the familiar smell of them. "Thank God!"

Her knees buckled, and they dropped with her to the grassy ground beneath a tree. Prim's arms came around her and gently pulled off her straw hat. Passion cried against her breast as Patience held her hand and murmured calming words in her soft voice.

They were here. She wasn't alone.

She wept until it seemed she had no more tears. Then she laid her head quietly in Prim's lap, and as Patience smoothed her brow, she told her sisters everything.

They listened with unwavering attention. They whispered words of comfort. They shed tears of sympathy.

She didn't stop talking until the whole tale was told.

"Oh, Passion," Prim breathed in a cracked voice. "Oh, my darling sister . . ."

Patience held Passion in her piercing green gaze. Her eyes were moist, and a frown marred her brow. "How are you doing this?"

Her sister's question could refer to anything or everything. But it didn't matter, because the answer was the same. "I don't know."

"I don't know either." Patience leaned closer and smoothed Passion's hair. "You should have the man you love. You deserve love." She shook her head. "You deserve happiness, not this terrible sorrow."

Passion almost smiled at her sister's tender vehemence. "And what of Charlotte?"

"Yes," Prim said thoughtfully. "What of Charlotte?"

"What of Charlotte?" Patience's frown deepened. "What of you? What of the earl?" Her green eyes sparkled. "This is love! This is happiness! This is everything your marriage wasn't. Are you going to walk away? Are you going to hand your love, your happiness, over to someone else?"

"Not someone. Charlotte."

"What if Charlotte knew?" Prim sat straighter, and one of her strawberry blond curls fell forward. "Would she still want this marriage, knowing it was forced?"

"It's not my secret to tell, Prim. Anyway, if this marriage doesn't happen, Abigail will publish the letter."

"That witch," Patience said low.

Passion twirled her finger in Prim's curl. "Besides,

Charlotte really does want him. She idolizes him for every cutting salvo he launches at her mother."

"I could idolize him for that, too," Patience offered.

Passion managed a brief smile. "I'm so glad you're both here. I've missed you more terribly than you could know."

Prim's sky-blue eyes looked down on her with concern. "We're here now, and we love you."

Patience pressed a kiss to Passion's brow and then smoothed it with her hand.

Passion let her eyes fall closed.

"Just rest," Patience whispered. "We're here."

Mark leaned against the trunk of an old oak and watched them. Passion lay with her head in one sister's lap—it must be Primrose, for the one with the red curls who held Passion's hand could only be Patience. They were comforting her, stroking her.

His chest grew tight. Since the night of the engagement party, it was the first time he had seen Passion so completely vulnerable. He wanted to go to her, to hold her and comfort her. To tell her . . .

But she wouldn't allow that. Her sisters guarded her now. They were her protection. They were her support.

He took a ragged breath. Yet his arms ached for her. His body begged for her. And his heart belonged to her.

If he could just offer it to her, maybe she would not reject it. If he handed her everything . . . Maybe then . . . Maybe then they could both survive.

"You have a visitor in the library," Matt said quietly as he walked up beside Mark. "It's Mickey Wilkes."

Mark shuddered. Did he have the letter? He gazed across the wide lawn at Passion. For him, it no longer mattered. It only mattered for Matthew now.

"Who are they?" Matt had followed his gaze.

"Passion's sisters. Patience and Primrose."

"Lovely names," his brother said idly as he stared

across the distance. He shook his head. "It's good they're here. She needs them."

"Yes. She does." Mark turned back toward the house. "Are you coming?"

"In a moment," Matt replied, his eyes still trained on the sisters.

Mark paused. "There's something about them, isn't there?"

His brother nodded, and a frown creased his brow. "Yes. What is it?"

Mark looked at Passion in the care of her sisters. "It's the lingering touch. It says, 'You are my first and only concern.' It whispers, 'I am in no hurry to leave you, and I shall stay with you for as long as you need.'"

"Yes," Matt murmured. "That's it."

"It makes you want to feel it, to experience it."

Matt looked at him. "Yes."

Mark nodded. "I have. It's the finest thing in the world."

He turned, leaving his brother behind, and headed for the house. He found Mickey in the library, trying to read the title on the spine of a book.

"Good'ay, milord." The lad pushed his black hair back from his brow and frowned. "You al'right, milord?"

Mark knew he looked haggard. "Do you have it?"

"No, milord. But I knows who does."

Mark frowned. "What do you mean?"

"I mean, milord, tha' the very let'er yer lookin' for be in the unexpec'ed possession o' yer fiancée, Miss Charlotte Lawrence."

Mark's frown deepened. "What?"

Mickey nodded. "Turns out, tha' th'upstairs maid I bin pumpin'"—he winked—"fer information, gave the let'er into 'er very 'and the day they lef' fer 'ere. So, tha' bitch, Lawrence, don't e'en know its missin'."

Mark pressed his fingers between his brows. What the hell did this mean? It meant she knew. She must, yet she had said nothing, revealed nothing.

"Why? Why did the maid give the letter to Charlotte?"

"She says she gave i'to 'er 'cause they all likes 'er so much. They wan'ed 'er to know what was what, so's she wouldn't be caught unkowin'. She said, much as it might 'urt 'er, Miss Charlotte ought t' know 'er mum's true col'rs."

Apparently, knowing made no difference to his fiancée.

"An'way, milord, I's thinkin' i'should be easy as pie t'ge'it now. She jus' go' 'ere. It'll be in 'er things."

Mark nodded but remained silent. Did Passion know her cousin had the letter?

"I's'll ge'it when e'ery one's 'avin' supper. Yeah." Mickey nodded. "Yu'll 'ave yer let'er tonight, milord."

What then? Mark looked at Mickey. "Where was the damned thing?"

Mickey pointed to the ceiling. "Tha' bitch 'id it behind a piece o' ceilin' moldin'. I's addin' tha' t'me list o' 'idin' places." He crossed his arms over his chest. "Only reason th' ser'ants found it was 'cause the butler saw 'er comin' down from a lad'er lef' be'ind by th'upstairs maid, who 'ad jus' finished dustin'. An' they knew she wouldna be climbin' no lad'er fer no reason."

Mickey scratched behind his ear. "Which brings me to me next point, milord. As I mentioned t'ye, tha' 'ole 'ouse o' ser'ants 'ates tha' bitch, Lawrence. An' I can tell by the shushin' an' whisperin' tha' some'in more is afoot."

A muscle in Mark's neck cramped. "Like what?"

Mickey shrugged. "Don't know. But it turns out she's been playin' 'em wrong fer years. Besides treatin' 'em like shit, she docks their wages fer no good reason. Las' wint'r, she dock'd the whole 'ouse'old. She also fired a dish-maid af'er she fell down th' kitch'n stairs an' broke 'er leg. It were th' dead 'o wint'r an' th' gel could'na get no work, so she were forc'd to start liftin' 'er skirts in alleys fer any passin' coin . . . crutches an all. She were th' niece o' th' downstairs maid"—Mickey shook his head—"but now she's a gin-swillin' whore. There's more, o' course, but tha's prob'ly one o' the wors' thin's she's done."

Mark pressed his hand against his forehead. It shouldn't surprise him. Cruelty walked hand in hand with evil—and that's what Abigail Lawrence was, evil. She took people's lives away. He couldn't hate her any more than he already did.

"I knows them ser'ants are up t' somethin'. Does ye want me t'go back af'er I get the let'er? See if'n I can't fig're it out?"

"I suppose." Mark's head ached. "Yes. Get the letter, then go."

"Al'right, milord." Mickey backed toward the door but then paused. "You al'right, milord?"

Mark looked at the boy. "No." Another muscle cramped. "Get the letter, Mickey."

The boy nodded and disappeared out the door.

Mark shoved his hand through his hair as he paced the library. The letter was here, in his own house. Charlotte had it. He would have it soon. What the hell else could Lawrence's disgruntled household be scheming? Perhaps it had nothing to do with him. Perhaps it did.

Slipping his hand into his jacket pocket, he fingered Passion's hairpin. He would have the letter tonight, but for them, it would make no difference. There was only one thing he could give her now, only one thing that might matter to both of them.

Hope and despair walked with him hand in hand as he left the library. He needed to tell her now.

He passed his mother in the vestibule. They neither looked at each other nor spoke. But he paused as he saw Patience and Primrose coming down the stairs.

They wore wide-brimmed straw hats, and though they had very different coloring, he could see Passion's beauty in their faces.

Their eyes never left him as they descended, and when they stepped from the stairs he bowed. "Miss Patience.

Miss Primrose. Welcome to Hawkmore House. I am your host."

They curtsied and thanked him for his hospitality.

They both smiled versions of Passion's smile. And their eyes, though different from hers, reflected a similar depth of spirit and intelligence. Even the curve of their brows and the set of their chins were tracings of Passion. It disarmed him. For despite the similarities, they were completely different.

What made Passion "Passion," was missing—her refined elegance, her subtlety, her gentleness, and the quiet strength that masked her vulnerability. And then there was the way she looked at him . . .

"Please, forgive me for staring." His voice was rough. "But I see so much of your sister in both of you."

"Forgive *me,* my lord, but you look as heartsick as our sister." Patience's green eyes looked into his. "And I fear for the life of a broken heart."

"So do I, for the thing won't stop beating. Somehow it beats on. Pumping just enough blood to sustain life, but not enough to live it." He shoved his hand through his hair. He was so tired. "I promise you both, I would mend Passion's heart if she would let me. I would pick up all the pieces and hold it together with my bare hands if she would let me. And as long as hers were whole, I could live."

"Tell her that, my lord." Prim indicated the stairs. "Go to her and tell her everything that is in your heart. You both deserve that, at least."

They opened a space for him to proceed up the stairs.

Stepping between them, Mark ascended. At the top of the stairs he turned in the direction of his own room. Once there, he crossed to the fireplace and, lighting a lamp, pressed the panel that opened the hidden corridor to Passion's chamber. A past earl had built it so he might have discreet access to his mistress. Now, he followed its brief path to Passion. His heart pounded, and his pace alternately quickened and slowed.

As he faced the panel that opened into her room, he paused and tried to quiet his breathing. He leaned his forehead against the cool wood and prayed for strength.

With a soft click, the panel opened and he stepped silently onto the Aubusson carpet.

His heart thumped and his gut tightened.

Passion lay in bed in her undergarments. In the filtered sunlight, her hair was a shinning auburn river across the pillows. He took a deep breath. Hints of vanilla and orange blossom hung in the air.

He wanted to say her name, to call to her, but he couldn't seem to make himself speak. A long-ago pain that he could barely remember kept a tight hand over his mouth. *Don't call,* it murmured to him. *Don't! She will reject you.*

He closed his eyes. But this was a different woman, a different time. He must call or lose her forever. He must.

He formed her name on his lips, but no sound came. He drew a breath and pushed air through his constricted throat, but only a whisper escaped him.

Damnation! He swallowed and, closing his hand around her hairpin, he forced out her name on a hoarse croak. "Passion . . ."

She bolted up in bed. Her hair fell around her shoulders. "Mark!"

"I—" Where was his damned voice? He swallowed again. "I need to speak with you."

She stared at him and myriad emotions seemed to touch her features. "This is not the place." Her voice quavered.

"It must be. There is no other."

She eased from the bed and moved slowly and deliberately across the room toward where her gown lay on a chaise.

No! Anxiety shot through him. "I need to tell you something. I need to tell you something now."

She kept her eyes lowered and picked up her gown.

No! He began to shake. His chest felt bound in iron. "Passion, I must tell you. I must . . ."

"I will meet you in the garden," she said softly and, turning, she walked toward the dressing room door.

No. She couldn't go. "But I need to tell you," he said, following. "You must stay!"

She reached for the handle.

No. He gasped for air yet could not say the words. "A moment only . . ."

She pressed down on the handle, and the door opened.

No. He couldn't breathe. He couldn't breathe!

No!

He drew a shuddering breath and forced out his last hope on a ragged whisper. "Please . . . Please, don't go."

She froze, and her gown dropped to her feet.

Tears that belonged to a boy welled in him. "Please, Passion, don't run away from me."

She turned and gripped the door frame. Her lips trembled. "I won't. I'll stay."

His sore eyes shut for a moment in relief, and he closed the small distance between them.

She was so close.

His heart thundered in his chest.

If he didn't say the words now, he would never say them.

Yet old fears and old pains burned with a new intensity.

His head swam. He looked into her beautiful eyes—eyes that regarded him with tenderness, pain, longing, and hope.

Hope—his only hope. "I came to tell you—I came to tell you that I love you."

Passion's face crumbled, and with a sob, she turned her face against the jamb and wept.

"I love you," he repeated.

With a choked cry, Passion threw herself into his arms.

Oh, God! His heart burst and his legs buckled. He dropped to his knees and clung to her. "Please, don't cry," he murmured, pressing his cheek into the curve of her waist. He felt his tears on his face, but his voice was un-wavering. "Once, long ago, I begged for love. I swore I would never do it again. But I'm begging you now, Passion. Please, love me." Her hands slipped through his hair, and he pressed his face against her. "Please. For, I love you. I love you with all that I am and all that I will ever be. I love you in this life and the next. I love you. I love you."

She bent over him, and her voice was full of tears. "You never need beg me for love. Never! I give my love to you freely, with a full heart. I love you, Mark. I love you."

He squeezed his eyes shut, but still, he wept. They collapsed together to the floor, and years of sorrow, grief, and neglect poured out of him.

He had waited a lifetime for her words. He had waited a lifetime for her.

He knew now that love was the radiance that had been unreadable to him before. Though he had observed it in her face and studied it in her drawing of him, it had remained a mystery. How could he recognize something he'd never had, something he didn't even acknowledge? Now that he understood, it was too late.

Finally, he had won a woman's love—Passion's perfect love—and now he must live a lifetime without it.

He sobbed and sobbed against her breast as she held him and rocked him. And for as long as he cried, she held him. And the only words she spoke, over and over, were "I love you."

Passion had no idea how long she held him. Though he lay silently in her arms, she held him still. He had given her the only gift she could accept from him. The only gift she could not deny. His love. "I believe I loved you from the beginning," she murmured. "Our last day together, I almost told you." Her tears trailed silently down her cheeks. "And then everything fell to pieces, and I thought

I would never tell you. I thought I would love you forever, yet never have your love in return."

Mark's arms tightened around her. "I would have told you before now. I didn't recognize my own feelings." His voice was rough. "But these days without you have been so painful, that I knew. Only love hurts this much."

Passion sobbed and dropped her cheek against the top of his head. "I want you to know that my heart is yours forever. No matter what occurs, I will always, always love you."

"Then I shall dream of your love."

Her heart rent anew. "And I of yours." She threaded her fingers through his hair and breathed the subtle lemon verbena that she would always associate with him. "When I met you, my heart was dead. I lived only in duty and obligation to others. But you brought me back. You made me alive. You made me remember my dreams—made me remember myself." She closed her eyes on her tears. "Despite this desperate end, I was wrong to nurture regrets. You are the most splendid thing that has ever happened to me." She kissed his brow. "I didn't think I was going to survive without you, but you have given me the one thing that makes it possible—your love. With your love, I can survive."

"Then that must be enough for me." His voice was replete with sorrow and resignation. "And when I look upon your cousin, I shall remind myself that kindness to her proves me worthy of your love."

Passion sobbed and her stomach turned. "I love you." She tightened her arms around him. "I love you."

She would have to stay away. It would be too impossibly painful to see him in Charlotte's smiling company. Though this was what she had wanted—for him to treat her cousin with kindness—she could not watch it. She must stay away. Forever.

She took a deep, shuddering breath. "Come. Let me show you something."

Mark pulled away from her so slowly and Passion's

heart stopped when she looked into his face. Misery was written in every feature. His beautiful eyes were red-rimmed, swollen, and shot with blood. He breathed through parted lips, and the sensual curve of his mouth was drawn down deeply at the corners. His hair fell over his brow, and his hand shook as he extended it to help her up.

Keeping his hand in hers, she drew him to the small easel she had placed in the corner of the room. "This is for you," she managed.

Carefully, she withdrew the sheet from the finished painting. The light fell across the portrait, and Charlotte looked back at them—Charlotte, in all her loveliness, her sweetness, and her poignant sorrow and insecurity.

Mark stared at it. His expression didn't change as his reddened eyes moved over the picture.

"I thought . . ." Passion bit her trembling lip. "I thought if you could see her as I see her . . ."

Her voice shook too much to continue.

"It's magnificent."

His voice was flat and desolate. He looked at her, and his eyes welled. "But I would that it were a picture of you. I shall look at it and I shall see you. I shall look at it and I shall dream of you." Tears fell slowly now. "I shall look at it and I shall remember the brief but joyous moments I spent in your embrace. And as I live out my life in the company of your cousin, I shall yearn for the life that might have been—a life with you—a life with love."

Passion could barely see past her tears.

Mark's hand slipped behind her head, and he pressed his lips, hard and firm, against her brow. Then he grabbed the painting and disappeared through the opening in the wall. The panel closed silently behind him.

Passion bent and covered her face with her hands. Her stomach cramped and her head spun. She felt sick, so sick, but her tears wouldn't stop.

Oh, God! Her stomach heaved. She ran to the basin. She gasped and panted.

But there was no help for it. She purged her unending grief into the bowl.

Mark ascended the stairs slowly. He had ridden all afternoon, trying to ease his mind of the pain and the loss. He had tried to think only of her love, but thoughts of that led to thoughts of all that he would never have.

He was miserable and exhausted, and each step was a labor.

"My lord!"

He turned and found Charlotte looking up at him from the vestibule.

He didn't want her. "Yes?"

"May I have a word with you?"

No! "Now?"

"If you please, my lord."

Mark turned on the stair and walked back down. Charlotte met him, and they crossed the hall to the library. After closing the door, he walked to the windows and looked out over the rear garden. Abigail Lawrence strolled through his roses. He turned away.

Charlotte stood right behind him.

He drew back. "Yes?"

She looked nervous. "You appear to be very tired, my lord. So I won't take much of your time." She reached into her pocket. "I just wanted to give this to you."

She pulled her hand from her pocket and held out an aged letter bound with a faded green ribbon. Mark stared down at Abigail Lawrence's address penned in his mother's familiar hand.

The letter. He felt relief but no joy.

His hand trembled as he slowly took it from her fingers. Pulling the ribbon, he opened the faded paper and let his eyes skim over the words. The original read exactly like the copy Abigail Lawrence had sent his mother.

Finally, the damned letter—handed over to him by the very person who, for all she knew, had the most to lose from doing so.

He looked at Charlotte. "Why are you giving me this?"

"Does it mean anything to you, my lord?"

"It does."

Charlotte wrung her hands. "One of my maids gave it to me, my lord. She found it hidden in my mother's room and advised me to read it immediately. She said there was something in it I should know about you."

Mark frowned. "So now what, Miss Lawrence? I ask you again, why are you giving me this letter?"

Charlotte looked up at him, and her gray eyes were shiny. "Because I am trying to love you, my lord. And if I am ever to love you, and if I am to be your wife, then I should only know the best of you." She shook her head. "I did not read the letter, my lord."

Mark's frown deepened, and another shadow fell over him. "What?"

"I said, I did not read the letter. And I don't want to." She gripped her skirts. "I've been agonizing over what to do with it, vacillating between temptation to read it and determination to burn it. Then I realized that I should just give it to you. The fact that my mother had it hidden away makes me certain that, at some time, she intended to use it against you."

Mark stared at her, stunned. This, he *never* would have predicted.

"As your fiancée . . ." She blushed. "As your wife, my allegiance is to you, my lord. And if I can protect you from any ill will, including my mother's, then it is my duty to do so—indeed, it is my pleasure to do so."

Mark didn't know what to say. He stared into Charlotte's gray eyes and saw her for the first time. He saw a wounded girl who, despite constant criticism, still carried hope and some sense of herself. He saw innocence and virtue—so much innocence that the connection between the letter and their engagement hadn't even occurred to her. He saw the beginnings of strength beneath her timid shell. He saw her, finally.

It had been easier to hate her. Yet he couldn't do that

anymore. Slowly, he took her hand in his. "Thank you for your allegiance," he murmured. He pressed a kiss to the back of her hand and then bowed his head. "Good afternoon."

A small smile and a frown battled for preeminence on her face. She bobbed a curtsey. "Good afternoon, my lord."

When the door had closed behind her, Mark crossed to the fireplace. It had already been lit in preparation for the evening. He took one last look at the cause of his ruin, then tossed it in the flames.

He watched until the hungry fire had turned every bit of it to ash.

Matthew was safe.

Chapter Seventeen

GOOD-BYE

Passion threw up into the basin. While she expelled the small breakfast she had consumed, Patience rubbed her back and held up her hair. Prim mopped her brow.

When nothing was left in her quivering stomach, they assisted her back to the comfortable chaise and sat on either side of her. While Prim poured fresh tea, Passion took a moment to close her eyes.

But for daily walks with her sisters, she had kept mostly to her room in the three days since she and Mark had declared their love. Her heart was too raw to risk running into him. She had neither the energy nor the will to participate in lengthy meals with him and Charlotte and the wedding guests, who had been arriving in droves.

She took her meals in her room but made sure to visit with her cousin every day. Though Abigail continued to plague her, Charlotte had new hope for the happiness of her marriage. She had explained to Passion how she seemed to have finally won her fiancé's civility by turning a certain letter over to him.

Passion had listened with a sore yet satisfied heart as

Charlotte told the story. She was proud of her cousin's actions and enormously relieved for Mark. He was out from under Abigail Lawrence's thumb, and Matthew's parentage would not be exposed. It had to be one less weight upon his shoulders.

"Darling . . ." Prim said softly.

Passion opened her eyes and took the cup of tea Prim offered her. She sipped it and sighed. These daily battles with her stomach were draining. She smiled weakly at her sisters, who where both looking at her. "I assure you, this will pass. Please don't fear you will have to mother me forever."

"And who mothered us all the years after Mummy died?" Prim reminded her.

Passion smiled at her sister's kindness.

"Darling"—Patience patted her leg—"this brings us to the very subject we wanted to speak with you about."

Passion lowered her cup. "What is it?"

"You've been ill every day now," Patience said.

"You're exhausted," Prim added.

Passion frowned. Need she defend her suffering? To her sisters? "These days have been a great trial," she murmured.

Prim leaned forward and took her hand. "Of course they have. Your grief is reason enough for your illness. But . . ."

"Passion." Patience looked at her directly. "We think you're with child."

Passion gasped, and her teacup rattled violently in her hand, for the moment she heard the words, she knew they were true.

Prim took the clattering china from her, and Passion pressed her hands protectively over her abdomen as her vision blurred with tears. Her wounded heart filled with sublime joy. A baby! A baby in *her* body! Mark's baby! She closed her eyes. Their baby.

She wept tears she hadn't known she had, and, again, her sisters were there to comfort her.

"I have believed I was barren for so long," she sobbed on Patience's shoulder. "It hurt so terribly, but I didn't know how much until now—until the measure of this happiness."

Patience brushed the tears from Passion's cheek, and her own eyes were shiny with moisture. "It *is* happy, happy news. And you shall be the most wonderful mother." Patience looked at Prim, whose face was streaming with tears. "And we shall be aunts."

Prim smiled and cried and laid her head against Passion's stomach. Passion held her and shared a glance with Patience. Prim had been young when their mother had passed, and this was a childhood reflex that had moved from their mother to Passion. It was a bid for comfort, and over the years it had remained with her.

"Will you tell the earl?" Patience asked.

Now Passion felt wrenching sadness. This was the dim side of her joy. "How can I? His life is set." She blinked back her tears. "Knowing would only increase his grief."

Patience frowned with concern. "But, surely, one day . . ."

Passion nodded and stroked Prim's brow. "Yes. Perhaps, one day . . ."

"What will Papa say?" Prim asked.

Passion shook her head. "I don't know," she said slowly. "I feel terrible trepidation about that. Papa will be incredibly disappointed in me," she whispered. "I can hardly stay at the vicarage. Where shall I go?" She turned from Patience to Prim in anguish, her tears running afresh.

Patience took her hand. "We'll go to France. Aunt Matty will come with us. We ought not leave Papa entirely alone, so Prim and I can trade off having visits with you."

France. The idea of her child being born in a foreign country pained her. The idea of being so far from home pained her even more. But she must be far away. And she must stay far away, for she could not shame her family.

Prim sat up, and it was almost as if she had read Passion's thoughts. "But you mustn't stay away too long, Pas-

sion. After a time, you must return home. The child should
know his aunts and his grandpapa."

Passion shook her head. "How can I? My presence and
the baby's would undermine Father's role. He could lose
the vicarage. We would all be shunned."

"Then we'll tell people we've adopted the child from
some destitute relations," Patience offered. "Or we'll say
you married again, but that your husband died."

Passion looked at her sister. It would be a lifetime of
lies. "I don't know what I'm going to do."

Patience stroked her hand. "We'll think of something.
But Prim's right. You and the baby belong with us." She
squeezed Passion's fingers. "Besides, the babe will need a
father figure."

Passion's heart twisted. A father figure, but not a father.
She brushed away more tears. "I will have to stay away
for a long time. And any decision to return will have to be
Papa's."

Prim smiled. "Then I am happy, for I know what his
decision will be." She rested her hand on Passion's stomach. "Oh, Passion. A baby! You're going to have a baby!"
Her lovely face was so joyful and her sky-blue eyes so
tender. "You know how I love babies."

Patience rested her hand atop Prim's. "Come what
may, this child could not have two more doting aunts."

Passion kissed her sisters and then rested her hands on
theirs. Her joy was bone-deep but bittersweet. Mark had
given her a child. He had given her not only his love but
also the living manifestation of his love.

She closed her eyes. This was proof that bliss could
blossom from misery—proof that God worked in deep
and mysterious ways. Yet for all her joy, a harsh sorrow
dampened her heart; for despite her sisters' love and support, she would be alone in this. Her father would be hor-
ribly disappointed in her. There would be lies and the loss
of home and country for an indeterminate period of time.
Her child would not know a father's love. And Mark
would not know the love of their child.

It felt unbearable and wrong.

Yet it was also wrong to knowingly and actively destroy the happiness of one person for the happiness of another. That had been her stance with Mark all along. And if that stance were right—which she believed it was—then it still was, child or no.

Praying for guidance, she found her first answer.

She looked to her sisters. "Tonight, I shall attend the ball. Tomorrow, I'm going home."

Passion and her sisters entered the huge, glittering ballroom after the dancing had already begun. The beautiful room, painted in pale green, white, and gold, was lit by six magnificent chandeliers that hung from the twenty-five-foot ceiling. A long upper gallery along three sides of the room supported a full complement of musicians and offered an ideal place for guests to walk and observe the dancing below. Six pairs of tall glass doors on the far wall led to the balcony without, and two large doors at the end of the room led to the grand salon, where drinks and refreshments were being served.

Passion took a deep breath as she and her sisters moved into the crowded room. It was important that she pay her respects to Charlotte at this event, as she was not going to attend the wedding. But she planned to stay only a short time.

They knew practically no one, so they kept together, nodding and smiling at strangers as they milled toward the glass doors.

"Passion, is that Mark's brother?" Patience asked. "There, dancing with the woman in blue."

Passion recognized Matthew dancing with Rosalind. "Yes, that's Matthew. The woman in blue is his fiancée."

Patience paused. "Is she?" She frowned and then shook her head. "No. She isn't right for him."

Prim lifted her brows. "And how can you tell that?"

"See how he looks at her? But she isn't looking at him. She cares more about being seen than she does about seeing him." Patience nodded. "He needs someone who sees *him*."

"Mrs. Redington?"

Passion turned and found John Crossman stepping away from a group of gentlemen. She smiled, genuinely pleased to see him. "Why, Mr. Crossman, how delightful to find you here."

Passion introduced her sisters.

"Mr. Crossman is the gentleman I told you of, who so graciously saved me the night I fell ill at Charlotte's party."

"Ah." Patience nodded. "Allow me to thank you, Mr. Crossman, for assisting our sister in her moment of need."

A small smile turned his mouth, and he bowed his head. "I am only glad that I was there to be of service to her."

John introduced them to the party of gentlemen with whom he had been conversing and then asked Passion to dance. Patience and Prim also moved onto the floor with two other gentlemen from the group.

"How are you, Mr. Crossman? I've missed our outings with my aunt and your cousin."

John grinned. "Have you really?"

"Yes, I really have."

"Well, I think you might be relieved to know that I have paid my cousin's debts. And now that he has no more financial trouble, he has abandoned the idea of marriage in favor of making a try for the stage."

Passion smiled. "I think the theater might be just the thing for him."

John nodded. "I hope so." He regarded her as they danced across the floor. "How are *you*, Mrs. Redington? Have you been well?"

Passion glanced up at him with a small smile. "I don't look well, do I?"

"You're beautiful. But I was concerned for you before you left London."

Passion smiled at his graciousness. She knew she

didn't look well. Her eyes were shadowed, and she had lost weight. All at once, she decided to be honest with him. "Actually, I am not altogether well. I'm going to go home tomorrow."

He looked down at her and nodded. "I wouldn't be able to watch the person I loved marry another either."

Passion's step faltered so badly that John had to save her from tripping. As the couples dancing nearby looked at her, she blushed with embarrassment and lowered her eyes.

"I'm sorry," John murmured, whirling her onto a different part of the floor.

"How did you know?"

"Those last days in London, I could tell."

Passion's heart fluttered, and she felt her cheeks flaming. "Do you suppose anyone else noticed?"

"No. I was the only one watching you carefully enough to figure it out."

Passion raised her eyes to him tentatively. "Why were you watching me carefully?"

"I think you know why." He smiled a little sadly. "But let's not speak of that now. Will your sisters leave with you?"

Passion wanted to say something about her deep appreciation of him as a friend. But perhaps that was a conversation for a different time. She shook her head. "No. Aunt Matty is to arrive tomorrow. She will chaperone them."

"Why don't you let me escort you home, then? It's Lincolnshire, isn't it?"

Passion looked into his kind green eyes. He was such a good man—a kind, decent man. But she would never love him in the way he hoped. "Mr. Crossman—John—our brief friendship has come to mean so much to me. I feel as if we share the easy rapport of old friends. I wouldn't want anything to jeopardize that."

He held her in his gaze. "You'll have a maid with you?" he asked after a moment.

"Yes. My sisters came with our maid. She will accompany me."

He nodded and twirled with her into the center of the floor.

After a while he spoke. "Did I tell you I'm going to sea?"

Passion's eyes widened with surprise. "You are? When did you make that decision?"

He smiled gently at her. "Just now."

Mark stood with Matt and Lord Fitzgerald by the doors to the grand salon.

"I like the plans, Langley. You did a fine job with them. Frankly, I'm not particularly fond of a lot of gewgaws and fuss on a building. I appreciate the classical design you propose."

Lord Fitzgerald was saying all the things Mark should have been pleased to hear, but he found that he couldn't muster any enthusiasm.

"So I'm going to present your plan to the committee as my primary choice. Assuming they agree with me, which they always do, you'll get the commission."

Mark nodded. "My thanks, Lord Fitzgerald."

The older man waited a moment, no doubt assuming Mark would say more. When he didn't, Fitzgerald nodded. "Right, then. I'll inform you of their decision."

Mark nodded again. "I shall await word."

After the man had moved off, Matt spoke. "Christ, you really went on a bit too much. A little embarrassing how verbose you were. After all, it's only the commission for the National Library."

Mark looked at his brother, but suddenly Matt's attention was riveted upon something else. He followed the direction of Matt's gaze and found Passion and her sisters talking with Charlotte.

His heart began pounding, and his breath quickened. Since the day he had left her room, he hadn't seen her this closely. She wore a gown of dark green satin, and her pale skin glowed above the low neckline. She looked thinner. And though shadows darkened her eyes and her smile was slight, he found her beautiful.

She would be magnificent in the Hawkmore emeralds. They should be hers. She was the wife he would have chosen—even if that meant ending his line.

"The one with the red curls, which sister is she?" Matt asked.

Mark glanced at his brother. It seemed that Matt's interest in Passion's sisters had not waned.

"Her name is Patience; Miss Patience Emmalina Dare."

Mark looked at her. She was a striking young woman with the sort of obvious beauty that caught people's attention. Tight red-gold curls fell down her back, and her green eyes looked at people in such a way that one felt she knew and understood everything in the beat of a heart. She had a confident, determined air about her. And the almost tangible sensuality that all three of them shared was perhaps most palpable in her.

He shifted his gaze to Passion, and his blood rushed. She was the one. She was the model upon which her sisters had been formed. She was perfection of form, beauty, and grace.

He hungered for her and feasted upon the vision of her, but he hated the intrigued glances and admiring stares that fell upon her from passing men. He wanted everyone to know that she belonged to him—and that he belonged to her.

"She thinks she has everything figured out," Matt murmured.

Mark glanced briefly at Patience before returning his gaze to Passion. "Perhaps she does."

"Look how Montrose is fawning over her," Matt said.

"Yes. Rather reminds me of how you look fawning over Rosalind."

Matt shrugged, but he didn't smile. "Go to hell."

"I'm already there, Matt." Mark watched Passion hug

Charlotte and then move off toward the glass doors. He ached to follow her. He ached to pull her into his arms. "I'm already there."

Passion stood beside one of the tall pairs of glass doors and welcomed the breath of cool air that wafted over her. She had told Charlotte that one of the members of her father's parish was ill and asking for her. She was not a good liar and hated having to voice the false excuse. But it would be far worse to remain.

Patience slipped her arm around her waist. "Are you all right?"

"Yes. I'm fine."

"Would you like a glass of punch?" Prim asked.

Passion looked toward the grand salon. "Yes, that would be . . ."

Mark was there. She stared across the distance into his hungry eyes and felt his gaze touch her like a caress. Her heart thumped painfully and her body answered him with a spill of moisture between her thighs.

Patience and Prim both looked at Mark and then back at her. "Oh, Passion," Prim breathed.

"It's all right," Passion managed as she watched Charlotte approach Mark.

His eyes closed, and when he opened them, his face had become a mild mask. He nodded to Charlotte and, taking her hand, led her onto the dance floor.

Passion watched them. Though she wanted to run, she couldn't look away. Guests smiled and nodded, and her cousin beamed happily as Mark took her in his arms with the start of the music.

As her beloved turned Charlotte across the floor, Passion's gut wrenched with searing jealousy. *She* loved him. *She* fulfilled him. *She* carried his child. Yet here she stood, cold and alone, while Charlotte basked in the warm and public light as Mark's chosen bride.

Dear God, she couldn't bear it! She hated the sight of his hand on Charlotte's waist, for she knew the feel of his hand—she knew the press of it and the strength of it. She hated their proximity, for although Mark held her cousin at a proper distance, she knew Charlotte could breathe the lemon verbena that always clung to him. It was Charlotte who could see the dark blue flecks that gave his beautiful eyes their dimension. Charlotte could study the sensual curve of his mouth and dream of what his kiss would feel like on their wedding day. A black pall clouded her mind as her breath came faster.

Passion tried to slow her breathing. Her insides boiled with covetousness. She felt tears rising and her throat tightening. She turned slowly and looked at her sisters. "I'm going outside for a moment alone," she murmured.

Prim nodded and brushed her arm.

"We'll wait for you," Patience assured her.

Once she was through the doors, Passion walked calmly and carefully down the wide steps to the lower garden. Several couples strolled along the wide, well-manicured paths. The murmur of their conversations and occasional laughter floated in the air.

Passion moved past them, alone amongst lovers. She pressed her hand to her abdomen—her tears welled— alone in the world, while Charlotte lived out her life with Mark. An image of her cousin, naked and writhing in Mark's embrace, filled her mind.

With a cry of wrenching despair, she ran across the lower lawn to the bridge. Her slippers patted the ground, and her gasping breath sounded loud in the stillness of the evening. The swans that glided across the dark water of the moonlit lake craned their long necks to watch her pass. She ran until she reached the rotunda. Grasping her aching side, she passed between the columns and dropped onto one of the wide marble benches that circled the interior. Her breath was ragged, and her heart pounded.

Through her tears, she looked back at Hawkmore House. It was a glittering jewel box above the lake, its musical key endlessly turning. And inside, her beloved danced with another.

Tearing off her gloves, she covered her face and wept into her hands until all that were left were dry sobs.

Suddenly she sensed him as he straddled the bench alongside her.

She turned her head and met Mark's dark gaze. Pieces of her heart fell away. "I love you," she choked.

He took her hand and pressed the back of it to his cheek. "I love you." His eyes closed. "I love you."

Turning to face him on the bench, she rested her palm against the slope of his jaw. Her body leapt as he pressed a kiss into her captive palm and then another against her pounding pulse.

"Oh, Passion, I love you," he breathed, rubbing her hand against his cheek and his ear.

She trembled at the supplication in his touch. "I love you," she whispered, as she slipped her fingers through his hair and lifted her other hand to trace the curve of his mouth.

His eyes glittered as he kissed the tips of her fingers, then he pulled her hand against his heart. "Tell me something," he urged.

A shiver tumbled down Passion's spine at the familiar words. He had asked her the same thing the first night he came to her room. That night they were beginning anew. Tonight they were ending.

She sought his other hand and pressed it against her heart. "I love you. And so long as there is breath in my body I shall love you and you alone." She held his gaze. "Never think of me sharing a kiss or a caress with another, for I never shall. Never wonder if I lie in the arms of another, for I never shall. Never imagine me pledging my love or my troth to another, for I never, ever shall." The broken pieces of her heart crumbled to dust. "When you think of me, only remember our time together. Remember me in your arms. Remember me with my lips pressed to yours. Remember me with my body moving against you, begging the fulfillment only you provided." He sobbed and her tears spilled over. "Remember me telling you, 'I love you,' 'I love you.' 'Forever, I love you.'"

Mark's head fell forward. He wept silently. His shoulders heaved as he lifted his anguished face to her. "Tell me that you love me better for this. For I swear, if you do not, I shall throw all away. And I shall pursue you with a relentlessness the likes of which you have never seen, until I have driven you inextricably and eternally into my arms."

Passion flung herself into his strong embrace. "I could never love you better," she gasped, "only longer and more deeply." She smelled him and felt him, engraining every little detail of him into her memory—the softness of his hair, the texture of his skin, and the press of his body.

She must never forget, for as time stretched forward, she would need the memory of every touch, every kiss, every breathy whisper.

Music reached out to them from the house. It was a waltz.

"Dance with me," she begged. "Dance with me one last time."

She slid from the bench and pulled him with her to the center of the rotunda. They brushed away each other's tears. He took her in his arms. They danced slowly, their bodies pressed close together. Her gown swished softly as they turned, and his eyes never left her.

It was a far different night than the one in the garden of the Crystal Palace. Possibility and hope had bloomed that evening. Tonight, longing and loss hung in the still air around them.

But also love.

Passion curled her hand around his nape. "I'm leaving tomorrow morning."

Mark dropped his forehead against hers. They stood still, swaying with the music.

"I have never been guilty of such dire envy before this night," she whispered. "The thought of not having you is unbearable. But to watch you stand at the altar with my cousin would be impossible."

"I know," he said. He touched his lips to the wet corner of her eye.

God! She wanted him with a desperation born of grief and with an intensity born of the knowledge that she carried his child. Her body cried out for him.

She choked back a sob and laid her head against his chest. As he held her to him and pressed kisses across her brow, she felt his heart pounding. It beat as hard and fast as her own.

"Tell me something," she said.

He tipped her chin up to look at him. His cheeks were wet. "I shall think of you every day, a thousand times a day. I shall dream of you at night and speak your name when I wake. I shall relive every moment we ever spent together, and I shall invent ones we didn't." He held her face between his hands. "I shall write to you and speak only of us. I shall tell you every adventure we share and recount all the ways we make love. And in such a way, I shall create a life with you."

Passion closed her eyes on her tears.

"I hope you will write to me. So that I can know you are well—so that I can touch the paper you touch."

His thumb brushed her lip and then his mouth was on hers.

They kissed with a brief and breathless longing.

"I love you," he whispered against her mouth. "Never forget."

And then he tore from her arms and disappeared into the evening.

She watched his shadow move across the moonlit grounds. She laid her hands over her womb. "I'll never forget."

Chapter Eighteen

HEAVEN ON EARTH

"I can't believe you actually bought this huge screen," Matt said.

Bright sunshine streamed through Mark's tall bedroom windows. Already in his formal wedding attire, Matt stood by the tall screen, running his hand over the intricate carving. Mark's valet, Smith, moved efficiently around the room, tidying up as Mark adjusted his cravat.

He glanced down at the parure of diamonds and pearls. The set had been in the safe with a selection of other jewelry that had belonged to past countesses. They would have to do for Charlotte.

It was tradition for Hawkmore brides to wear the Hawkmore emeralds. But after leaving Passion at the rotunda, he had gone to her room and left the emeralds on her dressing table. She was the bride of his heart, and he wanted her to have them.

His head ached. Early the previous morning, he had watched her leave. Then he had gone to sit in her empty room. He'd sat there for a long time, writing her his first letter. It had been full of regret and sorrow, but he'd needed to put the words on paper. Before leaving, he'd taken her pillows. They were on his bed now.

"You ready?" Matt asked, crossing to him.

Mark snapped the velvet jewelry box closed. "No."

Matt smiled. "Don't worry. I'll stay close and keep you from bolting." He brushed a speck of lint from Mark's shoulder and extended his hand toward the door. "Onward, my brother."

Matt stood on Mark's left as he knocked on the door of Charlotte's room. A maid opened it and curtsied as his mother came to the door to receive the box.

Mark extended it to her. "For the bride—a token of my esteem in acknowledgment of this occasion."

His mother glanced at the box and frowned. Flipping open the lid, her frown deepened. "Where are the emeralds?"

"The emeralds are mine," he replied. "Where they are or what I do with them is none of your affair."

Abigail Lawrence rushed to the door, having heard everything. She looked in the box and her face reddened. She lashed out with the fury of a woman who still believed she had a hold over him. "Where are they? All Hawkmore brides wear the Hawkmore emeralds. People will expect to see them." She snatched the box from Lucinda's hands, snapped it closed, and threw it at Mark. "Charlotte *will* wear the emeralds!"

Mark's hands shook at his sides, and he stared at her with a rage that he no longer need contain. Even his mother took a step back.

But before he could respond with the venom that was upon his tongue, Charlotte appeared behind her mother. Garbed in a flounced gown of white lace, she lifted her chin. "I will wear what my lord gives me and nothing else."

Abigail whirled around and threw her finger toward the side of the room. "Get back into the dressing room! You are not to be seen!"

Charlotte continued forward without looking at her mother. Matt bent and picked up the box.

"Good morning, my lord." Charlotte smiled. "In honor of this occasion, I am proud to accept your gift."

Mark nodded and removed the necklace from the box. Charlotte turned, and he clasped it around her neck. The scent from the flowers in her hair floated up to him, and he jerked back.

Charlotte turned with a frown. "What is it, my lord?"

Mark's heart raced. "Those are orange blossoms you're wearing. I want you to remove them."

"She will not!" Abigail said.

"Oh, really," Lucinda scoffed. "Her hair and her bouquet are finished."

"Off!" Mark growled. "I want them off."

Charlotte turned to the maid as she began pulling pins and flowers from her hair. "I believe the rose garden is in bloom. Will you please arrange for some flowers to be cut immediately? Some white, some pink, and plenty of greens." She gave the orange blossoms to the maid. "You may throw those away."

As the maid hurried off, Charlotte turned to him with a smile. "There. That was simple, wasn't it?"

She was trying hard to please him.

"Thank you." He bowed his head and handed her the box, which still contained the earrings and bracelet.

She touched the necklace at her throat. "Thank *you*, my lord. I have never owned anything so fine."

Mark nodded. What else could he say to her? "You look lovely."

Charlotte smiled and began to speak, but her words were covered by a loud crash from below. Voices rose and then there was another clatter.

Frowning, Mark and Matt moved to the railing and looked down two floors into the vestibule. Flowers and broken china were strewn across the floor. Mickey Wilkes was trying desperately to convince Cranford of something.

"What a racket he's making," Lucinda said irritably as she joined them.

Abigail Lawrence glanced down, then paused and frowned.

Charlotte peered around Mark's shoulder.

"It's all right, Cranford," Mark called to the butler. "I'll see him."

Mickey whirled around and, before Mark could even step away from the railing, flipped a newspaper open and held it over his head. "It's in the papers, milord!" he shouted. "The 'ole bloody thing's in the papers!"

Mark's heart began to pound in his chest as Mickey raced up the stairs. It was out? What would this mean? Where would this lead?

Freedom? Passion? His blood rushed and his body tensed.

Abigail Lawrence looked pale, and a flush was darkening his mother's cheeks.

Matt gripped Mark's shoulder and frowned with concern. "What the hell is he talking about? Are you in trouble?"

Mark put his hand over Matt's. "No. I'm not."

Charlotte looked confused.

Mickey skidded around the landing and, gasping for breath, slapped the paper and another folded sheet into Mark's hands. "I go' 'ere as fast as I could, milord. I tol' ya. I tol' ya there be somethin' more." Mickey shook his head. "I's a'ways right, I am. A'ways. A gen'leman read me th' paper on th' train. An tha' there be one copy o' many o' another let'er. It's circulat'in, milord, as a scandal sheet."

But Mark barely heard him, for while he held Matt at arm's length, his gaze fixed upon the paper. The words *blackmail, forced marriage,* and *to save his brother* popped out at him. No names were mentioned, but he was the only "lord of import recently engaged to a commoner." It was all innuendo, but it was enough. At the bottom of the article it said Original Letter of Incrimination in the Custody of the Editor. What letter? He had burned the letter.

He opened the other paper.

"Copies o' tha' there be all o'er the streets, milord."

February 8, 1825

Dearest Abigail,

I am writing to inform you that I am, at last, delivered of my son. I can say "my son" because he is all mine and only mine. He is the child of my choosing and the child of my making. He is handsome and healthy and has his father's dark eyes. (And, I do believe, his father's other remarkable attribute as well!) Heaven forbid, though, that he take too much after him and begin running about with the pruning shears! I can hear you tittering, my dear. But never mind that, I shall raise him up to be a proper lord.

At this very moment, he is sleeping beside me in his bassinet. My darling Abigail, I cannot convey to you the sensual pleasure it gives me to see my little gardener's son swaddled in the Hawkmore linens. I consider his birth an unparalleled coup on my part against the injustice of my marriage to George, whom, you know, I never wanted.

I shall ensure my son has everything his brother has—and more if I can manage it, since he will not have the earldom (though even that could fall to him one day). I shall place him upon the pedestal of my heart and give him all my love. He will be what my first son is not—all mine. How ironic that I should hate my first son for his legitimacy and love my second son for his illegitimacy.

You shall receive a formal birth announcement shortly, but as you are the only sister of my secret, I had to write to you immediately and share my triumph.

Well, my darling, my hungry little boy is crying for his supper, so I'd best go to him. Please write to me of the Chesterfield party. And you must tell me if Lord Harrington is still pining after me. I may decide to take him back, as soon as I can shed the maternal mantle that currently enshrouds me. After all, I am ever so anxious to try out the

techniques you informed me of for preventing children—
and even more anxious for the act that necessitates such
techniques!

Yours,

Lucinda

Post Script: "My son" is christened Matthew Morgan
Hawkmore.

Mark shook with fury. He lifted his eyes to his mother.
She stared at him with her hand pressed to her chest.

"You swore to me that there was only one letter! You
bloody swore!"

"Letter?" Charlotte looked confused. "Is this about the
letter?"

"I don't know what the hell this is about," Matt said.

Abigail jerked around to face her daughter. "What do
you know of any letter?"

"Susan gave me a letter that she found hidden in your
room. She said it had to do with the earl, and she told me
to read it. But I didn't. I gave it to him." Charlotte
frowned. "I gave it to him, because I was certain you had
kept it for some wicked use against him. And it seems I
was right, for some ill news has appeared in the paper."

Mark scowled at Abigail. "You, madam, have been re-
paid for your foul and reprehensible evil by the servants
of your own household," he sneered. "People who would
have been loyal and respectful of you had you shown
them any decency have, instead, dealt you a fatal blow."

Matt crossed his arms over his chest. "Everyone seems
to have pieces of this puzzle but me. What the hell is
going on?"

Mark looked at his brother and his heart constricted.
This would be hard news. He turned to Charlotte. "Please
excuse us. I shall return to you shortly." He grabbed
Mickey's shoulder. "Go, I'll speak with you later."

Mark walked with Matt back to his room. Lucinda
trailed behind them.

Once the door closed behind them, Mark faced his brother.

Matt held his hands out at his sides. "Christ, what the hell is it?" A vague anxiety dimmed his eyes.

Lucinda glanced apprehensively at Matt but then walked to the windows.

"Sit down, Matt," Mark suggested.

Matt's frown deepened. "No." Mark could see his anger mounting. "I don't want to sit down. I want to know what the bloody hell is going on."

Mark looked at the paper and the letter and then at his brother. "I wish you never had to see these, but there can be no keeping them from you." Slowly and regretfully, he held out both items.

Matt glanced at them nervously and then snatched them out of Mark's hand.

Mark watched his brother's face move from a mere frown to a tight mask of pain and fury.

As his eyes reached the bottom of the letter, he closed them. His fist closed around the letter and his jaw clenched. And when his eyes flew open, they were red with rage.

He fairly leapt at Lucinda. "You bitch!" She threw up her hands as he hurled the paper and the letter at her. "You lying, adulterous, disgusting bitch!"

He flung up his arm to deliver a backhanded blow, but Mark threw himself between them and grabbed his brother's arm.

"I never expected this to get out!" Lucinda cried. "I didn't even know if Abigail ever received that letter! She never answered it—I thought it had been lost!" She curled her hands around the very arm he had raised against her. "I love you, Matthew. I've always loved you."

Matt yanked away from both of them and, sweeping up the crumpled letter, held it up. "You don't love me. I'm just your coup, your triumph over Father, who made the horrible mistake of being too old for you." He indicated Mark. "Who made the horrible mistake of giving you a fine son. Who made the horrible mistake of loving you and remaining faithful to you while you spat in his face with your affairs."

Lucinda lifted her chin. "You know I have always loved you. I know you do."

"Yes!" Matt cried. "And I am ashamed of all the times I excused your behavior and let you fawn over me while you slapped Father's face and treated my brother as if he were anathema." Matt shook his head. "You loved me for all the wrong reasons—just as you abandoned Mark for all the wrong reasons. Your love is a burden, because it is only for your own selfish, pitiful gratification!" He visibly shook. "I despise your love, and I despise you!"

She reached for his arm, but he snatched it away. "Don't touch me. Don't speak to me. And don't ever darken my door again. You are not welcome at Angels' Manor, and I shall immediately remove my things from the London house." His eyes glittered and his voice shook. "For I am *not* your son. And I do not know you."

He turned his back on her.

Lucinda lifted her chin even higher. She blinked back tears as she crossed the room. With a click, she closed the door behind her.

The room was silent. Matt stood looking out the windows, just as he had earlier. Mark waited for him to speak.

"You've been lying to me," he said, not moving.

"Yes."

"You would have thrown away your life—given up the woman you loved—to protect me."

"Yes."

Matt turned, and pain twisted his features. "Why? You didn't think I was strong enough to bear this?" He stepped on the crumpled letter. "Do you think I would want you to sacrifice yourself for me? Did you ever think about how I would feel if this came out, and I realized you'd given up everything for me? I'd feel like shit, that's how I'd feel." A bitter laugh escaped him. "Like I do now."

Mark nodded. "I did think about it. And I believed you

were strong enough. But I worried about your love. I worried that it wouldn't survive this. And I couldn't be responsible for taking that away."

"Fuck you! Rosalind loves me. She loves me with a love that's real and true." His fists clenched at his sides. "Unlike the woman who just left, Rosalind loves me for *me,* not for what I represent to her. Do you think she would give up our love? Over this?" He ground his heel into the letter. "You're wrong. Do you hear me? You're wrong."

Mark's chest tightened painfully. "I hope I am."

Matt swayed on his feet and dropped into Mark's reading chair.

"Christ," he murmured. "Everything makes complete and terrible sense now." He raised his red eyes to Mark. "How you must have hated all those damned lectures I gave you."

Mark frowned. "They were difficult. But most of what you said was right. Truth has a way of rising to the surface, even from a bed of lies."

Matt shook his head, and a sour smile turned his lips. "And there I sat offering to stud your heirs. I'm surprised you were able to stomach that, my brother." He looked at Mark and his eyes filled with moisture. "May I still call you my brother?"

"You *are* my brother, and you shall always be my brother. And if this day brings the end my heart prays for, I shall gladly petition to bequeath my title and lands to your heirs."

Matt's lips turned in the smallest of smiles. "Forgive me for keeping you. Go to Passion and take back your happiness."

Mark trembled at the thought. But he didn't dare dwell upon it for too long. "First I must go to Charlotte."

Matt nodded. "Go then. I will sit here and try to figure out who I am."

Mark gripped his shoulder. "You are nothing less than you have always been. You are a man of honor and nobil-

ity. You are Matthew Morgan Hawkmore. You are my
brother."

Matt raised his eyes to him. "Thank you. Thank you for
everything you tried to do. But never do anything like that
again."

Mark tightened his fingers on his brother's shoulder. "I
love you, Matt."

Matt's eyes dropped closed. "I love you, too."

Mark turned and made for the door. He paused and
looked back. Matt had rested his forehead in his hand. "Is
there anything I can get you—anything you need?"

Matt lowered his hand. His face was wet. "I—I need
Rosalind."

Mark nodded. "I'll have her summoned."

He paused. He shouldn't leave.

"Go," Matt ordered. "Go, and bring Passion back here,
so we can have a proper wedding."

Mark's heart raced and he hurried out the door. Lucinda waylaid him as he strode to Charlotte's room.

"Go, forward with the marriage," she urged, her voice
frantic. "If you don't, it will throw everything into question. You can still save Matthew."

"You mean I can still save *you*." God, she was insufferable. "But that's impossible, Mother. You have destroyed yourself. When you had the thoughtless,
unmitigated gall to put those sickening words on paper,
you chanced that the world would discover what a beast
you are. Now they have."

Her face contorted into a vicious snarl. "Go through
with it, or I'll make sure you don't get the commission for
the library." Her eyes narrowed. "Lord Fitzgerald has a
particular fondness for me."

Mark looked at her and felt only disgust. "Go ahead.
Do what you will. I'm sure once Fitzgerald gets wind of
your letter, he'll be positively rampant with desire for
you."

Lucinda paled.

Mark turned from her. "You're finished, Mother."

She did not follow as he continued on to Charlotte's room.

He found the door ajar, so he pushed it open. "Miss Lawrence?"

"I am here, my lord. Please come in."

Mark entered to find Abigail sitting stiffly in a chair. Charlotte stood before a long mirror, staring at her reflection.

"My mother has explained everything to me, my lord. She revealed her whole vile plot."

Abigail leapt to her feet and spoke to her daughter's back. "You don't understand what I am trying to save you from. You don't understand what it's like to never be quite good enough—what it's like to have enough money but not enough breeding to be accepted into the best of society. I was only trying to save you. We would have had it all. We would have been untouchable."

"No, Mother. *You* would have had it all. *You* would have been untouchable. This has all been for *you*. Not for me."

"It was for you!" Abigail stomped her foot. "It was!"

Mark stepped forward to shield Charlotte from her mother's rage, but he kept silent as Charlotte turned from the mirror. Her normally sweet face was filled with a fury that was all the stronger for how long it must have been held in check.

"Liar!" she cried. "This was all for your own sake—as everything always has been." She leaned forward and her hands gripped the lace of her skirt. "You! The great you, who must reign supreme over everything and all! You, who must find and magnify every imperfection in others, so as to divert attention from your own monumental failings. You, who crave the respect of noble strangers, yet spit in the faces of those who share your household." Her eyes filled with tears. "And I am among those of your beleaguered household."

Abigail's eyes were ice. "Weren't you just looking in the mirror, daughter? You don't look beleaguered to me."

"Hearts don't show in mirrors, Mother. But I suppose you wouldn't know that, since you have no heart."

Mark crossed his arms over his chest. *Well said.*

Abigail drew back and prepared to vent a tirade.

But Charlotte jumped ahead of her. "Where your heart should be is a knot of blackened hate and revenge. For this was as much revenge as it was anything else. Revenge against the countess, who snubbed you from her society and, therefore, from all noble society. And it was all for naught. Now that your evil machinations have been exposed, we are all ruined. So don't try to play this off as if you're some great martyr to my elevation!" She shook her head. "I doubt if marrying Prince Edward himself would erase the black stain upon our name now."

Abigail cheeks puffed. "You are a spoiled and ungrateful daughter. And if you do not hold this man to his promise to you, you are a fool as well."

"Get out, Mother."

Abigail paused.

"I said, get out!" Charlotte shouted.

Abigail stormed from the room, shoving Mark's arm as she passed. The door closed with a slam.

Mark looked at Charlotte and suddenly found that his breath came more rapidly. This was the moment he wanted and the moment he feared.

"Charlotte." His voice caught in his tight throat. "If you want it, I will proceed with our marriage. Perhaps it might salvage something of your good name." His heart thundered in his chest. "An engagement is a promise, and I will keep it."

Charlotte lifted her gray eyes to him. "You didn't promise me freely, my lord. You were forced to promise me. And therein lies all the difference." She pulled the lace fichu from the neck of her gown and let it float to the floor. "No wonder you could barely stand the sight of me."

"I was wrong to treat you so poorly," Mark offered.

"You were innocent." He shoved his hands in his pockets. "And I was angry."

"Of course you were angry. I'm angry, too." She turned to face him. "And I find that, despite my mother's lifelong attempt to demean me, I still have some sense of my own merit. I have no desire to marry and care for a man who would rather I didn't." She lowered her eyes. "I think my servants thought I would be spared some of the scandal if I broke with you first. I'm sure that's why they gave me the letter. But I doubt anything can salvage my name now—I don't want to try. Besides, your family name has been besmirched as well, thanks to my mother." She nodded. "I'll face whatever difficulty this brings. But I will no longer live one moment with someone who does not cherish me."

She paused.

Mark closed his eyes and prayed.

"So, I decline your gracious proposal, my lord. I willingly release you from your promise."

Mark's heart pounded and sang. Tears of sublime joy welled in his eyes. He went to Charlotte and pressed a soft kiss to her brow. "I think many will cherish you. And the one you choose will count himself lucky to have found a woman as fine as the one you have become."

Charlotte brushed away her tears. "Thank you, my lord."

"Let us be Mark and Charlotte, for we have been through much together."

Charlotte smiled a small but confident smile. "Very well, Mark."

He wanted to run—to run to Passion. "Charlotte, after I leave you, I am going to go to your cousin."

"My cousin?"

"Charlotte, during this terrible time, I fell in love with Passion. How and where we met shall all be explained, but neither Passion nor I knew of how we were all connected until the night of your engagement party. From that day forward, she shunned me. But I love her, Charlotte. I love her with my whole soul. And I must go to her now."

Shocked tears sparkled anew in Charlotte's gray eyes. "Oh . . ." she whispered. Her gaze turned inward. "Yes . . . Yes, of course . . ." She shook her head and smiled a little sadly at Mark. "Then go to her right away. For I love her, too, and I would not have her suffer another moment."

Mark pressed a last, firm kiss to her brow.

Then he ran.

Passion pulled her paisley shawl tighter around her shoulders and glanced up at her father's stoic profile. Samuel Dare's thick red hair waved back from his brow like a mane, and his strong nose and jaw completed the imposing character of his face. Yet despite his striking appearance and strict demeanor, he was the fairest, most compassionate man she knew.

She ought to have known that though he would be disappointed in her, he would never abandon her or impugn her. And he would always, always love her. Whatever occurred, whatever they decided to do, that would never change.

"Perhaps we shall all go to France for a long holiday," he said idly. "I haven't traveled in years."

"That's because you hate to travel." She looked up at him. "Father, you needn't."

He patted her arm. "I want to be with you when your time comes." He shook his head. "Your mother wouldn't like it if I weren't."

Passion squeezed his hand. "Papa?"

"Yes, my child."

"I love you."

He stopped walking and looked down at her. His sky-blue eyes were somehow stern and soft at the same time. "I love you, too, lass." His voice was gruff, and he brushed her cheek with his finger. "I'd best be getting back."

Passion nodded. "I'm going to walk to the lake. I'll be back for tea."

Her father turned and strode down the path that led back to the vicarage. She watched him until his tall frame disappeared around a corner and then she continued down the path to the lake.

When she was alone, she let herself cry.

It was the day after the wedding, and the night before, she had dreamt of her lion. He had roared to her from a distant hilltop and then he had run toward her. As he had approached, it had seemed that more distance had appeared between them. Finally, though, he had reached her. And when he had reared up on his hind legs, she had seen that his wound was healed. Then, in a soft blurring of lines and colors, he had transformed into Mark. He had held his arms out to her, and she had run to him. But she had awakened before reaching his embrace.

Even in her dreams, she denied herself the comfort of his arms.

The small lake stretched out before her. It was quiet and peaceful. "I would have married you myself," Mark had said to her that day at his home.

Passion closed her eyes. Would that he could have found her here long ago and made her his. Her whole life would have proceeded differently. She would have happiness. She would have her love. She rested her hands over her womb. And her child would have a father.

A breeze rustled the treetops and skimmed the lake. But though the air was cool, she suddenly felt warm. A tingle of awareness moved up her spine. Who was there?

She turned and her heart stumbled then raced as she stared across the meadow.

Mark!

He wore no hat, and his formal attire was disheveled. Oh, God, what had happened? Why was he here?

She inhaled a choked gasp as he ran to her. Had he fled the wedding? She should run away but she couldn't. Her heart soared just to see him. She wanted his embrace. She wanted him.

He bounded over a small log. Passion felt her shawl slip from her shoulders. She heard the sound of his feet hitting the ground.

Her head swam with joy.

His eyes were bright and vivid.

And then he was there and his arms swooped around her. She cried out and held on to him with all her strength as he turned with her.

She could smell him and feel him, and her body thrilled to be touching him. She curled her hand around his strong nape, and when she lifted her face to his, his mouth came down upon her parted lips with the force and fervor of a man starved for his love.

Passion's heart filled and her head spun as he delved deeply into her mouth. She moaned and tasted him and moaned again.

But then she tore away and looked into his jubilant eyes—eyes so jubilant that something wonderful must have happened. Hope descended from heaven and filled her heart. "What happened? Why are you here?"

He cupped her face in his hands, and tears sparkled in his eyes. "It's all over, Passion. No more scheming, no more lies." He touched her quivering lip with his thumb. "The whole disgusting mess landed in the paper. Everything is out, and I am free. Free to love you."

Passion gripped his wrists. Her heart thundered and tears welled. "And Charlotte? How is she?"

"She is well." Mark shook his head. "I offered to stay, Passion. I knew I could never come to you unless I did. So I put everything in Charlotte's hands and I prayed."

He smiled, and all the pieces of Passion's heart flew from their hiding places. "Your young cousin wants a life of her own choosing, not her mother's. She has formally declined to marry me."

Passion cried out in relief and her tears spilled over as she threw herself against him and took his mouth in a deep, heart-binding kiss. She kissed him with all the joy and bliss of a soul reborn. She kissed him with all the heat and desire of a woman in love.

Gasping and panting against his beautiful mouth, she smiled. "I love you! I love you! I love you," she breathed between kisses.

"Never stop telling me," he murmured. His hands tightened on her waist as he pressed kisses along her jaw and neck. "And for every time you say it, I shall repeat it. I love you. I love you." He kissed the hollow of her throat. "I love you."

She held him as he slid down against her and dropped onto his knee. He lifted his beautiful blue eyes to her, and her own blurred with another rush of tears.

"Passion Elizabeth Dare, I love you with all that I am. You are the woman who makes every day worth living. You are the woman who makes my world a paradise. And you are the woman who makes me a better man." His own eyes flooded. "Marry me. Marry me, and let us declare our love to the world. Let us step from the shadows and dance and kiss and love in the light."

Mark wrapped his arms around her and pressed his cheek to her breast. "Let me love you forever. Let me love you until we are frail and old. And then let me love you in heaven. For my love for you shall never cease."

Passion held him and kissed his brow and then tilted his face to hers. "Yes, I will marry you. Yes, with all my heart and all my soul." Her knees trembled. She brushed his tears away with her thumb. "Mark, you need heirs and—"

"No. I need you." He shook his head. "I need you and only you. The rest doesn't matter."

Passion kissed his parted lips, and her heart overflowed with bliss. "Then what shall we do with the poor babe growing inside me?" she said against his lips. "We can't send him back."

Mark froze and Passion pulled back to look into his stunned blue gaze. His eyes glistened, and his hands shook on her waist. "You're carrying our child? We're having a child?"

Passion nodded and smiled. "Yes."

"Oh, God!" His hand slipped over her womb, and his eyes closed. "A baby . . . Our baby."

Yes! Passion's body shuddered with desire and her heart blossomed. "Tell me something," she whispered.

He kissed her stomach, and a slow smile spread across his handsome lips. He pulled her down before him and lifted his hands to her buttons. His eyes held unparalleled happiness. "I shall spend all my days with you," he said softly, "and enjoy a thousand small moments in each one. I shall dream of you while you sleep by my side, and I shall speak your name over your lips when I wake."

Spreading her bodice, he pressed her back upon the grass and lifted her skirts. She gasped to feel the press of his body on hers.

"Oh, Passion, I shall live every moment of life's adventure with you. And I shall make love to you over and over until our bodies are more one than two."

She writhed beneath him as his hand moved between them.

"And in such a way, I shall live a life with you," he promised. "And I shall make life with you."

Then he kissed her with plundering ferocity. And as he slid into her shaking body, Passion moaned her exultation to the sky.

This was love.

This was joy.

This was heaven on Earth.

Epilogue

One Year Later

In his hurry to get out of his shirt, Mark banged his elbow against the screen. "Ouch, damn it!" He glared at the offending piece.

Passion laughed as she removed her pantalets from beneath her skirts. "Are you all right?"

He grinned and kicked off his shoes. "I'm fine. Just open your bodice."

Passion didn't pause but lifted her hands to loosen her laces.

Mark pulled off his socks and trousers as she slipped out of her bodice entirely. She wore no corset cover, and her luscious breasts were full and straining against the delicate fabric of her chemise.

He moaned. His blood rushed and his cock grew. "Hurry, my love." He wanted her. He was desperate for her.

She smiled and quickly removed the skirt of her gown while her hungry eyes kept dropping to his erection.

He peeled off his undergarment and kicked it aside with his shoes.

Passion licked her lips and struggled with her petticoats. Her face turned from ardor to distress. "Mark, help me."

He stepped forward with a warm smile and worked at her knot while he kissed her. Her sweet mouth opened and he tasted her and . . . and, damn it, he couldn't get the knot loose!

As they struggled with it, a knock sounded upon the door to their room. They both froze.

The nurse's voice called, "My lady?"

Mark groaned.

Passion extricated herself from his embrace with a giggle. "Yes, Milly?" she answered. "I'm here." She looked around the screen. "Come in."

Milly's voice floated over the top of the screen. "The young master is wanting his mum, my lady."

Passion smiled over her shoulder at Mark. "Don't go. I'll be right back."

Mark indicated his nakedness. "Where would I go?"

She gave him a saucy, head-to-toe look before stepping around the screen. He'd make her pay for that.

In the next moment he heard her cooing and it made him smile.

"Thank you, Milly," she said.

The door closed and Passion came back behind the screen carrying their son. Mark Samuel Hawkmore was plucking at her chemise, which they had discovered meant "Feed me now or I shall holler to the hills."

Mark watched Passion open her chemise and lift her milk-engorged breast from her corset. Her darkened, distended nipple dripped milk, and his cock pulsed at the sight. But his son knew what to do and quickly sucked his mother's sweet nipple into his small baby mouth.

Passion sighed and gazed down at their son with tender adoration. She loved him powerfully and deeply, and Mark loved to see every moment of her devotion. As a boy, this was what he had been starved for. This was what he had yearned for. A mother who would have protected him and nurtured him. A mother who would have raised him up with love.

Passion lifted her beautiful eyes to his, and they darkened as she looked at him. She leaned her back against the wall. "Come here," she said softly.

He went to them and stroked the soft auburn hair that curled over Samuel's small head. His blue eyes were closed in blissful gluttony.

Mark's heart filled with so much love that he could not contain it. It spilled from his eyes in two tears. One dropped on Passion's breast, the other on Samuel's arm.

Passion's hand curved around his nape and, drawing him down to her, she kissed him with a sensual tenderness. "I love you."

He nibbled her lip. "I love you."

"Then show me. Samuel won't mind. He's more asleep than awake."

He moaned against her mouth and, lifting her skirts, he slid eagerly into her.

She gasped, clenched around him, and murmured his name.

And there, behind their screen, Mark's heart roared with the exuberant happiness of a man who would never again hunger for love.

Turn the page for a special preview of
Lisa Valdez's next novel

Patience

Coming soon from Berkley Sensation!

Matthew swept her into his arms and turned her into the waltzing throng. Patience found herself leaning into him, both offering support and taking succor. He held her so closely that she could smell the vetiver that clung to him. She could feel the press of his lower body and the brush of his legs. She could feel the strength of his shoulder beneath her hand as he led her with unwavering surety. Her memories of how he'd felt in her arms had blurred with time, but now they came back into clear and precise focus. He felt hard, unyielding, and perfect.

She closed her eyes and would have laid her head against his shoulder had they been alone. Gracious, she hadn't realized how tired she was—so very tired of the constant onslaught of male attention. The wrong male attention.

"Look at me, Patience."

Her body hummed with sensual appreciation at the sound of his voice. She breathed in the light, powdery scent of vetiver. What was it about him? They were almost strangers.

She lifted her gaze and stared into his dark, heavily lashed eyes. What did she see there? Determination? Pride? Need? His eyes were more beautiful than she had remembered. *He* was more beautiful than she had remembered. Glints of gold lit his dark hair.

"What took you so long?" she asked, softly. "I've been waiting for you."

His nostrils flared. "I'm here now." His fingers pressed against her back. "Are you prepared to give me what I want?"

The deep, resonant tones of his voice stroked her like a caress.

"What is it you want?"

He didn't answer. Instead, his gaze dropped to her low, flower-strewn décolletage. "You're gown is lovely. As whom are you costumed?"

Patience took a shallow breath. "Persephone."

"Ah, how appropriate. Persephone, the herald of spring— the goddess." His low voice held her captive as he turned her to the music. "Then I am Pluto, god of the underworld—and I want you." His dark, beautiful eyes held her enthralled. His embrace tightened and his voice held her captive. "I shall steal you away and hide you in my shadow. I shall chain you to my side and demand your submission. I shall take everything from you and, in the doing, give you everything you desire."

Something dark and hidden reverberated in Patience's heart. Her lips parted on a silent sigh.

His gaze dropped to her mouth. "And you shall light my dark world," he said, quietly.

Patience remembered the women's cruel words and her heart tightened. "How shall I light your dark world, Matthew?"

His eyes returned to hers and they were unfathomable. "I don't know—perhaps by speaking my name as you just did." A spark tumbled from her heart to her womb. His voice was so tender. "Perhaps I have lost my way." He paused then drew back a little. "Does it really matter, as long as I give you what you desire?"

Moisture tingled on her thighs. "It matters to me." When he didn't respond she gave him a small smile. "Besides, just because we've shared a kiss doesn't mean you know my desires."

He didn't return her smile. "It was more than a kiss—it always has been and you know it."

Her blood rushed. "That doesn't mean you know my desires."

His eyes held her. "Oh, I've been watching you, Patience. You're the belle of the ball. Almost every man here wants you. They practically stumble over each other to get to you. Isn't that true?"

She felt her smile fading. "Yes."

"And isn't it true that your fawning admirers crowd you, almost beyond bearing, in their urgency to impress you. Isn't it true that they drown you in continuous compliments that are meaningless to you? Isn't it true that they suffocate you with their innocuous but unending attention?" His dark eyes seemed to reach inside her. "Isn't that true, Patience?"

She frowned into his almost hypnotic gaze. "Yes." The word came on a whisper. Did he hear it?

He bent closer. "And though you smile and sweep them off their feet . . ."

She breathed in vetiver.

". . . I think none of them inspire your passions . . ."

His cheek touched her temple.

". . . let alone your love."

Patience trembled with desire and longing. She lowered her gaze as he drew back. Love—elusive love. How long had she searched for it? How many men had declared it? More than she could remember. Yet they had all proven false. Or weak. Or they had failed to inspire any reciprocating emotion in her. She had begun to fear she would never find love.

Then she had met him . . .

Matthew's hand tightened around hers as they whirled amongst the dancers. She lifted her eyes and found his still upon her—such deep, compelling eyes.

Could he be the one? There was something undeniable between them—there always had been. She could feel it. It shivered in the shortness of her breath and trembled in the tender spot between her legs. Did he hold the key to her passions, to her heart? Did she hold the key to his?

"Everything you've said is true," she admitted. "But you can't know my desires. Even I am uncertain of them."

"No, you're not," he said softly. "You're just afraid to admit to them."

Patience felt her frown deepening. Was he right? She pondered for a moment, but answers evaded her. She shook her head. "I don't see what you see."

His hand moved on her back. "Then give me tonight— only tonight—and I'll show you."

Patience's heart pounded in her breast. How could she accept such an offer? Her cunt quivered. She wanted him so desperately. How could she refuse it?

When she didn't answer, Matthew turned her to the edge of the dance floor and clasped her wrist. "Come with me, Patience," he said.

She paused. "Come with you where?"

Hidden in the folds of her skirt, his fingers slipped around her hand. "Wherever I say."

Her breath quickened and her nipples tightened. It wasn't the answer she had expected. "But we can't just leave."

"Yes, we can." Matthew's dark eyes bored into hers. "I have borne the abhorrent stares of this throng tonight, because of the memory of your mouth against mine, because of the feel of your body and the smell of your skin. I came here for you, Patience. Only for you. Now, come with me."

Heat flooded her body. She wanted to go—yearned to go. It was as if there were an invisible string between them, and he was pulling it. "But how can I?" she breathed.

He bent close and his low voice was gentle. "You can because you hunger for something you don't understand. But I am going to make it clear and simple for you, because what you need cannot be asked for; it can only be taken. And I am the one to do the taking." He drew back. "Now, not another word." And then he turned and pulled her through the crowd with the simple pressure of his fingers against her palm.

Patience's blood rushed in her veins. His calm commands were surprising. But her reaction was more so. Part of her wanted to wrench free and turn her back on him. But the stronger part, or was it the weaker, felt a hot thrill and an urgency to follow.

Yet, if she did, what then? A kiss would only be the beginning. She felt an unusual and uncomfortable moment of indecision, but seemed unable to act. So, with a wildly beating heart, she followed him.

Pulling her arm through his, he led her in a leisurely fashion and they nodded to people as they passed. Smiles, raised eyebrows and speculative glances followed them. She thought of the anonymous gossips and lifted her chin. She was not ashamed to be seen with him. Indeed, there was no man she would rather be with. And why shouldn't they be seen together? He was her brother-in-law, after all.

But the closer they came to the wide ballroom doors, the faster Patience's heart beat. Pride and desire, uncertainty and trust, all struggled for preeminence. If she was going to refuse him, it must be now. Now—before they crossed the ballroom's threshold.

The doors loomed before her. Her step faltered.

Matthew glanced down at her and his dark eyes flashed. "Come, Patience."

No sweet-talking, no cajoling. He tightened his arm on hers and a heavy throb pulsed between her legs. His firm command sublimated her resistance in a way that no amount of coaxing would have. She stepped over the threshold.

They crossed the foyer and climbed the stairs leading to the third floor. Masked guests ascended and descended around them, moving to and from the upper gallery that overlooked the ballroom. Matthew nodded at two passing matrons. The elderly ladies wore no masks and Patience noted their curious stares. She averted her eyes. They looked like two ripe old tittle-tattles.

Finally, with a brief glance over his shoulder, Matthew turned her down the corridor that led to the family's private wing. Sconces mounted on the walls flickered with light. The noise of the ball receded. Taking her hand, he pulled her passed the hall that led to her room, and moved on down the corridor. She had trod this same path to visit with her sister in her dressing room. But tonight, her destination was . . . where?

Her breath came quickly as Matthew turned her down a second corridor leading away from familiar pathways. She had never been in this part of the house. It was empty and quiet. She could hear almost nothing of the ball and her breathing sounded loud.

She glanced at Matthew. His strong profile revealed nothing but a purposeful intent. He said nothing. And then, as they turned another corner, he pulled her in front of him and released her. Patience stared at a wall decorated with a large tapestry. Only two doors faced the short hall.

She whirled around.

Pulling off his gloves, Matthew regarded her with dark, hooded eyes. His sensual mouth was parted but unsmiling. She removed her mask as she tried to slow her breathing.

"Drop it," he said low.

Patience let the mask fall to the floor.

Her fingers trembled as he slowly approached. She saw that his trousers were tented by a formidable erection.

A wash of desire sluiced through her. She swallowed the moisture that pooled in her mouth and tried to calm her nerves. But he simply leaned against the door jam to her left and, reaching for the handle, let the door swing open. She looked into his dark eyes and then into the dark room. Some flickering light sent dim shadows dancing upon the wall. But standing in the illuminated corridor, she could see little else.

She remembered his words below. *I shall hide you in my shadow, chain you to my side, and give you everything you desire.*

She stared back down the well-lit hall. This was it—her last chance to escape. But escape to what? To insignificant conversations with men who were too busy gawking at her to care what she said? Endless talk with men who were more interested in telling her their opinions than discovering hers? Trifling associations with men who only wanted to get between her legs?

She met Matthew's gaze. Of course, *he* wanted to get between her legs, too. Suddenly, she thought of her sister. Dressed as Aphrodite, her sister's high-waisted gown didn't quite conceal her five-month pregnancy. This ball would be her last social event before her confinement.

Patience put her hand over her flat stomach. She met Matthew's stare. His beautiful eyes seemed to dare her. But she didn't know if the dare was to flee or to enter.

Her body railed against her procrastination. She spoke on a rush of breath. "I'm a virgin—and I intend to stay that way."

He raised his brows. "Forever?"

"For now."

He lowered his eyes and seemed to consider for all of two seconds before nodding. "Very well. I agree to leave you intact."

Patience looked into his eyes. She had refused so many and trusted so few. But she saw no hint of duplicity in his deep gaze, only desire, tight and tense. She recognized it because her own body was taut with it. She wanted him. From the first moment she'd seen him she'd wanted him.

She closed her eyes and took a deep breath. *God and St. Matthew keep her.* Then, with open-eyed determination, she walked past him into the room.

The door slammed behind her. Patience turned with a start. Unaccustomed to the dim, fire-lit room, she saw nothing until Matthew emerged from the shadows.

"Welcome to my underworld, Persephone." And then his arms were around her. She felt his power as he held her against the unyielding strength of his body. His arm was a vice around her waist and his thick erection ground against her pelvis. She barely drew a breath before his mouth swooped down upon hers. Her blood roared as his tongue thrust between her parted lips, and his hand, cradling the back of her head, left her no retreat from his demanding kiss.

But retreat was not an option. That moment had passed. So she clung to him as his tongue thrust and thrust again, stroking the roof of her mouth and skimming her teeth. She tasted a hint of brandy, while the smell of vetiver, green and powdery, filled her senses. Moisture trickled from her cunt onto her damp thighs, and she tried to gasp for breath as he drove his tongue more deeply into her open mouth. Like a river, all sensation seemed to course from his mouth into hers, then surge with unstoppable force to the pulsing well of her body.

It was just as it had been the first time—but more. It was hot, urgent and demanding, but this time there was no restraint, no pause, and no withdrawal.

Wild with passion, she sucked and tasted him as she felt the contours of his back through his jacket. Her head spun and she heard his low groan despite the pounding in her ears. She felt his hand tighten in her hair while his other moved to grip her chin. He urged her mouth wider as he drove his tongue deeper, seeming to test the depths of her. As more blood rushed to her pulsing clitoris and her air grew thin, Patience moaned beneath his heady demand.

He tore his lips from hers and, as she gasped and her knees shook, he traced his fingers across her trembling mouth. "I knew you were for me," he murmured roughly. "I knew from the first moment I saw you."

Patience's heart skipped a beat and then raced as he slipped his finger between her parted lips. Instinctively, she curled her tongue and sucked in a sensual exploration. And as she gazed at him, half-lit by the fire, he slid in another and then another finger.

"That's good," Matthew whispered. "Show me how warm and wet your mouth can be." His hips tilted against her.

Patience trembled with excitement and her clitoris pulsed as she sucked hungrily upon his long fingers. She remembered the times she and her sisters had spied upon their butler as he delivered his daily dose of ejaculate into the mouth of their upstairs maid. It had always fascinated and excited them. But it was she who had been most entranced. It was she who had actually spoken of daring to take the maid's place. It was she who had started sneaking cucumbers into their room, where they had all laughingly practiced the act they so avidly watched.

Now, as Matthew explored the moist cavities of her mouth, she surged against him to feel the strength of his erection through the layers of her petticoats. And as she laved his long fingers with her tongue, her breathless excitement flared into an even more urgent need.

He lifted his long-lashed eyes to hers and they reflected a fierce desire. "You understand what I want, don't you? In fact, you're hungry for it, aren't you?"

Patience moaned. His voice was a low, soft contradiction to the hard gaze he bent upon her.

"That's good. But I wonder"—he slipped his fingers more

deeply into her mouth—"how a virginal vicar's daughter knows of such things?" He brought his mouth close to hers. "What have you been up to, my little virgin? Are you more Impatience than Patience?"

She answered him with a slow swath of her tongue along the length of his fingers as he withdrew them. His mouth, so close, covered hers in a deep, breathtaking kiss. She breathed in vetiver and the throbbing between her legs increased. Her knees grew weak and her arms trembled as she clung to him. And just when she thought she might collapse at his feet, he broke the kiss and spoke against her gasping mouth. "Now, answer me. Just how many cocks have you tasted?" The fire in his eyes belied the calm of his voice.

Her cunt tightened. The opportunity had arisen more than once, but she'd never taken it. "None," she breathed. "None, ever."

His features hardened angrily and his hand tightened in her hair. "Don't lie to me. Whatever occurs between us, never lie to me."

She met his dark gaze. The scandal about him had broken upon a bed of humiliating, shameful lies. "I never lie." She felt her cheeks flushing. "But I've seen it done, many times. Our butler . . . and the upstairs maid . . ."

Matthew's expression softened in an instant. "Ah, the servants. They're invaluable teachers, are they not?" He kissed her again, thrusting his tongue deep before withdrawing. "Did it excite you to watch them?" he murmured against her lips.

"Yes." Her lips tilted as he filled her mouth with another probing kiss that was over almost as soon as it began.

"Did you dream of doing it?" he demanded. "Did you think of it while you stroked your pretty clit? Did you come as you imagined what it might be like to have a nice hard prick between your lovely lips?"

Patience moaned. The small bud of flesh between her legs felt like it was going to explode.

"Did you?"

She stared into his dark eyes. "Yes," she admitted on a whisper. "Yes!"

His jaw tightened. He took her hand and pressed it to his

erection. "You think you can get your pretty mouth around this?"

Patience gasped at the size and strength of him. He was hard and heavy, and so thick that she couldn't close her fingers around him. Sudden moisture filled her mouth and more trickled from her quim as she explored him.

His hips flexed against her. "Do you want it?"

"Yes." Patience pressed an urgent kiss to his lips. "Yes, please."

He stroked the back of his fingers down her cheek while his other hand moved soothingly against her scalp. "How politely you reply," he murmured. "But, alas, I will not oblige you."

"What?" Patience drew back in confusion. "But I . . . But I want to . . ."

"You want?" His brows lifted. "My sweet Patience, we are not here for what you want. We are here for what I want."

Patience blinked and tried to think past the barrage of poignant sensations that coursed through her. "But you spoke of knowing my desires . . ."

The softest, most beautiful smile turned his lips. "Yes, I did." He brushed his mouth against hers. "That's quite a puzzle isn't it?"

Patience gazed into his handsome face and felt her nipples tingle. "I don't understand."

He pulled her before the warmth of the hearth. "That's all right. You will," he murmured gently. Something flickered in his hand. "In time, everything will become clear to you." He moved close. "It's so simple, really."

She lifted her mouth for his kiss. But no kiss came. Instead, she felt a firm downward tug upon her gown. Patience gasped as her low bodice suddenly loosened and slipped from her shoulders. She clutched it and, looking down, as that Matthew had cut the laces of the provincial style costume. His arms came around her. She felt another quick tug at her waist, and before she could grab them, her skirts fell to the floor in a frothy heap.

Taking a step back, he closed a slim knife and put it in his coat pocket. Then he held out his hand to her. "Give me your gown," he ordered quietly.

Stunned, Patience looked down at her sagging bodice and the circle of fabric at her feet. But what point was there in refusing? As it was, the gown was of no use to her. Indeed, she would have to contrive some repairs in order to leave the chamber.

Shaking, she slipped out of her bodice and scooped up her skirts. At least she still wore most of her under-things. She handed the whole pile of discarded garments to him and then nearly leapt out of her skin when he tossed everything into the fire.

A small cry escaped her. The room immediately darkened. She could hear only her own rapid breath. And then the fire flared, higher than before, and Matthew was there. His hands reached for her and, with one hard pull, he ripped the fragile fabric of her corset cover. It, too, fed the greedy fire.

She felt both shocked and enthralled as she watched her beautiful gown blister into ashes. But when he reached for her pantalets, she grabbed at them. "No," she gasped.

His brows lifted. "No?" He met and held her gaze as he simply moved his hands to the slit in her pantalets and, with complete disregard for her protest, sundered the fabric down the center seam.

He muffled her startled protest with a sudden but soothing kiss. It was so soft, so gentle. Her arms came around him. It seemed in complete contradiction to what he was doing. Patience moaned.

"You don't say 'no' to me," he murmured against her lips, and then he shredded the legs of her pantalets until nothing remained but a few points of fabric peaking from beneath her corset.

Shaking with fierce, inexplicable anticipation, Patience threw her hands over the triangle of red curls between her legs. She looked wide-eyed at Matthew as he pulled her chemise down so that the high mounds of her breasts were exposed.

With his breath coming fast, he stood back to look at her. His handsome face was tight with desire. His dark eyes reflected the firelight, making them seem to burn from within. "Move your hands," he ordered.

Patience felt her blood rising to her cheeks and descending

to her already swollen clitoris. Her fingers trembled protectively over the little nub of pulsing flesh. She couldn't bring herself to put her arms at her sides. No one had ever dared even dishevel her, let alone expose her like this. "I cannot." Her voice cracked.

He looked at her and his gaze softened. "You must, Patience, or I will do it for you."

Patience squeezed her eyes shut. She should scream at him in righteous indignation. Where was her indignation? She tried to summon it, but found only a hot, undeniable passion in its stead. And yet, she could not move her hands. She shook as body and mind, passion and pride, raged inside her.

"Is it so difficult?" Matthew's whisper sounded from right in front of her.

Patience felt sudden tears well. She was half naked and vulnerable. It shouldn't feel good.

And yet it did.

"Yes." She lifted her gaze to his and her tears spilled over. "Yes, it is difficult."

A low moan seemed to catch in his throat as his beautiful eyes locked onto her face with rapt intensity. "Ah, my sweet Patience, I adore the struggle in your tears—for I value most what is not easily given." He moved against her side and she felt the brush of his hand as he stroked his cock through his trousers. His breath touched her temple. "Every tear you shed in the suffering of my demands, honors me. I cherish each one. But ultimately"—he lay a gentle kiss upon her brow—"your tears must always accompany your obedience. Now, move your hands."

Patience's cunt throbbed with a deep, almost painful, craving; and the pulsing bud of flesh that always brought her pleasure tortured her now with its burning need for release. Every word he uttered inflamed her more, made her want him more.

What was wrong with her? And why must she obey? Why did she *want* to obey? Her emotions warred within her but, somehow, the battle only served to heighten her need.

With great effort, she forced her arms to her sides. Her muscles were stiff and rigid with tension. Her fingers pressed against her thighs.

"There," he whispered. "That's good."

His praise, so quietly spoken, calmed and warmed her. But in the next moment, her chest tightened and more tears welled at the realization that his simple words could affect her so. What power did he wield over her?

She lowered her eyes.

"No." With a finger beneath her chin, he tipped up her face. "Hide nothing from me." He kissed her trembling lips. "Don't you see, I covet your every response. Each and every lovely reaction you have is a gift to me." His dark eyes moved over her tear-streaked face with an intensity she had never seen. No one had ever looked at her in such a way. "Do you begin to see what I want from you?" His warm hands moved up her arms in a soft caress that sent a shiver down her spine. "I want you to submit to me. I want you to give me all that I demand of you. And I want you to hide nothing from me as you do it."

A hot rush of desire coursed through Patience's body, leaving behind a raw need that was tinged with both exhilaration and trepidation.

He stroked his hands over her shoulders as he moved behind her. "I want to see every struggle and every victory. I want to see each precious tear and each magnificent smile." His hands moved over her bare bottom, squeezing gently, and she felt the brief brush of his erection. "I want all of you, every bit of you, all for myself." Patience shuddered and closed her eyes as he kissed the tender skin behind her ear. "Do you know why I want this, my sweet Patience?"

She moaned as he wrapped his arms around her and pressed his whole body against her back.

"Do you?"

She surged against him as his fingers slid into the red curls over her mount. "Tell me, Patience. Why do I want it?" His fingers slipped lower; her cunt throbbed. "Tell me and I'll touch you as you long to be touched."

A soft, mewling sound escaped her and her hips bucked. She knew the answer, but didn't want to utter it.

"Tell me!" he demanded.

Patience drew a gasping breath. "Because it is what *I* want."

"What? What do you want," he said by her ear.

Must she say the words? She tilted her hips, but he didn't move. God, why must he torment her?

"What do you want, Patience? Say it out loud."

Patience bit her lip, her hips twisted with need. Say the words. She need only say the words. "To submit," she finally breathed on a whisper. Tears filled her eyes. "To submit, completely."

He came around to face her and a hot fire illuminated his eyes. "You see, you do know your own desires." And then he kissed her, and as she tasted him and clung to him, her body leapt as his fingers slipped down over the throbbing, distended nub of flesh that fed her rampant desire. Once, twice, a third time he slid his fingers over her wet folds, and then he was rubbing her—in tight, firm circles he plied her tender bud.

Hot, stabbing pleasure shot through Patience's body. She moaned and curled her fingers into the fabric of his jacket.

"There. There you are," he murmured against her mouth. "Come for me. That's my sweet, Patience." He ground against her hip and she felt the thick column of his cock. "Come for me."

God! Oh, God! Her chest heaved and her cunt clenched. It was too much and she had waited too long. Everything drew up tight within her. And then, throwing back her head, she cried out and her hips jerked convulsively against the press of his fingers. Shards of brilliant bliss imbedded themselves in her shattered nerves, where they pulsed and flared unrelentingly. She collapsed against him, and had he not had his arm firmly around her waist, she would have fallen.

Sweeping his other arm behind her knees, he scooped her up and carried her to the bed. Patience looked at him from beneath half-closed eyelids. "Thank you," she breathed.

His dark brown eyes held hers as he laid her on the velvet coverlet. His jaw was tight as he braced his hands on either side of her, but his voice was soft. "You're welcome."

He bent low to kiss her, and the kiss was as full of passion as their first. Patience curled her arms around him as his tongue plunged deeply. She moaned as he bit down on her lower lip and sucked it. Then, as quickly as it had begun it ended. He pulled away, leaving her feeling hungry for more.

She turned on her side to watch him. He crossed the room and, opening a door, disappeared for a moment.

Patience waited. It appeared to be his dressing room. Was he undressing? Her pulse started to race again.

When he returned, he was wearing a dressing gown. A long, white scarf hung from his hand. He walked purposefully over to her.

"Give me your hands," he ordered gently.

Her eyes widened and her tender clit pulsed painfully. Did he mean to tie her? She froze.

A small frown turned his brow. "Give me your hands," he said again, this time less gently.

Patience's heart hammered in her breast as she slowly put her wrists together before him. His gaze grew tender and he kissed her softly. "That's very good."

He quickly tied her hands. She began to tremble as she felt the tightness. "You're doing very well," he murmured, drawing her bound hands over her head and tying her to one of the bedposts.

Patience's body tensed and her nipples hardened against her corset. God, what was he going to do?

She sucked in her breath and almost screamed as she saw the flicker of the blade. But then she gasped as he imbedded it in the same bedpost she was tied to.

When he pulled back to look at her, his gaze was hot and intent. He smoothed his hand down her heaving side and over her hip, and then let it rest upon her patch of red curls.

He studied her for a long moment. "Listen to me. You are a wonder and a beauty. There is something profound in you that calls to me." He shook his head. "I've never been with a woman I wanted more. Even when I thought I loved another, I wanted you. Even when I thought I loved another, I dreamt of you." He paused and stroked his hand down her arm. "But my dreams were as nothing compared to you in the flesh. You are more than I dreamed." He leaned low and spoke against her lips. "And your submission is powerful."

Patience kissed him and thrust her tongue into his warm mouth. His words were like a sensual touch and her body thrilled as both happiness and desire tore through her. Whatever it was between them, he felt it too. Her feelings were not unrequited.

She moaned into his mouth and arched against him as his hand began to stroke the moist folds between her legs. The press of his fingers, slick with her wetness, made her throb and quiver. He broke their kiss but his dark eyes stared into hers. She pulled at her bonds and lifted her hips as he continued to ply her swelling flesh. She gasped and thrust against his hand. His eyes never left her. Then, just as she felt her cunt being to pull, he stopped.

Patience watched, speechless, as he stood and crossed to the chamber door. She squirmed as her clit and cunt throbbed with aborted need. Then she blanched when he removed his robe and tossed it over a chair. He was fully dressed!

"Where are you going?" she cried.

He looked over at her and adjusted his cuffs. "I'm going downstairs. You will submit to my leisure and await me."

Patience gasped as he pulled on his gloves.

"When I return, I shall expect you to satisfy me in the manner your maid satisfied your butler."

Before she could respond, he was gone.

The lock clicked behind him.